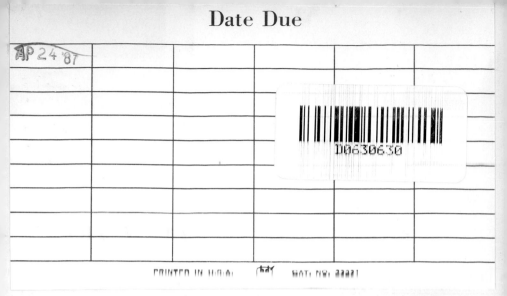

Riverside City College Library
Riverside, California

1. All members of the community are entitled to use the library.
2. Reference books are to be used only in the library.
3. Reserved books and circulating books may be borrowed in accordance with library rules.
4. The date due will be stamped in each book loaned.
5. Injury to books beyond reasonable wear and all losses shall be paid for by the borrower.
6. No books may be taken from the library without being charged.

BY LUDWIG BEMELMANS

published by The Viking Press

TO THE ONE I LOVE THE BEST

FATHER, DEAR FATHER

HOW TO TRAVEL INCOGNITO

THE EYE OF GOD

DIRTY EDDIE

HOTEL BEMELMANS

THE BLUE DANUBE

NOW I LAY ME DOWN TO SLEEP

I LOVE YOU, I LOVE YOU, I LOVE YOU

HOTEL SPLENDIDE

THE DONKEY INSIDE

SMALL BEER

LIFE CLASS

MY WAR WITH THE UNITED STATES

Children's Books

MADELINE'S RESCUE

QUITO EXPRESS

THE CASTLE NUMBER 9

THE GOLDEN BASKET

HANSI

THE WORLD OF

BEMELMANS

AN OMNIBUS BY

LUDWIG BEMELMANS

NEW YORK

THE VIKING PRESS · 1955

PUBLISHED BY THE VIKING PRESS IN OCTOBER 1955

PUBLISHED ON THE SAME DAY IN THE DOMINION OF CANADA
BY THE MACMILLAN COMPANY OF CANADA LIMITED

A number of the stories and sketches in this book
originally appeared in *The New Yorker, Holiday,
Harper's Bazaar, Town & Country, Vogue, This
Week,* and *Story,* some of them in somewhat different form.

Library of Congress catalog card number: 55-10472

PRINTED IN THE U. S. A. BY THE COLONIAL PRESS INC.

Contents

MY WAR WITH THE UNITED STATES

CONTENTS

SMALL BEER

THE DONKEY INSIDE

I LOVE YOU, I LOVE YOU, I LOVE YOU

viii   Contents
            NEW STORIES

My War with
the United States

FOREWORD

In December 1914 I was sixteen years old and came to America.

The quality of my mind and its information at that time was such that, on sailing for America from the port of Rotterdam, I bought two pistols and much ammunition. With these I intended to protect myself against and fight the Indians.

I had read of them in the books of Karl May and Fenimore Cooper, and intently hoped for their presence without number on the outskirts of New York City.

My second Idea was that the elevated railroad of New York ran over the housetops, adapting itself to the height of the buildings in the manner of a roller coaster.

These Ideas were the consequence of a very alone growing-up in the small villages of Tirol and on the lakes of Upper Austria. The last three years before coming to the United States were spent in a German boarding school.

The Captain of the steamer *Ryndam* persuaded me to return the guns. The shopkeeper in Rotterdam, however, would only exchange them for other hardware, and I traded them for twelve pairs of finely chiseled Solingen scissors and three complicated pocketknives.

On this steamer, the S.S. *Ryndam* of the Holland America Line, was a smoking room. The benches and restful chairs in this saloon were upholstered with very durable, gun-colored material with much horsehair in it.

My plan at the time was to have one strong suit made of this material. I reasoned that such a garment would last me for ten years, and in this time I could put by enough money to go back to Tirol and buy a sawmill which stands in a pine forest on top of a mountain in the Dolomites.

The chapters of this book were translated from the pages of my German Diary which I kept during my service in the United States Army.

2

The GUARDHOUSE
FORT ONTARIO

PLEASE DON'T SHOOT

Oswego is on Lake Ontario; it is a small town without tall buildings. There is one hotel, the Pontiac, a streetcar, also a theater, in which the Paulist Choristers sang yesterday. The town is very friendly, the air is strong and clear. We are stationed out at Fort Ontario. The grounds of this fortress are spacious; there is an immense parade ground.

The Field Hospital, Unit N, to which I belong, was recruited in New York. The men are all volunteer soldiers and the Officers, doctors. The men are mostly college students or graduates, not ordinary privates. Some of them are older, and professional men; for example, the one who has his bed next to mine in the barracks is a Professor of French at one of the large universities—it is either Harvard or Yale, I believe. His name is Beardsley.

I am very glad of his friendship; he seems to take the whole business we are engaged in as if it did not concern him, as a vacation, never has a serious thought. He takes a peculiar pride in having a very ill-fitting uniform and hat. These military hats are badly enough designed as they are, but he fixes his own so that the rim turns up off his face, which makes him look very inefficient; also he shaves only when he has to. Mostly he sits on his bed and eats a peculiar kind of small white nuts and crosses his legs.

All this is so fine because he is a man of great culture, and I like him so much because I have to think how unbearable a Ger-

3

man Professor would be here next to me. In the evening Beardsley looks like a Mexican bandit. He makes no effort to be assigned to better jobs, to win a promotion—he could even have a commission for the asking. But he is happy, and most so when we push a wagon with bread from the bakery back to the barracks every evening; then he sings and says that this is the best time he has ever had, that he is completely happy. Perhaps he has been in some terrible life and now feels happy because he is away from that. He tells me that Schopenhauer states with authority that Happiness is the absence of Unhappiness, which is so obvious and foolish that a backward child could make this observation, but he says I must think about it. I looked this up and it is right; only Schopenhauer says the absence of *"Schmerz,"* which is pain, and in German the word pain covers more than just pain—it means sorrow, trouble, unhappiness. And so Professor Beardsley is perhaps right.

They allowed me to bring my dog along. The Major said to the Adjutant back in New York City: "Say, Charlie, he has a dog, can we use a dog?"

The Adjutant asked: "What kind of a dog is it?"

I said: "A police dog."

Then he leaned back and said to the Major: "It's all right with me."

"All right, son, bring your police dog," said the Major. "What's his name?"

I am glad of this, yet I have never seen anything like it. I cannot think of a German Major calling his Adjutant Charlie and asking him about the dog—and all this time the Major sat in a chair and told me to sit down, and the Adjutant had his legs on the Major's desk. The Major smoked a cigar and smiled and then talked to me in German about beer and food; he also said how much he enjoyed a trip down the Rhine.

We drill here all day long, and workingmen are building new barracks and fixing the old ones up. There is a Colonel here from the regular army, a smart-looking old gentleman with white hair and a trim, well-kept body; he wears boots and spurs and behaves like an Officer. The men tell me that these are West Pointers and that you can always tell them, no matter how old they are.

We are being instructed how to take care of the sick, how to transport men on stretchers, first aid, and how to help in a Hospital.

In our free time we go to motion pictures and entertainments for the soldiers. One is as dull as the other. On Sundays we go to churches, and afterwards people ask us to their houses for dinner. In all these houses is a soft warm feeling, a desire to be good to us, and the food is simple, good, and plentiful. We also take walks together, and Beardsley has pointed out a piece of scenery which he named "Beautiful Dreck." It was a bitter landscape composed of railroad tracks, signal masts, coal sheds, a factory building and some freight cars, a gas tank, and in the background some manufacturing plant, black with soot. Some of the windows of this building were lit by a vivid gray-blue light and yellow flames shot out of several chimneys. "That is," he said, "beautiful Dreck, and we have lots of it in America."

Dreck is a German word for filth and dirt but it also means manure, mud, dirty fingers. It is a large, able word, *patois,* almost bad; it covers all that was before us, and thereby can be seen that Professor Beardsley knows much. He told me St. Louis had a particularly good portion of "Beautiful Dreck," but that the best he knew could be seen in the Jersey Meadows, where it covers almost a whole countryside.

One day the Wardmaster of Ward Number Three swam too far out into Lake Ontario and drowned, and I became the Wardmaster. This Ward was filled with oldtime soldiers; they call themselves "Oldtimers" and had recently been with Mr. Pershing in Mexico. They were distinguished from all other soldiers in that they had overcoats and uniforms of what they called the "Old Issue," a cloth of much better quality than the new and also of better color, and they were very proud of khaki uniforms that were almost white from much wear and bleaching. These uniforms of course they did not wear; they hung in their closets. They were middle-aged men, and those in our ward suffered from some amorous diseases which they mentioned with pride, considering those who did not have either the disease or the memory ot ɪt noɪ quite complete soldiers. Among my duties was to give them their medicines, to take pulse, temperature, and respiration, and the difficult job of turning the lights out at nine o'clock. They read, played cards, talked, and did not want to go to sleep. All objects they used had to be sterilized; I had to wear rubber gloves most of the time.

The first few nights after I took charge I said: "Lights out" when it was nine, turned the lights out, and went to the room outside, where I wrote out reports. But I could see that they turned the lights on again as soon as I was out of the room. This worried me a great deal, because "Lights out" means "Lights out" and there must be discipline in an army. I could not understand that these men who were "Oldtimers" did not understand that in Germany this would have been unthinkable. The third night I intended to do something about it. I walked into the room and waited until it was nine, then I turned out the light but did not go out. One of the men next to the light said: "Hey, buddy, turn on that light, like a good boy."

I told him that I was not "a good boy," but the Wardmaster in charge, and that the orders were to turn the lights out.

"That's right," said the Oldtimer, "but it doesn't say that you can't turn them on again!"

Then another shouted: "Turn on that light, Heinie"; then one of them came in his pajamas and turned on the light, pushing me against the wall, and they all laughed. When he was back in bed, I turned the light out again, and at that moment every one of them threw something at me, even two glass ducks, which is the name for the watering bottles.

I ran over to the barracks and got my Colt forty-five, strapped it around myself, and then I came back in the room with the gun in my hand. I told them that I would turn the lights out again and the first man who would come near me, get out of bed, or even make a noise, would be shot. I turned out the lights again—it was about ten o'clock. They howled with joy, threw all the rest of the things they had not thrown before, and I shot twice into the room over their heads. As yet I did not want to hurt any of them, but I would have shot the first man who came near me.

There was silence after this and then people came running, nurses, orderlies, patients from the other wards, and the Officer of the Day. He took my gun away from me and told me to consider myself under arrest and go to my barracks. The next day at ten o'clock an orderly told me to come to headquarters and see the Colonel.

Most of the Officers were in his room. I saluted in correct military fashion according to their rank, first the Colonel, then the Major, the Captain after, and lastly two First Lieutenants, each with a click of the heels and a slight bow from the waist, which was both elegant and correct and as I had seen the German Officers do.

The Colonel sat behind a desk; he was the very little man who always made speeches about an irrigation project in some country with malaria which he had been responsible for—I think it was Manila, but we heard this speech so often that I have forgotten just where it was.

He started to say, looking out of the window: "The basic function of a Hospital, Private Bemelmans, is to cure men, not to shoot them."

Then he turned around and laughed, and asked me to tell them how it happened. They laughed loud when I told them and said that after all I had done the right thing, in intention that is; they agreed that discipline is the first requisite of an Army, and when I informed them that either one had to enforce it or leave it alone and let the patients run the hospital, they nodded and laughed some more, and the Colonel said that he thought I would do more good to the service if I were outside the Hospital on the guard, since obviously I was a military man and not suited to ward duty. My gun was on his desk all this time. He gave it back to me and said: "But please don't shoot," and then he said that he would take care that I was transferred to the guard.

From then on, he, the Colonel, and all the Officers smile when they see me and it makes me mad.

But apparently there is no room for me on the guard as yet, and Beardsley and I have no particular assignment except to drill with Captain Pedley. He is a fine man, he has a likeness to President Wilson on account of his teeth, and while he is not a military man, he is not altogether so foolish and amateurish as most of the others are when they drill us—particularly the fat Officers who are squeezed into creaky leather puttees, get out of breath, and are unable to get us back into formation once they have given two or three commands. The regular army sergeant has to help them or they dismiss us and make us fall into our "original places." Also they lack that distance which must be in an army, because at rest they talk to the men about all kinds of things, even the movies; and one of them even lay down in the grass with us and picked his teeth while he told us about how he bought a house in Flushing and all the woodwork was painted, and when he had some of it scraped off there was some genuine kind of wood under the paint that is very valuable, and how mad it made him that the former owner was so stupid to cover it up and now he had to have all the wood scraped, it cost a lot of money.

Of course all the men are from colleges or as good as he is, but then they are privates now and he is an Officer. He also spoke to me at that time in German—*"Wie geht es Ihnen?"* he said and a few sentences like that—and he tells us that he has been in Heidelberg and Vienna and that the post-graduate courses in Vienna are a fake, but very fine for drinking and girls. Afterwards we drill again. This seems wrong to me.

None of these Officers can ride, fence, or fight; most of them wear glasses. Only the Colonel is a West Pointer, but he is very old and continually makes speeches, mostly in Oswego, on that irrigation project.

We have a Glee Club and there are dances. Beardsley and I do not go out much; but there is one from New York, a very tall man, in fact the tallest of all the men, who takes leaves over the weekend and says he goes to New York. He keeps to himself, has a silver hairbrush, and says he is in Society. He is an architect; but Beardsley, who knows New York and Society, says that he is not in the Register, but that he thinks he has seen him at some parties where everyone can get in.

Beardsley has found a fine way to fool the Officers. At inspection, they look at the bed to see if the linen is clean. We have to wash it ourselves and that is a lot of unpleasant work, so he has told me how one keeps one sheet clean by putting it in paper and carefully away. On Saturday, then, we take the usual sheets and the pillowcase off and we take the clean sheet out of the paper and fold it so that a quarter of it covers the top of the mattress. Then it is turned back, comes up over the blanket as if it were the second sheet, and then the end is tucked in around the pillow and the bed looks snow-white and passes. After inspection the white sheet is carefully folded up again and put back into the locker for next Saturday and the old sheets are used during the week.

We are now on the roster for Kitchen Police and this is a miserable job, particularly as the cook—his name is Lichten—burns the beans to the bottom of two square tin tubs which are as deep as an ashcan. When we have washed them we have to go with head and shoulders to the bottom of these receptacles and with a teaspoon scrape the black crust from the bottom. The water is greasy and not hot and it is a filthy job.

The nurses that came up from New York are not what we thought they would be. The one at the head of them is a crude person with a revolting fat body and the face of a streetcar conductor; she also has a stupid walk and a common voice. She teaches us how to make beds, take temperatures, and change the linen of patients in bed without moving them. All the men detest to be taught this by women and much more so when she does it; they are very clumsy at it and cannot make the neat corners that seem so simple to women. But because they know this, they make us feel silly. There is only one . . . she is young and lithe and has lovely black hair.

On Sunday afternoon they all sit down at the edge of the parade ground and look out over Lake Ontario; from far away they look like gulls at rest in their white dresses. I want to show them that we can do some things that they can't do and also impress the little nurse, and I have arranged to get a horse from the livery stable. Down close to where they sit is a wide ditch and I will ride up, gallop, and jump that ditch. The horse I got is seemingly good enough to do that. I rode along, then let him out when he came to the ditch. He stopped so suddenly that I was thrown over his head, taking the bridle with me; it came off and the horse ran back, jumping over two of the Major's children who were playing in front of Officers' Row. Then he ran down to where our mules eat grass and a quartermaster helped me get him. Next day there is a note on the bulletin board, saying: "Privates will not ride in front of Officers' Row," and it is signed by the Colonel.

the
Kitchen of
the ISOLATION HOSPITAL

FORT ONTARIO

THE OPERATION

We have two scarlet fever cases, and a sign is stuck on the bulletin board, that two men are wanted to take care of them, two men who have had scarlet fever and therefore are immune to it. Beardsley and I volunteer for this job; we both have had this fever.

The Isolation Hospital, a little brick building that has been given this title, is far away from all other houses. It has two small rooms for the patients, one for each, and a room for Beardsley and me, besides a bathroom, a combination kitchen and living room, and a porch. There is a telephone, and the house is stocked with linen, medicaments, hospital supplies, and dishes.

The patients are there already. One is a quiet, colorless man; the other, named Carey, is a mean, quarrelsome lout, without manners and stupid. We are to stay there, one on night duty, the other on day, never leave the building, and take care of the patients.

The house stands on a hill, on one side the old fortress, in front of it the lake, in back the parade ground; and anyone coming can

11

be seen long before he arrives. You have to cross the wide field on a narrow path. Along this path our food is brought, and after half an hour's exposure to cold and wind it is stale and not very good even if warmed up. The patients get milk and Zwieback. It is cold, and we have to keep a fire going all day long. Carey is in the little room at the right; on the left is the other man.

After the men had run through half the length of their sickness, the Doctor, who is a Captain named Grillmeyer, told us that now they could have food, that they must be built up with eggs, meat, vegetables. It is very fortunate that Beardsley can cook, and Captain Grillmeyer leaves us an order for the main kitchen and the commissary to supply whatever we need for the patients.

The big Hospital is filled; there are many patients, and Captain Grillmeyer is more a surgeon than a physician. He is busy operating all day and he will not come for a while, but will call up every evening, and if anything should happen we are to get in touch with him immediately.

We can order eggs, steaks, chops, vegetables, rice, noodles, sugar, flour, and many more things, even dried fruit and chocolate. In that foolish language which Beardsley and I talk, concocted of distorted words, elaborate gestures, Oh's and Ah's, the raising of eyebrows, and deep nods, we decide after the patients are asleep that we are more hungry than they and need building up ourselves, and that they can be kept without harm on a liquid diet for another week or so.

Beardsley is a fine cook. Many of the seasonings that he needs are missing, but he does well with what he has. The groceries and meats arrive promptly when ordered, the baskets are left on our porch, and we stand around the oven and fry and broil and stew ourselves into a contented after-dinner state twice every day, and have besides thick ham and eggs for breakfast. No wine, but cigars —Beardsley bought a box of them before we came.

Carey is troublesome; he smells the good food and all day long he wants to get up, so we have to chase him back to bed. Also we have read all the magazines and books that are here and talked ourselves out of everything we know that is interesting. This is dull, dead, rainy Saturday night. We don't know what to do with

ourselves; our patient is unbearably stupid. . . . But Beardsley
gets a magnificent Idea.

Beardsley went into Carey's room and looked at him with suspicion, felt his head, and asked him to show his tongue.

A while after he sent me in to look at him, I had to feel his
abdomen and shake my head.

Later we both went in and looked at him and then at each other
and walked out again.

The door was left open so that Carey could hear us and, after
we had eaten our—or rather his—custard, Beardsley said to me:
"I have seen it happen again and again; just when you think they're
out of it, this terrible complication sets in. God, I hope this poor
devil hasn't got it! Should we call Grillmeyer?" he asked himself
and then answered: "Not yet." He went in to look at Carey again.

Carey sat at the head of his bed, on the pillows, clamped to
the iron bars and ready to kick with his feet; but Beardsley calmed
him with oily words and then he allowed us to pull up the top of
his pajamas and feel his abdomen. He was white, his shapeless
mouth open, and he breathed heavily.

We went back to our cigars and Beardsley told me a loud story
of one man, such a one as this poor boy Carey, a case so identical
that the patient looked exactly like him, with precisely the same
symptoms and even color of eyes. The Doctor came too late;
he was dead in two hours—died in horrible pain—his spine con-
tracted to such a degree that his head was bent back between his
legs; he was like a ring with the navel on the outside—blue with
green spots all over. They had to bury him in a round coffin.

"But we're not going to take a chance like that with Carey,"
said Beardsley—and then in a low voice, as if he was afraid the
patient could hear and be upset, he added, pointing at himself:
"Not I, I'm responsible for this man. Close the door; I'm calling
Captain Grillmeyer on the phone, this minute."

I closed the door and we heard the bedsprings creak as Carey
climbed out of bed to listen at the door.

Beardsley came back from the phone and told me that Grillmeyer was standing by, that Carey had the unmistakable signs of

the dread disease, and that he, Grillmeyer, thought it best to operate. The room to work in, Operating Room Number One, would be kept free, a wagon sent over, and all this would take place in about half an hour.

We gave Carey enough time to get back into bed and opened the door. Beardsley asked him if he had any relatives and where they lived.

I put my hand on his head and Beardsley looked at him and said: "Steady, Carey, you'll be allright, just relax."

We brought him a pad of paper and a pencil, also an envelope with a stamp, turned out the big light, adjusted his pillow, put a white screen around his bed, and left him to go and drink more coffee and finish the cigars.

He was quiet. When he saw us, he looked down; he had not written anything but chewed on the pencil. He was almost green. I took his temperature again and his pulse, and asked him to say: "Ahh." Beardsley pressed his stomach so hard that he yelled. "Aha!" said Beardsley.

Then we made him use a bottle for Analysis and Beardsley came back with the result, in a small test tube. It was black coffee, but Carey gave only one quick look. Beardsley held it up to the light and said: "We might as well tell him now, this is the proof!"

For such an Operation, explained Beardsley, the entire cover of the stomach is removed, not with one incision but with four. He demonstrated this on his own person: two cuts ran from where the legs meet, left and right to the hips; the other two from there up to the neck. The entire covering of the abdomen is lifted off and with it also that which makes a man most proud of himself and which is no good after being replaced.

Beardsley went out, tied Doctor Grillmeyer's white gown around himself, stuffed cotton in his nose, and put on operating gloves. We washed Carey's stomach with soap and water and then shaved it and painted the area where the incisions would run with Iodine; then we gave him an enema.

It was too much; Carey turned gray and blue with almost the green spots of the dread disease on him. His eyelids fluttered like the wings of a young butterfly and the pupils almost disappeared under the upper lids. At this moment the telephone rang and

Grillmeyer called for his daily report. He also announced that he would be over tomorrow.

It was good for us at this moment that Carey was so without mind. When he came to, we informed him that sometimes in rare cases the crisis passes without need of the knife and that he looked like one of these fortunates. If he felt no pain for the next hour, he would be safe.

We both sat on his bed with watch in hand for the next hour. There was no sign of pain; he continually assured us how good he felt. He was enthusiastic about his condition even when Doctor Grillmeyer came the next day. We gave him a cigar for lunch.

SUMMER SPROUTS

We are going to produce an Entertainment at the Hotel Pontiac in Oswego. Private Pierre Loving is making the arrangements for it, the Society architect is also busy with it. Tickets will be sold; the beau monde of Oswego will be there, and the Officers and their wives; there will be dancing after the theater. The entertainment itself consists of two parts: the first is a play, *A Night at an Inn* by Lord Dunsany, followed by *Fauns' Rout*. I am to appear in this as faun; it is a pantomime, luckily I have little to do. I am painted dark brown all over and come out from behind a tree, then I dance a short while and during most of the action I sit on the side of the stage and play on my reeds. Beardsley laughs and I am not very happy at the whole business, particularly not since one of our soldiers has told me that I have a lovely body. He wants to help me paint it.

I will ask Evelyn to this party. She can bring her mother, watch the show, and afterwards we will dance.

I have known Evelyn for a month. She goes to Normal School in Oswego; I met her at a church party. On Sundays she comes out to the Fort and we walk around and sit on the lawn above the Fortress, under the flag in the shelter of a rock. The wind here is so strong that the flag up on the pole continually makes a fluttering noise—pupupupupupup—almost like a small motorboat. We look out over the lake.

One time I asked her to come earlier than usual and when she did not appear, I asked some of the men if they had not seen her. She has lovely white skin, red hair, and freckles which in Germany we call "Summer sprouts," so I asked the men if they had seen the girl with the Summer sprouts. Since then they call her "Summer sprouts." I have asked them not to, but they say it loud in the city—"Hello, Summer sprouts." She does not like this at all, but I can do nothing about it. She is very proper, and when I try to put my arm around her soft body, she wiggles loose, holds both my hands, and says: "Look at the lake."

Some days in the evening, when I am not going anywhere with Beardsley, I come to her house and the Family are very nice. They even leave us alone on the porch, but she only straightens out her dress and says: "Please don't." But they have my picture in an album on the table and under it is written: "Our soldier boy."

After she says "Don't," she arranges her hair and closes her mouth in a thin line with the lips almost swallowed. Her eyes are straight ahead as if she saw something, and she sits up stiff and straight. Beardsley tells me to ignore the "Don't"; he says it is part of a nice girl's routine, but when I ignored it, she slapped me harder than the game would seem to call for and called me a cad. Beardsley tells me that a "cad" is not very bad, to ignore the "cad" also. But I have had enough and we leave it as is and just sit quietly.

Evelyn loves to go with me to the New York Candy Kitchen, the most elegant icecream parlor in Oswego, where all the other girls she knows go with their fellows. None of them are soldiers. We always sit close to them and Evelyn converses in French with me loud enough so they can all hear it. When we walk out, every-body is quiet and looks after us, and at the door she turns and says something like: *"Ah—c'est dommage!"* She loves this word and uses it continually without need. Outside she speaks English again.

On the night of the entertainment, I came down early and looked for her. She sat in the second row with her mother to the left of her. I could see them through the opening between curtain and stage. Evelyn had on a lovely white dress of many layers of gauze, and out of her dress shone her red hair, her green eyes, and the lovely lines of her neck and shoulders.

The play earned great applause. For *Fauns' Rout,* I put on the brown paint and wear a thin strap around my middle with artificial leaves pinned on to it. When I finished dancing and sat down, I saw that a soldier who is not my friend was sitting next to Summer sprouts, very close to her; also he talked to her behind the program.

This man is related to some political boss in Pennsylvania and has gotten away with much already; also he has a room in Oswego and a car. I am afraid my evening will be ruined if I do not get out there very quickly.

After the curtain went down I ran to the dressing rooms that are below the stage and, because I was in a great hurry, I cleaned only my face and my hands to the wristbones; the rest I left brown and over it put on my shirt and Uniform and then ran up.

Evelyn sat with the soldier, but he got up and said a few nice words to me, to which I had no answer because I was too mad. He left to dance with another girl, also beautiful.

It became a lovely evening. The little Colonel was there and he was very pleasant; he did not make a speech. We had supper and punch that somebody had donated, the dancing started, and there was in this room a happiness that should always be, but seldom is, at such assemblies.

Among the dances was one called John Paul Jones and others where the ladies ran across the floor and chose their partners. Evelyn ran to me, I ran to her when this game was played the other way, and we danced more and faster and held each other tightly. Her cheeks were red with excitement, and the little hairs on the nape of her neck were lovelier than anything I have ever seen, also her ears. I looked at all this closely while we danced.

The orchestra played very fast pieces and it got very warm; we danced every dance. I had forgotten completely about my paint, and I think that this paint was not very good—with the heat and sweating it began to come off. It ran down my wet body to the elbows, to the wrists, and into the palms of the hand, from there to the fingers, and dripped down to the new white dress of my Evelyn. I had marked the white satin bodice of the dress with black fingers and palms all over. I think I could have kissed her often that night, but her mother told her about the dress, the soldiers stopped and laughed and said: "Look at Summer sprouts," and that was the end. She went home.

Entrance to the OLD Fort Ontario

THE GOOD PRISONERS

The Guardhouse at Fort Ontario is next to a long dipping road that runs into the Fort from an underpass, over which goes a railroad. The tunnel is long and of heavy stone construction. I am now on guard there; there is a strange way to do this. When someone approaches the Fort out of the tunnel, I wait until he is close enough, then I shout:

"Halt, who goes there?"

The halted one answers: "Friend."

Then I shout: "Advance, Friend, to be recognized," and the Friend advances.

This seems childish to me, as an enemy would hardly announce himself, but perhaps it is some form carried over from the Indian wars or something I do not understand.

I always have trouble in shouting the word "recognized." Most of the Officers laugh, and one night a new Major from Washington who did not know about this came into the Fort and when I stopped him he said: "My God! Are the Germans this far?" Then he laughed and said in that peculiar way Americans speak German, with the mouth too hollow and in back of the teeth:

"Wie geht es Ihnen, mein Herr?"

Since then all the Officers laugh, also the guards; they come out to see me do this and say: "Come on, Bemmy, go get him, do your stuff," and then roar with amusement, as if I were a comedian giving a performance, and they all imitate my "recognized."

We also have a duty that is called "Chase Prisoners"—walking six feet behind them. They wear stiff fatigue clothes of heavy blue canvas much too big for them, on the back of their coats a large P which means "Prisoner." They are not allowed to salute the Officers, which is no punishment, but we the guards must salute.

We have different places to chase them—to clean windows in the Officers' houses, shovel coal, deliver coal, collect garbage, collect ashes, cut grass, and many such kinds of work. They are not, of course, criminals or prisoners of war; they are soldiers who stay out late, get drunk, argue with officers, and their worst offense seems to be one called A.W.O.L.—which means absent without official leave.

Two of the prisoners, the nicest, are men who deserted the Army to join the Navy, or the other way round, and they are here for four months for this offense. They are my prisoners and we get along very well. They sing most of the time and make jokes, many of them funny, mostly when we work in Officers' houses.

The circumstances of Army Officers here—or for that matter in any other post—seem to me not overly desirable, very narrow and dull, and more so when there is no war. The houses are all alike, the wives also, and likewise the children. A poor kind of elegance is in these houses; it is made of white tennis trousers, bridge tables, a few magazines, and a piano. The furniture is bad, the rooms no better than in a house that might belong to a man like Evelyn's father, who is a repair man.

I feel there must be great jealousy among them, especially when one has what the others have not. There is one man here who drives a shiny black packard, which is too long for the garage and sticks out of the back all day. It seems to be an object of trouble. He also has a beautiful wife and better riding boots, and at his house the prisoners and I get cake and pie, which is against regulations.

The orders today are take the prisoners to the old Fortress and have them chop wood. We get two axes and I march them over.

I have noticed that among the grass in the old Fort and on the lawns that lead to it, many little flowers grow; they are like our own small field flowers in Tirol. Usually the grass in America seems to me just green, flowerless grass, but here are small white flowers, a little kind of bluebell, buttercups, and also sorrel.

The inside of the Fortress is beautiful America to me; I people it with such of this country's history as I have thought together for myself. It most probably is all wrong, because I hear that the Fort was built against the French, but for me they were Indians and I see them riding around outside shooting flaming arrows.

The prisoners are hot; they have taken off their coats and their hats, which are as foolish as the coats—like sailors' hats only without any shape whatever, or more like a baby's hat, blue, stiff, and would be difficult to draw, but it is necessary to complete the rest of the costume.

The men have chopped much wood, a large pile of it, and it soon will be time to take them back to the Guardhouse. In the past weeks the prisoners and I have become good friends; we talk always, even when I chase them, six feet apart. They talk loud ahead of them, as they cannot turn around, and I answer from the back.

The prisoners both have German parents, and they have German names, also blue eyes, blond hair, and the shapes of their heads are better because they are born here. They know many German words.

There is no one around; the Fort is in a close ring around us; and they ask if they can stop chopping. It's almost time to go back, so I say: "Yes, of course."

The sunshine is warm in here and there is no wind from the lake. We sit down together and rest and talk. They lay back and stretch in the sun and then turn around and eat blades of grass.

One of them asks me if I ever shot my gun off. I say yes and I tell them the Affair in Ward Number Three. They both agree that I did the right thing.

The other one, Walter is his name, says he is a gunsmith and small arms mechanic and that he knows all about automatics. He asks if I know how the gun is put together and taken apart.

I don't know; I have never taken it apart and I tell him this.

Then Fred, the other, says: "He'll take it apart for you and show you." Of course I know that this is a complete stupidity and against all orders to give a prisoner your gun; it is to laugh. But I like them so much and have such faith in them that I wish not to offend them, but give them proof of my friendship. Besides, if they wish to make trouble, here are two axes with long handles; and another thing is that they have only three more weeks to serve to be free.

Therefore I give my gun to Walter.

He pulled the magazine out, took the bullets out of it. With expert simplicity he changed the gun into little pieces, springs, bolts, screws; everything lay in his lap. He explained the why of everything, put it together, took it apart once more—it was very interesting—when we heard footsteps from the hall that leads into the Fort.

I took the part I had, which was the handle, and stuck it in the holster. Fred and Walter picked up the bullets, springs, screws, etc., etc., etc., and started quickly to chop wood.

The Officer of the Day was the one that made the steps. He is young, arrogant, and the only one that none of the men and not even his own brother Officers like. He looks much like a movie actor and wears such a kind of mustache with wax at the end of it.

He feels that something is wrong and does not go away. Then the whistles blow; it is noon over in Oswego and time to march the men back, but the Officer comes along, close behind me, and follows us to the Guardhouse. This is not as it should be.

After we got to the Guardhouse I locked the two prisoners in the big cage where all of them are together. The Officer of the Day is still around, but while he looks down to the underpass out of the door, I stand with my back to the cage so he cannot see it if he turns around and hold my hands open in back of me. Fred and Walter put all the missing parts into my hands. I keep them in back of me and walk over to the lavatory. There I lock the door and sit down. I have seen Walter put the gun together, fast and easy as a simple toy, yet I cannot do it. I am hot and nervous; every time I think I have it, it is wrong—the gun falls apart, or the spring jumps out, or I can't get the magazine in.

Therefore I come out again and move over to the cage. I hand the gun back through the bars, standing again with my shoulders against them, because the unpleasant First Lieutenant is still there. I give them the gun parts and all and Walter goes to his own lavatory with it; there he puts it together and gives it back to me.

Now I disappear again, to put it back in the holster, and then I can go into the Guardroom and hang it with my belt, up on a rack, where all the others are.

Uncle's Hotel in KLOBENSTEIN TIROL

MAD MAÎTRE D'HÔTEL

I have read on the bulletin board that a Hospital for the Insane will be organized in Buffalo, at Fort Porter. They need attendants there and do not wish to force anyone into this work; men are asked to volunteer for it. I am very much interested in this and only regret that Beardsley will not come along. My transfer is arranged and I leave in a few days.

The train from Oswego reached Buffalo at six in the morning and I took a streetcar that was filled with very strong-smelling Italian workingmen out to Fort Porter.

The Fort is not a Fort as one might imagine, such for example as Fort Ontario. It has no moat, ramparts, battlements, or any

25

military appearance at all. It is about half an hour's slow streetcar ride outside of the city of Buffalo and is a collection of army buildings, red and a grayish blue. A long house is the most prominent, in which are two large messhalls and kitchens. A smaller group, the non-commissioned Officers' houses, is on the most windy corner of the large ground and faces toward the river, also with an outlook toward the lake. On the corner between these two stands a square building, the Post Hospital.

Workingmen are busy making the houses over into an emergency Insane Asylum. The windows are heavily barred, the floors covered with a slippery kind of surface. One large room in the basement of the biggest house is made ready to give treatments in bathtubs that have a continuous in-and-out flow of water that is kept at certain temperatures. With these bathtubs go some kind of canvas covers to tie patients down on and in this is the first note of mischief or cruelty.

There is another room down there, a long one with a needle shower at the end that looks like a parrot cage with all the horizontal wires taken off. Away from it at the other end is a small marble table, on it a hose which throws a strong current of almost solid water, so tightly compressed is it. It can be shot at the other end, into the cage, as if from a garden hose.

There is cement mixing, carpentering, and hammering all over the place, and people stand around, as on all places where something is being built, and watch and give advice. So far, except for the bathing establishment, it is no more exciting than the building of any kind of a house.

I took a day off and went to look at Niagara Falls. It is perhaps because I took a streetcar out there that I felt they were about half as big as I thought they would be. The thrilling spot is where the water turns down and I made a shade of my hands and looked only on that, shutting out all the scenery. That was a powerful sensation. I am sorry that the Falls are surrounded by what Beardsley calls "Beautiful Dreck." Very interesting was a story that the conductor of the streetcar that took me back told me about the Falls.

A tug belonging to the Shredded Wheat Company, which makes a breakfast food and has a factory near by, broke its rudder and drifted toward the Falls, helpless. A little away from where the water falls down, the tug got stuck on a rock.

The Police and the Fire Department of Buffalo raced out to help them. This took a long time, and the men on the tug looking down could see and hear how the tug slowly moved inch by inch, scraping over the rock, either to be more firmly grounded, or also to go over and down. The Police came in the dark; they tried to shoot safety lines to the tug, but could not reach it. A heavy fog sat on the waters, and not until the sun rose were they able to shoot the line over to the tug. When they managed to get the men off, all of their hair had turned white from horror in this terrible night.

More soldiers are arriving; they know nothing of an Insane Hospital and also nothing of Insanity.

Today, a new group of men have come to us, Nurses, Attendants, and Doctors, and many more soldiers, also a Catholic Chaplain with a studious, earnest face; he is very young.

Many of the men are male nurses from the State Hospitals for the Insane. I observe them carefully—they are all strong, but I expected some sign of their profession on them, just what I do not know—this is, however, not apparent in them. They seem ordinary, normal, healthy people and talk of what anybody else talks of.

One of them, who seems the most important of the group, is a tall Irishman with a shock of flaming red electric hair that stands in a bush, sideway as if the wind were tilting it, or like the comb of a rooster on one side of his head. He has freckles, even on his fingernails, and a way of holding his head as if he were looking over a mass of people and listening into distance up and on one side, to the side where his hair points. He is immaculate; his arms and legs are like oak timbers, so strong they have a curve in them. There is also red hair on his hands, he holds them open at his side; he talks little, eats very fast, walks around the Hospital all day, and speaks a strong dialect, which of course must be Irish. It is an English with which he takes more air than is normally needed to say anything and, while it is loud, he seems to talk in, instead of out, with his breathing. I like him.

We have had several lessons in Anatomy. For this purpose skeletons have been shown, stereopticon pictures of the inside of the body. I attend these lectures with great interest and make drawings of all I see and read; therefore I soon know the names of all the bones, the most important muscles, and understand the body's construction, its contents, the position of the organs; and when I see people walk, or stand up after such a lesson, the solemn wonder of ourselves fills me with a deep respect. I feel that when I see children run, there is much happiness in understanding a small part of this organism. The Doctor who gives these lessons is addressing himself almost completely to me alone, as the others are not very excited about it.

The Insane Asylum is finished and the Irishman is really in charge. There are Lady Nurses, regular Army nurses of a dreadful caliber, women who look like what we refer to in Germany as *"Canaille."* They are gross and not women at all, particularly not in walk and voice.

Among the instructions we are given is this: never to leave the nurses unprotected or alone in a ward with patients. This seems like one of Beardsley's funny ideas; I am sure they could protect themselves and that no man would do them harm. I have never seen such formidable women, with shoes like they wear and legs like our barefooted peasants'.

There are more lessons and they are getting closer to the work. Always lock the door behind yourself when entering or leaving a ward. The most important rule is never, never to bring arms, knives, scissors, razorblades, razors, or any other instrument that might be a weapon into the wards. The patients are to be fed with spoons only.

The first patients arrived today. It was late at night, but many people waited outside on the street for the long train of ambulances and cars that came up from the railroad station with the patients and the guards that have been their attendants.

These men, the ill ones, seem stupefied and tired; some are in straitjackets and have a guard each. They are all taken to the basement where the baths are. I am told that they have been transported from Brest and, except for this evening, have not been out of their clothing. I do not know whether this is true, it seems possible. Their clothes are filthy, they have beards, also there is a sickening stench about them and their underclothing is foul.

They are bathed and then assigned to wards.

The Doctors do this. The red Irishman is in the middle of all this. To every ward there is assigned a regular State Asylum trained attendant and a novice soldier. The patients get milk, pajamas and bathrobes, and slippers that give them no foothold on the polished floors, while we have strong shoes with rubber so we can stand our ground when anything happens.

There are rows of solitary cells with what the Irishman calls "the tough customers" in them. They have what we believe to be mad faces, as bad as those that actors, mediocre ones, make when they are in horror plays. From that row comes howling. Some of these men have besides the mental sickness other vile diseases; it would be best to kill them, says the Irishman, that seems the kindest thing to do.

The night they arrived seemed very crisp with danger and excitement, but nothing happened. They sat on their beds and seemed no different from any other patients; some of them wept and mumbled to themselves.

It is a cruel thing to think, but I was disappointed, as were also all the other new men. We thought they might do some funny things, but the Irishman says to wait, they will, and too much of it, in a little while.

He has a definite, rough, and authoritative way with them; they are absolutely in his charge. He lets them know that by word and gesture and the tone of his voice. His personality seems to have developed out of doing this for years. It is in the way he stands and walks, also in the look in his eyes—they are water-blue and penetrate and are strong.

The patients have been here for a while now. I have learned to know their faces and many things have happened. They are not funny, but sadder than anything I thought could be and never in the least to laugh at. They are heavy, disturbing cases, mostly locked into their inner selves, their condition to be seen only in their eyes and also when they stand at the barred windows and look out into the trees and the street with free people walking up and down and trying to look in. They pace, and something of their unhappiness and condition jumps over to me. The Irishman says one must never feel sorry for them or understand, or attempt to understand, them and not to talk to them. But the transfer of their misery makes me limp and terribly tired.

The patients have small duties to perform—make beds, sweep, dust, wash windows on the inside. The men in this ward suffer from an illness which makes them periodically dangerous. It can be felt coming on; the unrest and disturbance in their minds gets out of all bounds and beyond their power to control it. They get irritable all at once and refuse to obey, grumble at any instruction given them. Then they have to be watched, and all at once without warning their control breaks, they jump and attack. In rare cases other patients are the object, but mostly the Wardmaster. They seem to go for the men from the back and, since they are soldiers and can fight, it is a great deal of work to overcome them. They are terribly strong once they have a hold, and in this state they cannot feel pain. At the least sign of fighting, the Wardmasters from the other wards come in and help. As many as six men fall on one patient; they choke him and hold him down until the man is blue in the face.

The first time I saw a fight I was unable to do anything but try and stand it. It is degrading and miserable, yet one cannot look away. After the patient is overcome, the men carry him down to the continuous bath, where he is left to soak in water in changing temperatures for, I hear, as much as twenty hours. When they come out, they are without any strength and then there is no trouble for several weeks. I have not heard of patients fighting together. This is strange. In almost all cases the others stand by and look; seldom do they help the nurse.

Those who howl in the solitary cells are left there. When the men go in to feed one of them, they rush in like a football team, almost on signal. One opens the door, the others go after the patient, to bring him food or to clean the place.

There are also two religious cases. One has worn the skin from his knees, sliding on them in continuous prayer. A new case has arrived and been put in with him; I went to see him. I have a pass-key and have become careless. I locked the door behind me, but the man I came to visit was around the corner of the room where I could not see him. This Hospital is a makeshift building; in a real Insane Hospital there are no corners around which one cannot see. As I walked forward, he jumped at me from the bed and closed his fingers around my throat.

I felt singing in my ears, not much pain. I could not breathe, I saw the religious patient for a while and he swam away into a darkness that was bluish. I felt a bang on my head and nothing more until I came to in another room of the Hospital. It had to be kept quiet because I had no right to go in there. The fortunate thing was that I fell against the door with the patient, and the loud bang brought the Irishman.

At first the attacks on the patients and the way they were choked into a corner made me hate the Irishman and all the other attendants. But even before the attack on me I already knew it was the only thing that could be done there and then. They are as kind as they can be, but they would be dead if they did not instill fear, and of course they fight only when they absolutely must. Also when the patients get out of the baths, the attendants are as nice to them as they are to anyone.

In this ward are also other interesting cases. There is a glass man. A mattress has to be kept on the floor next to his bed, because he is afraid of falling out and breaking. He moves everywhere with care, he screams when anyone comes too near him and sits down with great apprehension. And there are two men who are like puppets. In the morning they have to be sat up in bed, and they sit motionless. They have to be stood up, and if one were to take their arms in the morning and raise them over their heads, the arms would still be that way at night. Another patient repeats one word, the sound of which he likes, endlessly, over and over in monotone.

The most pitiful of all the men are several cases who suffer from persecution fear. They stuff magazines into their bathrobes and sit in corners; they are certain we wish to kill them, stab or shoot at them. They have to be forcefuly fed because they think that all food given them is poison. Or we have to eat a little of it ourselves in front of them or give them the trays of other patients who have already started eating. If they still refuse to eat, we sometimes just leave the food. They do not look at it, or curse and upset it, or smear it on themselves, but when we go out—in most cases it happens the moment we are gone—they ravenously eat everything.

They never sleep; at times they doze off in the middle of the night, but only to rise with horrible shrieks from their beds, and in the night these wards are most unhappy. God have pity on these men or let them die.

Of no use at all is religion or the young Chaplain; he feels that, I think, because he is unhappy himself. It made him mad that one woman who visited her husband here seems to be worried only whether he went to confession before he got insane. Yet I think, with its great promise of miracle and power and its character of mysterium, the Catholic religion would be the one most easy to help these patients; the transfer from their own make-believe horror to the church would be easier. I cannot explain this right, but this religion and their illness have something in common, like the texture of two tapestries, while other religions are not so, they are like linen or paint compared to it.

There is one man here who is continually searching for something in the toilet bowl, in a corner of his ward. He has his arm so deep in it that at times we can hardly get it out. He says his friend is down there. Also he talks through the barred window, never-ending poetry without rhyme and yet with a meter. His voice falls and rises with it and sometimes he yells the words. One poem I have remembered:

> The Cigarette Trees bloom over the clouds
> And Mainstreet looks like a melon,
> I am going to paint the battleships with Sarsaparilla,
> Do not forget me, the sun will melt this house.

He helps the Wardmaster in his ward, whenever one of the other patients gets out of hand. They are all violent cases and in this ward are only regular State Asylum men and the strongest. He is very strong, was a sergeant and killed an Officer in Europe. The attendants have allowed him to help in a pinch when they were hard up with two men fighting them, but the Irishman has warned them not to take help from the man with the toilet bowl, to watch that one.

The days are very short; the light changes early and at that hour the patients are depressed more than at any other time of the day; then also most of the fighting goes on and all of them walk around.

In this early evening I look out of the window and always wait for a certain little boy. He runs along home under the trees to a house at the end of the road, and in his thin legs and the little pants, fluttering in the wind, that hang down over them is the misery of all the world.

There is only tortured madness here, no single happy lunatic. In Tirol, in Uncle Hans's Hotel, we had a Maître d'Hôtel who one day became a happy case.

The Hotel stands high up on a mountain and is very elegant. The cogwheel railroad makes its last stop there. The name of the village is Klobenstein and the Hotel is named "The Old Post," *Die alte Post*. Further down, past the park and the tennis courts of the Hotel, is a low building, a peasant Inn; it has a little garden. We have a large one; our table cloths are white, theirs are colored with checks.

The Maître d'Hôtel always stands in front of the garden when the cogwheel railroad arrives, waits until the people come down, and smiles at them, bows, and seats them in the garden where they can eat and look at the scenery. The peasant Inn has no scenery as there are a hill and trees in front of it.

Uncle Hans first noticed that the Maître d'Hôtel was mad when one day he stood in front of the garden as the full train arrived and sent all the people down to the peasant Inn, saying we had no room, although the garden was completely empty and could seat over a hundred people. When one man with a family of six people, Prussians, but very well dressed, wanted to come in, the Maître d'Hôtel kicked him in the shins and shouted and sent him down to the peasant Inn. The little garden below was filled to bursting, they had not enough food and only one fat waitress. Some people could not find seats and started to come back, but the Maître d'Hôtel stood at the end of our hotel and picked up rocks. Then they sat inside the peasant Inn.

The next thing that happened, that same evening, was that he came into the salle à manger without even his shirt, stitch-naked, and chased Annie and the other servant girls around the room, which was filled with the regular "Pension" guests of the Hotel. Uncle called a Doctor, and the Maître d'Hôtel was locked in his room and put to bed. Uncle was very sad because this Maître d'Hôtel had been with us for twenty years.

In the morning he was gone. He had jumped out of his room through the window—curtain, glass, and all, without hurting himself—from the first floor, which is the second in America.

Aunt Marie was very proud of the Hotel park and gardens. They were neatly trimmed plots of greenery and flowers, bordered with rose trees and many fine plants, including tulips. This Maître d'Hôtel, although it was bitterly cold on top of the mountain in the morning, had used the early hours, working with great speed and the silver coupon shears from Uncle Hans's desk, to cut off every flower in the park. When we found him, he was on the second floor of the Hotel, hanging out of a balcony and cutting the geraniums in a window box next to the balcony. He had also cut them, stems, leaves, and all, on all the other windows. Uncle Hans took him by the arm and talked to him, and he answered reasonably, went to his room, and got dressed.

Because he had been with us for twenty years, Uncle Hans did not want to hurt him and gave him a good deal of money, after he was dressed and seemed allright again, and said: "Take a vacation, Herr Nolte." Nolte packed and took his money, but he came back again. In the village store he had spent all the money for every bottle of perfume he could get. This perfume was very bad, as it was bought for the peasants, that is, it smelled loud and of flowers, all sorts of them, sweet terrible scents assorted.

This he poured into himself in the reading room, into his overcoat pocket, into his bowler hat. He stuck a bottle, without the cork, upside down into his trousers and let the perfume run down there. He also drank it and rubbed some on his head, and all the time he cried and said: *"Ah, wie schön, wie gut, wie reichlich!"*

—"Ah, how beautiful, how good, how plenty!" Then he took his clothes off, ran to the church, locked himself in, and rang the churchbells.

And that is the way, I thought, the patients in this Hospital should be, not sad but filled with highest spirits. I could never feel sorry for Nolto and had enough to amuse myself for months when I thought of him.

The Irishman was right about the man who searches in the toilet bowl. He bit through the throat of an attendant while he was helping put another man down. They had to beat him unconscious, six of them, ramming their elbows into his nose and abdomen to get him loose while he shook all of them back and forth between the walls. The attendant is in the Hospital.

A happy case has arrived at last, a sweet little patient whom I liked at once. He comes into the Messhall for the first sitting. We have so many patients that we have two meals three times a day.

In the long double row of bent patients, he comes trotting like a gay pony, hopping up and down and continually smiling. He makes six hoppy steps to their one, and when he comes to the column that holds up the ceiling in the middle of the room, he dances around it, quick enough to be in his place again while the others just pass.

Next he has a little ceremony for his stool. He hops around it twice, shifts it into the right position back and forth, to the left and right and once around, with one of its legs in a certain place. And when he is finally seated he carries his attention to the dishes, he rubs the plate on his nose in a circle, three times, thereby giving it some power or just a greeting; then he rubs the back of the spoon on his nose also three times, this way and then the other way; then comes the cup, the bottom of that and then the rim. He whispers a few words into the cup and rubs it on the table. Then he mixes all the utensils and puts them in order and looks around, quickly like a bird. He smiles and nods several times as if to assent strongly to someone's words. But he is also a bedwetter and must be called out in the night.

MY BATHTUB
FORT PORTER

TO THE LEFT

At three o'clock is a concert for the patients, to be held in a long, windy porch. Rows of benches have been placed, a platform faces them. Nina Morgana will sing; they say she is from the Metropolitan or will go there.

The men were walked in with all the attendants available; they stand at the sides of the benches. Almost one soldier, nurse, or guard for every four men.

They watched every motion of the singer with interest; it was a change from ward routine, but I doubt whether any of the men have heard much music, would know any of its values. They seem appreciative out of duty. There is no disturbance; the guards keep their eyes on the men; it would be disastrous if anything happened here, at least very dangerous, and it is very brave of Miss Morgana to come here.

With her are the Officers, and I thought it tactless that they somehow managed to give the impression that they and Miss Morgana belonged together and were much above both the patients and the soldiers. This was shown on their faces.

Tomorrow the men who take care of the patients, the attendants, will be examined. There seems to be danger of some of them getting ill themselves. The red Irishman tells me that in

State Asylums the nurses get very long vacations and that a high
percentage of them go mad in the end; also he says that all the
Doctors are half mad. I have not been able to observe this myself;
they are peculiar and there is a tendency to assume that they are
not normal, which I think is a wish, not a fact.

We are being examined; two Doctors test reflexes, cover our
eyes and then look into them quickly. We have to find the tip of
our noses with the index finger of the right hand and eyes closed,
and other such tests, also of course the knee test.

After we pass the Doctors, we are ordered to get into two lines,
one on the right, one on the left. The line at the right is long, the
one on the left very short. After a while, the ones at the left, with
whom I am, are told to stay, and the right line is dismissed. I am
fortunate for there is confusion while the dismissed pass by us,
and I manage to leave with them, stepping out of my line.

I have done the better thing; the men at the left were again
examined, more thoroughly so, and five out of twenty-four are
being held back. They pack their things, and that evening they
are in bathrobes at one of the tables in the patients' Mess and in
a ward. Dreadful as it is, some of the other men have a hard time
to conceal laughing at this.

No one, however, asks them anything, and they look down at
their plates and feel ashamed. One of them in the middle of the
meal throws his cup against the wall and sobs and then screams.
The red Irishman is quickly behind him and holds him tightly.
He fights, and then two more help to carry him out. My knees
are weak, my hands not my own, I feel in danger.

Yesterday afternoon, as I walked across the parade ground,
someone shouted my name loudly and right in back of my left
shoulder. I turned and there was no one there, all around the
mile-wide field.

I stood still motionless and with loud heartbeat; there was a
bitter taste in my mouth and my hands felt loose again; so did my
arms and my whole body, then hot and cold and wet, and tears
came to my eyes.

Then I walked to my quarters and there again I heard my

name called by the same voice, as distinct, and again in back of my left shoulder. I turned instantly—there was no one there again.

The barracks in which I live have a hall and a wide straight stairway leading up. This stairway started to turn itself around me in a yellow light. I fell.

Luckily no one saw this; I came to my consciousness again and slowly walked up and lay down on my bed.

In the last month two men in this room have jumped up in the night and became patients. I see them every day in the Messhall; I think they will not come out again.

For two hours I lay straight on my bed and looked at the ceiling. I thought of going to a doctor in Buffalo, but he might only give me away; besides all the psychiatrists are from Buffalo and work here, I would most probably run into one of our own men.

Also would I hold out as far as Buffalo? Now that the mind is loose from its moorings, I think it best to end my life rather than go into the wards. I have formed this plan; if only I can carry it through and hold on that long, because I am afraid to even move.

I know where the Guardhouse is, I know where the guns are. I will walk down the stairs, straight out the door, across the lawn and into the Guardhouse. There are men there, but I will manage to be plain so they will notice nothing, go into the lavatory with a gun that I will take from a holster, and then shoot up into my brain through the roof of the mouth.

I get up and start to walk down the stairs and out of my quarters with my mind fixed on this Must of death and afraid that a second of thinking, of reasoning, of hope, might mean weakness and change of mind.

I go out of the Barracks and fall over a cat and the cat does not run and everybody laughs loud.

An order had been issued the day before to get rid of all the cats, of which we have a plague. Two soldiers collected them all over the Fort and brought them back in their arms, then dropped them into an ashcan that is outside our Barracks. When they thought they had all the cats in there, they went to the Hospital and got four cans of ether and poured them in over the animals, then clamped the lid down, put a stone on it, and left. Some cat friend who did not like this came and took the stone off, upset the barrel, and the cats came out and regained consciousness.

They are wandering around in a stupor, lean against the ashcan, and look cross-eyed. Their motions are so funny, at times like half wound up toys, at others, particularly the black cats, who are wet with sweat and ether, they look like caricatures of cursed souls. None of them can stand up; it is so strange and funny, everyone laughs; so must I, and it seems so silly and useless to think that one might want to die.

I have never heard my name again although I have waited for it, with a mind, inside my own, that is on watch all the time and dreads this. The front mind does the duties and thinks.

I have found a way to calm myself: I go myself to the long baths. There is a bathroom for the men that is not much used, as they prefer showers. I lie in it whenever I can, and I have started to think in pictures and make myself several scenes to which I can escape instantly when the danger appears.

These are all scenes from my childhood. Best of all, whenever the bitter taste, the tugging inside, and the prickly fear in hands and temples arrives, is a walk from the Castle Tirol down to Meran. I have taken this walk often. I remember almost every tree and the turns of the road, the sound of the churchbells from Meran below and from the village up above, the light on the mountains at different times of the day and the season.

I make it a practice to walk through Tirol every time I am in danger. I start from the door of the Castle and go down past the highest vineyards—there I place a little girl with bare feet—to a field on the mountain slope, where oxen drag a plow, and to an Inn, where I stop and sit down. I drink wine and eat boiled chestnuts, and I have built all this with desperate detail and clarity and as if I were painting it. To this end, the color of the red wine, the shape of the bottle in which it comes, the pattern of the chairs and the table, the lamp and the foliage of the tree, are things that hold my mind and have to be thought about.

I go there in sunshine and in rain, in summer and in winter, to vary the play, to change the clothes, the room, the people. We are inside the Inn in winter. I people this room with the group of peasants that appear in Defregger's paintings and on the covers of the *Fliegende Blätter*. There are hunters with dachshunds and guns, gendarmes, children; and the detail of the room—with ivy growing out of pots high over the windows and running along the ceiling—the detail goes to flies, to the design on the buttons of the gendarmes. In all of this is protection, and time is gained; in this warm water is not only rest for the body, but for my mind, a bath for the soul.

In six days I have constructed six such Islands of Security: the Inn in Klobenstein, with the red sunset of the Dolomites and many people I love; a walk on the Danube from Regensburg, Bavaria, to Kelheim and a ride back on a slow train; a visit up and down to the Hungerburg, over Innsbruck in Tirol; a performance of a group of the Peasant Theater in Munich, and a visit to a small restaurant in back of the Church of Our Lady; also a ride in a landau through Munich and the English Gardens.

I intentionally think little of my brother, my mother, my friends, because in this I sense a bridge to the dangerous state. Pictures I want, instant happy pictures that are completely mine, familiar, warm, and protective.

I have bought some colored crayons, and make some of the sketches, but this is inadequate. The mental pictures are luminous, alive, and real, while the drawings are inadequate; only they help to recall detail. There is a window on the peasant church in Klobenstein, Tirol, which I had completely forgotten until I made a picture of the church. This helped me to reconstruct the entire scene.

There is a poor Jew in the Hospital. He is pretty bad, in a solitary cell. He is occasionally beaten up, that is, he must be subdued and then taken to the bath, where he screams, as they use the cold spray on him. It is not because of his religion, but the same treatment as all other cases receive who are violent as he is. However, he has clear moments and no one comes to see him; he is all alone.

Rabbi Kopald is at the head of a Temple, called Emmanu-El, it is on the best street, the Avenue, in Buffalo. I visited him and told him of this man, that it might do good to see him, that he would perhaps be able to find his people and get him out.

I expected to find a man with a little black cap and sore eyes and a mumbling beard, which was my mental picture of a Rabbi; but he is tall, elegant, with the manners of a nervous scientist or surgeon, and seems to be completely unreligious, without the behavior of benediction and salvation in his speech or movements.

He is a great surprise to me, in his freedom. He has given me several introductions to houses, some of them Jewish and some Christian. He seems to know everybody in Buffalo and be in high esteem. I attend some of his services, and always enjoy the blessing at the end, which is very simple and well written, most so the words: "And may the Lord lift up His countenance, and give you peace."

We speak of religion and I am glad to hear how free he can be, how without hocus pocus his acceptance and his preaching of religion are.

There are dances at the Temple for the soldiers. I go to all of them. The girls come from nice families and are very lovely and most of all very simple. Simple and unaffected as they are, I cannot talk to them, and this seems stupid. It is also, when I think of it, remarkable that you can walk up to one you have never seen before, take her around the waist, and dance and press her, only because this is a ballroom and there is music. Anywhere else one would have to be very well acquainted and alone. One of the girls at a dance in another place, at a large house, is more beautiful than all the others. This is at a Presbyterian Church. My hands are moist and my cheeks burning, and when we have danced, I eat icecream. I have nothing to say, that is, I can't say it, but in the bath I take her, Doris, with me from the Castle Tirol to Meran.

There are more invitations. I have bought a Uniform in Buffalo and have it pressed one time very week, also gloves and several white bands to wear inside the collar. The Chaplain has a list of people who wish to entertain. He sorts out the guests and keeps in mind what people would like which kind of soldier. He sends me to nice houses, I think to the best, and almost every evening is taken up.

Many of the larger parties are very dull and all alike—a dance, icecream and cake, then some terrible singing. But the American soldier songs are humorous, not like the Germans', which are filled with blood and iron and the Kaiser. Here they are: "Johnny, Get Your Gun," "If He Can Fight Like He Can Love," "Fritzi, Pull Your Shade Down, Fritzi Boy," "They Were All Out of Step but Jim."

This singing is well meant but it makes me feel embarrassed. I always feel bad when I see many people do the same thing, that is, marching, playing, singing, particularly marching; and when I see children marching, and certainly so with a band, my eyes fill with tears, why I don't know.

After we have sung and eaten, there is a march around and after that more dancing; then the band plays "Good Night, Ladies," and it is over.

The soldiers have to go home alone. All the girls, even the unfortunate looking, are protected and taken away by parents or chaperones. They are all of nice or better people, and our men as they go home complain about not being able to get them. They say that very plainly and exchange their opinions as to how well it would be to have this or that one and why. They do that still in the dark in their beds, and the phrase usually is: "I betcha that blonde would be a good love," only a more direct word is used for "love."

I can talk now, particularly to Doris; her parents are German. They have a very feudal estate on the shores of the lake, several automobiles, servants and factories, also horses and a billiard room.

The chauffeur, who is also German, calls for me in the high Pierce Arrow car, and the food there is extremely good, also the wines, mostly good Moselle and Rhine wines. One of the rooms in this house is decorated like a Bierstube, and the old Gentleman head of the family is a Doctor, plain and elegant, and his wife is kind, motherly, and very plain in her dress. We speak mostly, in German, of Germany, of Munich, of the Rhine, also of Meran and Tirol. I think the war makes him sad and he is glad a soldier who is a German visits him.

On Sundays when the sun is out we go riding, and when it rains we sit in the house and read. Doris is proud of having a soldier. There seem to be no Officers around or at least none she likes better, and she says that, if we wanted to get married, her father would do nothing about it, because I am in the Army and an American Soldier and Citizen. Also because I am German it would make him happy anyway, and so it would be pleasant all around, but nothing became of it, because I was afraid to ask her.

There is much work at the Fort, new patients have arrived, many of them, new barracks are going up, the kitchens are enlarged, and the Messhalls made twice as big as they were. Everyone is working very hard.

What with this work, the Rabbi Kopald, the parties and Doris, her horses and the country, the fear has almost gone and appears only in the middle of the night when I awake trembling and wet from toes to the top of my head. But now I am so well trained that even without preparation and the bath I can hang my pictures over the terror, quickly, and blot it out.

The great misfortune is over there in the Hospital. Instead of locking the patients up together, marching them around to the ugly Messhalls where they must be quiet, and then having them sit on their beds all day long, where they are stuck in misery and illness, and when this overcomes them fighting them down, if each one could be taken away alone with somebody who cared and taught them how to think their way out of this, they might be helped. That is the hopelessness of the Asylum. They should be far away from it, from their own kind, and if they have no good memories to think of, then the present should be made happy and light for them. Their cure need only be a landscape, a decent person, even a dog or a horse, but it should be some one thing they can love outside of themselves. But of course I cannot see myself how this could be put into practice.

UNCLE JOSEPH AND HIS DOG

TIROL IN BUFFALO

By accident somebody left a wooden crate, in which oranges are delivered, in the baking part of the oven last night, and in the morning it was toasted without being burned. It was made of thin pine wood, and when I came into the kitchen, I felt heartsick because it smelled just like my sawmill in Tirol.

When I close my eyes and smell a little piece of wood which I have broken off the crate, I can see the mill, the road that leads to it, the water that comes in through the roof. This water runs along in a narrow wooden river that is carried along on heavy beams and sometimes built onto strong trees. This is done to keep it high and then give the water much drop, so that, when a wooden partition is pulled out, it shoots down through the roof onto the wheel that is thirty feet high and begins to turn it.

Not all the water goes that way; some of it is left below in the bed of the brook. This water is crystal clear, the bed is covered with fine sand; ferns and waterplants stand in it, and little lizards, jet black with flaming carmine patches, also many frogs, green as grass, with golden eyes. And little fishes live there.

In the valley stand the highest pines. The road winds in and out on the mountain side, only teams of oxen can go along to drag the heavy loads; they are slow but much stronger than horses, and the wagons they pull have two little wheels in front and long beams that drag along and act as a brake, because the road is very steep and always changes up and down.

Over the entrance of the mill is a statue of the Lord; He sits resting His chin in His arm and is very sad. The statue, like all the Christuses along the road, and there are many of them, is the work of a peasant artist. The artists have made the Christuses so earnestly that the suffering they themselves felt has gone over into the wood. They carve on them their own faces, and they are beautiful, honest, simple, and look sorry for the whole world. The design is not always good; the dimensions are wrong—sometimes they are a little too fat, or the legs are not long enough—the part from the knee to the ankle is very hard for them to carve.

Because of this, the statues are humble, and each one, with his little house around it, which is seen only in Tirol and Austria, is a private, different Christus and much stronger than the good, heroic ones that are too beautiful and too much alike.

At the base of all these Christuses are flowers from the fields that peasants put there—the lovely yellow cowslips, blue gentians, crocuses—willows—and, in the winter, pine branches.

The trees here about, and they are almost all pines, are free of branches almost to the top. This is because the peasants are poor; they cut the branches up to a height of thirty feet, trim the wood in the center for fire, and use the small ends with the needles for the stables. That is why the stables here smell so lovely.

No one believes me that the cattle on the high mountains have much more intelligent faces than in the valleys. This is also true of the people, even of their dialect. In the narrow valleys they are sullen and gruff and hardly speak; up above is more sun, lighter air, high voices, and much room, and they are happier, sing and dance. And the cattle grazing along dangerous precipices must think more; the oxen and the cows have serious and beautiful faces; they are also better in construction and much cleaner.

The finest place to see all this is on the hill in back of the mill, with the water flowing into the roof and coming out as spray below, with the sound of the wheel turning. From here a whole world can be seen—houses far below, little and littler; a church on the mountain opposite with a tower sharp as the point of a pencil, its bells clearly heard. Behind it soaring into the sky is the ring of mountains that change colors all day long and are glowing purple and carmine when the sun sets. All this I see with the little piece of wood under my nose. I can even ride back to the hotel with it and see the German tourists who always stand in groups, after they have written postal cards, and argue about the names of the mountains. They do that with printed panoramas in their hand, pointing and get very mad. They don't believe even our head waiter and look into the Baedeker to see if he is right about the height of each mountain.

The cogwheel railroad that runs from Bozen up the Ritten, to the last station, which is Klobenstein, has an electric locomotive. The car is a streetcar, really, that runs through Bozen and up on the mountain under its own power, but when it takes the long steep mountain climb, the little locomotive gets behind it and a man attaches three different safety couplings. Then the conductor blows a little trumpet that sounds: "Baehh," and the car tilts upward, and slowly it moves up, very slowly. I have found out that when I call long distance on the telephone the same sound as that on the locomotive, a howling, electric noise, is heard. Therefore when I get very homesick, instead of forgetting about it, I call long distance to hear this and then hang up.

I think if anybody would find out in this place about the little piece of pine wood which I heat and smell and the long distance calls for no purpose, I might have difficulty.

When the danger is of the worst kind, then my safest Island is Uncle Joseph. He cannot hear. He is up on the mountain and a simple peasant priest, and people from far away come to him because he is so good, and to confess to him because it is much easier. He watches their lips and forgives everything when they stop talking.

He has a little dog of no race, salt and pepper colored, with short legs, ears like a bat, and a face like a very old disgusted man. With this dog Uncle Joseph takes his daily prayer walk, with a little book out of which he reads. He always carries an umbrella that swings in back of him as if he had wheels inside and it were the pendulum. He speaks little, I think, because he feels that nobody can hear him either, but when he speaks he says everything very loud. Mostly he speaks with his eyes. He must be seventy years old, but he is very hale and sometimes, for no reason, on a long walk, he skips and jumps a few steps and then turns around to smile. He has permission from the Pope to wear a beard, because he has a goiter, but in Tirol a goiter is something almost to be proud of, because all the peasants have them and therefore speak with a deep basso.

The dog is also very old; he does not go to trees any more, and when he has to stop, he just spreads his four legs with his little belly on the ground and makes water and, doing this, his lips tremble and he looks more miserable than he does all the time.

When Uncle Joseph sees a little flower along the road, he stops and silently points at it, or at a bird in the air, and again smiles. He is a holy man. On Sunday in his little church he preaches, and when a peasant comes in late, he stops the sermon and speaks to him from the pulpit, and it is the only time I know that he gets mad. He points up to the ceiling of the church and speaks for the Father in heaven and says: "Franzl, where have you been again?" The peasant is then ashamed and hides behind a pillar, and after the service when Uncle Joseph walks through the church with holy water and a silver-handled brush to bless them, he takes an extra large dip and rains it on that peasant.

Uncle Joseph has other troubles. He has very little money, he lives plainly, all he can spare he gives to the poor or to many causes.

Another is the painting of the Christuses. There is a very good religious man with a beautiful white beard, who is a house painter and carpenter, and he has also to go around during the year and paint the many statues so they will not be eaten by the strong air, the heavy snow, and the cold. This man tries very hard to do this right, and when one watches him paint, he mirrors the face of the statue on his own. He is so deeply attached to this work. He does it the way children paint, with the mouth tightly closed, but unfortunately he is a very bad artist.

First of all, he mixes a terrible color for the statues; it is too red, and sickly red, as in a fever, or too pale, yellowish, and then the worst thing is that, when he comes to the face, he sometimes makes the eyes not right. All his Christuses have bad eyes; some of them are cross-eyed, and others look away to both sides at the same time. And then he cannot make the mouth sad; this is very bad, because some of the Christuses almost smile.

When Uncle Joseph comes to a newly painted one, after he has removed his hat, which on warm days he carries on a clip in a buttonhole in front of his chest, he points at it and shakes his head; but he is too kind to say anything to that man or to have someone else do it.

On these walks, little girls in wide skirts and flaxen hair come running out of houses, and make a curtsy and kiss his hand, and they say: "Praise to God in heaven," and Uncle Joseph blesses them with his hand on their hair and answers: "In Eternity, Amen."

This fills me always with an inner trembling, and a warm love for him, and, although I cannot believe in his religion, in the evenings, when he goes through the deep forests to a dying peasant and in his folded arms carries the Host, the altar boy ahead of him swinging a little lamp and ringing a silver bell, then I know, with certainty, more than I know anything, that he is of God.

GARDEN IN
GMUNDEN
SALZKAMMERGUT

DAVID

Lieutenant Doyle and the Chaplain have arranged for outings for the patients. On certain days cars will come to the Fort; in them will be one patient and one attendant; then they will all drive in one long line to the country and make a tour for fresh air, coming back again in several hours.

Lists are made out, so that this can be done properly. I manage to arrange with the Sergeant clerk, who writes out these lists, that Doris will drive my patient; his name is David.

David is a young Negro; he sits quiet and content in a chair and looks down on the floor, at all times, straight ahead of his chair. He has on his young face a constant smile; his face is of distinguished and fine formation and for his race I think one of the best, purest.

He never says anything, but when he is given something, he looks at it intently as if he has never seen it before, for a long, long time. He thanks you with a nod and with his eyes and goes back to the quiet smile and the stare. He looks forever as if he were posing for a black statue of St. Anthony.

Because a strong wind blows in from the lake, David gets a

warm cover over his bathrobe, and over this a coat. Doris brings a two-seater; he sits between us after we are checked out. All through the long drive he looks at the spot where the clutch comes out of the floorboards, never at the country.

On the third such round ride, Doris brought him some chocolate, for which he thanked her with silent, great dignity. Also there are a pair of big fur mittens to put on his hands because it is very cold in the open car. We have to stop to put them on and in this time the train of cars with patients passes us and is far ahead.

The regulations forbid this, but we drive our own way, out to the country. It is nicer; we can go faster and it is more fun than continually watching the car ahead. We come to many nice places and stop at one to walk through the wood. David we leave in the car and we make him comfortable with a blanket. It is a quiet deserted road.

We were not far at any time, or gone long. When we came back and looked into the car, David was gone. Doris ran to the right, I to the left; we shouted his name into the woods and fields; there was no sign of David.

This will surely mean the Guardhouse; it's a serious offense, even if David is not dangerous, or perhaps he is, very much so, and has only been waiting for this moment.

We climbed into the car. There he was, the top of his head stuck up over the side. He was sitting out on the running board where we had never looked, his hands folded on his lap, with the saint's smile.

After this they did not let us take him out again. The committee crossed Doris and her car off the list. I was reprimanded, and David went out in another car with another attendant.

I can visit him in his ward, bring him custard and chocolate, and feed it to him. His Doctor says he is not getting any better, and in another week he is put to bed.

Davy is very ill; he looks straight ahead of himself, somewhere about twelve feet in front of his face, and seems smaller. His hands rest silently and loose at the sides of his body. It is feared he will die. The young Doctor whom I like and who is very kind to David has little hope for him. He seems not to want to live, and late one night he almost dies.

The Doctor took gloves of rubber and with his forefinger reached up into the sick boy's backside. There must be a nerve center there, because he reacted and almost sat up straight. Then two days later his breathing changed and in tho middle of the night he died. It is not sad though it is the first time I have seen it happen.

When I was very little, a stupid nurse took me on Sunday afternoon to the cemetery. Behind great windows lay the dead, and among them the one I will always see, a very little, old, old Countess. Her feet were in thin paper shoes; two candles burned at the sides of her plain, black, wooden coffin; her little hands were folded over a black crucifix; and between their fingers were wound the beads of a rosary.

I have never been able to forget this, because her eyes were wide open, a fly circled over her face and landed in the middle of the eye; the fly walked around over the staring pupil, and I waited for the face to move. But the little lady was so dead that the fly was undisturbed; it walked down the bridge of the nose, into one of the nostrils, came out again, and left the face.

That seemed complete death to me and made me angry. The cemetery was on a hill over the town; it was filled with broken columns, weeping stone angels, crosses, big and small, white and black, and young trees. It was raining; the bells of the mortuary chapel had a high homeless sound; in the hall, behind the large windows where the dead lie on view, stood several people, curious and staring. Against the walls leaned flags, lanterns, and a crucifix on a long pole; all this was used for the funerals, and the most ugly of all things was the smell of cooking that drifted into this corridor from the end of the hall where lived the caretaker. It was Sunday, and the smell was of goulash, coffee, and beer.

The Countess was so very dead to me because I had seen her alive. I lived at the time alone with a French nurse in a little walled garden in Gmunden on the shore of the Traunsee, in the Salzkammergut.

Although we were in Austria and I was five years of age, I could hardly speak German. On the waters were swans, many white, a few black; in the garden stood immense chestnut trees that formed a green roof over it. And the little old lady fitted so well into this; she wore a black velvet ribbon on her thin neck, stood and sat straight, and had the character of a turtle in her face. That of course was the wrinkly skin, a proud mouth without lips, and the nostrils that leaned back. Ugly as she was, I loved her. She spoke beautiful French, had in her appearance a commanding little General's military correctness and elegance. I remembered her in all her motions.

But David's death was not like this.

There is a man in the Fort who apparently has no duty to perform; he is never asked to drill or put on the guard detail. He is a Corporal and, now that we have a dead soldier, he appears to be the undertaker.

David is in a room; he lies naked on a table and the undertaker is draining the blood from his body and pumping some liquid into it. He sits at the head and feels David's ear, to see if it is getting stiff.

In the evening David is most beautiful; he has the form of a statue, much finer than any white man I have ever seen. Blue lights play over his body; the part from the chest to his knees is the finest; even his organs are well designed, small, compact and part of his loins. His legs and arms look strong, as if polished steel were covered with a thin layer of cloudy wax, opaque, yet transparent. It is a fine pleasure to look at him; he does not look at all dead.

I have watched some operations in Oswego on colored men. When their abdomens are opened, there is snowy whiteness inside for several centimeters, and only when the surgeon cuts down deeper, does the dark blood come up and fill the cut.

The knowledge of Anatomy explains David's body. I know little of it but enough to respect its wonder. I know where heart, lungs, intestines are, where the bones lead to and where they are joined. The forms of all this can be felt through his skin.

I go to him as often as I can, just to stand and look at his death.

He never ceases to be young and strong, and somehow there is consolation in this room, it is like some of the music of the Bruch Concerto.

The soldiers are decent. It is the first death in the Hospital; they take it seriously and play taps for him, give him an escort and drape his flag over the coffin. One man has to take him home. They all seem sad to me, their mothers' children, and very small. This is most evident in the way they dress and clean their shoes and are quiet for David.

THE MESSHALL IN FORT PORTER
BUFFALO

THE MESS IN ORDER

I have been given the management of the Mess, that is, under Lieutenant Doyle. I have also no worry with buying food or supplies; that is the business of the Quartermaster Sergeant. We feed many patients and soldiers, all together almost two thousand people. The patients' Messhall is separated and in another building. The Messhall for the men is here close to the kitchen.

The cooks are good men. One of them is English and thin; he speaks a wonderful Cockney dialect, and says he has to make himself a "heggnogg." We have lots of cockroaches; they crawl to the ceiling, so at night the windows and doors are left open and they freeze to death and are swept out in the morning, but there are new ones the next day; also again those many cats everywhere.

In other posts there are periodic assignments of all men to Kitchen Police, but here, because of the nature of this house, we have a steady crew, men who cannot be used for better work, and they are difficult.

These men are all friends; they come from the Brooklyn waterfront, were drafted. The worst one is Mulvey.

Mulvey sings all day, so that his song—it is the same one—has become part of the kitchen, like the cooks and the oven. We cannot drive it out. It is a dreary piece and he draws it out, singing mostly into the dishwater. The words go:

> Take me over the Sea—
> That's where I want to be—
> Oh, my, I don't want to die,
> Take me over the Sea.

There is also something about "I want to go home" in it.

His friends join him in that line while they are busy with their dishes. These come in endless stacks all day long, after breakfast, luncheon, and dinner.

They love to insult each other in play and call themselves by the vilest names, all in fun; and at times, while the water is running into the tub or they are waiting for the towels to dry, they box without touching each other, dancing on their toes and, at the most, disarranging their opponent's hair. In their free hours they are visited by girls that are as terrible as they themselves are —ragged women, young enough, but with thick ankles, in shoes with blunt toes and sideway heels, with pimply faces, wide hips, and fat lips. With them they sit on a row of benches facing the river. But they are always together and behave toward the rest of us with great condescension, as if they belonged to an exquisite club that is very hard to get into. So far as I have seen, all they do out there with the girls is sing again this song, sit on the benches where they insult each other, and shout the same insults of short words after anyone who passes. Their girls sit with knees far apart and love to be pushed and mauled; they scream with happiness.

The Ideas of morality that people have seem so confusing. The men here are all so lonesome; the kitchen gang knows nothing else but to box and this business of which they constantly talk by one word. And after all it is only the itch that is in their bodies which marches in front of the command to have more people on earth, and of course they don't want any children, but it itches them just as hard. But these thoughts always confuse me, and I think of women, of girls I have seen at dances and swimming, and most I think of the muscles that run down to the knees on the inside of their upper leg; they are I think the most exciting part, much more so than any other part of their bodies, in young girls most certainly, in women they become flabby, and of porous texture.

When the kitchen gang are through washing the dishes, they have to set the tables in the Messhall. After meals, the three-legged stools on which the men sit are turned upside down and placed on top of the tables so that the floor can be mopped. These stools are taken down; then one man runs through the lanes between the tables and places the plates from a pile on his arm. He does this fast from much practice. The plates dance awhile and then settle down. The next one runs around with forks, another with spoons, knives, and another with tin cups. One can hear with little experience what they are doing without being in the room. There are, of course, no napkins.

For some time there have been complaints that the dishes are greasy. They do not wash them well enough, the same with knives and forks and the cups. The Officer in charge took a clean towel, slipped the end of it between the prongs of a fork, and showed me how dirty it became. He streaked a plate with his glove and, tilting it in the light, the path of his finger could be seen across the plate—it was fatty.

I told this to Mulvey, out in the kitchen. He turned from his tub and looked at me with small eyes; he has a way of making them look perfidious. Also, when he is told something, he assumes a position of great ease, leaning on the edge of the dishwashing tub and crossing his legs, his body as in a hammock, leaning toward me. With his free hand he scratches himself. This performance is chiefly for his friends, who stand around him and have great admiration for such a show of indifference.

After I have told him all this, he has to turn around and go on with his work, and he does it very slowly, looking into the faces of all his friends, taking a deep breath, and he says as if he were very tired: "Oh—well." He spits in the dishwasher and continues to wash the dishes in it.

I am sorry I cannot box, but I will not allow him to get away with this. The next day is Saturday and there is a football game; they love football games; their terrible girls always come for them and hang around the front of the Messhall. They hurry on that day and don't sing, and I will teach them a lesson. Before they can go off duty, they must ask me for permission.

The best part of this Saturday afternoon is that, when they have almost finished the dishes and started to set the tables, the top Sergeant, the Polish one, comes in late and eats in the kitchen. They are afraid of him; he has a voice like a bear, can beat them up one and all together, and on top of it lock them in the Guardhouse until their bones ache.

I walked into the dining room after the tables were all set, and one of them came to ask if they could go. Mulvey was already out of the door. Of course they could go if everything was done, but everything was not done, not right. I showed them the dirty forks and the greasy plates. Mulvey was called back. I made them take all the dishes and cups, the forks, spoons, and knives back, to wash them over again. They still thought they could make the game.

Mulvey used steaming water and raced around the room to help them. The plates danced down again, the top Sergeant nodded to me, the men were mumbling curses, audible enough for me to understand that they were not insulting each other. When they were finished they asked again to go.

I pointed at the tables and stools. "What is this?" I said. "Look at it, what a disorder! And the plates and the forks!"

Mulvey was sent to get a long string and two pieces of wood. The top Sergeant leaned against the door of the dining room and grinned, with his hands in his pockets.

The string came, and with a pencil I divided the first and last table in each row of tables in as many places as there were men sitting at them. Then we put the first and last tables in correct position, laid the string over the row of ten tables on each side, and first of all pushed the tables so that they were absolutely straight. The Polish Sergeant helped by bending to the edge of the first table and closing one eye, like looking down the line of stomachs of soldiers. He gave a signal with his hand for each table until they were quite in line.

Then with the string we aligned all the stools, the plates and cups of each man, also straightened out the knives and forks.

When this was done, I told them now they could go and from now on we would do it like this at every meal. By that time it was time for supper. But they ran out to their girls who had waited.

After supper they again hurried and set the tables. I felt sorry for them.

I went up to my quarters to get the leather leggins to go out. We can wear spiral puttees, if we buy them, but not leather leggins. We should, however, according to regulations, wear the canvas leggins which are furnished by the service.

Uniforms we can also have our own; I had one made in Buffalo. There is only the terrible campaign hat; no one is allowed to wear a cap or hat like the Officers have, but I have bought myself a Stetson campaign hat which at least holds its shape and has a somewhat better color. Besides it does not turn up at the corners like a cooked mushroom.

My leather leggins, which are forbidden, I have in a bag and, carrying it under my arm, I leave the Fort. Next to the Fort is a park, and there is a bush where I sit down and change the canvas for the leather leggins and hide the canvas ones until I get back. I have also spurs in my pocket. When this is done, I wait for Doris's big car. It is a Pierce Arrow with the front seats apart so one can walk between them from the back seat and sit with the driver.

As I sat down under the bush, a blanket fell on me, and then I was hit on the head by a plank. It was from the kitchen gang. They kicked and trampled with boots and clubs until I was insensible. I woke up in the Hospital and could not see out of my eyes; my head swam and all my limbs hurt.

I sent for the Polish Sergeant and asked him to have the kitchen gang arrested. He gave me a chocolate bar and said No, he would not do that, because I had it coming to me. "It will do you good," he said, "this is America."

The Buttermachine

THE BUTTERMACHINE

There are two Doyles here—one a Sergeant, the other a Lieutenant. The Sergeant is efficient and thin; the Lieutenant is fat, with the face of an old lady and little eyes that easily turn hard with offense. He always looks past my face when he speaks to me. The soldiers have invented a very right and beautiful name for him—his trousers have given them this idea—they call him "Satchel Ass." A "satchel" is a portmanteau and "ass" is a donkey but in this case it is the army word for derrière—it fits well. When he walks, it looks as if this portmanteau were constantly opened and closed, and when he sits down, it flows over the chair. When he has been around, they do not say: "Lieutenant Doyle was here"; they say: "Doyle was here." Question: "Which one?" Answer: "Satchel Ass Doyle."

Lieutenant Doyle is the Glee Club leader and Mess Officer. He complains all day long about the flies, looks into the ice-machine and the iceboxes, and his pet is the buttermachine. He looks at it twice a day with affection. He bought it himself and he shows all the other Officers or some friends of his that come visiting how it works. "That's a great little piece of machinery there," he says to them.

The buttermachine has been here ten days. Before that we cut the butter with a small square frame over which a row of thin sharp wires were stretched, making about sixteen squares. These wires run from left to right and up and down. One man and a tub of water with ice is all that is needed to cut all the butter for the men, the patients, and even the Officers' Mess; and all this takes is at the most ten minutes.

Now we have to first rinse the buttermachine with hot water, fill it with ice, then trim the blocks of butter, because as they are they do not fit the round cylinder inside the ice. The cylinder is long and round, the blocks of butter are square and short. One and a half of them, after they are trimmed, fit into the machine. When they arc in there, a tight cover is attached, the heavy lid clamped down, and then the work begins.

A man has to stand in front of the machine and work a little lever from left to right and back again to the left; and every time these two motions are completed, one little square of butter falls out of the machine.

I have told Lieutenant Doyle that it is a waste of time, that the butter was cut in ten minutes before and now it takes two hours to do it, and twice a day; it is ridiculous. But he says: "That buttermachine is allright."

I have detailed Mulvey, who is the laziest of the K.P.'s, to this work, and he is now in the dining room and sings his awful song in there and makes these little butterpieces. Mulvey soon finds out that, with making a little fuss, he can stretch his work so that he has nothing else to do, and when Lieutenant Doyle comes in and sees him cleaning the machine very carefully, he stops and smiles and he tells me: "Mulvey is a good man." But I will fix that.

We have one Mess .table that has a broken leg. After midday meal, when the dishes are washed, would be a good time to do this, but then there are too many people and I think such things should always be done alone with no one around for confusion when somebody asks questions later on.

Sunday is the best day, then all is very quiet, everyone is out.

On the next Sunday, when I am not invited out until late in the evening, I move the table with the broken leg over to the door and change it for the one on which the buttermachine sits. This one has good legs. There is a corner of the table which meets the door when it is opened—soldiers rush into rooms—and on that corner is the machine. It is very heavy, about one hundred and fifty pounds.

After this is arranged, I go up to my quarters. There was a crash as soon as I got up there, but I dressed and left, because it was time to meet Doris's car.

The next day when I am back in the Messhall, the cook says: "Somebody busted the buttermachine. Lieutenant Doyle is wild and wants to see everybody who works here."

The best thing is to go right over to headquarters and look surprised and make a face that asks: "Who could have done this? Let me think."

Mulvey is there already answering questions. The buttermachine is there also, but I am afraid that it can be repaired; one of the pig iron legs is broken off, and the machinery under the cylinder, where the lever goes back and forth and the butter comes out, seems mangled, but it looks good otherwise.

Lieutenant Doyle has no suspicion; he points at the machine and says: "What do you think of that?" but he asks no more. Mulvey has told him when he saw the machine last and another man how he found it. Whoever opened the door and broke it is not to be determined because he would not report himself and no one has seen anybody else.

All questions and answers are filled out on a long printed statement which the Army issues for all things that break or are lost or worn out. Mulvey is back washing dishes and we cut the butter the old way for some weeks. Then Lieutenant Doyle comes and takes Mulvey away from the dishwashing. He comes back with a small table with very strong legs. Lieutenant Doyle has picked out a corner where to put it; near this corner are no doors. Outside is a truck, with a new buttermachine.

François Marie Arouet de Voltaire

1694 — 1778

NIGHT ON GUARD

The Flu Epidemic has cost many lives and it is to keep the men that work here well that we are changed from one duty to another.

Yesterday the red-headed Irishman and I were working in the Post Hospital carrying the dead men down to the cellar on stretchers. We wear long white nurse's gowns and a cap, also a pad over mouth and nose and look like ghosts. The cellar stairs turn and are very steep.

The Irishman was in front of me, walking ahead down, when the dead man slipped and his feet went into the Irishman's back.

He said: "Sit down or I knock you down!" This kept me from screaming or dropping the body.

Down in the cellar is a room and in this we have brought the corpses. The Irishman takes the feet when we lift them off, I take them by the hair as I do not wish to touch their faces or neck, which is stupid of me, but the hair is better, it is not so dead. The post undertaker now has a lot of work, he has the assistance of several undertakers from Buffalo. I wonder if he has a girl.

There are not enough men to mount guard, the posts are reduced, and although I am a Corporal I must stand guard.

The third night I am down in the cellar again, now as a night guard. The dead must be watched, there is a regulation to this effect, they cannot be left alone.

The cellar is dark and lit by a loose gas flame, this flame is on the outside of the room where the dead are. They lie in rows and no one has had time to close their eyes. In the white of these eyes dances the reflection of the gas light. I sit as close to the wall as I can squeeze myself and I am terribly afraid, so afraid that I have taken my gun out of its holster and point it at the dead men. The safety catch is off and it makes me feel safe. If anyone of them will move, I'm afraid I'll kill him, I don't see why they cannot be left alone, or locked up over night, or why there aren't at least two of us.

The Epidemic is much better and almost over; now I have an altogether new duty. I am stationed at the Guardhouse and I see that the men who have been on leave report for inspection before turning in. They come in at all hours of the night. Some of them have late passes, which I have to collect as well.

After all the soldiers are inspected and have gone to bed, when everybody except a few men out on posts are asleep, I have time to myself.

After the reports are in order, I read, mostly Voltaire, Goethe, a little book of Schiller's poems, and on Napoleon.

Later I go out; the air is so cold that it bites inside the nose, and when I come back I am much thinner.

It is also difficult to walk because the roads are icy, and at times I must quickly slide to a tree, or the wind would take me along across the frozen parade ground.

The clouds race past the moon; there are more stars than I have ever seen in America. In the metallic light, the roofs of the Hospital buildings seem to float in the air in one flat green-silver row of tilted panels; under them the Hospital is quiet most of the time. At times there is a scream from the bad section and then the figure of a nurse passes the lit windowpane, but that happens not very often.

Around the Fort is water, lit as the roofs are, and in this scene is a dangerous ecstasy, an elation which begins as the fear does. It swells up in back of me, high and wide, and as if I were standing in front of an orchestra with rows of instruments wildly playing.

In this excitement many doors open to walk out of the house of reason. The mind becomes acutely clear. This goes through the body, as if the brain, the fingertips, all surfaces, were sandpapered and the nerves laid bare to every sensation. The mind was a little cup and now it is as big as a tub. This happens every night. First of all I feel years older, and whatever I think seems crystal clear. Also I seem able to do anything.

I have had this feeling mildly before, when coming out of a motion picture in which the acrobatic hero has swung himself on a curtain up the side of a tower and jumped on horseback across the parapets. For half an hour afterwards I have felt like doing the most difficult things in play, to jump, to take hold of anything and swing myself up to the next electric sign on Broadway, to successfully punch anybody in the nose that seemed not worth liking.

Here, now that the Islands of Security are where I know I can reach them, there is the constant wish to walk out further on the thin plank of reason, to gamble with the chance of not being able to come back.

The highest joy, and it is always a boundless happiness, is when the sun rises. It remains resting on the horizon for a long while and then frees itself, floats freely. I feel then a sense of the miraculous logic and divine bookkeeping that makes all things in this world a day older—myself, my mother, the sawmill, the patients, the dead grass under the snow, the trees—and for all these things wells up a rich affection, so that I must put my arms around a tree and feel its being. I also feel the sun, where it has been, with unbelievable detail—the shadows it has thrown past the church in Klobenstein, on the Christuses, on Uncle Joseph who is out with his dog, on the ventilators of the ships on the ocean, and here now on the snow past this tree.

Shortly before the sunrise there is a blue light all over, somewhat like in a theater, where they change the light from night to morning too fast. Unreal, humid and inky, and spattered with yellow street lamps; when you squint your eyes, the streetlights rain gold over the scene. In this light a milk wagon horse clops up the street and a man who has to go to work early comes out of a house always in the same fashion: he yawns, closes his collar, and lets a small dog out after him. He walks down the steps and sees me and lifts his hand in greeting, and then, and always in this same order, bends down to speak to his dog. The ill-formed, unkempt, many-kinds-of-dog makes a creaky sound, scrapes and scratches, and is beside himself with gratitude. He shows this with all his might, wiggling so that one moment his head looks at his tail on the right side of his body and then on the left. It is his daily morning prayer to his master and for himself to show how glad he is to be alive and how grateful to be a dog.

Then the sun rises, it places light on ice-covered branches and on a young oak leaf that has stuck through wind and winter. It is curled like the webbed claw of a bird and becomes liquid and gilded.

Then the prisoners arrive; they go from the Guardhouse to the Messhall to get food. They are dressed in the wonderful fatigue suit, blue with the lovely large Prison "P" handpainted on its back, and they have the foolish fatigue hat—fatigue is so right for this. They also show their prisonness in their walk. Behind them goes the guard; they all hurry to get into the warm kitchen, to warm their hands. I always follow them and love their walk, their faces, their words. Hat, coat, tray, all speak. They say: "We are prisoners, not bad fellows. We only drunk too much, or fought, and it's nice in the jail, but hurry up, kitchen, so we can get a little coffee and sit by the oven." The guard is much less eloquent.

In the kitchen they look around to swipe something from the cook. They get an extra cup of coffee here. The cook is the thin low-class Englishman, with the lovely London dialect. He is simpleminded, and in all simple people is a securing, restful quality. When he looks in a pot, I can read on his face whether it is clean or dirty inside.

There are some specialists, who have a right, or just a claim of their own invention, to a cup of coffee here early. Their faces appear on the side of the door, and they look at the cook, to find out whether he is in the right mood, if he will give it to them.

In all this, the appearance of the horse, the little dog, the prisoners, and the cook, is wonder without end. In them also are the strongest weapons against illness of the mind, against even just a low mood. There is an ever present quiet humor; one must only sit and listen carefully and look for it, but of course I think one must have been very ill to be so grateful. I am no longer afraid. After breakfast I go over to the Guardhouse to sleep. If the danger comes, it is now controlled. Physically it is the same—quickly changing temperature, fast pulse and respiration, cold sweat and bitter running of water down the inside of the cheeks—but mentally it is much better. It is now about the same sensation I have when looking into a shopwindow of artificial limbs, or when seeing an ugly child weep somewhere alone.

Another experience like the sunrise is Voltaire, who is again so vivid; himself, his clothes, Sans Souci, Frederick the Great, the affair with the diamonds, are all alive as if he were sitting over in the Headquarters building. Sentences of his malicious sacred writing are before me, clear and free as if I could read them in fine letters on the façade of a marble temple. He is for me clarity, truth, and highest freedom of thought. Because I must return the book, I have copied a picture out of it, a good bust of Voltaire. I wish I could paint. I carry it with me always. I have also drawn what I think Thunder-ten-tronckh, Cunégonde, and the wonderful Dr. Pangloss look like, but torn them up because they were poor.

Doris has sent me *The Italian Voyage* of Goethe, and mountain stories of Tirol by Peter Rosegger. I cannot keep my mind on any of this, with all the disturbance that this new duty brings. I will have to replace *The Italian Voyage,* because yesterday I pushed a bottle with ink over and it made a big splotch in the book; besides it smells already of this place.

In the book of Poems by Friedrich von Schiller is "The Song of the Bell," a long ode without feathers in its wings. The books lie next to each other, but of course it is unfair to compare Schiller with Voltaire. But in Germany, Schiller's poetry is so eminent and compulsory that if one will say to a little boy, to a soldier, a lady washroom attendant, or a streetcar conductor, or any German rich or poor, anywhere in this world: *"Festgemauert in der Erde,"* or any other sentence from "The Song of the Bell," the so addressed will take it from there and recite it to its faraway end, in the rigid form that has been carved into his mind and voice on the first schoolbenches.

In German one cannot say the elegant candle-lit phrases. My affection for German is that which one gives to a box full of cobbler's tools; they are not always well used when speaking, for example Schiller in his "Ode to Joy":

> *Seid umschlungen, Millionen!*
> *Diesen Kuss der ganzen Welt!*
> *Brüder, über'm Sternenzelt*
> *Muss ein lieber Vater wohnen.*

This word *umschlungen* is better suited for a lady at a Fair with a snake around her; *diesen Kuss der ganzen Welt* is hurtful; and *Brüder* is a word that belongs better in a restaurant, as, for example: *"Trink, trink, Brüderlein, trink."* Even worse is this from Schiller's "Song of the Bell":

> *Von der Stirne heiss*
> *Rinnen muss der Schweiss,*
> *Soll das Werk den Meister loben;*
> *Doch der Segen kommt von Oben.*

I like German words best when a simpler man uses them; for example, the good Wilhelm Busch writes:

Links sind Bäume, rechts sind Bäume,
Und dazwischen Zwischenräume,
Durch die Mitte der Natur
Zicht sich eine Pappelschnur.

In this humble, humorous employment the German landscape stands so clear that one can almost walk into it, into a happy picture of many years ago. I see a teacher with a string of children going out to look at Nature from their meeting place at two o'clock sharp, with no one late, happy, but very orderly. *"Eins, zwei, drei, halt.* Here is a butterfly." "Emil, tell us what you know of butterflies," and on the next day a composition about *"Was wir gestern auf dem Schulausflug beobachtet haben."*

The thought of German children is one to weep over.

The frame of mind that makes things so beautiful always widens into hatred when I think of someone I dislike, for example our Professor of Design who was at the German school in the few miserable years I attended it.

He prided himself upon the faultless discipline in his classroom. No boy ever asked to step out; the hour there, which might have been one of few happy ones, began with the wordless entrance of the pupils, at the minute before the hour, after they had formed themselves into a column of two rows outside the door. We marched in, turned sharply at our assigned benches, and sat down erect, with both hands, palm down, in front of us.

The Professor stepped up to his desk and tapped with a pencil. This meant to put pencil number one, the soft graphite, on the table; the next tap brought pencil number two, the harder; the next tap, the eraser; then the dust cloth, and after that the drawing block. Then he ran around; pencils were held up to show that they were properly sharpened; the Primus of the class was allowed to bring out of a box a wooden sphere for each student to draw.

This evil teacher ruined whatever free talent there was in his class, helped us to hate paper and pencils, and most of all himself and his room and the building he was in.

It is hard when thinking of Germans, without considering the war and other nations but themselves, to rhyme them with themselves.

The dear old ladies that sit in Munich on streetcar crossings and switch the tramways, they have apple faces and alpine hats; the ease and wellbeing in my Grandfather's house, he is a Bavarian brewer and loves everybody; the rightness of a simple life; the Sunday promenades with new hats; concerts, and in the evening singing excursions out to a simple tree-shaded summer restaurant. Mild, kind, and good, content with so little and altogether respectful, those of course are the people. The brutality comes from the Uniform, the policeman, the official. I love half of them, the other half I detest.

A TRIP TO MISSISSIPPI

Some of the men are released from here as cured, others are transferred. One man was released for some reason that no one can
understand. He has murdered a man, is degenerate and awful
looking. He is not sent home but allowed the freedom of the Hospital, and they have sent him to me for work. I have put him into
the kitchen, where he peels potatoes. He has the little knife in
his hand, and I am afraid he will use it some day, but it is the
only work we can give him. Even the kitchen gang is scared of him
and they watch him from the side. He shouted at Mulvey to stop
singing, and Mulvey, who would not stop for a sane man twice
the size of this patient, was quiet for a long time.

The men who are sent home have in most cases a guard to
take care of them and deliver the patient safely. In this way our
men travel all over the country.

There is a considerate arrangement to give all the men trips,
and turns are taken. Most men are chosen so that they can take
prisoners to places which are their own homes or in the vicinity
of the cities from where they come, and in this again is evident
the interest in the men and the latitude the Government allows
in making the duty of Army life as easy as possible.

Besides, there is great generosity on the part of the Government in conducting these trips. On overnight or very long trips sleepers are provided. Meals may be taken in the dining car, and even short rides are luxurious, in upholstered coaches, not as in Germany, where soldiers travel in the baggage car or in the fourth class, which has benches of wood. Besides that, our pay is good, our meals are fine, we receive ten percent extra because there is a war, besides a few dollars more for this or that, and it is altogether very decent and liberal.

I cannot believe myself to be an American, just because I have a citizen paper, even if I am in the Army, but I could not think of myself as a patriot for any nation. This is interesting to me and I am thankful that there is little or no patriotism among the soldiers. They will fight and even be killed, but they do it, even the crude ones, with the same feeling as if they were repairing a truck and it rolled over them. This seems a bigger field of sentiment and thinking than the Germans are capable of and I think it makes men better soldiers. The Germans are tied up with three little holy grails; they constantly shout and march around with them, and it seems too few to me. Also they are too subordinate and think too little of themselves; they are willing to be kicked as long as there is someone below to whom they can pass that kick.

But this is also wrong because there are magnificent people among them, and I have often set my mind never again to speak or think of nations in the mass. Even if there are only a few among them that are good, it is unfair; and it is fine of the Americans that now, here in the War, they let me speak German, tell me that Germany is beautiful, and don't say a word that I have a stack of German books and many German Ideas. I am truly thankful for all this and respect it. I have often talked to Beardsley of such Ideas, that I do not believe that all men are created equal, and many other things; he calls that "Nickel Philosophy." A Nickel is a five-cent piece in the meaning of this criticism.

On the railroad stations of Buffalo and all other cities are buffets with Red Cross ladies who stuff the soldiers with cookies, chocolate, and candies, also coffee, and one does not have to take a train to get that at any time. They speak a lot and are too sweet, but they mean well and some of them are even young and beautiful.

It is my duty to take a man back home. I think this is because none of our men come from Mississippi and I have told the man who assigns patients that I would like to go anywhere, far away, if possible to the State of Wyoming, Montana, or Colorado, but this trip is to Mississippi.

Mississippi is filled with colored people and so is the patient I am taking there.

This man, the Negro, is a maniac of the violent type. He has not been a soldier, but a civilian employee who was apparently mad when he got into work for the Army. Therefore he is not under the complete protection of the military, but he is a United States Citizen and his part of the country is responsible for him. Although he is not a soldier, he has a Uniform.

My orders are to deliver him to the civil Authorities of Purvis, Mississippi. Nobody here knows where that is, but I have a long ticket—it is about three feet and of many different colors and at the end of the many connected papers is one printed: "From Jackson to Purvis, Mississippi." Ahead of Jackson come many towns; in one, Cincinnati, we have to change trains.

I receive the papers, an order in which my authority and instructions are made clear, a paper which is the receipt from the Government for my patient, and also the instruction to bring the straitjacket back with me.

The red-headed Irishman gives me some advice before I go. I asked if it is possible at times to let the man loose in his straitjacket because the trip is long and his arms in them must become dead, but he forbids this under all circumstances, not even to undo it one notch. Then I see the man; he is very big and already tied up in his jacket. It has a stiff collar and his arms are tightly bound to his sides. He is being fed. The feeding is the same procedure as with all these cases: the attendant takes the man's head in the crook of his elbow and with a spoon goes quickly into his mouth when the patient opens it, which sometimes he must be forced to do. The spoon is then taken out very quickly or he will chew it up and not let go.

I am not very certain now that this will end right. The man is a good deal higher than I and I think much stronger. Even with his arms bound he has the use of his legs and his teeth. But the Irishman says he is stupid, and not to be afraid, and not to let him ever know I am afraid. Besides I want to make this trip very badly. I also have my forty-five Colt with me—the Authorities here know nothing about the experience in Ward Number Three. Here again America is fine. I remember in Germany, in the boarding school, a little boy had done something bad in the first class; his teacher put remarks of this and about his character into the papers and they traveled with him all through his school years, so that every new teacher knew what he was like and he never could enter clean into a new classroom and start with freedom.

The complete authority over another human being such as I have now frightens me. I make up my mind that I will be more than kind to him.

The Ambulance of the Fort Hospital takes us down to the train in Buffalo. I have talked to the patient in quiet words, as the Irishman talks when there are no troubles, but he does not hear or answer me. He rolls his eyes, and I hope, if an attack comes off, it is here in the ambulance where I have trained aid, someone who knows what to do.

As I get him on the train and have both hands busy pushing him up the stairs of the car, a little boy comes and wants to take my gun. His mother just pulls him away; these children need a little order in their lives, I have often observed that.

When we are on the train, the porter says that I cannot go into the sleeper with a colored man, but I explain to him that we must be together and that it is the order of the United States Army. That seems not to impress him, but he looks at our tickets and, because he is a colored man himself, he changes our berth to one close to the door and below one which is not occupied.

After dinner is served for the other passengers, we go into the dining room and order some food for the patient. Then I have to feed him. I have so far hidden his straitjacket under his Army coat, but now I have to put the coat away so that I can hold him. All the waiters in this dining car are colored, and they all stand around while he is fed. He does not look at them or say anything while he eats; only his eyes are like those of a scared horse, and he gets ahold of the tip of the spoon, but I manage to bend it out of his teeth. The waiters are ready to help me; they all look as scared as the patient, and they cannot go away and do their work; they seem very unhappy.

To go to bed is a large problem. The bed is wide enough and I am tired and don't mind sleeping next to the man, but I am afraid he might bite my ears or nose off during the night, and there is also the possibility that he might get loose.

We have some straps that the porter got me and rope and strings; with these I tie my patient loosely to his corner, where the baggage net is. This net comes off and I put it over his head. Then the porter tells me that I can have the vacant upper berth, so I take a long piece of string and bind it around the man's neck and have it run up to my berth, where I attach it to my wrist in case he should break loose. But I cannot sleep and neither can he; therefore I sit up and untie him again and talk with the porter. As to everybody, I have to explain to him why I am in the American Army and not in the German.

The next morning I wash the patient and give him his breakfast; there are some people here in the dining room and again I have to explain the whole business to them and they ask me if I am not afraid. I am no longer, but I was up to now.

We are coming into Cincinnati. At a station just before we get there, arrives a very elegant young woman, who is smartly dressed, with an intelligent, direct face. Of a very efficient body, she wears a suit of smoky gray with some color, that of eggplants, in its design. This color seems also to be in her eyes.

This young woman comes over to the table after I have fed the patient again and is the first who does not ask questions but talks, and I find out that she has been to Innsbruck. She knows also the cogwheel railroad to Oberbozen, also Munich. Of this city she knows all my favorite streets, the radishwomen, the women who sit in the rain and change the tracks of the streetcar, the little restaurant behind the Frauenkirche, and she has been to the lovely

Marionette Theater of Papa Schmidt on the Promenade Platz. She lives in Cincinnati and there is a stop between trains of almost a day before I can go on to Jackson.

In Cincinnati there are again the "Welcome, Boys" signs and the ladies. We get coffee and cake. There is also a large dance that evening at a house of the girl's friends, and she asks me to dinner. There is only the patient, whom I cannot very well bring. He is completely absent in mind and has not said a word all this time. He follows me wherever I go and makes no sign of trouble.

This party seems to be fine. On the station are several more girls; they all have lovely ankles, well ordered hair, and good clothes. Therefore I have an Idea. I ask a policeman where Headquarters are; then we get one of the girls' cars and drive to this station. It is in a large building in the center of the town up a hill from the depot.

A Lieutenant of Police is at the desk. I ask him if I can leave the patient with him for a day. This is of course an offense, but the man can do no harm with a lot of big police around him, and besides I would mind it only if he were aware of it. In his eyes is nothing, nor in his entire person; he is numb and does not know what goes on around him or where he is, or who he is.

First I have to explain to the Lieutenant and to all the police why I am in the American Army and not the German; then they speak German to me, almost all of them, and finally the Lieutenant says I can leave the patient. It is allright with him and not against regulations, only I have to pay 75 cents for his food and keep. That is allright. They all laugh again because I still have a purse to keep my money in. On it is a picture of Klobenstein in Tirol and under it in golden letters is written: "Greetings from beautiful Klobenstein." Then I am given a receipt, and they take the patient away. This is a guilty thing to do, and I feel as if I were leaving a child alone, but they promise to be nice to him and also not to open the straitjacket. He has eaten and I will feed him when I get back again.

We took a trip up a little mountain in the vicinity of the City. It has a cable car like some mountains in Tirol and on top is a museum. At the entrance of it stand two knights that are copies of the silver knight in the Hofkirche in Innsbruck, and they make me feel very far away. Around this hill is much of Cincinnati's "Beautiful Dreck."

The dinner is very fine, the dance also; everybody in this city seems to be German and at least talk it. They also know Doris and her family in Buffalo. They are brewers, so was my Grandfather a brewer. When we drive back to the station I think of the kitchen gang and how rough they are with their terrible girls, and with this to strengthen me I kiss the girl in the car, without asking for permission first, and this seems to be the way to do this, because she allows it and holds still and only says it's too bad I have to go.

The Lieutenant at Police Headquarters takes me up with a lift to where the patient has been all this while. He says he would gladly pay for having him stay.

On one of the upper floors is a large iron construction like a huge birdcage and in it are lots of people—small crooks and harlots that have been locked up for minor offenses, also peddlers and beggars that come here to keep warm.

In this room the police say is a continuous deafening noise and much cursing, whistling, and booing and many fights, but not since my patient is here; now it is quiet like in church.

For all the time he has sat on one side of the cage, and they, all together and close as they can get to each other, opposite him. They stared at him and he at them. He must have known that they were afraid because he rolled his eyes and made faces, also growled. All this time they have been in terror, and when he moved, sliding a few inches, they moved a few inches to keep the most distance between him and themselves.

I have a little more time. My patient is fed, but first we have to remove his trousers and clean them. This has happened three times on this trip so far. When they are clean and dried, we are ready to go. The Lieutenant said: "Auf Wiedersehen," and gave me back the 75 cents, also some cigarettes, and asked me to stop any time I came to Cincinnati.

The coach in which we ride next is filled with noises; it wobbles, and, except for the patient and myself and at times the conductor, who is not inclined to talk, it is completely empty.

The train stops frequently. I think it has a woodburning engine because after a stop we always pass a pile of cut timbers. Also there are at times scrubby forests, but they are irregular, not like the deep forests around Munich and in Tirol, where each tree stands behind another one in a straight orderly line and is tall and even. The trees do not look too healthy, and when a patch is passed, there comes again a wide stretch of red land. It lies in waves like the sea in a wind that is not yet a storm.

Over this landscape the sun sets redder than I have ever seen it and also twice the size it is in Buffalo. Far apart are houses, shacks of unpainted wood. For some reason the fallen apart ones do not look half as unhappy as the ones that are lived in, with smoke coming out of them. That is because I feel lonesome for whoever has not moved away from there. This scene is again like a melody, of violins that play on deep strings. The man without mind that is my patient is in his bundle so good and quiet, so sad and lost, it seems it would be kindest to shoot him rather this minute than the next and bury him in his land here, so that he could find release and go back to the earth.

There are no civil Authorities in Purvis, Mississippi. There is a sawmill and one street with chickens in it and two pigs. On both sides of it are filthy houses and sunflowers. In the houses that are covered with the red mud and are open to the four winds, people, all colored, animals, and many children live together.

After looking very close and long at him, they recognize the patient or admit he is one of them. He was well when he left them; now he is back, he recognizes no one. The people take me to one house; in there is his family. One woman shrieks and weeps, the children stare, and the men look at me with anger.

I tell them that he will be better, that this takes time, and that after a while the straitjacket can be taken off him and then he will be as happy as he was before. They weep and look angry and I wonder what to do. I cannot leave him here; my orders are to the civil Authorities of Purvis. Where are they?

The Authorities arrive, in the shape of a man with a dirty white suit and a sharp thin face. He has two horses with him and is some kind of mayor and gendarme. He also knows this man and of me bringing him here.

Over night he will take care to have him in a lockup and then take him away tomorrow on the next train. The little train on which I have come will be back again; it runs one day to the south, the next to the north, and stops one day altogether. I must go back with this train. First we bring the patient to the lockup. Somebody will stay with him through the night, and in the morning I will feed him and show this man how this is done. We also have to take care of his trousers again. His wife is going to wash them, and in the meantime he has others to wear. Then we ride away.

This Authority has a big house behind several hills. It has thick-leaved exotic trees and plants and is weathered but of fine classic design, with columns, one of which is missing. I get a room, the biggest I have ever slept in, on one of the upper floors.

In the morning we have a rich breakfast of fried chicken with sweet sauce and very fine coffee, then I get a receipt of the Authority for the patient, and also give him the papers.

As it is time for the train, we ride down to the lockup. My patient sits there in the morning sun, outside with somebody that is nice and kind, and I think, if anywhere, in this landscape that he must love as I do Tirol, he might get well. Three strong men are around him and they are his friends.

Now I have to get the straitjacket. I said to the man in Authority: "You take it off," but he says: "Oh, no, and you are not going to take it off him either." Then the train whistles; we have to hurry because I cannot stay here for three days.

In Buffalo the straitjacket is taken out of my pay; it cost $13.50.

INWOOD ON HUDSON

LEAVE OF ABSENCE

Everybody can have a leave of absence in the American Army, if he asks for it. Some men don't ask and just go away, which in wartime is desertion in any other Army and punishable by death.

Here it is different. If he is gone, they wait if he will not come back himself within the short while of a few weeks; if he comes back himself, little happens to him, at the most a few days in the Guardhouse or he is docked his pay or demoted if he has any rank; after six more weeks he is officially absent without leave, then when he comes back himself he still is not severely punished, but he is courtmartialed and goes to the Guardhouse for several weeks; only after a long while, I think it is six months, does he become an official deserter, and they start looking for him.

We are given frequent leaves of absence because of the nature of the Hospital. I have saved up my allowance to be able to go to New York. Why I want to go there I don't know, except that, since I landed there and lived in that city first, I have been thinking of it as my home in America, and I think it is the Idea of going home, that everybody else speaks of so much, that I feel I need. Besides, I get transportation if I take a patient along, and I have also some money. We are well paid and cannot spend any money, at least not much, because we are always invited. There are very few soldiers in Buffalo and many patriotic ladies who need them for their entertainments.

The house in which I lived in New York belongs to a lovely old lady, German, with a daughter who is very young and pretty. Her name is Ada Bach. The house is away from New York, near the Botanical Gardens and a park. It is reached with the subway and a streetcar; it is old and roomy and peculiar; it was the mansion in an estate. Trees stand around it, and in front is a lawn out of which stick a few rocks. There is a hill to the right, no other houses around, and a vegetable garden in back. I lived here chiefly because I could take my dog for runs in the country and because it was quiet.

Ada sometimes writes to me; I have been thinking much of that house and my room and of Ada, and lately I have thought and pictured how I will try and see if I can make love to her.

The nightly talk of the soldiers in their beds made me of the opinion that the way Mulvey and the kitchen gang do it is the best way, that is, without much ceremony, a few words and gestures, but complete indifference and confidence, as if it were accomplished before one starts. I know the formula by heart, it is simple and does not ask for much effort or imagination. It either works or one knows soon that it doesn't.

After I delivered my patient in New York, I took the subway home, and near the park I had to change to the streetcar. This streetcar passes a riding academy, and I got off to hire a horse to start things right. It is a short ride, and Ada was home, and I managed to ride in and be very much admired. I tied the horse to a tree and we had dinner. Mrs. Bach had cooked something very fine, Ada had on a lovely dress and kissed me, and so far it was very successful. Only during dinner Mrs. Bach asked whether I rode the horse all the way from Buffalo.

Afterwards I had to take the horse back, and it was soon evening. Many relatives came and nothing happened, except that I thought everything would be allright by my first of all being very certain of success. There was one difficulty—Mrs. Bach and Ada sleep in the same bed and in the same room—so I had to think of something different.

The next morning is Saturday and Ada asks me to go to the City with her. We ride in the subway, arm in arm, and everybody smiles stupidly at us. We ride very far downtown. She wants me to see her Office and her boss.

This man is a lawyer by the name of Mirror, and he says we must come to dinner at his house that evening.

In the Office I am introduced to another girl and a young man. Ada sits down at the typewriter and writes, and smiles at me to show me how well she can write without looking at the machine, and also chews gum at the same time. The other girl is allowed to see all this and I get a chair. Ada can go early and Mr. Mirror calls up his house and tells his wife that we, Ada and I, are coming with him to dinner that evening.

The house in which he lives is on East 193rd Street; it is called Oxford Hall. Towards the street it has a very imposing façade; around it, two feet away from the building on the sidewalk and sunk into thick concrete posts, are swollen brass pipes. A court opens into the building from the street; in its center is a cement fountain, and left and right of the door are two cement lines.

In an outer hall are rows and rows of names, and the one we look for is written out: "Stanley B. Mirror, Councillor at Law."

The upper part of the foyer is decorated as if someone had smeared an unthinkable material with his five fingers on the wall; up to the chest it is of white marble. In the middle stands a gold painted elevator shaft. A boy in uniform with "Oxford Hall" written on him is inside of it when the elevator comes down.

He takes us up and there is a long corridor. All the way up in all these corridors I see baby carriages; there are four on this, the top floor.

I would like to run away because I am certain I don't like this, but it is too late. At the door is a card, again with "Stanley B. Mirror, Councillor at Law," written on it. The door opens and we step into a long narrow hall at the end of which is the dining room.

The furniture in this room is of a period called Mission; it is so big and the room so very little that we all sit glued to the table. Mr. Mirror is a little man, the table is high, the sideboard is close behind him, and the grapefruit on the table is almost in his nose. His face has no more identity than the grapefruit. It is decorated with thickly rimmed glasses and a small mustache, but that only makes it more like all such faces that I have seen everywhere in New York.

They are good people and it is unkind to not be grateful and polite to them, but I feel a strong repulsion in me, against all this, the house, the furniture, Mr. Mirror, and I would like to get up and tell them that I do not like it and go away. But this is of course impossible.

Mrs. Mirror also has glasses, thin ones with a little chain; she is a woman who is not a mother, not a girl, not a mistress or wife type. She is ordinary, unlovely, and only female in an unhappy sense. Her flesh is white, bloated, and porous; she must be hideous in the bath; her voice is metallic and too big for the room, and her hands are common.

The conversation is mostly of Mr. Mirror's making; he had an argument with the superintendent of the building in the morning, and while he eats he tells how he told that man to see that there was enough hot water or some such business, also about a radiator. He insists on being heard. He says over and over again: "Listen to me, listen to me," at any time when everybody's attention is not his. If that doesn't help, he takes hold of his wife's arm or my sleeve and pulls. He starts every sentence like this, three times mostly: "Then I said to him, then I said to him, listen to me, then I said to him, you know what I told him?"

At one time I turned around to look out of the window, which was behind my chair. Outside was a suicidal picture, millions of bricks, run this way and that and up and down, and they became narrow lines far below; they ended on a metal roof with a skylight; rows of windows were along the shaft. When I looked back in the room he still went on: "He always gives me an argument, that guy." For the rest the conversation here is as if it were written on building blocks that are thrown from one person to another; nothing is ever said.

Ada seems to be at home here; she can join in and say the things to which they answer easily and in which they are versed and secure. Sitting next to me, she eats with one hand. So must I because she has my hand in hers, except when she cuts a piece of chicken. Whenever anything comes to the table she says: "Oh, it's so delicious." In saying this she pauses at the letter L, leaving her tongue against the upper teeth for a moment too long. It sounds: "Dee - llicious." She does the same with "Beautifu - ll" and to the icecream she said:

"Oh, I think it's the most dee - llicious thing I ever put in my mouth."

But that is not all; they wish to come tomorrow and visit Mrs. Bach's house. Ada says they will be delighted, and I can't very well say otherwise. Mr. Mirror will bring his camera and take pictures of us, and afterwards we will go to the Botanical Gardens and after that to a movie on 168th Street.

Ada says once more that everything was "so dee - llicious." We leave the house and I am glad of the fresh air after we get out of the golden elevator.

We took a taxi. It was not far from home, and since I no longer wanted it, I could have my way on this first evening. Just to try out their value, I used one of Mulvey's phrases and gestures; she seemed to know it, followed in words and motion, and seemed willing to comply.

But all desire was gone.

The typewriter which she can work without looking at it, Oxford Hall, and Mrs. Mirror have done it. Now there is a relaxed dumbness in her face. She is a sweet-smelling animal without will. The lower lip hangs loose, the line of her neck is clumsy, the ankles are too thick, but my dislike fastens itself chiefly on the "Dee - llicious."

I try to think of Mulvey's terrible girls—they are so much worse than Ada—but that is better, they are at least strong—and I also say to myself: Why be so very choosing, after all it is not a pleasure of the mind. But it is.

in MR. SCHILLINGS HOUSE

THE WIDOW FROM SCRANTON

Frau Bach has a brother, and he has a son who is a riveter in the Navy Yard, but is not a sailor. He lives at our house and has a little car. I know his father, who was a barber and is an old gentleman, little, fat, with very light blue eyes. The father's name is Lorenz Schilling and the son's Eddy.

It is perhaps from working with a riveting gun that Eddy has a strange way of speaking. He chops the air in a quick move of his right hand, which travels back and forth at the height of his chest the moment he starts saying anything. If he is mad or intent, which often happens, then the chops are shorter and faster. He does that even when we drive, holding the steering wheel with his left hand while with the right he upsets the air. He calls me "Ludy" and he always seems to be mad. Just now he has a piece of steel in his right eye; he says that happens all the time and that they are going to pull it out with a magnet, and then he gets a fortnight off and will take me along up to their farm in Pennsylvania. Mr. Schilling has a frugal chicken farm near a place called Mayfield.

When the steel was removed, we drove up. It was very cold, but Eddy is a tough hard person. When we had to leave a good highway and turn into sideroads that lead to his father's house, he lost the contour of the road, in a place where the wind had evened out the snow. Eddy got out and with his bare hands and without gloves shoveled the snow away, and we both pushed the car a little and it was on the road again. He never said a word until he was in the car; his fingers did not seem to be cold, because he kept on talking and chopping the air again as he had done all the way up. He has mostly talked about a woman with two children, a widow, who lived in a house which he pointed out to me along the road and has since moved to Scranton, but sometimes in the summer comes back here. He has been in love with her and when he speaks of her he says either "the widow," or "the widow from Scranton." It's a very long story and he has repeated the details of it several times.

Mr. Schilling could see us far away because there is nothing around his house except a long chicken barn and a few lilac bushes. The landscape is very beautiful; the property is on a high plateau, and around it in a ring and far away are hills that seem almost mountains.

It's a little warm and friendly house. It has thin walls, and the oven must be kept going all day and night. The windows are clean, with white curtains. In the kitchen at a window is the barber chair and on the sill bottles of different tonics, brushes, and combs.

The first thing Mr. Schilling wants to do is cut my hair; he cannot shave me yet, as I have no beard. He makes a joke about this: he says I have to rub chicken manure and chocolate on my upper lip, the chicken manure inside, the chocolate outside, one pulls and the other pushes. He laughs very long at this joke and then he cuts my hair. He tells me some of the great people whose hair he has cut, and he is very proud of his work.

Mrs. Schilling is a silent wife, but with a shrill voice, worried. Her eyes wander around from the oven to the little pantry. She has asked Eddy five times to get some water outside while I am in the barber chair. He says: "Ah, get it yourself," but finally, when he is through reading, he takes the pail and goes out.

Eddy also has a dog here, a sad, loose animal, a setter. Its name is Girlie, and this dog slips up on him like a rug and tries to cover him all over, and while doing this moans with affection and licks his face. After much wiggling—the dog is very big—it finally succeeds in sitting on Eddy with its head over his face. I can see this in a mirror and the dog moans more, like someone with a heavy weight on him.

Down in the cellar are rows of preserves that Mrs. Schilling makes in the summer—pickles, tomatoes, chopped up sour things, pears, and apples—rows on rows of this—and in a corner coal and firewood and three barrels of a terrible drink called "elderberry wine." It is sweet-sour and contracts the lips so one cannot whistle, and I was given a big glass of it when I came in. It gets dark early, and we have a very good dinner and fine *Apfelstrudel* afterwards, also a cigar for me, and Mr. Schilling goes down for another bottle of the sour elderberry wine. He is going to brew some beer next week.

In the living room is some furniture of a kind that seems to be cut out with a jigsaw, and the grain of the wood is polished up in some varnish that is very bad in color and looks like dark mustard.

After dinner—and Mrs. Schilling has brought everything to the table and sat with us but said nothing—Mr. Schilling goes over to his easy chair. It is a curious piece of machinery; he bought it out of a catalogue and loves it very much. It has a lever on the side, and when one sits in it and pulls that lever, it folds back like an operating table; and when it is that way, Mr. Schilling talks up to the ceiling. The moment he was in this chair, Girlie jumped up, and he scratched the dog behind the ears and talked about his military service.

He did his service in Dresden and is also very fond of the King of Saxony. He speaks, as if praying, of the Kaiser who rode past him in a review. Then he pulls the lever, the dog jumps away, and the chair falls into another shape with a loud bang and stands him up. This is very funny, and to show me how it works, Mr. Schilling sits down again, pulls, and is laid flat. Before Girlie can jump, bang, he stands on his feet again. Then I have to try it, and after this Mr. Schilling walks over to a closet and takes out a broom. To show me that he has not forgotten the manual of arms, he commands himself: "Present arms! Right shoulder arms! Left shoulder arms!" and when he is through with this, he dismisses himself and puts the broom away.

In this room, on the wall, over the mechanical easy chair, hangs a picture of Heidelberg. It is a paper calendar with a pocket under it on which is written the advertisement of the firm that gave them away. A castle is pressed out into relief and is covered with a glassdust, the color of Lifebuoy soap; around the castle is foliage.

In the middle of the room, over the table, hangs a petroleum lamp. Mr. Schilling turns the light down low. The lamp has one of those artless glass shades that are found on drug store counters; they are inlaid with many colors. He turns the shade until a red glass is in the light, and now the castle sparkles as it did when it was festively illuminated for patriotic purposes. Then Herr Schilling sings *"Deutschland, Deutschland, über alles,"* and *"Röslein auf der Heide,"* and winds up an old gramophone with a scratchy record that plays: "Must I leave, must I leave my little city?" While this music is playing, he fills my glass and his own with elderberry wine. "Bottoms up," he says and drinks it down with me, after looking into my eyes and clinking glasses as the code requires.

The music plays and he looks on and on at his castle until two tears run down his lovely face. He does not wipe them away, and I have to go out of the room because it is so sad and lonely.

Eddy had been reading a Western story all the time, with his dog moaning and sitting on him, out in the kitchen, and his mother has washed and dried the dishes and is now looking through eggs and wrapping them.

When it was time to go to bed, we walked upstairs into a room with a slanting floor, a low ceiling, and two iron beds. It was icy here, the beds moist and cold. I had many covers and Eddy went to bed with his warm underwear on although he seems to be so tough. The moon was full and shining into the room, and in its light it was colder still.

I could not sleep and neither could Eddy, and we talked. In a short while Eddy sat up and started again with his widow all over at the beginning, which I knew so well. He has difficulty in telling how very beautiful she was because he knows only a few words or does not wish to use the right ones.

He described the size of her eyes by making a circle with his index finger and thumb and the firmness of her bosoms by making both his open palms tremble about a foot in front of him.

He also told how frequently and well he made love with her, and he said that with Army words. He was with her every day and sometimes all of the night, sometimes from Friday to Monday, and one day she asked him to give her some money to have her hair done in Scranton, in a beauty parlor.

" 'I like you the way you are,' I told her," said Eddy and chopped the air again, "but she wanted ten dollars, see?

"So I give her ten bucks and she goes to Scranton to have her hair fixed.

"When she comes back, she says to me: 'Eddy, how do you like me this way, how do I look?'

" 'You look like Hell,' I says."

He says this with his lips drawn back, tearing the words sharply with his tongue and teeth, and he likes it so much that he repeats:
" 'You look like Hell,' I says to her.

"But, Ludy," he continued in soft tones, "she was a pippin, beautiful like nothing you ever laid eyes on, with her hair done up in curls."

Eddy showed the curliness of her hair with his hands as if he were tickling the back of someone in front of himself.

Well then, Eddy had to go away on some work for several months, and while he was away, a man who had been hanging around the widow for years with serious intentions and whom Eddy did not like and who also had a farm, some money, and wanted to take the children and also marry her, which Eddy did not want to do, became her friend. He became so bold because Eddy was away and also because the widow was now so beautiful with her big eyes and the curls.

Eddy in the meantime had saved his money and worked very hard and he had bought himself a new suit, shoes, hat, and necktie, and when he came back, the people told him about the widow and the other man. Eddy wanted to go right over and beat him and the widow up, but then he thought differently about it. She was not worth it, no woman is, he told me, and he stayed home. But he planned his revenge.

On the way up here, whenever Eddy came to this part of the story, he would drive to the side of the road and stop the car. Now he got out of bed, and went on.

There was a dance in the next village, to which he knew the widow and this man would go. It was called a "Social," to celebrate the Fourth of July.

And Eddy, dressed in collar and necktie and the new suit with the straw hat, went to the Social.

Eddy was very worried that I might not have a clear picture of this. He showed me the suit hanging under a curtain and described at length the hall in which this party took place, how it was decorated, with flags and streamers and balloons, and how it was illuminated, and how everybody was there, with music and refreshments, all the people in the neighborhood sitting around the room along the wall on benches. To show this, he runs around the little room on the sides of his feet, because the floor is very cold. "Here was the orchestra, there was the door, and along the wall the people, all the people. Do you get it, Ludy?"

He waited until the party was well under way and then walked in with his new suit. The music stopped and everybody wondered what would happen. The widow laughed like this: "Haha," and walked over to him.

" 'Hello, Eddy,' she says to me, like as if nothing happened. 'Hello, Eddy.'

"Now, Ludy," he went on, "here I was, in the middle of the room with everybody looking, and she was there beautiful like anything with my curls that I paid for. I would have bust him in the jaw right there, but he didn't come out. He sat in the back and looked dumb like.

" 'Hello, Eddy,' she says to me.

" 'Lady,' I says, without even looking at her but so everybody in the room can hear it, 'Lady, you are talking to a man what don't know you,' and I walked out. I didn't even take my hat off."

Then he went to bed. "Tomorrow, Ludy, I'll get you fixed. Got any money? I know some swell dames. You tell Ma you got to go back."

Foyer *Polish Kate's*

POLISH KATE'S

The next day after breakfast we go over to the barn to inspect
the chickens. While Mr. Schilling goes inside, Eddy shows me a
torn rubber boot in which he has hidden a pint of whisky. He
winks and says: "For tonight. You'll be surprised, Ludy!"

The landscape in the morning light is lovely, the air is biting
and clear, the horizon wider than yesterday. All objects, even
the faraway ones, stand out in clear line and strongest color, almost as if looked at through the sharp lenses of a fieldglass. Girlie
is joyful at the still new return of Eddy and gallops through the
snow with foolishness and suddenly stops with all four paws outstretched, takes a mouthful of snow, and eats it with joy as if it
were icecream. But country is not country without a horse.

Of course Mr. Schilling is glad he can have the chickens, the dog, and his food in order and paid for. His is not an easy life, I think. Feed for the fowls is high, he does not get much for eggs, must clean, grade, and pack them, and the farmers around have their hair cut only once in six months.

Mrs. Schilling comes out of her house, then goes in again; she works without ever halting and since I have been here she has not spoken more than the greetings when I came, yes and no, good night, good morning, and the five-times repeated: "Get me some water, Eddy." She seems not unhappy and is just made the way she is.

Eddy has told me that he knows a house, down in the coal region, where women are kept, he says the most beautiful girls in the world, more beautiful than the widow even. But I am afraid all women are alike to Eddy, because again these girls have the eyes which he described last night as belonging to the widow and also the bosoms two feet in front of him, but we will see. In the meantime it is very exciting to wait for this.

When the light changes, we say good-by and drive off. The car is open; for a while it is bitter cold and we have to drive a long time. And then appears the most beautiful "Dreck" I have ever seen. The snow is smudged; little houses are unbelievably dirty but with much character and warmth; in small towns rise the steeples of Russian churches with onion tops; and behind all this are mountains of black coal with blue lights playing on them. The shapes of crushers rise as high as the towers of Neuschwanstein and much more forbidding; beside the road flows a river, also black. It is as if all the colors had run out of this corner, except a rusty red, black, and indigo. Wherever there is a poster, a lamp, a firebox, it sings out its color and makes the black blacker.

Then we drive up a hill into a town, over railroad tracks. As sad as the moan of Eddy's dog is the sound in the night of the bell on American locomotives. It is like a pulse beat of loneliness, but how beautiful are the engines below! The signal lights have the electric color of Christmas tree glass ornaments, the rails are silver; and the swinging lanterns, the voices of men who shout at each other—all this belongs rightly in this picture.

Past the bridge, a little higher up, we turn past a gas station,

and drive into an alley where Eddy leaves the car. He has been
quiet all the way down. He says we need one dollar each, and
that he has a girl in mind for me, not his kind, he says, but just
right for me.

We come to a house in a narrow alley in which all houses are
such as the one we enter.

Eddy is known here. The girls—there are two in a little room
in front that looks out on the alley—put their arms around him
and lean on him, and he is very proud of this ease and welcome.
He pats them on the backside, and says to me: "Have I been
lying Ludy?" He hasn't; the light here is dim, but the girls are
young, have smooth limbs, firm bosoms, and big eyes. It happens hereabouts that Polish men marry Irish women and from
them come children that are pale skinned and very beautiful.

Eddy goes downstairs and says he will be right back; he is going to see if Julie is in, that is the girl he has for me. But she is
out, and the two girls in the hall say: "Why don't you take either
of us, at least until she comes back?" But Eddy comes up through
the door and on his hand is another woman and he says:
"No-o-o—you don't know what's coming, you sit here and
wait, Ludy." The woman with him is again beautiful, really so—
she is obviously mostly Slavic with a soft rich body, not one that
would look well in clothes on the street, but so generous and
warm that it makes the blood hammer at my temples; her lips
are moist, the eyes black, black, her skin clear and white. Eddy
slaps her on the wide haunches, and they walk up a narrow stair.

"You wait there until she comes and don't give her more than
I told you," says Eddy and disappears with his woman.

There is a foolish little sofa with a summer slip cover on it in
the entrance hall where I am sitting. On the right of it, and so
hot that one can only sit on the far end of this couch, is an iron
stove, small with a round belly and heated to glowing in the
most beautiful color. This room is about ten by eleven feet, but
the heat goes up mostly. In front of the stove are the two girls.
They lean out into a box that is built into the window out on the
street, so they can look up and down. When a man passes, they
play a small pantomime and knock and then wipe the film of vapor
from the pane so they can see again. From where I sit I can see

them; they have bare legs in mules, two loose robes as if in a bath house draped around them. They lean over forward with their legs wide apart, and in this position is much sensuality. It also portrays how much they love the warmth of the oven in back of themselves.

From below comes a mixture of voices and the cry of a baby. There is a wallpaper in this room that I will never forget, just as anything I will see and feel in this house will always be with me. I have never been so beautifully nervous on any day of my life, and I have lost the sense of guilt which I felt walking up to this house.

Then Julie comes in from the dark street; she is again what Eddy promised, not more beautiful than the others, who are lovely in the manner of peasant girls. She has slim heels and a finer face. I do not know the rules of behavior here, whether I am to introduce myself and how to ask her, but that is all done for me. One of the girls says: "He wants you," and she says without looking: "Just a minute," and disappears downstairs.

She had a raincoat buttoned high with a belt in the center, ashen hair, and a hat like a southwester that sailors have. When she returns she has a long simple emerald-colored dress with a small ornament that catched the folds of the dress in the center of her loins. The dress is exquisite in cut and I wonder how it can be bought by girls who cannot have much money. Besides, it is in best taste.

"Come on," she says; she has a strange voice, and I wonder whether there is a spell in this house that all things seem so wondrously beautiful.

The upper part of this house is divided into compartments, many of them with thin walls. We come to one in which Julie turns on the light. She holds out her hand first of all. "Give me the money," she says. I give it to her, more; because one dollar seems disgraceful. "I'll get you change afterward," she says.

In this partition of the house is a bed. It has a mattress without a cover and a pillow covered with waxcloth. There is a chair, a bureau with a stack of towels on it, about twenty of them; on the chair is a basin; a stout colored woman comes in and fills the basin with water. There is also a little glass jar with some disinfectant in it and from this the room smells of carboleum.

On the floor are six different kinds of linoleum, small pieces put together like in a game; pasted on the wall are pictures of John Barrymore, Jack Holt, William Farnum, Pauline Frederick, Norma Talmadge, Mary Pickford, and Theda Bara. They are cut out of rotogravure sections, and their cheeks and lips are colored with rouge. From the ceiling hangs a naked electric light bulb on a black wire, and a piece of black electrician's tape along the bulb.

It is obvious for what reason I came here, but again I feel like a child. What is the next thing to do? I must look at her; even in this unkind light she is so beautiful. I sit down at the bed; she lies down next to me and folds her arms under her head, and then I do the same. Afterwards I turn my face and look at her and she turns her face and looks quietly, with her eyes looking at my mouth. Outside are the coal hills, the ring of the train bell, and there must be a stable in back of the house because I can hear the sound of horses when they change their positions. The ceiling of the room at which I look is painted blue, a light color with much white in it, most probably a bad job by anybody around the house, but because of that it has the marks of the brush and is nice.

My long problem with life on earth is here again. I think that it is not like Schopenhauer says; I think that in this life we have few and far apart completely wonderful happinesses. Here and now is one such moment, in which all things are right, even the six pieces of linoleum on the floor, the coal hills outside, and the bells—who would ever come here to find it?

Such moments come not only in love. I have felt them at concerts, mostly when the orchestra, after its fullest playing, leaves a space of silence between the pulses of the kettledrums, the pause between the dull thuds half a second apart of two soft "booms" on the copper drums, which often happens in Wagner music and is filled with melody although there is not a sound. The quiet pauses between words, here with Julie, were like that.

Through the thin wall next door come voices; there are another man and a woman, and some of the talk is silent, but when they speak loud it is again in words that belong so well in this house. The woman talks most of the time; she is apparently jealous of some other woman, and the pieces of talk go like this:

"He knows I'm sitting here boiling."
"Let's not spoil the whole thing, I said to him.
It's the thing that counts."
"You're up against a stone wall, I said to him.
You know what a stone wall is."
"It's not fair for a guy like that to go to a girl that's been brought up in the church and say: Who is God? How do you know it's true? A guy like him, that's been practicing atheism for years."
"Well, honey, you wanted Steve, here's Steve.
I'm on my way, I told her."
"I thought she'd soften up, women like her soften up sometimes. But not that one."
"Allright, I said, if you don't believe me, maybe you'll believe my lawyer. Oh, gee, Joe, don't laugh. It ain't funny a bit, not for me it isn't."

All this time, Julie has been looking at me and at the loud parts of the lament next door, making grimaces of sorrow, amusement, and mock anger. "This goes on all the time," she said. She has been holding my hand all the while and abruptly she says: "Do something for me, will you?" And when I ask her what, she says: "Kiss me, I never kiss anyone."

Her body is young and firm; her back with the contour of the spine, the shoulder blades, and the pelvis of finest modeling; her abdomen, the armpits, the inside of the elbows, soft and without fault. I have always thought that such a life would waste all beauty.

"Why don't you put a shade on that lamp?" I asked her, as if I had known her all my life.

"The chiselers would take it right along, they take everything when they're drunk. We had a beautiful standing lamp down in the hall, a guy walked right out with it the first night. There was a kid here, a week ago, he didn't like the light either. He took his socks off, blue they were, and pulled one over the light, but it got hot and went on fire. The time we had! The room was full of smoke."

We had to laugh at this.

"Look what I can do," said Julie and stood on her head in the bed.

"Why do you do that?" I asked.

"Oh, I don't know," she said. "Just for fun. And look"—she pointed at her toes and spread them like two fans.

And after this I have to sit up and laugh, and nothing can happen. It is strange that this business of love demands solemnity, one cannot do anything with it laughing. It has, I think, something to do with breathing or nerves; it needs absolute concentration. Ever since Julie has been funny and wiggled her toes, everything is impossible.

She buttons me up and kisses me again. "Here's your money," she said and pushed it into my pocket. "Come down with me. I'll make you some coffee."

There is a bent and twisted stairway down the back of the house, and in the basement is a room with an oven in it and in a crib a little baby that belongs to the stout colored cleanup woman. Two girls sit and look at it and point their lips and follow its eyes with their faces. It is very, very young, with fingernails the size of a grain of rice. Over the tiny face wander trembling changes —a wide grin from ear to ear, then, with great effort and clenched fists, the face of scorn and suspicion. The little pale eyes wander in a wide arc and try to look around two corners; when it has done this, after an undecided pause, the lower lip quivers and falls away in a bitter helpless cry. It was well comforted; one of the women carried it back and forth, the other walked along, up and down, and spoke to it softly.

There is also a man with his hat on and a wardrobe trunk full of exquisite evening dresses. They come from New York, from debutantes and society women. He tells with each dress the name of the lady who owned it, and of course each name is one that everybody knows. Now I know where the lovely emerald one comes from.

Eddy comes down and asks me how it was. He has to go home to the farm, and I am going to get a room at the Y.M.C.A. and take a train the next day to New York.

In back of the house is a stable in which the old horse made the bumpy drum noises as it changed its position. I go in to him; his stable smells sweet, and the horse is plain and strong with flaxen hair. I have an excuse to go back to the house for sugar. I want to hear her voice once more, to see if she is so lovely, if her hair and her eyes are what I saw before. She is all that.

Hospital in FORT PORTER BUFFALO

THE ARMY IS LIKE A MOTHER

The Army is like a mother; one cannot go hungry or without a bed. It is my home. I like the patients and love some of them; in their illness they are so alone, and the madness, even when it is dangerous or unfortunately amusing, calls from me not pity but some kind of respect. They seem more grave and interesting, stronger; they appear to me like actors with half their make-up on.

The Army issues a book of a few pages in which almost all things are taken care of. Punishment and reward, advice and consequences, are written into sober paragraphs for the guidance of the men. The spirit of this book is clearest in the advice given to non-commissioned Officers on how to make men who have quarreled friends again. On this problem the book states that the men are to be put to the duty of washing windows, one outside, the other inside, washing the same pane. Looking at each other they soon have to laugh and all is forgotten; they push up half of the window and shake hands. It works, I have tried it. Soldiers are terribly childish and forgive easily because they have no rent, wife, insurance, etc., to worry them down.

On the train back to Buffalo I have many hours to think over the last days. Whenever I think of Julie, I feel as if I were back in the young days of my childhood, standing on my toes with arms back and face up, breathing deeply and singing, or looking into the clouds, without a wish other than that this happiness might last forever.

Beardsley told me once that "our dubious Society, and mostly that in the West," was mothered by women out of such houses. The hard men that went out to settle the wild lands married them chiefly for the reason that women were then very scarce out there and even back here.

I can understand that and like it, even without the reason of scarcity. Immoral seem to me the breed of women like Mrs. Mirror and undesirable girls like Ada. I have often seen open enmity and disgust in the faces of married people. I have seen so very seldom an unreserved frank admission in their eyes that they are glad of each other or even interested.

In the subway in New York I also remember the dreadful deadness and stare and the inner upset and drive that is clearly written in the way they sit and move their lips silently, or look constantly as if they have forgotten something and were trying to remember where it was. Free of this seem only sailors, soldiers, some policemen, and most Negroes. They have privacy and seem not to care about much.

Another thing I wondered about is how much they dislike any person that seems not to be like themselves. In one train a man came in and sat down; he had a funny hat on and gaiters on his shoes, also a collar that was not the kind anybody wears—it stuck over his chin left and right. He read a little book and blew his nose on a large blue handkerchief. The people who lined the seats along both walls watched him with displeasure from the moment he came in; their eyes all swam over to his shoes and up and down him as if he had stolen from them. I wished he would take a big gun out of his pocket and scare them to death.

On the train up I also have imperial Ideas again. I think that America needs someone like our King Ludwig, who was a little mad, but made his country beautiful. Someone who has arrogant power and says: "I want a wide avenue through the City of New

York, three times as wide as Fifth Avenue, with light, monuments, fountains, and parks!" who gets the finest artist, not one who ruins the scenery with bad work, but the best, no matter whether he be in Paris or anywhere.

"Make the Hudson beautiful from the Palisades down, forbid such houses as Oxford Hall, and do away with the Jersey Meadows!" The Hudson is much more majestic than the Rhine. It is not always so beautiful, for the Rhine is lovely in the Spring because of the many trees in blossom that go down to the banks and also because it winds much more and, of course, the castles and ruins are nicer than the factories.

All things that are for utility need not be ugly, and it can only be done with great and absolute power. Some people might lose something for a while, although there is no need even for that, but in the end New York and America could be the most beautiful and proudest land in the world.

But I fear this is a leftover of my German heritage and training, and wish to settle everything and have absolute order. Perhaps Mr. and Mrs. Mirror are happy and should be left alone in Oxford Hall, and so with everybody else. That is, I think, Democracy, and besides I have found that Beautiful Dreck is really very fine. Think of Scranton and the trains racing through the Jersey marshes, also the colored flames, the smoke from the lighting plants there, and the mist on the ground. It's just as well to leave it as it is.

In New York two detectives have brought a man on the train between them; he was handcuffed and looked somewhat like Mulvey. I no longer dislike Mulvey and his gang; they are rough but, I think, out of having been made so, and I also think in their way they are honest. I am glad to go back to the Hospital again.

I am most happy to go back to the friendship of the little Chaplain. I can see his gait always. He is so young that I can never get myself to call him father and always get around it by saying either nothing or "you"; I cannot very well call him Philip yet. He is so young that he whips on his toes as he walks along, a very gentle motion one sees in boys. They step as he does, touching the ground first with the front of the shoe, then with energy lifting the palm of the foot, and then heel goes down. That walk is much of his person. I imitated him on a little walk and he blushed and smiled. He is altogether good and fine, but he will not like my ideas on Morality and it will be best not to upset him with Polish Kate's house.

Barracks Bayonet School

BAYONET SCHOOL

The Army needs Officers very badly, and a general order has been issued from Washington to the effect that each post can send one out of a given number of enlisted men to Officers' Training Camp. A board of Officers here gave me a very kind examination; I also passed the physical test—all through my good friend the young priest—and then I received transportation and orders to report to the command at the Officers' Training School at Camp Gordon, which is near Atlanta, Georgia.

Here blows a different wind. The day is cut up into minutes, and from the early morning to the hour of retreat almost every step is counted. It is almost German. In a short period they must make Officers out of civilians and get as much West Point training into them as possible.

To every eight men a young Officer is assigned. He is like a governess, but a strict one. He has a little book with the names of his men in it—we are called candidates—and he watches us

103

all day. These men, who are Second Lieutenants, are somewhat arrogant, and the only consolation is that in a short while we can hand it on to the next group.

Demerits are called "skins." A button undone, a book on the shelf over the bed out of alignment, a shoe under the bed not laced up (even without the foot in it), or looking down when marching at attention to the faraway drill grounds—any of these things means a skin. Sixty of them is the limit during the training. One more, and the Benzine Board, as they call the Faculty, takes prompt action and throws the candidate back into a Sergeant's Uniform.

I get by and go to the Bayonet School; a berth here is very much envied because we can wear spurs, although we have no horses. Not much happens that is funny, because the work is very exacting, leaving no time for jokes. I have gained weight, feel wonderful, and my only sorrow is that when I drill the men, they sometimes have to laugh. I can shout: "At hease!" so it flies across a whole battalion clear and right. We have practiced this in the woods, shouting commands for days, but I have great trouble in other words; "Attention!" is all right, but "Forward march!" is bad.

Our Major is a compact man; he has hardly a neck and is very energetic. They say he was a ribbon salesman before the war; he doesn't know much about soldiering except that he has enduring drive, and he thinks that to ride a horse well means to ride fast. I see him always galloping. He gives frequent pep speeches, and they have introduced a system of making men mad that is childish. Every candidate has to accompany the execution of a command with a grunt, ugh—"port arms, ugh" "at hease, ugh!" I think it does nothing to improve drilling.

This ribbon salesman Major has another wrong Idea. In the evening when we march the men back from the bayonet field, he sits on his horse, takes the salute, and as the companies pass, praises those who have the most broken bayonets. It is to him an indication of good work.

But bayonets are easily broken; I have shown my men how. When charging the dummy, just press the butt to the side; the leverage will snap the bayonet right off in the center. I could march home without a single blade intact, but I don't carry it that far.

The Major is nice and when not in the saddle or on the drill grounds one can talk to him. I have observed how easy it is for men in the service here to acquire the spirit of the military. The young men from colleges absorb it quickly. There is a Captain here who is very young and out of Georgia Tech for a short while; he is every bit as arrogant as a German Lieutenant, bearing, voice, vanity, and all.

The Major addressed the Bayonet School; he said with his face purple: "When you see a German, you are looking at the worst so and so that God has created," and he spoke long and bitterly that way. Afterwards he turned to me and out of the side of his mouth said: "You know, I have to do this. This is a war."

He did another surprising thing. We have long latrines with many seats in a row, and there is in our barracks a young man who, because he has an uncle who is a Senator, manages to get leave to go to Atlanta when no one else can go or will, because there is so much to study. In consequence of this leave, he was behind in his work, and of course the Benzine Board would have flunked him even with the Senator uncle behind him; they do not fool. Well, this candidate went to the latrine and sat there with his drill regulations in one hand and the gun in the other, which he polished at the same time while studying in the book.

The Major passed by and shouted at him: "Hold it, hold it, stay there!" and then he ran out, and we who were outside had to come in. "Look at him, you guys," shouted the Major, "ten percent intelligence and ninety percent ambition is all you need in this man's army. Here's an example!" From then on he was the Major's pet.

In the evenings there are social functions of a very disappointing kind. The songs that are sung are below anything I have ever heard sung. One is so embarrassing that in the beginning the men only sang it with half voices; now they blare it out because they no longer think about the words. It goes:

> I want the Bars, just like the Bars that my Lieutenant wears;
> They are the Bars, the only Bars, and so on. . . .

It refers to getting a commission as a Second Lieutenant, who wears little gold bars on his shoulders.

We eat many chocolate bars, and at noon drink a colored liquid called Coca-Cola. In the beginning I hated this drink, but it was the only thing at the stand and I was very thirsty from the sun and the exertion of bayonet drilling. Now it must be drunken, I long for it, and afterwards sit down in a very fine restful ease.

The food is good, the barracks crude but airy.

The landscape is not remarkable, but the climate is. In the morning when we march out, it is so cold that the men's fingers get numb, and at the halt some drop their guns because of this; at noon it is oppressively hot.

There are Negro labor battalions here, and I have much pleasure watching the colored men that are on guard. They creep along with bent knees as if held up by invisible strings, and they have found out how to carry their guns so that they float without effort over the shoulder. The gun lies on its side, the balance is worked out so that a little more weight is in back than in front and thus the butt holds up the hand. This hand is long, and the last joints of the fingers are pasted to the end of the gun. Their eyes are open but asleep; I am always afraid they will fall or walk into a tree; and the most wonderful performance is when they change the gun from one shoulder to the other. They hate to do this and go through the right motions but like in a dream. I am so fond of Negroes because I have never seen one until I came to America and they are therefore rare and interesting.

Since the latrine incident, they call the ribbon salesman Major "Ninety Percent." For some time now, I have observed on his side a feeling of suspicion towards me. At times he stands with other Officers; they speak together and then look at me. Most of them laugh and walk away. I am going to get mad about this laughing one day and tell them a few frank opinions.

The Senator's nephew has asked two of us to come along to a party. They say since the Army is here all the good families have left Atlanta, but a few without daughters have remained and we are to go to a house for a party.

We have not been drinking anything except this Coca-Cola for a long time, no beer, no wine, but at this house are these drinks, also whisky. I drink a glass and it shakes me like a wet dog. But the other two are drinking it; they are more at home with this strong beverage. Spalding, who has been with me mostly on the bayonet field, is soon wobbly, and he says to me: "You're my pal."

But later on he comes again, and says: "You're my pal, but I'm not your pal! Oh, no—I'm not your pal!" and also: "You're going with me, but I'm not going with you."

And again, when I ask him why, he says: "You're my pal, but I'm not your pal!" and finally he takes his glass, and bangs it on the table, breaks it, and says: "Because you're a German spy."

The Senator's nephew, who can drink more, because he is always going out, told him to shut up.

We went home and I heard for the first time that there was a rumor that I was a spy, but that everybody laughed at that.

I was very angry and went to the Major and told him that, after all, the Germans weren't that stupid. He was sorry and everything seems allright again.

Today a Colonel from Headquarters sent for me; he invited me to sit down and spoke of many things, but nothing of the Army. He gave me a cigarette and then out of the blue sky asked me to tell him the Story of the Elephant Cutlet.

I had told this story only to Beardsley and the young priest. This officer knows Beardsley from the University, and how he heard of the story is very interesting.

Somebody in New York informed the police that I was a German spy. The police, not knowing me, informed the Army; the Army turned the information over to the Intelligence Department in Washington. Beardsley has been transferred to that branch of the service in Paris. Checking up, the Army was very thorough and among other things got in communication with Beardsley. His correspondence came to Camp Gordon with the rest. The Officer here wrote to Beardsley and Beardsley answered and wrote him to have me tell the Story of the Elephant Cutlet. Again I love America, because it's wonderful that in a great War like this, such nonsense can go on in looking for a spy.

I told him the story, and since then have had to tell it to so many people here that I am tired of it. It's about two men in Vienna who wanted to open a restaurant.

THE ELEPHANT CUTLET

Once upon a time there were two men in Vienna who wanted to open a restaurant. One was a Dentist who was tired of fixing teeth and always wanted to own a restaurant, and the other a famous cook by the name of Souphans.

The Dentist was however a little afraid. "There are," he says, "already too many restaurants in Vienna, restaurants of every kind, Viennese, French, Italian, Chinese, American, American-Chinese, Portuguese, Armenian, Dietary, Vegetarian, Jewish, Wine and Beer Restaurants, in short all sorts of restaurants."

But the Chef had an Idea. "There is one kind of restaurant that Vienna has not," he said.

"What kind?" said the Dentist.

"A restaurant such as has never existed before, a restaurant for cutlets from every animal in the world."

The Dentist was afraid, but finally he agreed, and the famous Chef went out to buy a house, tables, and chairs, and engaged help, pots and pans and had a sign painted with big red letters ten feet high saying:

"Cutlets from Every Animal in the World."

The first customer that entered the door was a distinguished lady, a Countess. She sat down and asked for an Elephant Cutlet.

"How would Madame like this Elephant Cutlet cooked?" said the waiter.

"Oh, Milanaise, sauté in butter, with a little spaghetti over it, on that a filet of anchovy, and an olive on top," she said.

"That is very nice," said the waiter and went out to order it.

"Jessas Maria und Joseph!" said the Dentist when he heard

the order, and he turned to the Chef and cried: "What did I tell you? Now what are we going to do?"

The Chef said nothing, he put on a clean apron and walked into the dining room to the table of the Lady. There he bowed, bent down to her and said: "Madame has ordered an Elephant Cutlet?"

"Yes," said the Countess.

"With spaghetti and a filet of anchovy and an olive?"

"Yes."

"Madame is all alone?"

"Yes, yes."

"Madame expects no one else?"

"No."

"And Madame wants only one cutlet?"

"Yes," said the Lady, "but why all these questions?"

"Because," said the Chef, "because, Madame, I am very sorry, but for one Cutlet we cannot cut up our Elephant."

Small Beer

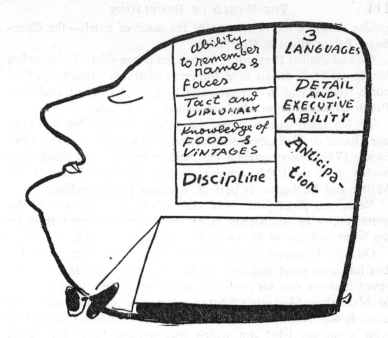

"NO TROUBLE AT ALL"

The world is full of maîtres d'hôtel, many of whom are able, well-informed men. But only one in a hundred thousand is blessed with that rarest, most priceless of qualities so generously evident in Gabriel, the Maître of the Cocofinger Palace Hotel in New York.

We see this peculiar talent in the profile above, behind the ear, under "Detail and Executive Ability." It is the faculty of "Anticipation," an astral clairvoyance with which to sense catastrophe, anywhere in the wide realm of his authority. Not only to feel it ahead, but to prepare for it and minimize the effect thereof.

One more look at the graph, and it is evident to anyone why, with such talents, Gabriel has come up, up, up, from the position of third piccolo at the humble "King Wenceslaus" in Przemysl, through the pantries and over the red carpets of Madame Sacher's, the Negresco, Shepheard's, the Meurice, Claridge's, up to the

113

golden doors of the restaurant of the hotel of hotels—the Coco-finger Palace Hotel in New York.

Gabriel smokes Dimitrinos, he has ten dozen shirts, Lobb makes his boots, he is driven in a Minerva, thinks in French, his hats come from Habig in Vienna, and both Noel Coward and Cole Porter have asked him who builds his fine tail-coats.

To his many subordinates, he speaks through his assistant, one Hector de Malherbes, who at one time worked for Max Reinhardt. (This temperamental aesthetic experience has fitted Malherbes most admirably for his present position.) Between the Maître and Malherbes is perfect, wordless understanding.

Never was proof positive of Gabriel's great talents and of the mute felicity of Malherbes more clearly demonstrated than on the night and day of February the twenty-fifth, 1937.

On that Thursday at three-fifteen in the afternoon, when the last luncheon guest had left, Gabriel leaned on his desk with its seven drawers, one for each day of the week, and nodded gently to Malherbes. Malherbes bent down to the drawer *Jeudi*—because it was Thursday—and took from it a salmon-colored folder with a sulphur label, on which was written, "Birthday Party, February 25, 1937, Mrs. George Washington Kelly."

Gabriel carried the folder up to his room, Malherbes bowed and left. In his room, Gabriel took off his fine tail-coat, which was rounded from much bowing, hung it up, sat on his bed, and carefully unfolded the bills that five-, ten-, and one-dollar patrons had pressed into his hand. He added them up and entered into a little crimson book, "February 25, *Déjeuner*, $56." Then he took off his boots, leaned back into the pillows, stretched his toes in the sheer, black Sulka silk socks, and opened the salmon-colored folder.

Madame George Washington Kelly was a difficult and exacting client.

The Italian waiters called her *bestia,* the French *canaille,* and the Germans *die alte Sau.* She had a desperate countenance, partly concealed by a veil; behind this, her face shone the color of indigo. Her skin had the texture of volcanic rock seen from the air, with dirty snow swept into the crevices.

She dressed with complete immunity to fashion, except for the Beaux Arts Ball. On the night of that elaborate *affaire,* she had come with her friend, the "Spirit of the Midnight Sun," and together they had engaged the rooms and made the preliminary plans for this birthday party, of which Malherbes had said to Gabriel in *sotto voce* French, "It is not a birthday party—it is a centennial celebration." Gabriel had stared him into silence.

After many more visits and consultations with architects, stage designers, and florists, Madame had decided to build, at one end of the ballroom, a replica of her Miami retreat, "O Sole Mio," in its original noble dimensions. This was to be set among hibiscus, poinciana, and orange trees in bloom, surrounded by forty-foot royal palm trees and fronted by wide terraces. Cutting through the center of the room, from the terraces on the north to a magnificent flight of stairs on the south, ran the lagoon, filled with real water, and in this water was to float the genuine gondola which Mr. George Washington Kelly had brought as a souvenir from Venice and taken all the way to Miami. The stairs on the north end rose to a balcony; from there, a birthday cake was to be carried down, placed on the gondola, and rowed across to Sole Mio, where Mrs. Kelly's own darkies would bring it to her table to be cut.

The gondola was in Miami, also the royal palms, also the four white-haired darkies, brothers named Morandus. The Fire Department had sent a captain to study the position of the hydrants and windows, to connect a pumping-truck, and to fill the lagoon, which, it was estimated, would take fourteen hours.

To do all this properly, the complete entertaining facilities of the hotel had been rented for the three days preceding the party and for an additional two following it, to clear away the debris.

Since Monday morning, the house was filled with drafts from open doors and windows, tall ladders, and empty smilax crates. Careless carpenters, careless stagehands, careless plumbers and florists, ruined the peace and the carpets of the hotel with hammering, riveting, and soldering together the two-hundred-foot tank. Following on the heels of the plumbers came the painters, who painted the sides of the lagoon emerald-green and a pattern of underwater scenery on its bottom. An eminent artist from Coral Gables supervised this.

The menu for this party was dictated by Madame herself, without benefit of Gabriel's advice. It was in the tradition of her entertainments and composed itself—at twelve dollars a cover for four hundred guests—of the following: *Caviar aux Blinis, Borscht, Homard Sole Mio, Faisan Miami, Purée de Marrons, Pommes Soufflées, Salade Georges et Marthe, Bombe Washington, Café.*

For the one thousand five hundred additional guests for supper, she had chosen an equally unfortunate repast. This, at five dollars a cover, consisted of *Velouté Marthe aux Croûtons, Poussin en Cocotte Washington, Nouilles Polonaise, Petits Pois Parisienne, Bombe Sole Mio aux Fraises Cardinal, Gâteaux Georges, Café.*

Breakfast was to be served from four o'clock on, at one dollar and fifty cents per person. Provision was also made for eighty musicians' suppers, suppers for chauffeurs, maids, the secretaries at the door, and the announcer and detectives, at one dollar per person.

Cocktails were to be served during the reception: a fantastic, violent drink of Madame's own invention, named "High Diddle," the secret formula for which Madame fortunately gave to no one. Closely guarded, her trusty darkies—the Morandi—were to mix this, bringing most of the ingredients themselves.

After Gabriel had read the papers and made several notes, he rose, looked into a mirror, and took a loose smoking jacket from his closet. He slipped on a pair of white gloves and walked below. Malherbes was waiting for him. It was six o'clock.

Gabriel nodded, and his assistant followed him with a silver pencil and a morocco portfolio.

They walked through the kitchen, where the cooks fished red lobsters out of steaming casseroles and chopped them in half. From there they went on to the cellar—here, men broke open cases of *cordon rouge* 1921, at eleven dollars a bottle, put them away in tubs, and stood them on top of one another. From here, they walked up to the ballroom proper. The tables, seating eight guests each, were set to the left and right of the lagoon. Sole Mio was finished, and, on the lower terraces in front of it—as indicated on the plan—was the crescent-shaped table, facing the room. Here, Monsieur and Madame George Washington Kelly and their son, George Washington Kelly, Jr., as well as their most intimate friends, were to sit.

Two painters were busy pouring and stirring fifty gallons of turquoise ink into the lagoon, to give it the precise color of the waters in Miami. The Coral Gables artist had left with them a sample of that shade on a piece of water-color paper, and, from time to time, they compared this and then added more ink. Up on the balcony of Sole Mio, two electricians were focusing spotlights across the room, up to the magenta curtain on the other side.

From the street could be heard the last *"Poooommmph,"* *"Puuuuuuumph,"* *"Poomph"* of the Fire Department pumping-truck. The lagoon was filled.

Gabriel, walking into the hall, saw the last of twenty royal palms—in tubs, with their leaves carefully bandaged—being carried upstairs, and below from the street appeared the neck of the Venetian gondola.

The great Maître nodded to Malherbes. Malherbes ran down to the door and told the men, "Watch out for the paint, you." Later on, in the office, Malherbes made certain that a gondolier had been engaged. Yes, he had. He was to report at the ballroom in costume, with a knowledge of how to row a gondola and ability to sing "O Sole Mio."

Gabriel went back to his room, lit a cigarette, and rested in his bath for half an hour. Then he dressed.

As on every evening, so now he received the dinner guests of the hotel at the door of the restaurant.

Madame George Washington Kelly's party over in the ballroom was in the able hands of his third assistant, Monsieur Rudi, a withered, one-time stable-boy of Prince Esterházy.

At regular intervals, a courier crossed from the ballroom and whispered to Malherbes, "The guests are arriving." Then again, "The cocktails are being passed." After this, "The guests are entering the ballroom." Then, "Madame George Washington Kelly is very pleased," and on to "The guests are sitting down," and "The soup is being served." These bulletins were translated into French by Malherbes and whispered on to Gabriel, who nodded.

Dinner was almost over in the restaurant when Gabriel went into a little side room, where, on a table behind a screen, a plain meal was prepared for him. It consisted of some cold pheasant, cut from the bones, field salad with lemon dressing, and a plain compote of black cherries cooked without sugar. In ice under the table was his favorite wine, an elegant, slim bottle of Steinberger Kabinett, Preussische Staatsdomäne, 1921.

In the middle of his meal, before he had touched the great wine, Gabriel rose abruptly and quickly walked across the restaurant. Malherbes, who had eaten out in the second little room, swallowed quickly and followed him. Almost running, they crossed the entrance hall of the ballroom and went up the staircase, to the third palm.

Gabriel stopped and beside him, as always, stopped Hector de Malherbes. The dessert had just been served, the remnants of the *Bombe Washington* were being carried from the room by the waiters, and, as set forth in the sheet of instructions, the lights were lowered.

Two heralds sounded the *Aïda* theme as a command to silence and attention.

The heavy magenta curtains sailed back, and high above the audience appeared the birthday cake. It was magnificent, of generous proportions, and truly beautiful. The masterpiece of Brillat Bonafou, *Chef Pâtissier* of the Cocofinger Palace Hotel, twice the winner of the Médaille d'Or de la Société Culinaire de Paris, Founder and President of the Institut des Chefs Pâtissiers de France. In weeks of patient, sensitive, loving labor, he had built a monument of sugar, tier upon tier, ten feet high, of raisin and almond cake. Of classic simplicity, yet covered with innumerable ornaments that depicted scenes from a happy sporting life. Up and down the sides of the cake, dozens of cherubim were busy carrying ribbons; these—Bordeaux and emerald—represented the racing colors of the G. W. K. stables.

But the most wonderful part of the wonderful cake was its top. There, complete in all details, stood a miniature replica of O

Sole Mio, correct as to palms, orange trees, the lagoon, the gondola. Under the portico, an inch high, smiling, hand in hand stood
Monsieur and Madame George Washington Kelly: Madame with
a bouquet of roses, Monsieur with his ever-present cigar, an Hoyo
de Monterrey, at the end of which was a microscopic tuft of
cotton.

That was, however, not all. Over the miniature Sole Mio
hovered a brace of doves. In their beaks, most artfully held, were
electric wires, so arranged that flashing on and off they spelled
first "George" and then "Martha"—"George" in green, "Martha"
in red. Five lady midgets, dressed as the Quintuplets, carried the
cake downstairs in the light of the amber spotlights.

The Hawaiians played "Happy Birthday to You, Happy Birthday to You." Everyone sang, and all eyes were moist.

The gondolier started to punt down the lagoon to receive
the cake.

At that moment, with all eyes upon them, one of the Quintuplets, Yvonne, stepped on an olive pit, and turned her ankle. The
cake trembled, swayed, and fell into the lagoon, taking the midgets
with it. *"Ffsssss-ss-hss,"* went the electric wires.

But where was Gabriel?

He stood under the royal palm and nodded quietly to Malherbes. Malherbes lifted one finger and looked up at the man
with the spotlight.

The amber light left the lagoon and raced up the stairs. Out
came the trumpeters again and sounded the *Aïda* theme, the curtain swung open once more, again the Hawaiians played "Happy
Birthday to You, Happy Birthday to You."

As if the last dreadful minutes had never been on the watches
of this world, there appeared to the unbelieving eyes of Monsieur
and Madame George Washington Kelly and their guests and
friends—THE CAKE again, unharmed, made with equal devotion,
again the work of Brillat Bonafou, identically perfect and complete, with the scenes of the happy life, the cherubim, cigar and
smoke, lagoon and gondola, doves, lights flashing the names in
green and red, and carried on the shoulders of a new set of Quintuplets.

The miserable first set of midgets swam to the shore of the

lagoon, scrambled out, and tried to leave the ballroom in the shade of the tables.

Gabriel hissed *"Imbéciles!"* to Malherbes. Malherbes hissed *"Imbéciles!"* down to the midgets.

The new cake was rowed across, besung, carried to the table, cut, and served. Not until then did the great maître d'hôtel leave the protecting shadow of the royal palm. Now he walked quietly, unseen, to his room, for, in spite of possessing every talent, and besides the gift of "Anticipation," Gabriel was a very modest man.

DOG STORY

For many years our summer vacations were spent in an old peasant house, and everybody who came to see us was breathless, partly on account of the beauty of the scenery, but chiefly because the house stood atop a steep hill, overlooking a village on the shore of a remote Austrian lake.

The landscape was as simple as bread and water. A ring of dark green mountains which anyone could climb reflected themselves in the silent lake. At one side of this lake, a string of gay rowboats shifted back and forth in the currents of the green water. Each boat had the name of a girl painted on its side, and from the end of the pier to which they were tied I went swimming while Wally, my dachshund (she was so small that I carried her home in my coat pocket whenever we had walked too far), slept in one of the boats, in the shade of the bench that spans the center. Wally disliked both sun and water.

From the pier one walked into the garden of the White Horse Tavern, a cool space, filled with yellow tables and chairs, shaded by an arbor of wild grapevines.

Here usually sat a man of good appetite; he was a butcher and Wally's best friend, a plain fat man with a round shaven head, a large mustache, the caricature of a German, and certainly a butcher. He owned the house to the left of ours, on the hill.

After he had finished eating and laid knife and fork aside, he would take a piece of bread, break it into two pieces, call for Wally, and, mopping up the rest of the sauce on his plate, carefully feed it to the dog.

He paid his bill, said good morning, blew his nose into a large blue handkerchief, finished his beer, and took his cane from a hook, put on an alpine hat, and in a wide circle walked around the baroque, salmon-colored church.

Next to the church was a fountain, with a statue of St. Florian, the patron saint of firemen, standing on a tall column above it. As the butcher passed this fountain, the lower half of him was always hidden by the wide basin and only his hat, coat, and arms —rowing in the air—seemed to walk up the street. In a while we followed him up the hill.

The sounds of this remote place were as comfortable as its panorama. In the morning twilight, Wally was at the garden gate, barking at the cattle that were driven up to the high meadows. From their necks hung bronze bells, suspended from heavy, quill-embroidered leather straps. The bells clanged away into the distance, and their place was taken by the church bells below calling to early mass at about seven.

The little motorboat that zigzagged back and forth over the lake had another bell, which announced its first departure half an hour later. The bell on the schoolhouse rang at eight.

As the sun rose over the high wall of mountains it changed all the colors in the valley and lit up the underside of the clouds that hung in the thin clear air above. Children sang in the schoolhouse, the birds in the trees, carpets were beaten in gardens, and the cobbler started hammering.

At half-past ten followed the screech of the small wheels of the daily train from Salzburg as it slowed down to negotiate the sharp curve which carried it into the village. At this sound Wally sent up a long, high flute-like cry. She took that up again for another sound that came from the same direction as the train, the tearing howl of the whistle which announced that it was noon in the saw-mill at the far end of the lake.

The worst sound, one that made the little dog's hair stand on end and sent her for protection under a couch, was the music that started at one, Mozart, Bach, Haydn, Schubert, and Beethoven. It came from the house on our right. In its living room, little girls, in one-hour shifts, glared at études, cramped their small fingers into claws, and performed awful concertos on two old Bechstein grand pianos.

This went on until four. When the last of the little blond girls had left, Frau Dorothea von Moll, the music teacher, came out of the house, held her temples for a moment, and then walked slowly up and down in her kitchen garden. She wandered between even rows of spinach, kohlrabi, beets, celery, peas, and carrots and the large leaves of rhubarb.

She wore a severe black costume, on cold days a mantle trimmed with worn Persian lamb, an old gray bonnet, and a watch on a long thin golden chain. She looked like someone deliberately and carefully made up to play the role of a distinguished old lady in reduced circumstances.

She went out little; a few gentle, little old ladies formed a group that met in her garden house on Thursdays. She entertained them with coffee and Gugelhupf, a native cake, and with anecdotes of musicians and the great people she had known when her husband, the famous pianist Arnulf von Moll, was still alive.

As soon as the pianos were stilled, Wally ran down the steep stairs that led to Frau Dorothea's garden as if to thank her because the terrible concert was over. Wally seesawed down the incline—front legs first, back legs after. Then she squeezed through an opening in the fence and attended the Thursday teas, eating cake and drinking milk. On other days she just walked up and down between the rows of vegetables, behind Frau Dorothea.

Wally's initial cost was very small, notwithstanding the fact that her father was the Bavarian champion Hasso von der Eulenburg, and that she personally was entered on her distinguished pedigree as Waltraut von der Eulenburg. However, she became expensive almost immediately.

One Sunday morning she pulled the cloth off the breakfast

table and with it every cherished cup and saucer of a Sèvres tea set. The hot water from a falling pot scalded her, and Wally walked about for a week wrapped in bandages. As soon as this was forgotten, she ate a box of matches, and when she had recovered from that experience and come back from the veterinary, she worked a whole night to rip the satin cover off a Biedermeier love seat, took all the horsehair carefully out of it, carrying small tufts of it all over the house, down to Frau Dorothea's, and over to the butcher's garden.

There were many more nice things in this old house of which we were very fond, and it seemed best to send Wally away to be trained. One day a forest ranger, who had trained many dogs, took her away in his knapsack. To this experience I owe the knowledge that dogs can recognize a picture, a fact often disputed.

The forest rangers are government employees; they wear green mountain uniforms and faded felt hats with plumes. Most of them have Santa Claus beards, and usually they smoke long pipes that hang down the middle of the beard and end over heavy silver watch chains that are weighted down with old thalers. They carry knapsacks and over their shoulders hang double-barreled shotguns.

This forester found Wally more stubborn than any dachshund he had ever trained. He was very strict with her, rubbed her nose on the floor whenever she had done indignities to his clean house, gave her a few slaps on the backside, and threw her out into the forest.

Wally came back to us a few weeks later a completely changed dog. A model dog. Soon after her return a new tobacco was put on the market. It was called "Forester's Cut" and was wonderfully and widely advertised. Large posters were pasted up everywhere; on them appeared a package of "Forester's Cut," and the picture of a forester smoking it with delight. He wore the rakish hat with the plume, the grass-green uniform, the white beard, the shotgun, and was just such a one as Wally had been living with.

Wherever Wally saw this picture, she went for it. She strained on her leash, the little hairy chest became a bellows and started to work in and out, the lips were pulled up from over her teeth, and long rolls of thunder came from her throat. She shook with anger and looked like an old woodcut of the devil in a peasant Bible. She did nothing about the picture when it was shown to her in magazines, where it appeared in full colors but was reduced to half a page, nor did she recognize it when she saw a poster that was life-sized but printed in black and white.

At the end of that summer's vacation, we took Wally to America with us. It was not a happy idea and we should have followed the advice of Frau Dorothea, who wanted to keep Wally for us until our return. Wally hated the big liner. She was in a good kennel and had the company of two theatrical black poodles, good-natured animals, used to travel, and able to ride a bicycle and to count up to ten. The food was excellent, the sailor who took care of her a friendly fellow. But Wally remained curled up in a corner of her compartment, an unhappy, defiant coil of dachshund. She looked with mistrust at the ocean, with despair at the masts, the funnels, and the ventilators of the ship. She never played with the other dogs and stopped trembling only when she was wrapped up and resting on my lap in a deck chair.

Wally did not like New York any better than the ship. Her memories were a nightmare of fire-engine sirens, revolving doors, backfiring automobiles, the absence of grass and bushes, the rarity of trees. We decided the next summer to leave her with Frau Dorothea, who took care of our house while we were away.

This also was a sad arrangement. Frau Dorothea wrote that Wally came home only for meals, that she ate little, became thinner and thinner, sat in front of the closed door of our house, and that even her friend the butcher, leaning over the fence from his side of the garden and holding up choice pieces of meat, could not console her. Once she almost bit him when he came up to the house to speak to her.

We asked a dog specialist for advice and he suggested that we send her some piece of personal wearing apparel. A pair of old slippers, an old skiing mitten to which I had lost the mate, and a sweater with a few holes were dispatched with the next mail.

This helped a good deal. We read in happier letters that Wally now had a basket on the porch of our house and busied herself packing and unpacking it. She carried the slippers or the glove proudly through the garden, slept inside, under, and on top of the sweater. She still sat on the porch waiting for us until dark, but she ate now, slept at night in Frau Dorothea's house, and the butcher was allowed to come into the garden, was welcome, with a bone, or even just as he was.

We did not open the house the next summer; it was the year of the Anschluss. From letters we gathered that the village was not noticeably disturbed; a new strategic highway was being built along the lake, new songs were being sung, some people had become very quiet and others too loud, and a few places had been renamed; but to a dog, Hermann Göring Strasse and Adolf Hitler Platz are as good as Heinrich Heine Strasse and Dollfuss Platz.

Early the next year, Frau Dorothea had a visitor at whom Wally barked. He was a portly, serious business man from Salzburg and he offered to buy her house. The man's name was Hermann Brettschneider.

Frau Dorothea said that she loved her home, had no reason to sell it, and would certainly never sell it at the price he offered her. She told him that our house was for sale. He did not want our house. He left.

A few weeks later he came back again, this time in the parade uniform of a captain of Storm Troopers, the medal of the Order of the Blood, highest Nazi decoration, on his chest. He sat a long while in her garden house and talked, and he left finally, red in the face. Frau Dorothea still did not want to sell.

Soon after he was gone, the piano lessons stopped, the little blond girls were forbidden to come. The old ladies also sent their regrets and stayed away on Thursdays. One night windows were broken, and then the butcher was arrested because he had come out of his garden to beat up a young man in uniform. The young man in uniform had been busy with a pail of red paint and a brush; he had lettered on the wall of Frau Dorothea's house, "Get out of town, Sarah—make haste, go back to Jerusalem."

On the first of the next month the house was newly painted, the windows repaired; the balcony broke out in Nazi bunting, and Herr Hauptmann Brettschneider gave a garden party bright with uniforms.

Frau Dorothea moved out of the village, to a house near the sawmill, and during the daytime she stayed indoors or in her little garden.

Wally, of course, was Aryan. She could run around and she made the long run to our house twice a day. She climbed to the terrace, unpacked the dirty slippers, and carried the skiing glove about. The butcher was in a concentration camp, but the Brettschneider housekeeper gave Wally occasional pieces of ham, ends of sausages, cuts of pork. Storm Troopers kept good kitchens.

When it was time for her to come home, late at night, Frau Dorothea usually walked to meet her in the dark. It was a rather dangerous place to walk. It was a freightyard of a place; its contours were an uncertain smudge, much like a charcoal drawing. There was a lamp about sixty feet from the spot where the railroad tracks crossed the new cement highway. It was here that the wheels of the train screeched at half-past ten in the morning. The highway entered the village in a blind, sudden turn, something the engineers would have liked to avoid, but the alternative would have been to drill a tunnel through two mountains. At the side of the highway, on its outer curve, the ground was soft and the terrain dropped down to the rocky bed of a river, the outflow of the lake. About where the lamp was, the water thundered down over a dam. It was an ideal setting for accidents, this place.

The accident happened on the night of March 7, 1939. A battery of tanks was being rushed to the Eastern Front—Front is the right word, for Germany was in a state of war—and came to the sawmill somewhat ahead of schedule, at the moment that Wally was about to cross the highway.

The beams of the strong headlights, the hellish clatter and tumult of the machinery, and the apparition of terror that a tank is, must have frozen the little dog to the middle of the road.

The driver of tank Number 1 tried to avoid her. He suddenly put on the brakes, that is, he retarded the left tractor belt and advanced the right. Four of the tanks behind him piled into one another, and his had turned too far, left the highway, and rolled over three times as it went down into the river bed.

It went into the shallow water (the sawmill closes the locks at night, to have more water for the turbine the next morning) right side up, and the two men in it, in overalls, loosened their belts and climbed out of the machine. Tanks Numbers 2, 3, 4, and 5 were somewhat damaged.

From the tower of tank Number 6 jumped a baby of a lieutenant with his first mustache. The men had climbed out of the other tanks and stood in a ring about Wally. The lieutenant picked her up, patted her head, spoke soft words to her, and held her to his cheek.

When Frau Dorothea came forward he clicked his heels, saluted, and smiled. "Dear lady, so sorry," he said, and gave the dog to her. While the mechanics set to work repairing the damaged tanks, the young lieutenant lingered a moment or two, asking the dog's name and talking to Frau Dorothea about her. Then he went over to the edge of the highway.

At his direction, pulleys and spades appeared. Chains and cables were carried down the embankment. As two bugs might pull another, a dead one, under a leaf somewhere to eat him, two of the tanks above, without effort or strain, dragged the tank up out of the river bed and set it on the road. The lieutenant waved at Frau Dorothea and Wally as he got into the top of his machine. Tank Number 6 started forward, then the other tanks fell into line, one by one, and the procession continued on its way to the Czechoslovakian frontier.

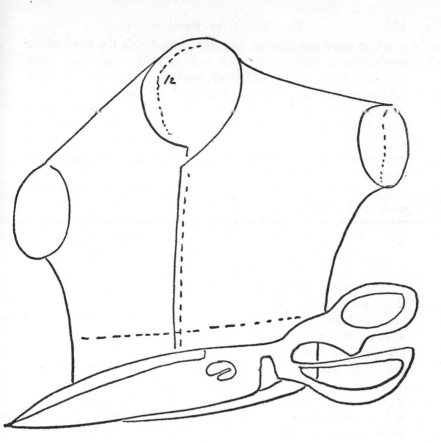

MY ENGLISH SUIT IN PARIS

I had always wanted to own an English suit, a garment that was cut and shaped to the sound of Big Ben's booming, whose buttons were sewed on in a historic street of tailors not far from where the Guards trooped their colors.

At long last the wish came true. I locked my little flat in Montparnasse and with several letters of introduction in my pocket I went across the Channel to the fumed-oak fitting room of a firm of tailors so old and well established that in a century of polishing their name had been rubbed from the brass plate at their door.

There were two fittings, and at the final visit the head of the establishment, followed by two assistant tailors and the cutter, who carried pincushion and chalk, walked around me three times, rubbed his hands, nodded, and released the garment.

Complete with new boots from Lobb and a Lock hat, I stepped from a plane at Le Bourget a fortnight after I had first started out. In my right hand was an Anthony Eden umbrella over whose handle, correct and elegant, hung the loose fingers of hand-sewn capeskin gloves. I was a new man.

I watched my passing reflection in the mirrors of Maxim's bar and had stopped for an instant in front of Thomas Cook's windows to adjust my new homburg when a man came very close to me, leaned over, and asked me where the Madeleine was.

I turned and pointed at the church with my new umbrella.

He seemed surprised and said, *"Merci, monsieur,"* and started to walk along with me. His voice had changed to the hum of confidential conversation. He spoke English and asked me whether I had a desire for a small pleasure. I thanked him and kept on walking down the Rue Royale. He stayed with me and continued to talk. Almost inaudibly, and out of the side of his mouth, he informed me that he knew of a wonderful place.

It had a smart swimming pool of gold filled with perfumed water, around which was built an exquisite bar. This pool, he said, was filled with the most beautiful girls in Paris, the hand-picked beauties of the Folies Bergère. It was lighted from below, very artistically, and the girls, without any bathing clothes whatever, swam around in it, even turning and rolling like dolphins, this way and that, while cocktails were served and the music played. He took both the lapels of my new English suit in his hands and blocked my way. He said that this was not all that was marvelous about it: the most exquisite feature of this bar was that there was no charge for any of it, it was free, it cost nothing; all I had to do was to go there, to follow him.

I had lived in Paris for a long time and never before heard of this philanthropic paradise. I thanked him again. It took all the way to the Place de la Concorde to get rid of him. I turned left and he walked back to Cook's.

But around the corner there was another man. He wore a cap

and he came from behind the second of the stout, square columns that hold up the front of the Ministère de la Marine. He raised his eyebrows and said a small "Pst!" From the shredded edge of his overcoat pocket he pulled a deck of photographs. He bent them and—prrrrrrrt!—let them race past my eye with the expert motion of a card-player.

I thanked him, and another like him, and a third, and all the others like him who, spaced like Santa Clauses in a New York December, stood at their posts all the way to the golden statue of Jeanne d'Arc. Every one of them—pst, prrrrt—showed his collection.

In the old blue serge and wearing any of my other hats, I had never been aware of the number and industry of these dirty-art dealers.

A policeman upheld his arm and stopped traffic and I fled into the Tuileries and started to walk over toward the Seine. Tired and worn, I headed for a horse-chestnut tree and in the cover of its late-afternoon shadow I sat down.

A motherly old lady was feeding the large, fat, blue-gray birds that live in this park. She was with a young girl. In a little while the old lady sat down next to me. The birds followed her and sat on the ground and all around us on the armrests and the back of the bench. She threw her last handful of bread crumbs to them and asked me what time it was. The young girl walked up and down and smiled.

"She's a nice girl," said the lady. She went on, proudly, "I have accommodated several English and American friends—every one of them a gentleman—and they have all said, 'How do you do it, Madame Benoist?'

"Yes, these gentlemen, sometimes, when I was arranging things for them, have said, 'No! Not this beautiful, simple child who looks like a virgin! Oh, I am afraid to ask her. Do you really think she will do it; that such a nice girl will go with me, the first time? So lovely and with such charming manners? Madame Benoist, how do you do it?'

"But they all do it here in Paris; it is only a matter of price.

"Lovely material," she went on, and rubbed a piece of my suit with her fingers.

"Of course," she said, "one can say that it is always the same thing in the end, and that it is foolish to spend too much money for it. After all, they say all women are alike. True enough, my young friend, but how about when you get old, what memories will you have? You'll want nice memories. I always say, detail is important. I like things nicely done. That makes for nice memories."

I agreed and she motioned with her head to the young, nicely perfumed girl with the custom shoes who was doing sentry duty between the chestnut tree and the Musée du Jeu de Paume. "Marie-Claire is her name," sighed the lady, and I ran for a bus on the Quai Voltaire to go to my favorite street corner.

It is the wide piece of sidewalk whereon stand the red marble-topped tables, the wicker chairs, and the old waiters of the Café des Deux Magots. From it you can look undisturbed at the chalk-colored walls and the tower of the church of St.-Germain-des-Prés and against it watch the stop and go of the grass-green buses. Nuns with white butterfly hats come out of the church; spahis, sultans, priests, and delivery boys pass by. An old couple tows a black oilcloth sack of carefully selected comestibles between them, a bushel of soup greens hanging out of it. Behind them walks a little girl holding a five-foot loaf of French bread with a small paper wound around its middle.

Every evening there passes a living Lautrec, an aged man with gray beard. He wears a washed-out linen duster, pushes a small baby carriage, smiles at the baby, then waits for the traffic to stop. He smokes a foolish pipe. On his feet are blue felt pantoufles, and he reads a paper-covered novel held close to his eyes.

This corner I love best of all in Paris, and here I sat down in peace. Waiter Number 8 brought me a glass of vermouth and I leaned back to listen to the conversation at adjoining tables and to wait until the Lautrec walked by with the baby carriage, passed up the street, and disappeared, and the lamps were turned on.

I had hardly given the order when a man who sat at the table next to me leaned over and said, "Have you a match?"

I gave him a light, and then in one breath he said, "Thank you very much, my name is Georges, you are English, you don't mind,

I would like to sit with you, I understand English very well, but I speak it so badly."

"Oh, no," said I.

"Oh, yes," he said.

He snapped his fingers for the waiter, ordered a Pernod, and looked around in back of us. Moving his chair closer to mine, he leaned over my drink, squeezed the sleeve of my new suit, and in a secret voice said, "I am in big trouble, I would not tell you this, but I can see by your clothes, your hat, your shoes, you are a gentleman, a sport. I have a big box of German marks, smuggled out of Germany for a Jewish friend who died, poor fellow.

"Every day I ask myself what I will do with these damn German marks, it is so difficult for me to get rid of them, because they are all ten-thousand-mark bills, and I look not too good, in this old suit and not shaved, but for you, my friend, it is different, we could make a nice little business together, I will sell you these marks cheap.

"I would not tell you this, but I like you, you are a *chic* type, anyone can see this, and I am not lying, look here."

He reached into his coat pocket and with great caution slid out an imitation pin-seal wallet with gilt edges and from it took a ten-thousand-mark note, one of the worthless bills issued during the inflation fifteen years ago. He looked around and told me to be careful, to feel it and touch it and look at it and give it right back to him.

"I have," he said, "lost twenty-six pounds since I have this money in the house, afraid that someone will steal it."

I told him that he need no longer be afraid, that the bills were worth little then and nothing now.

He looked surprised and said that this discovery was terrible news to him and he slumped back into his seat, bit his thumbnail, and looked out into the street.

The old Lautrec with the pantoufles and the baby carriage was just going up the street.

All at once Georges came to life again, sniffed the air, sat up, and leaned over to squeeze the sleeve of my other arm. "Just the same," he said, "I will sell you the marks very cheap."

"What will I do with them?" I asked him.

"That is very simple," he said. "The first time, I will show you, after that you can do it alone. Listen carefully!

"You buy the German marks, the whole boxful. I put on a new suit and take a shave—you will be surprised when I come back. Also I will change my French so that I speak with an American accent. We are supposed to be two rich Americans who come back from a trip to Germany.

"Next we go to the lobby of a fine hotel, one of the best, and we sit down on a sofa and wait for a girl. It must be a *poule de luxe,* not one of the little hungry beasts that run up and down the Boulevard Sébastopol—those ones are too smart. We want a big girl—they are stupid. I don't mean big size, I mean nice— one with a fur cape and a dog and clean gloves. I know them from far away.

"I start a conversation with her and you order the drinks and we talk of our trip through Germany. Then we ask very loud for the bill. When the bill comes, you take out your wallet and open it and you say, 'This is terrible, I have forgotten to change my German money.' You look around in your wallet and hold it low, so she can see that it is full of German ten-thousand-mark bills.

"She will say, 'Oh, please, monsieur, let me pay for this.' So she pays for the drinks.

"Then we go to eat a good dinner and see a show and after, if you like to dance, we go to Florence's. Always the girl pays. After the cabaret I run along. 'You will excuse me,' I will say, 'but you stay.'

"The next day you say to her, 'Don't wake up, darling, don't wake up, but I must leave you now, I must go.' You kiss her on the shoulder and say, 'This is for you, my little poppet,' and you slip one of the ten-thousand-mark notes under her pillow. 'Keep it all,' you say, 'it is all for you. You have been very kind. You have made me very contented, I have been extremely happy with you—good-by—good-by!'

"It is easy—nothing to it, as they say in American films," said Georges.

Just then the evening shift of waiters came on duty with clean napkins. Our new man counted the saucers and asked us if we wanted anything more, and we ordered two more drinks. When he came back, he leaned down and spoke into Georges' ear.

Georges explained later that the waiter was one of his customers and sometimes bought small things from him, a watch, a cigar lighter, a bijou, a fountain pen—little things.

"He wants to buy a camera," Georges explained. "I have a very fine camera for sale, and a ring. You need a camera?"

"No, thank you."

"I will sell you this one cheap. It's a very fine camera," said Georges, and produced from his coat pocket a used candid camera of German make.

The waiter looked at it over our shoulders, and when I gave it back, he offered five hundred francs for it. Georges said it was not for sale for less than a thousand, being worth three thousand. Finally they compromised on seven hundred. It was all very confidential, like the German-mark deal.

The waiter went to get the seven hundred francs, and when he came back he handed Georges the money in a tight little packet under the table, and Georges spirited the camera under the waiter's tray and into his hand. The waiter left and Georges sighed and unfolded the bills in the shadow of the small table. He counted them once, then once more, then his voice became shrill. He brought the money up into the daylight and screamed, "The head of veal! The thief! Look, he has given me only six hundred francs!" But his voice became assured and calm as he added, "I am so glad I took out the lens!"

These words had hardly been said when the waiter came rushing out, red-faced, the lensless camera in his upraised right hand. I could not see what happened, it happened so quickly. There was the sound of broken glasses, a splash, a scream. Somebody pointed and shouted *"Voleur!"* And Georges was gone with money, camera, and my umbrella.

PUTZI

They thought he had asked for more volume, but Nekisch, the conductor, had caught a raindrop on the end of his baton and another in the palm of his hand.

He stopped the orchestra, glared up into the sky and then at Ferdinand Loeffler, the Konzertmeister.

Loeffler reached out for a flying-away page of *Finlandia,* and the audience opened umbrellas and left. The musicians ran into the shelter of the concert hall carrying their instruments, and Herr Loeffler walked sadly to the back of the wide stage and took off his long black coat and shook the rain out of it.

There Nekisch arrested him with his baton. He stuck it into Herr Loeffler, between the two upper buttons of his waistcoat, and held him there against the tall platform. Ganghofer, the percussionist, could hear him say, "You're an ass, Herr Loeffler, not

136

a Konzertmeister, an ass; it's the last time, Herr Loeffler; you can't do the simplest things right; we have a deficit, Herr Loeffler, these are not the good old days, Herr Loeffler—I am telling you for the last and last time: *Inside! Here* in this hall we play when it rains, and *outside* when the sun shines."

Herr Loeffler silently took his blue plush hat and his first violin and went out and waited for a streetcar to take him to that part of the city where his wife's brother Rudolf had a small café, The Three Ravens.

Frau Loeffler sat in a corner of the little café reading the *Neue Freie Presse* out of a bamboo holder. She stirred her coffee.

"Ah, Ferderl," she said, and squeezed his hand, "but you are early today." She could read his face . . . and she looked with him through the plate-glass windows into the dripping street.

"Outside again," she said, and turned to the front page of the *Freie Presse,* and, pointing to the weather report, read, *"Slight disturbances over Vienna but lovely and bright in the Salzkammergut.*

"Inside, outside," she said, over and over again. These two words had taken on the terror that the words death, fire, police, and bankruptcy have for other people.

Behind a counter, next to the cash register, sat Frau Loeffler's sister Frieda. Frau Loeffler pointed at her with the thumb of her right hand. "Look, Ferderl. Look at Frieda. Since I am waiting for you she has eaten three ice creams, four slices of nut tart, two cream puffs, and two portions of chocolate, and now she's looking at the petits fours."

"Yes," said Herr Loeffler.

"Ah, why, Ferderl, haven't we a little restaurant like this, with guests and magazines and newspapers, instead of worrying about that conductor Nekisch and inside and outside?"

"He called me an ass, Nekisch did," said Herr Loeffler. " 'It's the last time,' " he said.

"Who does he think you are? The Pope? Why doesn't he decide himself, if he's so smart! I go mad, Ferderl—I can't sleep for two days when you play, reading about the weather, calling up, looking at the mountains, even watching if dogs eat grass. I tried to ask farmers—they don't know either. You can never be sure, they come from nowhere—these clouds—when you don't want them, and when you play inside and hope that it rains outside, the sun shines, just like in spite, and they blame you!"

They put their four hands together in silent communion, one on top of another, as high as a water glass. Frau Loeffler looked into her coffee cup and she mumbled tenderly, "Ferderl, I have to tell you something." With this she looked shy, like a small girl, then she told him into his ear. . . .

"No!" said Loeffler, with unbelieving eyes.

"Yes! Yes, Ferderl!" she said.

"When?" asked Herr Loeffler.

"In January. About the middle of January . . . Dr. Grausbirn said. . . ."

Loeffler guessed right about the weather for the next two concerts. The sun shone. Outside, it was. Nekisch was talking to him again and Loeffler walked to the concerts with light steps, whistling.

One day at a rehearsal of *Till Eulenspiegel,* he could hold it in no longer; he had to tell them. They patted his shoulder and shook his hand. Even Nekisch stepped down from his stand and put both hands on Loeffler's arms. "Herr Loeffler," he said, just "Herr Loeffler."

And then one day, after the "Liebestod," Loeffler, coming home, found in front of his house the horse and carriage of Dr. Grausbirn.

Loeffler ran upstairs and into the living room, just as Dr. Grausbirn came out of the other door, from his wife's room.

"My wife?" asked Herr Loeffler.

"No," said Dr. Grausbirn. "No, Herr Loeffler, not your wife." Dr. Grausbirn washed his hands. Herr Loeffler went to kiss his poor wife and came back again.

"Herr Doktor," he said, "we won't—I am not going to—"

Dr. Grausbirn closed his bag and slipped on his cuffs.

"Pull yourself together, Loeffler. Be a man," he said, "but you won't be a father—"

"Never?" asked Herr Loeffler.

"Never," said Dr. Grausbirn.

Herr Loeffler sat down on the edge of his chair. "We are simple people," he addressed the table in front of him. "We ask so little of life. We have always wanted him. We have even named him—Putzi, we call him—why, Annie has burned candles to St. Joseph, the patron saint of fathers." He sighed again.

"Why does this happen to me?" he said. "And how could it happen? We ask so little."

Dr. Grausbirn pointed out of the window. "There, Herr Loeffler," he said. "It's like this. Do you see that lovely little late-blooming apple tree? It has many blossoms. . . ."

"Then comes the wind." Dr. Grausbirn reached into the air and swept down. *"Schrumm*—like this—and some of the blossoms fall—and the rain—takes more"—with his short fat fingers the doctor imitated the rain—"and brr r r, the frosts—more blossoms fall—they are not strong enough. Do you understand, Herr Loeffler, what I mean?"

They looked out at the little tree: it was rich with blossoms, so rich that the earth below it was white.

"That blossom, our little Putzi—" said Herr Loeffler.

"Yes," said the doctor. "Where is my hat?"

The doctor looked for his hat and Herr Loeffler walked down the stairs with him.

"If you are going into town—" said Dr. Grausbirn, opening the door of his landau. Loeffler nodded and stepped in.

At the end of the street a lamp post was being painted. The carriage turned into the tree-lined avenue; a column of young soldiers passed them. After the lamp post, Herr Loeffler talked earnestly to Dr. Grausbirn, but the doctor shook his head— "No no no, no no, Herr Loeffler. Impossible—cannot be done." Herr Loeffler mumbled on, "We ask so little." He underlined his words, *"the only one*—never again—my poor wife—love—family"— and all this time he tried to tie a knot in the thick leather strap that hung down the door of the wagon.

"No," said Dr. Grausbirn.

The driver pulled in his reins and the horse stopped to let a streetcar and two motorcars pass. Herr Loeffler was red in the face. Under the protection of the noises of starting motors, horns, and the bell of the trolley, he shouted, "Putzi belongs to us!" and he banged with his umbrella three times on the extra seat that was folded up in front of him. The driver looked around.

"Putzi?" asked Dr. Grausbirn.

"Our little blossom," said Herr Loeffler, pointing to the doctor's bag.

Dr. Grausbirn followed the flight of a pigeon with his eyes. The pigeon flew to a fountain and drank. Under the fountain was a dog; he ate grass and then ran to the curb. From there the doctor's eyes turned to the back of the driver and across to Herr Loeffler—a tear ran down the Konzertmeister's face. The doctor put his hand on Loeffler's knee.

"Loeffler, I'll do it. There's no law—every museum has one. Properly prepared, of course . . . in a bottle . . . next Monday . . . *Servus,* Herr Loeffler."

"Auf Wiedersehen, Herr Doktor."

And so Putzi was delivered to Herr Loeffler. Herr Loeffler, who wrote a fine hand, designed a lovely label for the bottle. "Our dear Putzi," he wrote, and under the name he printed the date.

The next week Herr Loeffler guessed wrong again—rain for Beethoven outside—and sunshine for Brahms inside—and conductor Nekisch broke his baton.

"Go away, Herr Loeffler," he said. "I am a man of patience, but you've done this once too often. Get out of my sight, far away —where I never see you again, ass of a Konzertmeister!"

Herr Loeffler walked home. . . .

For a year Putzi had stood on the mantelpiece. He was presented with flowers on his birthday, and on Christmas he had a little tree with one candle on it. Now Herr Loeffler sat for hours in his chair, looking out the window and at little Putzi in his bottle, and thought about the weather, about the orchestra—about inside and outside.

The *Neue Freie Presse* was mostly wrong; the government reports were seldom right. Nekisch was always wrong—more often than when Loeffler had given the word—but Putzi in his little bottle, Putzi was always right, well in advance. . . .

It was not until months had passed, though, that Herr Loeffler noticed it. He watched closely for a few more days and then he told his wife. He took a pad and a pencil and he drew a line across the middle of the pad. On the lower half he wrote "Inside," on the upper half "Outside"—then he rubbed his hands and waited. . . .

Long, long ere the tiniest blue cloud showed over the rim of any of the tall mountains that surrounded the beautiful valley of Salzburg, Putzi could tell: he sank to the bottom of his bottle, a trace of two wrinkles appeared on his little forehead, and the few tiny hairs which were growing over his left ear curled into tight spirals.

On the other hand, when tomorrow's sun promised to rise into the clear mountain air to shine all day, Putzi swam on top of his bottle with a Lilliputian smile and rosy cheeks.

"Come, Putzi," said Herr Loeffler, when the pad was filled—and he took him and the chart to Nekisch. . . .

Herr Loeffler now is back again—Inside when it rains—Outside when the sun shines.

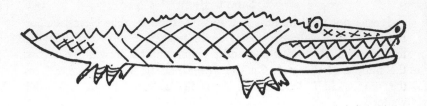

FANCY GREEN

On the Avenida Bolívar, in the mountain city of Riobamba, under the Equator, hangs a hand-hammered crocodile, the sign of the Café Chimborazo.

Under this crocodile is a door through which one enters an ocher-colored dump that smells like the winter quarters of the Barnum and Bailey menage.

The benches are covered with leopard skins—on them sit sunburned, bearded, weary, saddle-bred men such as one might find in the Foreign Legion and in the offices of Mr. Zanuck and Dr. Ditmars. Here sat a recently arrived Italian colonel of aviation, come to teach Ecuadorian cadets formation flying and aerial combat.

There are few women here to admire the colonel's uniform. It is Hussar from the waist up, with so many gold stripes below that they hardly leave room for pants and buttons. He rose to salute his guest, the famous explorer, Captain Cyril Vigoroux.

Captain Cyril Vigoroux was the comfortable size and weight of a champagne salesman; he was familiar to us; we had seen him often in full colors advertising cigarettes, photographed with his wife, both partly submerged crossing a stream. The explorer-captain holds his Winchester high above the turbulent waters, a frightened ape clinging to his upraised arm. Behind them is their smiling jungle porter with steady nerves, carrying the air-mattress, the folding tent, compass, maps.

Captain Cyril Vigoroux took off his tropical helmet, and said "Phew," ordered two bottles of Münchener Löwenbräu, stuffed his pipe, lit it in the frame of his umber beard, and started to fulfill the high promise of his appearance.

With brave words he spoke and with eloquent hands he kneaded into the pipe smoke a report of the jungles of the Oriente and the headwaters of the Amazon. Of leaves, the size and thickness of an Indian elephant's ears; of *lignum vitae* forests behung with orchids, enveloped in phosphorescent bark; of violets weighing three and a half pounds each; of swinging bridges, headhunters, vampire bats, and blue spiders big and strong enough to catch wild turkeys. Of gold in green rivers, and cool, crisp mineral water in others.

His hands danced the flight of the giant whistling butterflies, and he borrowed the air over our table to demonstrate the slithering, deathly stealth of an anaconda, sixty feet in length—the tip of its tail somewhere out in the pantry of the Café Chimborazo, its middle here over the table, where, with one well-aimed stroke of his machete, he cut the snake into two equal lengths, which disappeared north and south into the jungle.

Captain Cyril Vigoroux had succeeded in washing away my modest plans for a quiet voyage to Quito and back. He had shifted into its place his luxuriant reservoir of surprises.

Without shaving the next morning, I left to assemble my jungle trousseau. Two days after, alone, I bought a ticket for Baños, which is the last outpost of civilization, at the gateway to the Oriente.

Happy at the silver music of my spurs, I tinkled up and down alongside the train wherever it stopped, the silhouette of my tropical helmet swam around telegraph poles and along the sides of the dusty railroad cars, I swished my rawhide whip at flies, and felt with an inward glow the little bottle of quinine in the breast pocket of my blouse. This pleasure found its culmination in the appearance at my hotel in Baños of the four mules and the smiling Indian boy who answered to the name of Aurelio. Aurelio had hair like a shoebrush, he was barefoot, and he took his place about six feet behind me, remaining there always. He called me *"Patrón."*

Baños has a wild thermal establishment. Wild, because it is without benefit of *Kurmusik,* wheel chairs, *Wandelhallen,* and *Sprudel.*

From the side of its highest mountain, with no more ostentation than a common woodland brook, spouts the sulphur brine, steaming hot and opaque and the color of frozen honey.

It breaks up into a pool. To the edge of this pool come the fields; on them, under swaying eucalyptus trees, graze sheep and llamas. A little Indian boy in a cerise poncho herds them.

Free as the waters are the baths; no tickets, no one to tip, no fuss—take a dressing room and slide into the water. There you lay your head back on the soft stone that is the worn edge of the pool and look up and around and think how beautiful, how unbelievably beautiful, how much finer and more complete than anything I have seen on this earth.

There is rarely anyone there, but I found one happy face looking out of the pool. "Kam in, Señor," smiled its owner.

"Teik a seeeet, beautiful, no?" He swept the horizon with a thin hairy arm that came dripping out of the golden soup.

"Very, very beautiful, Señor," I said in agreement and sat down by him.

In this little benevolent land, everyone wishes to help you, to be your guide and adviser, to send you to a friend, to the friend of a friend.

There are only a few things to talk about and not many people, and in a short while we had arrived at the name and person of Captain Cyril Vigoroux, the explorer.

"You know him personally?" I asked with gladness and anticipation.

"Everyone here has the great pleishure to know him. How is he, and how big is his snaike?"

"You know about the snake, Señor?" I inquired eagerly.

"Ah—I have know this snaike for years. The last time I hear about him, the snaike is forty feet long. Now the snaike is how long?"

"Sixty feet, Señor."

"She still grow, ha! Oh, it was a leedle, leedle snaike the first time I hear of him, like so long." He stuck his two index fingers out of the sulphur ten inches apart. "You have heard perhaps the story of how the snaike bit the Capitán, no?"

"No."

Without any urging, my friend moved closer and started to tell me that, many years ago, when the "snaike" was just born and very "leedle," Captain Cyril Vigoroux was on his first safari into the Oriente.

Four hours out of Baños, behind the mountain under which we sat, he made camp for the night. His boy erected the tent and blew up the air-mattress, while the Captain walked up and down outside, with his meerschaum pipe.

Later, he went in to retire. He sat down on his folding chair, but, with terror in his voice, jumped through the side of his tent. It was then that the "snaike" had bitten him. Fortunately, he carried with him an elementary guide on surgery and medicine. Under "Snake Bites," he read that the first and foremost thing to do was to suck the wound.

This, of course, was impossible. He was all alone, the boy being down below watering the horses in the wild Pastaza. "Next," said the little book, "take no violent exercise." This the Captain did until his boy came back. Then they entered the tent, armed with machete and gun, and found, reclining on the seat of the folding chair, not a snake at all, no, no, but the Captain's spurs.

"And then?"

"He left. He has never been seen again in the jungle. He has a villa in Ambato, and everyone there has the great pleishure to know him."

My friend rose from the waters and came out a knobby, blue man. With his legs apart, he skated carefully over the wet terrace. Clinging to the withered muscles on his calf, his cotton bathing suit, much too big for him, covered his ribs and, I thought, a soul given to jest and loose words. He disappeared into his dressing room and came out, to my surprise, in the somber robes of a father of the Salesian Order—humble, truthful missionaries who serve the Indians throughout the jungle.

The next day, with the sunrise, we started off into the jungle of the Oriente. Myself on the first mule with the machete, gun, and whip; behind me, the pack animals, and, last, Aurelio. My beard was five days long. We swung onto the road to Río Verde, along the foaming Pastaza.

This river is wide enough and as loud as the finale of *Götter-dämmerung,* but one crosses and recrosses it on steel and cement bridges, and, for the length of that day, we rode abreast on the back of a perfect automobile highway. We arrived in Río Verde covered with the dust of passing cars and trucks. There stood a hotel. Aurelio slept on the floor outside my room and brought breakfast to my bed the next morning.

The second day was less of a funeral. The road was no longer wide enough for motorcars. Pasted alongside the mountains, it rose and fell abruptly.

The jungle came nearer. It turned into a green tunnel with walls of fat, immense foliage, a greenhouse without end. The light here had the hue of the inside of an empty Moselle bottle.

Butterflies as big as a baker's hand hopped through the air. The trunks of the wide trees were covered with moss and parasites. On their branches hung and stood baskets of orchids and miraculous flowers the size of an idiot's head. A cheap race of monkeys acrobated in this picture. From time to time, there was a roaring waterfall spewing its water down into the Pastaza.

Steel cables and ironwork on the bridges were hidden by tall ferns with leaves as long as Dr. Piccard, and somehow looking like him, with their many outstretched arms.

Beautiful and filled with wonder as all this is, one can only think "Ah—ah—ah" for five or six hours. It is like sitting in a theater with a magnificent stage set on which the actors have forgotten to appear. The second day, I began to wiggle in the saddle. The greenery and flowers looked as if the florists had thrown the end of a Hutton wedding down the back stairs. The wild orchids changed, in this estimate, first to geraniums, then to cabbages.

The parrots and monkeys were sparrows and cats, and for all the excitement (I saw a gray rainworm a foot long) one might be on a *tour dans les Montagnes Catskill.*

We found a fair hotel every night and, in between, places to stop for rest and a drink, but, on the fourth day, everything went wrong.

Aurelio had brought up my breakfast. The toast was muggy. I dressed and paid the bill while the boy took our sleeping bags and the tent out of the barn and packed them patiently on the two mules.

We started off at half-past nine and soon after crossed a river, in which a man overtook us. He had identical equipment: boy, beard, mules, and helmet, and he sang:

> Now you found someone that set you back on your heels,
>   Goody, goody,
> Now you know, hm, hm, hm hm hm hm hm, how it feels,
>   Goody, goody.

Between "your" and "heels," he managed to sandwich a nod and said, "How do you do."

After the last "goody, goody," he was out of sight and hearing. He rode fast, spurring his mule.

We came to a clearing. There we found, pressed close together, a church, four houses, and, hanging outside a little magazine kiosk, *Punch, La Revista Mundial, Die Schweizer Hausfrau, Time,* the *Saturday Evening Post,* and *Popular Mechanics,* the latter in both Spanish and English.

I bought the *Post,* some cigarettes, and some candy for Aurelio. We mounted again and stopped for luncheon at the next hotel.

Aurelio carried the *Saturday Evening Post* and carelessly left it on the porch of the Tivoli, where a hungry donkey took it and trotted off. I found him, almost too late, under a wild banana tree, and twisted the last few torn leaves out of his teeth. During luncheon I read:

(Continued from page 44) Then her voice came out of the impenetrable darkness deeply and quietly, "I'll warm you." He felt the blanket tugged gently and relaxed his grip. He was shaking terribly. The woman lay down alongside of him and pulled the blanket over them.

"How did this get by George Horace Lorimer?" I said in loud alarm to myself.

"Lorimer isn't with the *Post* any more," said the bearded man at the next table, looking out of his Irish stew. "There's a new man, what's his name?"

He snapped his fingers twice and then shook his head and shouted the question out of the window into the jungle.

"Wesley Stout," came back the answer from another explorer, who was saddling a horse.

We rode away and in the evening came to another hotel. The service here was not all that could be desired. It lacked tableware, and, for the second course, the same silver was used as for the first. The Swiss proprietor, however, offered an excellent marc with the coffee.

Later I walked into the jungle. My eyes were not accustomed to the darkness. Aurelio, who was his usual silent six feet behind me, came close and tugged my sleeve, whispering, "Look out, *patrón,* in front of you there is a horse."

I could not see this horse, but I heard two men speaking. Said one of them, "The purchasing agent had ulcers of the stomach, so I took her to the French Casino."

Aurelio took my hand and led me back to the hotel; as soon as we entered the reception hall of the Savoy, I said to my faithful boy, *"Mañana*—tomorrow, *nos*—we, *vamos*—go." I did not know the Castilian word for "back" and pointed three times down the road toward Baños.

"Bueno, patrón," said Aurelio.

I walked wearily up to my room. In it, over my bed, hung a sepia print, an advertisement common in this country. It was a good reproduction of the Botticelli *Madonna and Child.*

The baby is nude, the right hand of the mother supports its little pudgy haunches, and the left hand caressingly massages its back. Under the right hand, in bold Bodoni capital letters, is printed "Vicks VapoRub."

I lifted my eyes to the Madonna and mumbled a prayer with the hope that Captain Cyril Vigoroux might never come this far.

He would be inconsolably disappointed.

THEODORE AND "THE BLUE DANUBE"

Dinner was over, the room was filled with smoke and empty tables, the orchestra played "The Blue Danube," and a waiter cleared off the buffet.

"Sale métier! Bande de voleurs!" said Theodore Navarre *né* Navratil, the maître d'hôtel, and he thought of that dog Wenzel Swoboda, headwaiter many years back, at the restaurant in Vienna where he had served his apprenticeship. . . .

The tip of Theodore's nose was white with anger, he crumpled the list of reservations, tore a table plan into small pieces, and walked up to his dressing room. He counted the tips. Filthy money! Filthy profession! The end of "The Blue Danube" came up the stairs and he had to think again of that specimen of a dog, Wenzel Swoboda. . . .

Theodore had been young then, he had wavy blond hair and his first slim tail-coat . . . it was spring in Vienna. . . . The restaurant had a garden shaded with old chestnut trees that were in full bloom. Under one of them stood a buffet, a square table covered with a white cloth, and arranged on this were trays of pastry, peach, apricot, plum, and apple tarts, and a bowl of whipped cream with fragrant wild strawberries.

Wenzel Swoboda was the maître d'hôtel and to this restaurant came every day the not altogether young but American Mrs. Griswold Katzenbach. She always asked for Theodore; he served her under a large yellow umbrella.

One Friday afternoon a dark cloud floated past the hotel and

149

stopped over the chestnut tree, water came out of it, and together with the blossoms from the tree messed up the pastries, the tarts, and the whipped cream with the strawberries.

Swoboda saw this and looked for Theodore; Theodore leaned over Madame Griswold Katzenbach and pointed to the scenery.

The dog Swoboda danced to the table and kicked Theodore in the heel; then he himself pointed to the scenery and smiled at Madame Katzenbach, and while she looked he hissed at Theodore in Bohemian, "Clear off the buffet—son of a swine," and he kicked him again with more power and higher up.

The orchestra played "The Blue Danube." Theodore attacked the buffet, he cleared it with the speed of an acrobat, stacking tarts and pastries all over himself—in one trip he made the kitchen —strawberries and all—without dropping anything. . . .

Ever since then Theodore had suffered when he heard "The Blue Danube," saw a buffet, or came upon a chestnut tree in bloom. As for Madame Katzenbach, she lives upstairs in this very hotel where he sat on his bed in thought. She talks to him for hours in the dining room, where he stands behind her chair. When she meets him on the street, she stares at a lamp post or looks into a shop window until he has passed, but then they were all alike—and besides in two more weeks they could all go to the devil! In this hope Theodore mumbled a litany that went: *"Que le diable les emporte—j'en ai assez, moi—pique-assiette, pique-fourchette, je m'en vais, moi, je m'en fiche—foutez-moi la paix, bande de sauvages, salauds!"*

Every year Theodore Navarre went to Europe, first class in a modest cabin on one of the slow boats, because none of the hotel guests ever crossed on them. He took the Orient Express but would change to a slow train in Salzburg. It took him to a little village on the shore of a quiet lake and he walked to the hotel Alpenrose, and there he took the cure for his soul.

As soon as he arrived at the Alpenrose he went up to his room —Number 5, with a balcony—waited for his trunks, and came down a changed man.

He took a bath in esteem and respect, and this started in the morning when he appeared at the table for breakfast. Stefi, the waitress, with soft round arms and flaxen hair, wished him a loud and healthy "Good morning, Herr Direktor," and "How has the Herr Direktor slept?" and "What does the Herr Direktor want for breakfast?"

It would never do to live in this respectable hotel without a title. Everybody has one and Herr Theodore Navarre had written, where the register asked for his name, birthday, profession, domicile, and nationality—*Navarre, Theodore, July 6, 1878, Direktor, New York, U. S. A.*

Dinner was at noon, at a round table. Most of the guests came here year after year and they were, from left to right:

Herr und Frau Generalkonsul von Kirchhoff, Vienna
Herr und Frau Oberstaatsanwalt Zeppezauer, Vienna
Herr und Frau Professor der alten Philologie Leichsenring, Graz
Herr Direktor Theodore Navarre, New York

Supper was at seven, the ladies dressed in crêpe de Chine and chiffons; afterward there were parties, once a week the peasant theater, quiet evenings at the hotel—Schubert *Lieder,* cards.

Herr Direktor Navarre was invited to play, to swim, to dance, everyone listened to him—no one called him Theodore, he sat on a chair and important men took off their hats when they met him on the street and smiled and said, "Good morning, Herr Direktor —good afternoon, Herr Direktor—and good evening, Herr Direktor."

Herr Direktor had a good deal of trouble getting on and off his bicycle, but he stopped, even on a curve, for a few words with the gendarmes. They saluted and spoke to him with their heels together, their hands at the seams of their green trousers—it was good medicine.

On his birthday Stefi decorated the table with crocuses and Herr Direktor ordered twelve bottles of the young heady wine that was the best he could find in the cellar of the hotel.

The Alpenrose did itself proud with lake trout *au bleu,* Wiener Schnitzel with cucumber salad, and a pancake, big as a garden hat. The Generalkonsul made a speech, the bottles were emptied, and Herr Direktor Navarre sang.

After dinner it was decided to hire a car and go all together to the other side of the lake and take coffee there.

The automobile arrived and slowly turned the lake for them. Herr Professor Leichsenring, who sat next to the driver, pointed at a dark cloud, but the driver said that it hung too high and would pass.

On this other side of the lake, a table had been set close to the water; two rowboats bobbed up and down. The restaurant "On the Lake" was elegant; it had a waiter.

Herr Direktor Navarre stared at a loose button hanging from the man's shiny dress coat while he ordered Cointreau for the ladies and drank brandy with the men. On a painted platform played a small orchestra, zither, guitar, and fiddle. Frau Oberstaatsanwalt's cup was empty.

"Psst—more coffee." Direktor Navarre turned in his chair and looked for the waiter with the loose button.

He saw a large chestnut tree; under it stood a buffet, a square table covered with linen. Arranged on it were pastries, apricot, pear, and plum tarts, Apfelstrudel, wild strawberries, and a bowl of whipped cream.

The zither player plucked his strings.

The wind leaned into the tree, it swayed, the dark cloud hung over it, rain started to fall and with it the blossoms of the chestnut tree, like rose-tinted popcorn.

Without knowing it, Herr Direktor Navarre left his table and rushed to the buffet, he stacked cakes and pastries all over himself, took along the whipped cream, the wild strawberries, and disappeared into the kitchen.

The orchestra finished "The Blue Danube."

"Herr Direktor!" said Frau Generalkonsul. "Herr Direktor?" looked the others. . . .

He left with the first train, the one that carries peasants to Salzburg, and he never came back.

THE ISLE OF GOD

The train left the Gare de Montparnasse at seven-thirty in the morning. We changed trains at Nantes, again at La Roche-sur-Yon, and once more at Challans. As we left Paris, I had found, in the second-class compartment, an abandoned newspaper. Among the personal notices was this brief and double-spaced advertisement: "Financial gentleman would like to make loan to lady with *poitrine forte.*"

"*Tiens, tiens,*" I said to myself, "how honest, how simple, are love and life in France," and then I looked out of the window. Nothing exciting—a cathedral, some railroad scenery, children come to meet someone wherever the train stopped, a Connecticut kind of country, with an occasional château.

The last train, the one from Challans to Fromentine, is painted ivy-green; its engine is five feet tall. Whenever it enters a village, children run along and jump on the running board; at the end of the village the engineer stops to let them off. The train puffs over

153

marshland, white houses stand alone, the wind blows. The train arrives in Fromentine at about six in the evening.

Fromentine is between La Baule and Les Sables d'Olonne. There are three hotels here, one is as good as the other, all three of them smell of wet sand and bathing suits. Ours had the best view, a glass-enclosed dining room and a Spanish piccolo.

The dining room is a veranda, decorated with aquamarine fish nets, dried starfish, pink streamers, and bouquets of mimosa standing on the twenty tables. Out of the windows of this room one sees a beach, chewing-gum gray and halved by the scaffolding of a pier. Under this pier the sea rises and sinks; it drags garlands of water weed up and hangs them on splinters and rusty bolts and then takes them away again.

Landward stand three stucco villas, close together and resembling a spumone lying on its side; the first one is green, the second yellow, the third pink. In back of them rises the smokestack of a sardine factory, with "Amieux Frères" spelled out on it.

Partly on the pier and partly on the beach is a Chinese pavilion dedicated to the sale of sandpails, shovels, lighthouses, Eiffel towers made of seashells, and a postal card showing a fisherman leaning against a boat (Number 7036)—he wears oilskins and holds up a fifteen-foot oar, and the picture is entitled *"Un Vieux Loup de Mer."*

Back in the dining room, a half-grown girl and the adopted Spanish piccolo, who is about twelve years old, together with the proprietor, serve the fifty guests of the establishment. The dinner is announced by a bell with a black handle; it almost swings the piccolo off his feet. As soon as it rings, the seaside patronage arrives—vacation faces, matted hair, crying children, and ravenous appetites. The people of Nantes come here for two weeks of determined happiness.

The financial gentleman who wished to loan money would go bankrupt here with *poitrines fortes.*

It is a holiday of shirtsleeves, loud singing, and thumbs under suspender buckles. One shows that one knows how to enjoy life, toasts are drunk with *vin ordinaire,* arms wave, everyone smiles and bows to left and right. *Coquettes jeunes filles* squeeze between chairs to their tables with an extra wiggle of hips and shoulders.

The conversation drowns the sea, the phonograph, and the clatter and yelling in the kitchen.

At my table, to the right and left of a shivering, mouse-faced fox terrier, sat Monsieur and Madame Le Baron. Monsieur Le Baron—*"tout est bon chez Le Baron"*—was a *charcutier* from Saint Nazaire. He had the torso of a lion-tamer. His mustache, made of cast iron and painted black, was hard, heavy, and new. He crossed his arms so that he could scratch both his strong shoulders at the same time. The shoulders came out of a striped, half-sleeved garment which, Madame explained to me, was *américain*, was bought at the Bon Marché in Paris, and was called a "sweet shirt."

The ample menu began with *"les fruits de mer"*—mussels in a green cold sauce—followed by a fish goulash, highly seasoned and not bad. The soup plates were cleared away, Monsieur Le Baron wiped his mustache and lips with a piece of bread, ate it, and looked to the kitchen door. A murmur went through the room. Madame also looked up and then pointed to the door, singing, *"Ah—les crabes!"*

The Spanish boy staggered into the room carrying a casserole of steaming crabs. He wore an apron that reached from his chin to under his shoes. He brought six crabs, immense, the color and texture of imitation leather bags, each one with six legs, each leg three feet long.

The young girls arched their backs as he approached; the legs of the crabs reached out for their shoulder straps, for the piccolo's black hair, and for the mimosa on the tables. He managed to serve them without anyone's coming to harm; he had a great deal of practice. The *crabes* are the *spécialité de la maison;* this disastrous menu is served here every evening. Its price includes half a bottle of *vin ordinaire* and is thirty cents and certainly worth it.

My bed was filled with sand and the night with such songs as *"Ma femme est morte"* and *"Auprès de ma blonde, qu'il fait bon, fait bon dormir."*

The three villas and a few wailing children warmed themselves in the next morning's sun. The sea-going motorship *Insula Oya* tooted, the Spanish piccolo came running with the bags. He was also the hotel's *portier* and now wore a green billiard-cloth apron and a cap. He collected his tip, bowed from the waist, and the ship left.

Out of an hour of calm, green ocean appeared first a lighthouse, then a church steeple, then, seven kilometers wide and nine long, the Island itself. Another half-hour and the colors on the houses separated, windows and doors became visible, lettering was readable on the Hôtel des Voyageurs, the Café de la Marine, and the Buvette du Port.

The entrance to the harbor is like a bent sleeve. Where the elbow is stands a lighthouse. The entrance is so narrow that a chain is thrown from the lighthouse and fastened to the bow of the *Insula Oya*. The captain spins his wheel and she turns in her own length, slips through the passage like a hand into a pocket, and is fastened to the pier. Blup—blup—blup—a last puff, a white cloud, and the motor stops.

The Ile d'Yeu is immediately beautiful and at once familiar. Its round, small harbor is stuffed with boats; the big tuna schooners lie in the center; around them are sleek sardine and lobster boats. One can walk around in the harbor over the decks of boats. Only between bows and sterns shine triangles of green water. Twice a day there is a creaking of hulls and a tilting of masts; all the boats begin to settle, to lean on their neighbors; the tide, all the water, runs out of the harbor, and the bottom is dry.

The first house you come to is a small poem of a hotel. It has a bridal suite with a pompom-curtained bed, a chaste washstand, pale pink wallpaper with white pigeons flying over it, and three fauteuils, tangerine velvet and every one large enough for two, closely held, to sit in together.

The five-foot proprietor rubs his hands, hops about, glares at employees, smiles at guests. Madame sits behind an ornate desk in the dining room, her eyes everywhere. The kitchen is bright and smells of good butter, the linen is white, the silver gleams, the waiter is spotless. Outside, under an awning, behind a hedge of well-watered yew trees, overlooking the harbor, are the apéritif tables and chairs.

The prospectus states besides that the hotel has *"eau chaude et froide, chauffage central, tout confort moderne"*—all this is of no consequence, because you can never get a room there. The hotel has but twenty-six rooms, and these are reserved year after year, by the same people, French families.

Farther down is the Hôtel des Voyageurs, sixty rooms, the same thing, the bridal suite in green, the prices somewhat more moderate, the *confort less moderne,* but also all booked by April. "Ah, if you would only have written me a letter in March," say the proprietors of both places several times a day from June to September.

Walking down the Quai Sadi-Carnot, you turn right and go through the Rue de la Sardine. This street is beautifully named; the houses on both sides touch your shoulders and only a man with one short leg can walk through it in comfort, as half the street is taken up by a sidewalk.

At the end of the Street of the Sardine is the Island's store, the Nouvelles Galeries Insulaires. Its owner, Monsieur Penaud, will find a place for you to live. Ile d'Yeu should really be Ile Dieu, Monsieur Penaud explained, "d'Yeu" being the ancient and faulty way the Islanders spelled "God." He established us for three happy months at a fisherman's house, at the holiest address in this world, namely: No. 3, Rue de Paradis, Saint-Sauveur, Ile d'Yeu.

Our house was a sage, white, well-designed building. Through every door and window of it smiled the marine charm of the Island. The sea was no more than sixty yards from our door. Across the street was an eleventh-century church, whose steeple was built in the shape of a lighthouse. Over the house a brace of gulls hung in the air; there was the murmur of the sea; an old rowboat, with a sailor painted on its keel, stood up in the corner of the garden and served as a chicken coop.

The vegetables in the garden, the fruit on the trees, and the chicken eggs went with the house; included also was a lady bicycle, trademarked "Hirondelle." It is a nice thing to take over a household so living, complete, and warm, and dig up radishes that someone else has planted for you and cut flowers in a garden that someone else has tended.

The coast of the Island is a succession of small, private beaches, each one like a room, its walls three curtains of rock and greenery. There is a cave to dress in. Once you arrive, it is yours.

On the open side is the water, little waves, fine sand; and out on the green ocean all day long the sardine fleet crosses back and forth with colored sails leaning over the water.

There seem to be only three kinds of people: sailors, their hundred-times-patched sensible pants and blouses in every shade of color; children; and everywhere two little bent old women dressed in black, their sharp profiles hooked together in gossip. Like crows in a tree they are, and rightly enough called *"vieux corbeaux."*

Posing everywhere are fish and the things relating to them. The sardine is the banana of the Ile d'Yeu: you slip and fall on it. It looks out of the small market baskets that the *vieux corbeaux* carry home; its tail sticks out of fishermen's pockets; it is dragged by in boxes and barrels. Other fish, the tuna predominating, wander by on the shoulders of strong sailors, tied to bicycles, pushed by pairs of boys in carts.

Stuffed and mounted fish hang from the ceiling of the Buvette du Port, and are nailed to the wall of the Café de la Marine. Carved in wood and brightly painted, they sail as weathervanes over houses and on the masts of ships. Even in the kitchens fish shapes are hammered into brass molds and serve as forms for the baking of soufflés and cakes.

The cooking on the Island is of the simplest. The Hôtel Turbé may be recommended. The specialty of the Island is, strangely enough, *homard à l'américaine*. It is served at the Auberge des Homardiers in Port de la Meule.

From where the *Insula Oya* docks to Port de la Muele is a three-hour walk. The Port is a crescent-shaped, rock-rimmed wild harbor that holds at most five small boats. The Auberge des Homardiers overlooks it. Madame Clamart, who owns this tavern, is a passion flower, with the hips, the nostrils, the voice, and the laughter of Lynn Fontanne. Before you are seated, she will inquire whether you are by any chance American. Say "No" if you want *homard à l'américaine,* or anything else. If you admit it, she will lean back, plant her fists in her hips, barricade the door with her shoulders, and, staring far out to sea, she will look past you and with the Fontanne laugh say that she has no table, no *homard à l'américaine,* or anything else, for you. In that case it's three hours back to the Hôtel Turbé, where you arrive too late for dinner and have to eat an omelet.

For this we have to thank a sailor, a first-class machinist's mate named "Swanky Franky." He arrived on board a United States submarine, which, with one of its engines crippled, limped into the Port de la Meule toward the end of the war. Swanky Franky walked up the hill and made himself at home at the Auberge. His favorite dish was *homard à l'américaine.* And while he waited for parts with which to repair his submarine, he translated, with the aid of a little book, his sentiments and his plans for the future to Madame Clamart. With his honest, big, red hands he rubbed her back and kissed her behind the ear while he whispered of a little house in Tenafly, N.J., of electric irons, vaccum cleaners, and even of a *voiture* Buick.

Three weeks passed. One day the parts arrived. The last of Swanky Franky and his promises disappeared into the submarine and went to sea. The old ravens of Port de la Meule carried the story all over the Island; everybody pointed at the Auberge. Madame locked herself in and swore a terrible revenge.

You can, however, get lobster and cook it yourself. The best is to be had at the far point of the Island. There stands the tall lighthouse, and to the left of it, its battlements in the sea, stands the Vieux Château, a junior Frankenstein Castle.

Between these two landmarks is a shack that reaches to the armpits of its owner, a man inordinately fond of America, American catchup, Americans, and most so of *le petit père* Roosevelt.

A novelist, and known because of his great kindness as "Bon Georges," he lives here with a donkey. The animal stands in patches of salt grass, answers to the name of Tin Tin, and is driven to town for bread, salt, wine, and cheese. Like all donkeys, he is slow and pensive when in harness. In the rare moments when Bon Georges is in a hurry, he leans forward from the driver's seat of his two-wheeled cart; the donkey lays his ears back to meet his words and hears: *"Tin Tin, que vous êtes beau! Faites comme un petit cheval!"* This flattery gets five meters of trotting out of him.

The inside of the shack is underwater green, an iridium light that comes through cracks between the boards and is filtered by a mountain of empty wine bottles which are stacked against the stormy side of the house. The wind sweeps the floor and dusts the typewriter; the typewriter is protected by an open umbrella. Two forks, two knives, two plates, and a picture of Léon Blum complete the inventory.

Outside, against the horizon, in the shade of an old sail, one edge of which is nailed to the house and the other held up with two oars, perpetually rests Bon Georges. In September he shaves, puts on a shirt, and when you see him at the Deux Magots in Paris he is much less beautiful.

He has two lobsterpots, and after some reluctance will trade for wine those lobsters he does not want himself. I came to get four lobsters one day and put them in a bag over my shoulder, and after a swim rode back to the Rue du Paradis and almost ran into Paradise itself. Pedaling along with the sack over my shoulder, both hands in my pockets and tracing fancy curves in the roadbed, I came to a bend, which is hidden by some dozen pine trees. Around this turn raced the Island's only automobile, a four-horse-power Super-Rosengart, belonging to the baker of Saint-Sauveur. This car is a fragrant, flour-covered breadbasket on wheels; it threw me in a wide curve off the bicycle into a bramble bush. I took the car's doorhandle off with my elbow.

I asked the baker to take me to the hospital in Saint-Sauveur, but he said that, according to French law, a car must remain exactly where it was when the accident occurred, so that the gendarmes could make their proper deductions and see who was on the wrong side of the road. I tried to change his mind, but he said, "Permit me, *alors,* monsieur, if you use words like that, then it is of no use at all to go on with this conversation."

Having spoken, he went on to pick up his *pain de ménage* and some *croissants* that were scattered on the road, and then spread aside the branches of the thicket to look for the doorhandle of his Super-Rosengart. I took my lobsters and went to the hospital on foot.

A doctor came, with a cigarette stub hanging from his lower

lip. With a blunt needle he wobbled into my arm. *"Excusez-moi,"* he said, *"mais votre peau est dure!"* I was put into a small white carbolicky bed. In the next room was a little girl who had had her appendix out, and on the ceiling over my bed was a crack that, in the varying light of morning, noon, and evening, looked like a rabbit, like the profile of Léon Blum, and at last, in conformity with the Island, like a tremendous sardine.

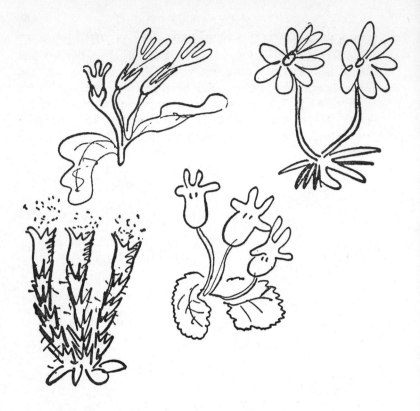

SACRE DU PRINTEMPS

The Undersecretary of the Division of Spring of the Ministry of the Four Seasons unrolled an ivy-green runner on the balcony of the Ministry of Strength-through-Joy at the precise moment that the Undersecretary of the Ministry of Discipline and Order placed thereon his microphone; then both listened to the bells strike seven in the morning and opened the door behind which stood, in proper uniform, with all buttons buttoned, the Ministers of Spring, of Discipline and Order, and of Strength-through-Joy. The Minister of the Four Seasons and the Minister of Discipline and Order announced the beginning of Spring.

Dutifully, with dispatch and promptness, there appeared blossoms in their proper colors on all trees in the land, buttercups growing orderly along the brooks opened their little faces to the sun, forget-me-nots in the forests, heather in the marshes, daisies among the fields, and even edelweiss high up in the mountains.

In the windowboxes of the workingmen geraniums bloomed, tulips in the gardens of the civil servants of the classes 1, 2, 3, 4, and 5, and roses in the classes from 6 to 12. Above that, in classes 13 to 15, there was no need of Spring—flowers were in bloom the year round in the winter gardens of generals, bishops, directors of banks and gas factories. Heartwarming and admirable was the success with which the state and particularly the Ministry of Strength-through-Joy, the Division of Spring of the Ministry of the Four Seasons, and the Ministry of Discipline had succeeded in the administration of all details, down to the orderly joy of the little girls, who marched out into the lovely greenery in proper white starched dresses and in battalion formation, starting at seven-thirty in the morning, the smallest in front, the tallest in back.

There the little girls stopped to sing the appropriate songs, simple *Lieder* written for the occasion. On this day there were sung: The *Lied* of the *Lindenbaum* for the linden trees, the song of the *Heidenröslein,* for the little wild rose. How good! How without problems was life ahead for the little blond girls! How provident was the Ministry of the Four Seasons and, for that matter, the Ministry of Youth, of Motherhood, and even of Love!

No one was forgotten. The railroads ran extra trains to take each and every citizen out into the Spring. And even the railroad was an example of the forethought and order of the provident State. There were first-class carriages with red plush upholstery and umber curtains; there were second-class compartments with green herringbone sailcloth; third class (a) with wooden seats, soft wood tailored to conform to the curves of the body; and third class (b) with hard wooden benches, non-conforming; and sixth-class carriages, to stand up in.

Malcontents, enemies of the Government, and scoffers told of a sixth-class carriage that had no floor—just a roof and sides— in which the passengers had to run along the tracks. That, of course, was not so. Besides, there were no malcontents left.

The unsleeping vigilance of the Ministry of Justice had run all non-conformists into the ground, or successfully converted them. That is, all but one man, the Outsider, the One, by name Kratzig, Emil, who walked alone in his own disorderly path.

When all the citizens were out in the Spring, Emil Kratzig sat at home with his curtains drawn and read forbidden books; and again when all were snug at home in the Winter, singing the songs of the "Oven," "Grandfather's clock, tick tock, tick tock," or *"Ich bin so gern, so gern daheim, daheim in meiner stillen Klause,"* he ran around outside in the snow and whistled.

There was a long official report under K—Kratzig, Emil. But while the Political Police shadowed him, they nevertheless left him alone. They did not disturb him. "We must save him," said the Minister of Justice. "He is the last one; we may need him as an example." Besides, Emil Kratzig was an old man, and a foreigner: his maternal great-grandfather had been a Frenchman.

So Emil Kratzig lived apart and sat alone. And on the street the policeman, Umlauf, who was stationed at the City Hall square to keep him under surveillance, filled his little notebook with the discordant reports of the goings and comings of the dissenter.

The leaves in the official notebook of Policeman Umlauf, pages 48 to 55, carry the story of the sad end of the incorrigible, insubordinate Emil Kratzig. . . .

On the sunlit morning of a green May day, when all in the city went out to look at the blossoms, take deep breaths, and sing in the new, light-flowered prints designed by the Ministry of Dress and Underwear, Kratzig, wrapped in a muffler, burdened with galoshes and heavy winter coat, fled alone to the meanest landscape he could find, a district that contained the municipal incinerators, the garbage trucks, and the streetcleaning apparatus. There he spent the day crossing and recrossing the cobblestones, with wild tirades; made free with the names of ministers, the Government, the nation as a whole, and that night came home and slept with open windows. That night, of course, there was a frost, and it was this frost which took many blossoms and reached out also for the life of Emil Kratzig.

The next day Emil Kratzig was ill. A cold turned to pleurisy of the left lobar cavity, and the Government doctor, who came the following day and ordered him to stay in bed, shook his head as he left the house. But Emil Kratzig got up again, in violation of the doctor's orders, and with a high fever ran to the City Hall.

"Aha," said Policeman Umlauf, and in his notebook he remarked: "The end is near and Herr Kratzig is coming to heel."

And it looked as if at last, indeed, this misguided Kratzig had decided to mend his ways. He passed by the Bureaus of Birth, Taxation, and Marriages, and properly opened the door to the Bureau of Funerals, on the second floor. He entered the room, removed his hat, and stood quietly in the line of citizens who had business with the clerk of that department. He patiently awaited his turn with hat in hand and finally spoke his desire . . . to make arrangements for himself.

The clerk pushed forward a chair for Herr Kratzig. On the top of his desk was a large album. He opened it for Emil Kratzig's inspection.

The Chief Clerk appeared and pushed a platoon of underclerks away. With his own lips he blew dust from the funeral album (this album was used only in extraordinary cases); he washed his hands in the air with anticipation, patted Kratzig on the shoulder, cleared his throat, and opened the cover.

"Now this," said the Chief Clerk, "is the first-class funeral." He pointed to the first of the many pictures and recited, "The first-class funeral is composed of the wagon, first class," indicating with the rubber end of his pencil the four angels of Annunciation carved in the teakwood, who stood at the four corners of the wagon, at the rubber tires, at the betasseled curtains of black brocade.

"This wagon is drawn by six horses, with black cloaks and black plumes. They wear this silver harness. There is, besides a bishop and two priests, sixty *Sängerknaben,* a band, the bells of all the churches ring, there is a salute of guns, incense, and, at the high mass, twelve of these golden candelabra are used with scented beeswax candles. But this is not for you. It is for the classes 13 to 15 of the Civil Service."

He turned the page of the second-class funeral. "Here we have the same car, rubber tires, four horses with black cloaks, black plumes, and silver harness, three priests, but no bishop, forty

Sängerknaben, incense, six of the first-class candelabra at the high mass, the bells of half the churches, no guns, and, in the first-class candelabra, plain unscented candles."

Again he turned a huge page. "Now we come to the third-class funeral," he continued. "There is a different wagon, but also very nice, with one mourning angel sitting on top, cretonne curtains, two horses with nickel harness, black cloaks and plumes, two priests, no *Sängerknaben,* but a male quartet, nickel candelabra, of course no guns, but the two bells of the cemetery chapel and one priest with two apprentice priests, incense, and a very nice grade of candles, not beeswax but scented. But that is not for you either."

He shifted the weight of his body to his left foot and his voice changed. "The fourth-class funeral is somewhat plainer. We have here the wagon of the third class, one horse with cloak and plume and nickel harness, one priest, one singer, two altar boys, and incense. For the mass, organ music and two candelabra with candles.

"The fifth-class funeral," he went on, "is here." And he turned the page. "Here is a strong solid wagon, and one horse, no cloak, no plume, but it is a black horse, an apprentice priest, and one singer, one altar boy, incense, no music at the mass, and two wooden candelabra with used candles."

He paused.

"And finally we come to the sixth-class funeral," he said. "Here again you get the wagon of the fifth class, the black horse, an apprentice priest, no singer, one altar boy, two wooden candelabra with used substitute-wax candles, a little bell." And he turned the page to show a drawing. "And with this funeral goes a rented coffin—it saves you buying one."

A working drawing of this imaginative, melancholy piece of black carpentry was attached, also photographs showing its economical performance. It looked like any other frugal coffin, but had an ingenious device—two doors at the bottom opened when a lever was pulled. Once occupied and having been carried to its destination, the coffin opened at the bottom and the occupant was dropped into the grave. So the rented coffin could be used over and over again.

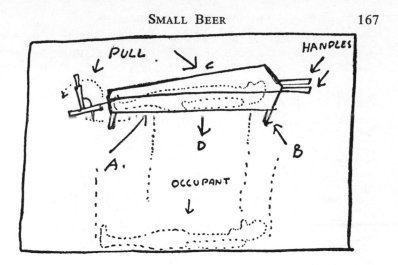

"Very simple, after all," said the clerk and, turning, he left the sentence open, because Emil Kratzig was gone.

Emil Kratzig was not seen again until the middle of next night. Policeman Umlauf, standing in the center of the market square, saw a pale man coming toward him. The man was dressed in a long, white nightshirt. On his head was a top hat. Tied to it with a piece of crepe was a black plume. In his hand he held two burning candles and he carried a shovel under his arm.

"I am Emil Kratzig," said the man. "I died last night. I am going up to the cemetery. This is a seventh-class funeral."

DEAR GENERAL, WHAT A SURPRISE!

My friend Anthony produces plays. I meet him about once a year, usually on Times Square, running to or from a rehearsal in a sad, unbuttoned overcoat, which he has owned as long as I have known him and which he never takes off.

Last season we met on Forty-sixth Street. He slapped me on the back and pulled me out of the sidewalk traffic into a white-tiled grotto on whose walls were mats of artificial grass. Pineapples hung from the ceiling, and on a counter were a stack of cold frankfurters, a mountain of coconuts, and a radio, framed in mustard pots, playing a Toscanini concert. It was Saturday and late.

When Anthony says anything he smiles so widely that he has to close his eyes—big, black eyes, which when open interfere with the mask of complete happiness that announces all things, good and bad, alike. Anthony smiled and said, "I'm doing an anti-Nazi play. There's a part in it for you. Wanna be an actor? It opens in three weeks. I'll send you the script in the morning."

The play was in the next day's mail, bound in blue cardboard. Next to it was a small pocket-sized folder. Outside the folder was printed: 'German General." Inside, held by a clip, was half a sheet of transparent typewriter paper and on this was written my part. It read: *The Germans enter. First a platoon of soldiers followed by a Lieutenant. The Lieutenant is followed by a Colonel. The German Colonel introduces himself to the Austrian officers.*

An orderly offstage: Attention! *You enter.*

The German Colonel: His Excellency Graf Ottokar von Sporentritt zu Donnersberg—Commanding General of the Garde Grenadier Regiment zu Fuss Nummer Eins. *You salute.*

The Austrian General's wife enters. Austrian General's wife: General—what a surprise!

You are surprised, you turn, bend over her hand, and kiss it.
You: Dear lady, I am delighted to see you again.
You mix with the officers.

A line under this ended my part.

I had barely spoken the lines a few times when the telephone rang and I was instructed to be at the Belasco for rehearsal at eleven o'clock.

Promptly at eleven, I sat at the edge of the ground cloth of the Belasco. A man came toward me, asked my name, nationality, the place of my birth, and for fifty dollars. He was from Equity and he made me a member.

After the Equity man had congratulated me and gone, another actor introduced me to the members of the company, and then we watched an earnest young man make chalk marks on the floor. He was the stage manager. When he had finished marking he sat down at a table at the side of the stage and opened the typescript of the play. The rehearsal began.

A newly engaged actor came late. He was to play the part of an American journalist, and as he took his coat off he said, "Oh, they're on their feet already." This meant that the rehearsals had progressed far enough for the actors to walk about and speak their lines or read them out of little folders such as I had left at home, for which there is a fine of five dollars. I also learned that "up-stage" is in back of the stage and "downstage" is in front, nearer the audience.

My friend Anthony from that day on always sat in one of the fauteuils in the first row of the orchestra. Behind him sat two men, one in gray flannel slacks, yellow shoes, and a tweed jacket, a long ivory cigarette holder in his teeth. The other man had a mustache. Both had pads and pencils, and most of the time they held their heads sideways in the position in which one admires a rare vase, a good picture, or one's cute child. These two men were the authors.

After we had rehearsed for two hours, Anthony sent out for ham on rye and a paper container of coffee. This was his diet for the next three weeks.

The authors, who came from Hollywood, went to lunch at "21," the actors to a cheap lunchroom which seemed always to be directly across the street from the stage door of whatever theater we rehearsed in.

For three weeks we moved from one theater to another, into little and big theaters, theaters with plays in them and empty theaters, and most of the time I sat on a chair at the back of the stage and waited for the third act and my cue.

The chairs and boxes on which I sat were always broken and dirty, it was drafty and dark. Next to me on other broken chairs sat and whispered the other actors, who also waited for their cues.

When the long rehearsals were over, the stage manager called the actors together and said, "All right, you can go now. Be back here at eight o'clock," or, "You can go now. Be back here at eleven tomorrow. That's all."

After the second week's rehearsals were over (there was no pay for the first), the actors all received envelopes with twenty dollars in them. I spoke to one of them about the twenty dollars being very little. He fished the money out of the narrow envelope with

two fingers, caressed the bills, folded them carefully after counting the money, and then gave me a curious answer.

"My dear fellow, don't be silly," he said. "This is absolutely
marvelous. Why, a few years ago we received nothing for rehearsals
—not a penny for five weeks of rehearsals. This"—he unfolded
the bills again—"is extremely generous—it's wonderful!"

"Shhhhh!" said the stage manager.

My confidant, a gentle, precise Englishman, bent closer and
whispered, "There was a time, you know, when we had to buy
our own costumes—wigs, gloves, and what not. Oh! I must tell
you a funny story about a pair of stage gloves, about a pair of
lemon-yellow gloves—"

"Quiet, back there!" said the stage manager.

My friend shrank a little and was quiet for a while, then he
leaned over again and whispered into my ear, "Years ago, in London, I played opposite a very important actor, comedy of manners,
Haymarket Theatre. He played a lord. I was his valet. We had to
furnish our own wardrobe. In the second act he called for his
gloves, a pair of lemon-yellow gloves. He had to put them on so a
lady would recognize him by them. We had a bit of a tiff over these
gloves: he insisted that I buy them; I said it was he who should,
because he wore them. He pointed to the script where was written,
'Valet enters with gloves in his right hand, hands them to Lord,
who puts them on.'

" 'You can't come on without them,' he said, 'so you must buy
them.'

"He absolutely refused to do so himself. And, mind you, he
was drawing twice my salary.

"Came opening night, and I taught him a lesson, the bounder!
Last minute before curtain time I ran out to a fruiterer's, bought
three bananas, peeled them carefully, and hung the skins out of
my right hand. From out there, they looked more like gloves than
real gloves. When he called, 'Jarvis, my gloves—my lemon-yellow
gloves!' I handed him the peels, hü, hü, hü!"

"Shhh! Quiet back there!"

"Cured him," added my friend almost inaudibly, as if under
the protective bedcovers of a nursery.

A few days before the opening of our anti-Nazi play we started to rehearse the third act. I walked up and down in the wings and tried my lines.

"Dear lady, what a surprise!"—no—"Dear lady, I am delighted to see you again."

My cue came, I marched in, saluted, looked surprised, bent to kiss her hand, kissed it, and said, "Dear lady, I am delighted to see you again." With my most elegant gesture I pulled a chair that stood a little to the right, for the lady to sit down on.

The play stopped the moment I touched the chair. The stage manager ran in from the wings. He stuttered, waved in the air with both hands, and when he had found his breath yelled, "For God's sake don't touch that chair! Don't ever move that chair again! Don't move anything! You'll throw the whole play out of gear." He took the chair back again and carefully placed it on its chalk marks.

The actors looked at one another and shook their heads, in an oratorio of surprise, shock, and pity. The authors had come down out of their second-row chairs, leaned over the footlights like two worried mothers watching a child drown. Anthony shook his head and looked at his watch. The stage manager wiped his head and said, "All right now, that's all. You can go now. Be back at three o'clock."

After everyone had left, the famous actress who played the lead, the role of the Austrian General's wife, smiled, walked toward me, took my arm, and said, "Look, dear, watch me carefully, slowly repeat after me 'I am delighted to see you, dear lady'—or how does it go again?" I told her, "Dear lady, I am delighted to see you again."

She said it for me once more, effortless as music. As liquid pearls on a string the words came from her lips. It was a superb reading of my part and I repeated it after her three times. "That's much better," she said.

"Now look, darling," she said in consoling tones, "never, never, never move anything on any stage. That, my dear, is the first thing for you to remember. Secondly, don't twitch, don't dance, don't wiggle or move, don't start talking, until I have crossed over to your side. Acting is timing.

"Don't mind this, dear, but I feel someone must tell you this.

You see, the audience out there, they are like little children. If you move a finger, they take their eyes from me to your hand. They want to see what you are going to do next, and I might as well not be on the stage. It kills my lines.

"Just now, when we rehearsed it, you walked on my lines, dear. Watch your timing. Now let's try it again."

Anthony, wrapped in his overcoat, sat out in the audience with his ham on rye and his nose in the container of coffee.

"Oh, another thing," said my mentor, "don't ever play with your back to the audience—don't ever!"

We tried it again.

"Oh, General—what a surprise!"

I turned and looked surprised. She walked across the stage, lithe and free as Le Gallienne in *The Swan*. I bent over her hand and kissed it, counted to five, and said, "Dear lady, I am delighted to see you again."

"You see," she said, "it's very simple."

We went out to celebrate the simplicity with lunch at the Algonquin and even sat at a table next to George Jean Nathan's. At three o'clock we went to another theater to continue rehearsals.

The stage manager made chalk marks on the floor, the authors came backstage, and the one with the cigarette holder asked me to step aside with him. The other author waited in the gangway. One was to my left, the other to my right.

"They'll never hear you out there. Louder, much louder," said the one with the hunting jacket. "You're a general, see? You're the big cheese. When you come on like this, see, with your chest out, you walk in as if you owned the place. They're all scum as far as you are concerned—a lot of weaklings. You're taking the place over, you're headman. Know what I mean?"

"More schmaltz," the other said.

"But you're also a gentleman," added the first, "so when you see her, you kinda drop the military air a little. You're surprised, like this, pleasantly, but not too friendly." The author showed me on his face how a German general is pleasantly surprised. Both of them stood aside to let me try it.

"Dear lady, I am delighted to see you again." I did it with gestures and pantomime.

Both of them shook their heads and looked worried, and one said, "I don't think he was cut out to be a German general. Too soft." Turning to me, he added, "Not Prussian enough, and you haven't the right accent. Try it this way: 'Dear lady, I am delighted to see you again.'" He screamed in the accents and voice of Lew Lehr of the newsreels.

They both escorted me to the ladies' room. An electrician was called to turn the lights on and I was left to practice. I had several visitors during the rest of the afternoon. The authors came twice and said, "Much better." The famous actress came and said, "Remember the timing." The Englishman with the yellow-glove story came and said, "I hope you don't mind, but I feel I must tell you this: when you speak your lines, look at her face, not at her navel. Otherwise your words will drop on the floor—blup, blup, blup—and die there." Last of all, Anthony came: "Louder, still louder! You have to project yourself. You'll never get across. They won't hear a word in the fourth row."

After the stage manager had dismissed us that night, I took a bus. I must have said loudly, "Dear lady, I am delighted to see you again," because everybody looked at me and the woman next to me said, "Why, I have never seen you before!"

I excused myself, explained that I was an actor going over my part. The woman got up and went to another seat.

The next day we moved to the theater in which we were to appear. The scenery was up. In the flies above hung the scenery of another anti-Nazi play that had folded up there a few days before. "You can have it for two bucks," said the stage-door watchman; and he added that the producers of that play had not enough money left to have the scenery carted away.

Our theater had been rented out to a theatrical society from the Bronx who had bought out the house for a preview that night. In the dressing room which I shared with my colonel hung my uniform—a splendid garment, its breeches bearing the wide, carmine stripes of the general staff, the coat laden with the Iron Cross first, second, and third class, and the order Pour le Mérite. There was an exquisite pair of boots and an elaborate cavalry saber with golden belt and chased buckle. Over all I wore a cape weighted down by a sable collar four feet wide. My colonel was only slightly less magnificent; his cape had a mink collar one foot wide.

All day the first and second acts were rehearsed, the actors were let go one hour sooner, at six, and we were back at eight to make up and dress.

My colonel hung up his street clothes, took off his old shoes, and, sitting in his underwear, showed me how to smear grease paint over a layer of cold cream. He himself used olive oil out of a small bottle for a base because, he said, it lasted longer and was cheaper and if the play closed you could make salad dressing out of it, or use it to cook. He showed me how to put blue shadows over and under my eyes, and finally he traced my eyelids with an eyebrow pencil so worn down that he had to hold it between his fingernails.

We helped each other button up the tight uniform collar, slip on the boots, and tighten belt and spurs. Then we went down and stood in the wings to watch the first two acts.

Everybody wished everyone else good luck. The slim German girl who played the heroine spat three times—toi, toi, toi!—on my sable collar, the Continental actors' way of wishing good luck. She also said, *"Hals und Beinbruch!"*—a phrase that skiers and acrobats shout to each other as they go up into the snowfields or to their trapezes.

The curtain was still down. Outside was a humming sound like a swarm of bees flying past, a dangerous noise punctuated by the sound of seats being pushed down and the rustling of programs.

The stage manager said, "All right, first act." The actors walked on the stage. For most of that act the American journalist had to hide in a telephone booth and spy. The actor who played that part went into the booth and closed the door. My colonel leaned down and whispered, "Poor fellow! It's all right now, but it will be hell in there next summer." The curtain went up, the play was on.

The first two acts went by, the third act and my cue came on with the speed of a car that is going to run you over. My feet and legs left me, my mouth was filled with cotton, and I repeated over and over, "Dear lady, I am delighted to see you again—don't touch that chair, don't wiggle, you're the big cheese, timing, don't walk on her lines— Dear lady—" The gentle Englishman squeezed my hand and said, "Go out there and give it to them!" Then came the cue: "His Excellency Graf Ottakar von Sporentritt zu Donnersberg, Commanding General of the Garde Grenadier Regiment zu Fuss Nummer Eins!"

Somehow I was on the stage, saluted, kissed her hand, "Dear lady, I am delighted to see you again——"

But it would not have mattered what I said. From the moment I came on, the audience hissed, booed, and stamped their feet.

We had never had time to rehearse what I was to do after I had said my lines. I said them in the center of the scene, almost at the footlights, and I would have remained there, but for my English friend. He came and took my arm with a patrolman's determined grip and said something about going out into the garden, because the audience had just begun to listen again, and he carted me to the back of the stage and out.

"You walked on my lines again, dear," said the actress, wagging a finger. "And, darling, on opening night please don't wiggle that sword. You'll ruin everything. Everything depends on you in this scene."

I went home. I could hardly speak. I had shouted myself hoarse. The next morning I had a fever, but I thought, "The play must go on!" and went to gargle and took some quinine, until I read in the *Times* that I had laryngitis and that another actor would take my place and play the General at twenty-four hours' notice.

That evening, like a murderer to his victim's burial, was I drawn to opening night, to hear another man say, "Dear lady." He did it very well, with perfect timing, without walking on her lines or wiggling his sword.

After the show I went backstage. The famous actress put her hand on my shoulder. "But I tried to tell you how to play it, dear," she said.

The press agent said, "You shouldn't hang around here. You should be in bed, for Christ's sake." And he added, "What the hell you care? Be glad you're out of it. It's a flop. This is a coffin, this theater. Anybody wants to be an actor is nuts."

The play lasted one night.

When it was over and the audience had left, I looked for An-

thony. He sat in the last row of the orchestra in his old coat—cold
and alone, like a wet mouse. He has the theater for an illness.
With his eyes closed, he smiled his wide grimace and said, "I
guess I'll have to look for another play."

The authors had left, one for Jersey, to shoot pheasants, the
other for Hollywood. They had not said good-by, even to Anthony.

Up in our dressing room my colonel, who had worried a little
while ago about the summer's heat in the telephone booth, packed
up, put on shoes with their heels worn off. His threadbare coat
hanging from his shoulders, he stuffed the little bottle half full of
olive oil, the eyebrow pencil stub, his dirty powder puff, and the
rest of his make-up into a battered biscuit tin and then walked out.

On the dressing table we had shared was an envelope, torn
open with his name on it. Some figures were written on the back
of it. It was the twenty dollars for the last week's rehearsal, and
deducted from it was the cost of two tickets for opening night,
seven dollars. That left him thirteen dollars.

The Donkey Inside

THE S.S. *MESIAS*

"I am only stating that the food here was foul until they killed the cook," said a big man, a Hollander. He turned and, as if it were a rare animal that he wanted to catch without hurting it, he advanced to the rail of the ship with outstretched hands. He took hold of it, held it tightly to test whether it was solid, and then sank his huge body down on it. He was short-nosed, a man with shrimp-colored skin and a pink mustache, and he was drunk. A bottle of Mallorca stood on the table.

A dog came, a mongrel the color of a fox. He stopped, smelled the cuffs of the Hollander's trousers, and with stiff, dancing legs ran away, disappearing around a table.

The table might have stood in the family corner of a third-rate Italian restaurant. It was covered with cracked oilcloth on which stood greasy salt and pepper shakers; a river of red wine, half dried up, wound itself around a vase of breadsticks; and from the rim of a bowl of grated cheese blue flies and little bugs took off, circled under a lamp, and landed again on the neck of the bottle of Mallorca.

Mallorca smells like absinthe. It gets milky when you pour it over ice and mix it with water. It's cheap enough for Indians to buy, and whole villages in Ecuador are in a stupor on Sundays and holidays, thanks to its powers.

The Hollander clasped and unclasped his hands, and sank to his knees between the pink and white filigreed columns that held up the ship rail. He tried to reach one of the six chairs that stood around the table, and fell headlong on a couch whose back rest leaned against a wooden wall of a most beautiful arsenic-green. A decayed awning patched with a raincoat shaded him.

A cow, hanging in a brace of canvas, came down past the awning, and for a while turned in silent circles, its eyes wide with hysteria. Then it dropped in a sudden lurch of a winch and turned again over an old Lincoln touring car. The Hollander snored and the little dog came back. He was surprised by the cow. He stopped and watched it for a second and then he ran on.

Nothing happened but the snore of the Hollander and the take-off of bees, mosquitoes, and small bugs from the cheese bowl. It sounded like a military airdrome, very far away in memory and space.

Down my hand along the little finger walked a fly, a small, common fly with gray wings. She sailed from there for the rim of the cheese bowl and climbed up to its cover. Upside down, hanging from the metallic ceiling, she went along looking for food and stopping. She came to the edge of the lid and walked along it with six legs, I think, three of them on the inside and three on the outside of the lid. She hopped to the knob of the lid, stopped there to clean her wings with the last pair of legs, and then took off again.

With a humming drone she wrote some word in immense letters into the space between table top and awning. The last letter ended up near the raincoat. In the small circle of light over the lamp, like a performer in a circus, up under the roof of the tent, she stood still, and then with the sound of tearing cloth she dived down straight through the narrow space between the glass chimney and the shade, avoiding a bug that came from the opposite side, and soared up again into the warm air and the brilliant light under the lampshade. She gained altitude once more and in two wide arcs shot down into an empty liqueur glass. I thought she would surely crash there, or get stuck in the slush at the bottom of the glass, but she had calculated in millimeters. She almost touched the glass, almost the walls, but in a maneuver too fast for observation she was out and had looped and set her course through the back rest of two bentwood chairs, over my nose, for the shining gold disk in the drunken Hollander's ear. There she stopped to clean her wings once more.

The raincoat patch on the awning moved, a small hairy hand came in, and then a golden eye looked down through a small opening. A monkey, with the motions of a woman taking off a tight dress, wiggled down through a hole no larger than a child's fist. With soft searches, carefully groping with his long legs and arms, and watching in back of him with the tip of his tail, he came down. Grimacing and pulling the skin above his metallic eyes into pleats and quickly straightening it out again, sending furtive looks to left and right, he advanced over the table, stole a piece of sugar without stopping or looking at it, dropped it, and voyaged on to the shoulder of the sleeping Hollander. He reached into the man's pockets, found a coin, stuck it into his right cheek, then went to the man's face, looked into his ear and tried to pluck the small gold disk from it, pulled the lips apart, and examined the teeth. The mongrel dog came on his third round, looked under the table, recognized the Hollander, looked into the kitchen, and ran down the deck, which was split and uneven, like the floor of a neglected bowling alley.

The *Mesias* was occasionally chartered for trips to the Galápagos. She took mining machinery up the Magdalena River, underbid freight rates of the established steamship lines, and was suspected of smuggling gold and helping people arrive and disappear. Most of the time, like a submerged old woman carrying above water only a garish hat decorated with banana leaves, she paraded up and down the coast from Chile to Colombia.

Her crew was half a dozen unshaven men who slept and drank and sang, and whose brown limbs hung out of the carcass of the boat wherever the planking was gone. They lived on bananas, rice, and the fish they caught. The Captain was an amiable Italian with an upper and a lower stomach, divided by a belt. Since his cook had been killed he attended to the food himself, and first class were his spaghetti, risottos, and soups. The Captain's life was made cozy by an Indian girl, barefooted, with a pair of tinkling brass anklets on her right foot, and small hands with which she poured red wine into the Captain's cloudy glasses and served Mallorca. She smelled of cheap soap, and her cotton housedress was too big for her: when she bent to serve someone across the table, her firm little body stood in it nude, with a small appendectomy scar and a medal of the Virgin hanging between her breasts.

I boarded the S.S. *Mesias* in Arica, a small, clean town beside a high cliff. The mile-wide cliffs change color from black to white as the birds fly away from them in an endless living cloud. They blot out the town, the liners, the horizon, and the sun. Out over the green waters they drive, in close formation, their wings touching. It looks as if an immense carpet with an all-over design of birds were suddenly unrolled into the sea.

Hundreds of pelicans in reflective moods line the gunwales of the barges in the harbor. Here and there one sits alone in the water. Seals swim about and play, coming up out of deep water without warning and bumping the pelicans. The fat birds look annoyed, then ruffle themselves back into their dignity and unconcern.

On the day I was on board the *Mesias,* a Chilean boat had caught fire off the coast. The cattle had been thrown overboard and made to swim ashore. (From this disaster came the hysterical cow.) The steerage passengers had been taken off in lifeboats and the first-class passengers in a motor launch. There were only two of these, an American and his wife, and they chose to take the *Mesias* to Callao rather than stay a night at the town's hotel.

They had smart luggage. The man was over fifty, well groomed and elegant—not a businessman. The wife was athletic, gaunt, handsome, and younger.

They seemed very fond of each other, and had great consideration for each other's comfort. The Captain came out of his kitchen and greeted them with his apron wound around the lower stomach. He offered them a drink; the Americans asked for a dry Martini, or some Scotch, but there was only red wine and Mallorca. They looked with suspicion at the glasses with the blue milk in them, tasted it, looked to left and right, and again at the glass, and drank it. "It's very cooling," they said.

The Captain then showed them to their cabin. They came back immediately and wanted to get off the boat, but the two planks nailed together that reached over to the dock had been pulled in, and by bending low or sitting down you could look under the awning and see that the *Mesias* was moving out into the green water, toward the endless line of flying guano birds.

The Americans visited the cow on the lower deck. Later they stood arm in arm to watch the copper mountains, and he tried to take some moving pictures. He found the light too weak, but he took one of his wife, anyway. The Indian girl set places at the Captain's table and rang a dinner bell. The American asked the Captain to let him sit at a separate table with his wife. The Captain arranged this. They sat down; he pushed the chair for her, and held her hand at the beginning of the meal.

The Hollander was awakened, and a Frenchman sat down at the table. He was in the diplomatic service and was visiting an oilfield at a place along the coast at which no large vessel stopped.

After the minestrone plates had been cleared away, and the table was loaded with risotto, salad, bread, and cheese, the Captain and the Indian girl sat down and everyone ate in silence.

The mongrel dog came again; the wife of the American petted him and talked to him and offered him food. He ran away on his stiff drumstick legs and continued his parade around the boat. The woman asked to whom the dog belonged.

The Captain wanted to give us some more of his risotto, and the Americans brought their glasses to the table, spilling much.

The Hollander was awake again, and he asked whether anyone wanted some rijstaafel. "Have you ever eaten pio pio?" he asked next. "That's buffalo hide with shrimp. You take the buffalo hide and cut pieces the size of a poker chip out of it, but not quite so regular. You then drop them in hot oil. The basis of this dish is rice also. Have you ever eaten monkey liver?" He turned to the Captain and said that he only wanted to point out that the basis of all these dishes was rice. He fell asleep again.

The Indian girl chased the flies away from him. The ocean was blood-red, the lamp lit. The Captain said that the dog belonged to the cook who had been killed. He waited for a while and looked around for someone to ask him to tell the story of how the cook was killed, and when no one did, he started by himself.

"We were loading cargo in Buenaventura. I was trying to sleep, when suddenly there was a loud scream outside my window, the sound of many feet running past, and much cursing.

"There was a German ship docked not far from us and our cook had gone over to drink German beer. While he was gone we had a visit from a union delegate, a Communist elected by one of the ships in the harbor. We talked about this and that and he had a few drinks here and then he started back to shore.

"Just as my cook comes back and wants to come up the gangplank, the delegate gets hold of him and they get in an argument about the German beer the cook had been drinking.

"The union delegate shouted, 'Down with the Nazis! Down with the Fascists!' My cook said, 'What difference does it make— German beer, American beer, or Jewish beer—what difference does it make?' Diaz—that was the name of the union delegate— pushed him in the face, and as the cook raised his hands to protect himself, Diaz slipped a knife from his belt and ripped him open. We got the money together to fly him to Panama, and there he died. It was plain murder, and that dog that runs around here is his dog. He's looking for him."

The cook's dog had listened to the story and looked up at the Captain, and then had gone on his rounds again, stopped at a dark spot in the planking, and howled out to sea.

The heat of the engine made the place comfortable. Over the swells of water, wide as avenues, ran a luminous band of light to the moon. The sea was studded with the fins of sharks, each one a gleaming, golden plowshare stuck into a black field.

The little Indian girl wound up a portable victrola and Richard Tauber sang *"Dein ist mein ganzes Herz."*

"I can't stand his singing," said the Frenchman to me. "He gives me the sensation of a waiter reaching up under my coat when I leave a restaurant."

The drunken Hollander pulled the Captain's sleeve. "Last time I heard that song," he said, "was in Magdeburg—Malta— well, I am pointing out it was not exactly where the plan says it

is. It was in Nell Sprout's, at the end of Kruger National Park.
We were coming into the Equator with sixteen parrots and two
monkeys; the ship's carpenter built the cages and the Governor
of Venezuela came on board personally. I bought some cheese
cookies. In the meantime the parrots were dying off. I was married
at the time. We had them right there in back of the anchor winch.
There were still fourteen parrots and two monkeys. One monkey
was dead and the other was dying. They were given a proper
burial at sea. The last parrot was buried off Southampton."

The Hollander made an involuntary underslung gesture with
his hand to catch his chin and hold his head up. He missed and
fell asleep. One after another everyone disappeared.

In the early morning light a fishing boat crossed our course.
The Hollander waved to it and climbed over a mountain of cargo
to the rear deck, where the carpenter was busy building cages for
his animals and birds. The dog followed him there, in advances
and retreats, uncertain of his footing but determined to look there
too for his master.

In a shelter that they had made of palm leaves, arm in arm,
sat the Americans. The little Indian girl came out of the Captain's
cabin and stretched herself in the sun in the little piece of cloth
that was her dress.

The Americans got off in Callao; the Hollander stayed on,
and left with the Frenchman at a small place just before the
Mesias turned into the Guayas River.

The boat fought upstream half the time, and then ran quickly
with the support of the tide. Small bouquets of water hyacinths
floated past down to the sea. Dugouts with Indians and half-naked
mulattoes and Negroes passed. Large rafts of balsa wood, complete households on them, with children, goats and dogs, and
hammocks, swam along the river. Brown and black legs and
banana leaves hung out of boats into the water, out of hammocks,
down over bags of coffee; everywhere siesta. In the dugouts were
oranges, pineapples, fighting cocks, pigs. Turkey buzzards sat in
all the trees along the riverfront. Over the water, and so close
that their bellies seemed to get wet, flew trains of pelicans, their
wingbeat like a dancing lesson—one, two, three, four, glide. A
cool wind came down the river; it began to smell of chocolate.

The Captain tinkled his engine bell, and the *Mesias* sighed in a slower tempo, turned, and, between launches that crowded together like young pigs feeding out of the same trough, she squeezed to a wobbly dock and made fast in Guayaquil.

"Stay—today I'll make some lasagne à la bolognese," said the Captain, who never seemed to wash himself.

To the pier came a group of youths and men with caps and rope. Two of them grabbed the lapels of my coat, others gave me a massage; they seemed to have their hands in all my pockets. They all wanted to take my baggage to the Gran Hotel.

I am always unhappy when I leave a place—a hotel, a house, a boat—no matter how bad. For the first few hours on arriving in a new place an emotional sloppiness comes over me; I sat lost and homesick for the greasy *Mesias* in my room at the Gran Hotel. This house, half-garage, half-hospital, is excellently suited to make you unhappy. I went to the dining room, which is on the roof. I tasted the soup and got up and reached for my hat and walked back to the *Mesias*.

The Captain stood in the kitchen preparing his lasagne à la bolognese. In troubled moments there is nothing so reassuring, so kind to the soul, as to watch someone repair something or cook. The Captain oiled the pan with his fingers, carefully placed strips of noodles along the bottom, and spread over them a paste which he had made out of ground beef and pork, some garlic, chopped onions, origanum, and a sauce prepared from Italian plum tomatoes. Over this he put another layer of noodles, and over the blanket of noodles he spread Mazzarella cheese. Then came more paste, another sheet of noodles, and finally he carefully trimmed with scissors the noodles that hung down over the pan and put the whole thing in the oven. He cooked a lot, and he needed it.

ON A BENCH IN A PARK

In the morning paper of Guayaquil appeared a small announcement of my arrival. The name was misspelled, but the text was one of cheer, of welcome and enthusiasm over the visit of a "most intelligent and precious North American Author." A picture appeared with the article; "EL SEÑOR BNELEMAAS" was printed under it, and, in smaller type, "Important North American Author"—but it was a picture of James Cromwell.

The reporter who had come to interview me the night before had asked for a picture. I had none, and he said, "All right, all right—I fix it up." James Cromwell seems to be the Ecuadorian ideal of the typical North American. I encountered his picture again in *El Comercio* in Quito, where he appeared as Russell Davenport, another important North American engaged in helping a presidential candidate.

I had hardly cut the notice out and looked into the mirror when a bellboy knocked at the door and came in with a visiting card on a small tray. The sender of the card, he informed me, was waiting for me downstairs in the lobby of the Gran Hotel. The name on the card ran from one edge to the other: "Don Juan Palacios, Conde de Ampurias y Montegazza"; and on the back a few words of greeting were penciled. I was also informed that Don Juan was the historian of Ecuador.

He sat in a chair and around it hung the fragrance of roses; he wore a white rose in his buttonhole and offered a hand cobwebbed with blue veins, the fingers cold and stuck together and the thumb away straight out, a moist, negative handshake. He pointed to a glass: he had ordered half a bottle of champagne. He told me he could read English, read much English and loved it for its economy and precision, but did not speak it; that he preferred to speak French, having spent much time in France, which

189

he loved, as a young man. Since I did not speak Spanish, we agreed to converse in French. "I am so fortunate, you are so intelligent," he said; "I am so glad you have come here. So few Americans speak French well enough to express themselves well. Ah, I am delighted." I bowed, he bowed, and then he offered to show me the city; and he said that he would send me the books he had written, which concerned the city of Guayaquil and the cities of Riobamba and Quito, and that he had also written a history of Ecuador. I bowed again, he bowed again and smiled, the tired smile of an invalid. He then took a silver-headed cane and got up with difficulty; and after this effort, when he could spare breath to talk again, he informed me with a mocking smile that his family was so old and so distinguished that two of his aunts suffered from hemophilia and that his uncle had had a silver hip. We both stood now, and he moved close to me and took my arm; he hooked himself to the inside of my arm with a grip which he did not relax until the end of a long promenade. He wore an old and out-of-date garment, a short coat, once called in France a *pet-en-l'air,* a well-tied four-in-hand, and a collar which in Austria was named *Vatermörder;* his waistcoat resembled the plumage of a starling. He walked with his small legs as if each shoe were a sandbag which he had to pull and then kick forward. It took six separate motions to clear the one step from the Gran Hotel's foyer down to the sidewalk, a delayed maneuver to turn to the right in the direction of the street. We advanced slowly past a box of greenery to a sign "Gran Hotel," to a bell labeled "Nightbell," to another sign which said "Entrance" and pointed back to the door of the Gran Hotel; and then came the adventure of crossing the street. It was done with a waving of the cane, increased pressure on my arm, and quick breathing. On the other side of the street he climbed the sidewalk again with great effort and then stood still. I looked around and was astonished at the number of casualties in this street: there was a man who had only one leg; a woman, blind, sat on the edge of the sidewalk, and a child of about ten had an arm and hand the size of a doll's hanging out of its left sleeve.

The burdensome parade went on and it had its compensation, for in this retarded progress there was time to see every detail:

the child with the withered arm, the man with one leg, and the blind woman. I noticed also the great number of drugstores: we passed three of them in short order. Most of the medicines in the windows seemed German. On one window a story in pictures was pasted. Obviously inspired by American advertising technique, this simple drama was adapted to South American conditions, in that the man seemed more important to the advertiser than the woman. It went like this:

In the first picture an old gentleman with a white beard sits at his window; he is sad. Through the window he sees the door of a club and two other men enter smiling with their arms around each other; a third man, also smiling, waves at them from the window of the club.

Second picture: A kindly friend comes to visit the old gentleman. He also has a beard, he speaks to him in great confidence, he says some Spanish words into his ear, and the old gentleman listens with surprise. The friend has brought a gift, a cake of pink soap called Lifebuoy. The visiting friend points at the soap while he delivers a long speech.

Third picture: The old gentleman is in the bathtub, shoulders and arms covered with soapsuds, the head and beard now no longer at an unhappy angle. He smiles; the soap is on a chair next to the bathtub and has a few things to say.

Last picture: The old gentleman is in the club, surrounded by his friends with their arms around him. The cake of Lifebuoy soap has a face that smiles and points at the happy ending.

Inside the window of the drugstore are several posters showing people with headaches and malaria; pictures with religious motives advertise aspirin, quinine, anti-flea lotions, and Vicks VapoRub. We went on, and between the last drugstore and a shop for Panama hats and souvenirs cut out of ivory nuts, I saw a large brass plate with the name of a veterinary. I have never heard of one who was better named—it was "Dr. Aníbal Carrion."

Farther on came a film-renting agency, with Shirley Temple, Wallace Beery, George Raft, and Dolores del Rio on the posters that hung over the desks. Down at the end of the street some pelicans went by, and it began to smell of cocoa. Turning the next corner we found the street covered with cocoa beans, and two men, using their feet as plowshares, walked up and down the length of it, turning beans in the sun.

Near the water was a park with several benches, each shaded by a tree which seemed especially trained for the purpose: it grew straight up and then spread like a square umbrella to shade all who sat under it, allowing for outstretched feet and people who leaned back or over the arm rests.

We sat down here and Don Juan pointed at a boat in the river, with a large C painted on its bow.

"That," explained the Count, "is one-third of our Navy. We have three battleships, *A, B,* and *C.* This one, *C,* is an old Vanderbilt yacht. It has a bad sternpost but it has six bathrooms and eight open fireplaces, and is the ship most sought after by our officers because it is the most comfortable. You will notice that it has no gun; it had a one-pounder but we took it off because it almost knocked the boat apart when it was fired. The other ship, *B,* is most probably in the Galápagos. We can go to the Galápagos now; we have engaged a man who almost graduated from Annapolis to act as pilot and advise the Captain. Once before, when they went without him, they came back and said that they could not find the islands, that they had disappeared. We had a group of prisoners to send there. The next time we tried with that American, he found them, but that time the Governor of the islands said that he did not like to have the criminals on his islands and they had to be taken back again. Now it is all arranged; he takes them and the boat goes and comes back again and everybody is happy, including the prisoners, who have nothing to do but go fishing all day long. The battleship *A* I have not seen for a long time, I do not know where it is, no one has seen it; perhaps we have only two.

"But look around and you will see many automobiles. When I was very young my family owned the first car here in Guayaquil. At the time it was pure folly to own a car, because there was only one street to drive in and it was not very long, only a few blocks.

"The Americans developed this country. Our car was American. The Americans built the first gas factory here, the locomotives on our railroad are American, the streetcars and the first boat that went up this river, and now the electric works—all American.

We are in many ways very advanced: you can have a divorce here for the asking, without trouble, and for a long time, hundreds of years, we have allowed our soldiers to bring their wives into the armory with them, a great improvement on the comforts and the morality of barrack life. Our temperature here is about 79, the dry season lasts from June to December or January, and the evenings and nights are very cool, even cold.

"History—what do the French say of it again?—is a fable agreed upon. Here, the fable is bloody and colorful, with violent incident, with gold, Incas, treachery, and a scoundrel unmatched—at least until recently unmatched—I am speaking of Pizarro. But we also have handy things, lovely memories, good names, and deeds to remember. We are a small country, we have little more than three million people, and the Indians outnumber us ten to one. Most of our people cannot read or write; our records for the most part are unreliable and our statistics largely guesswork."

He was almost serious for a little while. The thin tired smile came again when he said, "We have a revolution here every Thursday afternoon at half-past two and our Government is run like a nightclub. We owe some two hundred and fifty million sucres; but who pays debts these days?"

A man came and offered to change some money—he began by offering the sucre at thirteen to the dollar—but the Count said, "Wait—let's ask that man over there. Oh, Don Luis, one minute, please," and while the man he addressed got up from another bench to come over, Don Juan said, "He was Minister of Finance in the last Cabinet; he can tell us all about it." The ex-Minister advised us to change at the rate of seventeen sucres, and went. "They all fell out of the fat last week," Don Juan remarked, "and now they are sitting on the benches in the parks in Quito and here, and the President is riding in a streetcar. That is democracy."

An old lady and a man sat down next to us, speaking in French so that we should not understand them. They were from the Midi, judging by their dialect. The mother gave her son a long lecture:

"My dear child" (the child was about fifty years old), "your father and I founded our *affaire* here, thirty years ago now, in one room; we enlarged ourselves and took two rooms, then we engaged employees and a few of these are still with us. We have established ourselves in this place with a reputation of honorability and honesty, and the products that carry our name are the best and we are proud. These Germans offer a good price but if they take over the business, will they continue in the same manner? We have gained a fortune sufficient to our simple needs, our employees are like our children, we are a large family perfectly happy. What more do we want of life? Believe me, my son, let us guard our little house—with our Ideal. Let us be satisfied with that which we possess."

"Do you think Hitler will win?" asked the son.

"Yes and no," said Maman, "but it makes no difference, don't sell the *affaire* now, with the sucre falling, it is now seventeen and might go lower. Makes no difference—like this or like that—what happens in Europe. Here, the Americans will fix it, there will be a conference and they will buy the *chocolat. Cet homme Roosevelt, c'est un phénomène,* wait for him." A young girl with soft blond hair came and kissed the woman, and they got up and walked away.

"Ah, how lovely, how logically, how clearly they can think!" said Don Juan Palacios. "And to hear them talk, no matter what, makes it hurt me here, under my ribs. I become homesick." He looked after the girl. "Did you see her, the blond girl? When I see a blond girl I grow warm like soft chocolate inside—helpless. But one should never bring them here, never bring a beautiful woman into the tropics. Look at her legs! They wear thin stockings and the black flies bite them and lay eggs under the skin, and then it swells up and they squeeze and scratch it and the whole girl is covered with hard red patches, and ruined.

"Ah, but in France . . . You know we love France so much here that at one time the natives and the servants thought that outside Ecuador and Peru there was only France, and the only other city besides Guayaquil and Quito was Paris. In Spanish, 'Frenchmen' is easier to say than 'foreigners,' too, and so all foreigners were called Frenchmen.

"When I was a young man here, I fell in love with a beautiful girl, I wanted to marry her badly, but my father was against it. He went to Quito to investigate her family, and found out that the girl's great-grandfather came as a servant with the first Chiriboga. That was when my family arrived, at the same time as Pizarro, or soon after. Now they are accepted in Quito—at any rate, nobody minds them—but that was four hundred years ago. They even have an escutcheon now; my father almost died laughing when he heard of it. They made a special trip to Spain to establish a title. In those days the King of Spain would hand out papers for money, but he asked too much, and so they came back with a story that the title was there and that they could get it if they wanted to, and they brought along this escutcheon. The father even became President—but who doesn't here? At the time it happened, I was very unhappy. They sent me off to France. . . . Ah, la Place de la Concorde, les Tuileries, the perspective down the Champs-Elysées, the little restaurants in the Bois and in back of the Madeleine! I fell in love. . . . Ah, her little footprints in the sands at Le Touquet! We took a villa in Biarritz—it was covered with a peculiar kind of fawn-colored rambler roses; there were roses everywhere. Suddenly it was all over. I was a madman for a few days, I wanted to die, I was so beside myself that I thought of joining the Foreign Legion and I went there to enlist. It was Saturday afternoon and they told me to come back on Monday. On Monday I felt somewhat better. Ah, Denise, I have never forgotten her. I had my architect build me a replica of the villa in Biarritz. It is on my hacienda, up along the Guayas River. I made the sketch myself, from memory. I found a man in Quito, with extraordinary talent and imagination, a Mexican, who helped me with forgotten details on doors and windows and on balustrades. I watched it grow, and one day it stood there in the true color and shape of its original. It was raspberry-colored and covered with roses. We had trouble raising the roses here; they grow well only on one side of the wall, to the east—but from there at five in the evening it looks and smells like France. The sky drawn with blue chalk, the vanilla color of the doors and the stairs, it is all as it was and I go there to be lonesome, to feel the ancient ache. I don't see the wild land at the back of it. When I built the house, the river that runs past it was filled with crocodiles; like a raft of old logs they lay there, one next to the other, and at night their eyes shone. The eyes of the old ones were red and the eyes of the young ones green. They laid their eggs on the edge of my garden, and the gallinazos swooped down and dug them out. They helped me get rid of some, and the rest I shot, all of them. I made my gardener wear a big hat and a blue coat, so that he was like the one we had in Biarritz. . . . I would ask you to come and stay with me at the villa, but my wife Hortense and the eight children live there, and it is a madhouse."

We walked back and he promised again to send me all the books he had written, and gave me a small volume that he had brought along for me. It was a travel book on Ecuador, written by Friedrich Hassaurek, who was American Minister to Ecuador, and published in 1867: *Four Years among Spanish Americans.* I was very grateful for this gift. I have always tried, when visiting a new country, to get hold of an old book, because it extends the view, it helps one to see into the land in much greater perspective, gives one another life almost—one can look around and compare and say, the last time I was here this was so and so. Everything takes on new form and stands out in the round.

Above all, an old book, written with attention to detail, is a consolation, a proof that the most important things remain unchanged through all the immediate terrors. Down over these a benevolent curtain sinks, and on it is painted the unchanging landscape; it is made up of children, of the games of children, of cooking, of dances and music, and the climate; it even has in it the labels on the boxes of food or medicine, the architecture of a house, words that are used nowhere else, the sound of the bells of the nearest church. The storm passes on, these things remain —and through them we heal ourselves again.

The Count asked me to dine with him, and we wandered back into the town together. We crept past a row of two-story houses, most of them wooden, almost all painted green with simulated marble veins, the upper stories seemingly all window, and decorated with a kind of wooden lacework. It was evening and getting cool; we were followed by a horde of half-naked children who wanted to shine our shoes and sell us lottery tickets. *"Veinte mil sucres,"* they cried, "twenty thousand sucres"—the amount you will win next Saturday if you buy a ticket from them.

We passed a fire company, firemen in red shirts, polished apparatus, half of them modern and half museum pieces.

"This town," observed Don Juan, "burns down frequently; its history is one of sacking and fires. For a few sucres you can become a lieutenant of bomberos—for a few more a captain, and that entitles you to the pleasure and the honor of appearing in a beautiful uniform, with music, and marching at the head of all the parades and important funerals. But when the city burns, as I have told you it frequently does, you stay home and let the muchachos climb the ladders and run through the streets; that is what they are paid for."

He climbed into a cathedral next, which was built entirely of wood, painted to resemble granite. Inside the church, barefooted Indian fraters prepared the interior for a requiem. Long curtains in black and gold, reaching from roof to floor, were pulled up to cover the windows. Angels made of cardboard appeared and were set to the left and right of the catafalque; a choir practiced a miserere to the accompaniment of an organ; a monk fell off his bamboo ladder and sprained his ankle.

"They love death in this country; it's like a dance to them, they cry for six months. Wait until you see the flowers, the relatives, the wagon with the black angels—and the darkened church. Fires will be lit here and there, blue flames, six priests. It is a wild fiesta of grief. . . ."

I went to my hotel to rest. There was a large bouquet of white roses; the invitation to dine was for nine. I found out in the meantime that here one says "hola" instead of "hello" to the telephone, that while a crocodile in all other languages is a crocodile, in Spanish it is a *cocodrilo;* and that a question mark is put in front of a sentence as well as at the end of it. I found also that the Spanish language is very objective. The back page of the newspaper which I tried to read had a local news report of a tragedy: a young girl had jumped or fallen out of a third-story window. The headline read: "YOUNG GIRL DESCENDS THREE STORIES."

I dressed and went to the address of my friend. He lived in a street of very old and severe houses. A woman in a shawl opened the door and showed me through a long corridor. I passed a second open door, and from the dark room came Don Juan's voice: "Please wait in the next room until I wake up."

A table was decorated with white roses, and fawn-colored ones were in two vases on the wall. A picture of the villa in Biarritz also hung there, a daguerreotype, the sky almost black, the house copper-colored and out of focus, and in the foreground a woman in a large white hat. An old servant looking like a dark imitation of Beatrice Lillie, who was enceinte and walked in large soft slippers, finished setting the table and then Don Juan Palacios came and we sat down. He told the woman to open the champagne. She was afraid of the bottle. He tried it but his fingers were inadequate and then he gave it to me. It was a bottle of Chilean champagne, and though it had been cooled for several hours, almost all of it came out in a high fountain.

The menu opened with some cold hors d'œuvre, things I could not make out, all of them pickled sour things, some like fish, some like meat, including pieces of cauliflower and two slices of beets, sliced onions sprinkled over all.

"You don't have to eat it if you don't want to," said the host, "but I find that of all things of which one is afraid, cold things are easiest to eat: the vinegar is a kind of protection."

A good red soup came next, with eggs and corn in it and large pieces of tomato; then a fish. There came a dish of rice with lamb and cold stringbeans, and afterward a dessert made of pie crust with jam inside of it, and coffee. During coffee Don Juan fell asleep.

THE GUAYAQUIL AND QUITO RAILWAY

To take the train for Quito, you are called at five in the morning, and an old and twisted ferryboat carries you across the Guayas River to Durán.

The traveler here beholds a picture, lit by the rising sun, that is a hundred years old and like the finale of an operetta that has been dressed with second-hand costumes. Only the orchestra, the score for *The Count of Luxembourg,* are missing. Here is a station-master with a coat cut *en taille* and a "haby" beard. Nuns walk up and down dressed in the colors of several convents, predominant among them the Sisters of Charity of Saint Vincent de Paul, under immense butterfly hats. Between them clatter officers' sabers, hanging from young men of Schnitzler format—garde du corps, Vienna about 1898—their gloves with the fingers almost worn through. There are others, with broader swords, képis, in tight litevkas crowded with frogging—a kind of Hussar. Half a dozen monks, fat and happy, stand talking with folded arms, and aside and serious stands a Jesuit, his eyes on a little book. Commercial people, clerks in bowlers and threadbare black suits, large families with handkerchiefs ready for tears, embraces, and train-whistling, conductor running up and down, salutes and crying and waving of the handkerchiefs.

This train is a curious affair with little wheels and a lid hanging on the side of its chimney. It was manufactured by the Baldwin locomotive works in Philadelphia and the cars that go with it are wooden, red, with elaborate fences around the platform and banisters up their stairs that belong to an old brownstone house. But here is the same train mood as in Victoria Station. It comes from the poom-pah, poom-pah, of the engine, a deep iron breathing and a small mechanical click in between.

An engineer, his face smudged before he starts, looks out of the cab and under the shed that covers the station; smoke creeps along, and the air becomes a kind of champagne for the lungs— carbonated air that makes breathing a pleasure. It expands the chest, one is tempted to cough, but it does not go that far. It is the exhilaration that comes from the tuning of a fine orchestra, rather than from its playing, and it finds its high point in the first two tugs of the engine, when the landscape outside begins to jerk and then slowly move.

Out into the large leaves of banana trees—clatatatat, clatatatat, shaking and trembling and about half an hour late the red train runs. Its most luxurious accommodation is the last car, called an observation car. You can observe out of six barber chairs, three on the left and three on the right, made of genuine mahogany, each one with an immense brass cuspidor next to it, on a green linoleum floor. At one end is a little water fountain, overhead sways a lamp, and in the back through the open door the rails run away and tremble in the heat.

The prospectus of the Guayaquil and Quito Railway informs us that we are in a land of Old World charm, courtesy, and hospitality, a land with a delightful climate to suit every taste, ranging from the tropical to the temperate; that verdure-covered hills are set like jewels among snow-capped mountains; that the distance from Guayaquil (Gwah-yah-keel) to Quito is 462 kilometers; that the railway is the result of the initiative of General Eloy Alfaro and Mr. Archer Harman, a far-seeing North American; that the railway traverses banana and cocoa plantations, coffee and rice and tobacco fields; that the train stops in Huigra and that from there on is the most interesting part of the trip, where the road goes up over the Devil's Nose in a five-and-a-half-percent zigzag and eventually comes to Riobamba, which lies at an altitude of 9020 feet; that the population of this city is 30,000, that it is the capital of the province of Chimborazo, and that it has many fine buildings, parks, statues, and excellent hotels.

The finest of these, recommended to the discriminating traveler, is the Hotel Metropolitano. If you have neglected to order a car to take you on to Quito, this is where you must spend the night.

This violent inn appears to have come out of a story conference of the Marx brothers; it shakes and trembles, it is full of cracks and cold drafts, and the plaster from the ceiling rains down on your face at night. The railroad engines switch cars through its lobby and engineers pull the cords of their whistles whenever they want a package of cigarettes, coffee, the morning paper, or a drink of chicha; the old engines operate with every mechanical noise and chuff back and forth relentlessly. Late guests come in singing, and by the time the last one's baggage is dragged upstairs, a boy calls you and it is time to get up for the second part of the trip to Quito.

The floor is cold, the shoes are outside the door, there is a washstand under the window, the kind one sees in charity hospitals, made of enameled bent wire which embraces a basin, a chipped pitcher standing under it.

There is of course no soap, and the towel hanging at the side is muggy, gray, and the size of a tabloid newspaper. The boy comes with haste, a cup of lukewarm water in his hand for shaving, and throws the baggage down into the lobby. *"Buenos días,"* says the manager and presents the bill.

The scene at Durán the day before is repeated here with everyone freezing, the officers with their coat collars up over their ears, their hands in their pockets; the nuns are blue in the face. At six, again the train rolls on; here in Riobamba the wind is fresh and the air is light and everything is crisp and clear. The train passes between fields of clover and barley, there is wheat and corn, and Chimborazo appears on the left.

Except for its unforgettable name, it is not a very impressive mountain. It is snow-covered, an immense hill with smooth sides, a fat kind of Fujiyama. A biting wet wind comes down its slopes, so strong that at times it blows mule and rider away. The Indians wear chaps made of sheepskin, they are plump and most of them wear handkerchiefs across nose and mouth. There is dust on floor, chair, hat, and coat, one can write one's name anywhere, and breathing has become difficult on account of the altitude.

Somewhere hereabouts is a watershed—and long before the railroad was built, a Viennese traveler, Madame Ida Pfeiffer, the author of *A Lady's Second Journey round the World,* noted in her diary:

"I got off my mount and climbed a little way down the western side of the mountain till I came to water, when I filled a small pitcher, drank a little, and then took the rest and poured it into a stream that fell down the eastern side, and then reversing the operation carried some thence to the western and amused myself with the thought of having now sent to the Atlantic some water that had been destined to flow into the Pacific and vice versa."

A little farther on the railroad descends into lovely valleys, into a delicious landscape of geranium trees, of roses everywhere, of white volcanoes, a sort of geological Soufflée Alaska, hot inside and snow-covered outside. The sky is blue as it is in the South of France; it has been described as the land of eternal spring, but it is more like the last golden days of September, and the smoke that rises everywhere on the mountainsides supports this idea— it is like the burning of autumn leaves. All along the way there have been little restaurants—in Huigra is one with a sign that says "Hays Krimm" (Ice Cream) and I have seen others, "Airistiu" (Irish Stew) and "Wide Navel Wiski" (White Label Whisky). These, however, are luxury establishments that cater to the discriminating traveler.

The natives and even some of those who travel first class patronize small itinerant restaurants, places set up beside the train, consisting of a table, a sand-filled box on stilts which serves as the kitchen, and a piece of sailcloth over the whole business. There is a pot for soup and a fire on which the meat is roasted. Chickens and guinea-pigs are cut up with a small hatchet; the cook, in a greasy blouse and a hat such as bricklayers wear, licks her fingers and picks up pieces of meat which she arranges on plates that are wiped but never washed.

Under the oven are several dogs who wait for the bones. The entire personnel of the train storms these field kitchens whenever we stop for a while. A well-dressed man who sat in chair Number 4, next to me, assured me that the food was excellent; he had some roast pig brought to the train and ate it with good appetite.

The engine of the train went for water frequently. Once there was a delay on account of a rail that was loose. Half an hour later the maid of the Pension Hilda in Ambato waved a flag and the train stopped to take on a passenger, who kissed his family and embraced his friends several times, contemplated how much to tip the assembled employees of the Pension, and then discovered that he had forgotten his light green coat and sent the maid, whose name was América, back for it. The green coat arrives after a while—the good-bys are repeated.

"*Vamos!*— Let's go!" shouts the conductor, and the train goes on, over a bridge along a river, over a hill in a sudden wide curve, and Quito is in its embrace.

QUITO

Quito, the oldest city in the New World, is seemingly built over a sunken roller coaster. Up and down in wide curves and sudden drops go its streets and white houses; the base of one monument is above the spray of the fountain in the next plaza. It is at once like Tunis and like Bruges, and its near-by backdrop of mountains reminds one of Innsbruck.

I have often expected, at night, that out on the roof of the cathedral, under a foolish golden cockerel that turns in the silent wind, would come Rimsky-Korsakov's star-hatted magician and sing the prologue of the *Coq d'Or*.

It has been said of Quito that it had one hundred churches and one bathtub. There are more bathtubs now, but the churches are still ahead—and they make themselves heard. Their bells are high and insistent; they start ringing for early mass with the crowing of the roosters—clank-clank-clank, bim-bim-bim-bim-bim-bim, bang-bang-bang-bang, and ping-ping-ping-ping. They sound more like large alarm clocks than church bells. The deepest give off a sound like that of a bathtub hit with a sledgehammer;

the others are nervous and quick, and none of them has much music—one right next to the hotel goes: "Beany bunk, beany bunk, beany bunk."

In the early Sunday morning hours, when you ride above Quito to the foot of the volcano Pichincha and look down, the city appears as if made of marzipan crawling with numberless black flies. The flies are priests and little women in black shawls running to and from the churches, and in this respect it is like Bruges; but in Bruges the little women walk in twos, and here they walk alone.

The churches are crammed from floor to dome with gold and statuary; their walls are like pages from the Tickhill psalter. The dogs go to church here, they wander in and out, and during the midday heat they lie on the cool floors and sleep in the confessionals. The Indians unpack their children here, sit close together, and everyone prays half audibly—the church seems filled with the flights of bumblebees; fleas hop from one Indian to another. Santa María, Santa María, Santa María, they love the Virgin most and to her they sing and pray, and they believe that a child nursed in church is particularly blessed. They slide on their knees to their saints and light candles and hold their hands aloft in rigid poses of adoration and prayer.

The sacristies are elaborate apartments, filled with statuary, gilded again and behung with paintings and rows of closets that hold magnificent robes.

The sacristans, complicated bent old men, acting their parts like grand pensionaries of the Comédie Française, creep around in faded soutanes, carting silver candelabra, hanging up brocade curtains, arranging plants, and lighting or snuffing out candles— always followed by the large dark eyes of the Indians. Altar boys run around and chase one another except in front of the altar— they are Indian boys with black hair and brown, round faces over pink cassocks and white surplices. They finally line up at the door of the sacristy—one has an old and heavy silver censer which he begins to swing, another holds a set of small bells, and the one in the middle carries a tall, thin silver and gold cross. He has discovered that a ring of gold at the height of his nose, when touched with his tongue at the same time as the silver, gives out a tingling sour taste, and so he licks that part like a small dog during the procession and the mass.

Bim-bim bim-bim, the bell up above begins. *Vamos*—let's go —and they march into the church. The Protestant religion, they told me, never made much progress here, because the pastors lack the power to forgive sins; but the Catholic Church is busy all day long. One mass ends, another begins—there are litanies, sermons, adorations, vespers, benedictions, novenas, forty-hour devotions, rosaries, all day long. Bim-bim-bim. Bang-bang-bang.

Even the poorest sections of Quito have music and design. From the most decayed hovel leaning against its neighbor comes the sound of a guitar, and the building is made interesting by several coats of whitewash, each a different shade, as if three large bedsheets of varying degrees of use, one above another, were draped over it. Other houses insist on a character of their own by being painted with the left-over colors of some better abode, coming out red, blue, green, and mauve. People here are brave with colors, and magnificent names are written over the doors of the humblest houses.

The roofs are universally nice, bent, of tile so old that it is green and gray, with small fields of light and blind, smoky sides with the edges worn. The tiles are curved, two rows with the concave side uppermost and between them a third row, reversed, covering the joint. The evidence of the hand and of play is everywhere; exactly the point where someone grew tired of painting his house is visible in a final upward stroke of the brush. There are peculiar designs above windows and doors; benches are built into walls; chimneys lean and balconies sag.

The houses, good and poor, all have patios. In some of them are chickens and workbenches and in the others pools of water or a fountain, an arrangement of palms, cacti, and tangerine trees. You find floors done in colored tiles, inlaid with the vertebrae of oxen, walked on until the bone has taken on the feeling of old ivory, and so arranged that the inlay forms a design or spells the family name, the date of the house, the name of a favorite saint, or a motto.

Some of the patios are also painted with landscapes or naïve, bright designs done with great individuality, sometimes by the owner of the house. There are majolica vases with a thousand small cracks in them and banisters, doorways, columns, and cornucopias which show restraint, good judgment of space, and a quiet humor. It is all old, worn, bleached, and made by hand.

With these ancient, fine, and practical examples in front of you, it is doubly saddening to go into the modern quarter, into what is the elegant suburb, and see what they have done there. A pastry-cook of an architect who has become fashionable has been let loose here and built a street in which he has carefully assembled everything that is bad and awful.

The first house is a Moroccan château, pink and green, with a memory of the Taj Mahal injected somewhere among its doors and windows. Next to it he has given shape to the nostalgia of a German émigré and perpetrated a Black Forest chalet that lacks only snow, Christmas music, pine trees, and a wolf with a basket in its mouth. The third exercise of his unhappy initiative is modern, a pastel-colored bathroom turned inside out, a shiny small box with oversized round windows, oval doors, and a chromium ship's rail on its roof. This row of houses, each one a few feet from the other, ends in a stone sentinel, a midget Lohengrin castle. Every one of these villas has been indulged with a wall or fence, lanterns, doorknobs, bells, and landscaping to match its character—the fixtures seem all personally selected by the architect.

Happy to be out of this street, you run into another architectural disaster a few blocks to the north—one that is even more depressing because you cannot even laugh. In a superb landscape that is difficult to equal, an ambitious builder has set down two rows of houses facing each other—about twenty of them, alike as foxterriers, built of stone, painted red, with carefully drawn white lines dividing the red surface into bricks. Each little house has the same number of windows, the same door, and the same mat of grass to the left and right of the entrance. They accomplish the heartlessness of a company street in the Pennsylvania coal districts.

The owners of all these properties are extremely proud of

them, and one can console oneself by thinking of their happiness
and by riding away in any direction. In one short hour from
Quito, to the south, is a replica of the road from Nice to Monte
Carlo; to the west, Africa with bananas, Negroes, monkeys, and
malaria; to the north, the badlands of the Dakotas; to the east,
Capuchin and Dominican monks in sandals, walking over soft
carpets of green grass like those along the Danube between Stift,
Melk, and Linz.

ABOUT THE INHABITANTS OF QUITO

On page 110 of a geography book that is used in the schools of Ecuador, written by Professor Juan Morales, the character of the natives of Quito is described in detail.

I requested one of the pupils to translate the passage into English and here is the paragraph verbatim:

"About the inhabitants of Quito: The character of his [Quito's] inhabitants is laughing, frank and sincere, noble and full of these qualities that are a gift and they are learned. Is besides extremely patriot and lofty and incontaminated by any moral misery, but we must call attention to a quality in this noble town that is called 'Sal Quiteña,' is a quality that every Quiteño like to make joke of every word they talk and like to smile with their funny word."

He forgot to say that they are also extremely generous, polite, hospitable to a fault, and proud.

They certainly are patriots—no people on earth can love their city more. They will take you by the arm and hold you tight and whisper, *"Lindo, no?*—Is beautiful, no? You love my country, yes?—Ah, you are so intelligent!" And then they will say, "We Quiteños, when we die, we hope to go to heaven, but we will go there only if we know that in the floor there is an aperture, where we can kneel down and look at our beautiful Quito."

The old Quito families stay in their homes and on their haciendas. They love their children and the children love their parents, deeply, genuinely; they care little for fashion.

The social life of Quito centers in and flows through the bar, the palm court, and the foyer of the Hotel Metropolitano and is mostly made up of foreigners.

Isaac J. Aboab, the energetic proprietor of this hotel, has assembled under its roof some hundred potted palms, uncomfortable beds, employees who are very obliging and run around all day with Flit guns, keeping the house free from flies and bugs. The kitchen is passable, there is always hot water, and an elevator runs day and night.

The palms stand in the palm court, their leaves gray and dead, the stems wound with old coco-matting. A row of splintered spreading wicker chairs, almost black with countless coats of varnish and sticky with a recent one, leans left or right of the palms between which they stand; they are upholstered in green velvet and decorated with a doily for your head to rest on. Next to each chair is again a brass spittoon, large enough to hold a bouquet of lilies. A landscape done by a native artist represents a waterfall along the Pastaza; the effect is very modern—like noodle soup running down over a green couch. At the door and between the chairs, in front of the elevator and on all the floors, are boys in caps with "Hotel Metropolitano" lettered in gold; they open and close doors, address the guests by name, jump here and there to catch a falling pocketbook, light cigars and cigarettes, and deliver messages. The service is excellent.

On Sunday afternoon, the solid bourgeois families, consisting of husband and wife and their two marriageable daughters, gather here to admire the scene and the people of fashion and importance and to drink tea. The girls wear wide-brimmed sailor hats and middy blouses, and hide their long, black-stockinged legs from the glare of the Italian Chargé d'Affaires. Quito, little town of churches, of tradition and above all of family ties, is jam-packed with legations and the cars that belong to them. The mail is shot through with engraved invitations:

"*A l'occasion de la naissance du prince héritier, le ministre de Bulgarie et Madame Popoff prient, etc. etc.*" "*Der deutsche Botschafter beehrt sich, Herrn und Frau—und so weiter.*" "The American Minister and Mrs. Longworth invite all Americans to celebrate the Fourth of July."

Luncheons, dinners, dances, receptions, visits, and presentations of credentials, the feasts of all the saints of the Catholic Church and of several local Madonnas, the celebrations of the various independence days and great battles, the birthdays of

Sucre and Bolívar and the current President, keep Quito in a beflagged mood the year round and cut schooldays down to 79 a year.

There are palace intrigues, counter-intrigues, fidelities and infidelities among the foreign set, but among the Quiteños there seems to be some kind of regularity in family affairs.

"Here in Quito," the father of a large and distinguished family and a former President said sadly, "we have not to offer the passing, loose pleasures of the big city. Here in Quito, Señor, either you love your wife or you go to visit New York, or if you are very fortunate to Paris; but, alas, Paris and New York are so far away, the exchange is so bad just now . . . next year, perhaps, when the Germans can buy our coffee and chocolate again, we can go to Paris."

A lieutenant was even more gloomy. A careless sunburned man, his eyes covered by dark lids and lashes, he looked down at the table, slowly unpacked a box of matches and put them back one by one, and sighed:

"It is terrible here, Señor. First you must make love to this girl you want until your nose bleeds; second you must make love not only to her but to her mother, her father, the butler, and the parrot, and in the end you always must marry her."

"Always?" I said.

"Always," he assured me bleakly. "The town is too small— for otherwise, with a desirable girl"—he put up his hands and counted the obstacles—"she is religious, that is one fence you must jump over; she is beautiful; she is rich, that is the third fence —but the worst is that the streets and the windows are full of relatives who watch her. There are three Pizarro aunts, three Ayora aunts, two Chirimoya uncles, and a Rio del Pinar family of twelve head, and her father—he is worse than all of them. He had the cheek to ask the British Minister for a list of his guests before he accepted for her—what do you think of that?"

Outside of the marriage market, things are not too difficult, at least as far as boys are concerned.

"My wife is a modern woman," said another family man. "She reads American magazines, she has a subscription to the *Woman's Home Companion,* and they are full of these things, I mean about certain big diseases, and she is afraid that our boy Anselmo will get it, too.

" 'Do you know,' she says in the middle of the night, 'that ninety percent in this country have it, and the other ten are getting it?' She is like a dictator when she says these things. 'We must know,' she said, 'with whom he goes, or else he will run around and ruin himself. Look at your cousin Alfonso,' she said; 'he is sick and he has difficulty in walking; they say that it is rheumatism but it is that sickness. Good, it will not happen with our Anselmo.'

"Anselmo at the time was nineteen years old and a quiet boy; he was not sick, he was not fat, his voice had changed, but nothing happened. At one time at least we thought that something had happened with Clemencia the maid, a very quiet girl; but no. What will we do?

"All at once my wife thought of my brother who lives in Guayaquil, where these things are arranged more easily than in Quito. My brother is a man of the world, and he found a nice girl, very agreeable and serious, and he rented a small apartment and arranged a party. My brother first took Anselmo for a long drive and told him all about love and how things are between two people, and then he took him to the little place. The girl was properly presented to Anselmo and the arrangement seemed prudent; it lasted several weeks, until Anselmo got homesick and came back. The girl cried a little but made no demands, and my brother sent her a gift and flowers and Anselmo did not get the big illness, only the little one.

"And all this began with Mother, who was afraid of syphilis. 'I hope you are content now,' I have said to her."

Entertaining, among the elect families whose names are cut into marble plaques on the side of the cathedral, is difficult in Quito on account of the fact that all of them are related to one another, and when someone dies half the city is in mourning for six months. By the time they discard their black clothes, someone else is dead.

The more worldly families and the diplomats entertain mostly in their homes. With the few exceptions of French and Belgian hostesses, who trouble themselves with their kitchens, the dinners are starchy sessions of course after course which leave their traces in soft round arms, matronly profiles, padded wrists and fingers.

A clique of some hundred people forms the café society of Quito. Twice a day they repair to the bar of the Metropolitano; on Wednesday evenings they attend the gala performance at the Cinema Bolívar. You meet them on Sunday at the arena watching bullfights, and far into the night they sit at the tables of the nightclub that is currently in vogue. Here they repeat the meager gossip of the town and stare at newcomers with an insolence that is unmatched even in Berlin and Budapest restaurants—they all but come over to your table to read the labels of your clothes.

Of all the women here, perhaps half a dozen are beautiful and four of these dress with taste.

The last and most interesting group is a small circle of ever-changing characters, a formidable array of talents and personalities, who immediately recognize one another, link arms, and sit down together.

They are explorers, English remittance men, ex-Captains of the Foreign Legion, Hollywood stunt men, deep-sea divers, and promoters of various imaginative enterprises. Each one of them has a biography, brief and risky and as if clipped out of a magazine, and the man is usually a good illustration for the article.

Among this group was a pretender to the throne of Austria, for Quito, like every other metropolis, has its own outcropping of the Affaire Mayerling. Franz Josef's local grandson had some claim to authenticity: his accent was correct, he clicked his heels in the real sloppy Viennese fashion, he was heavy-lipped, and appeared always to be unhappy. At a reception, when he came to the buffet to get some hors d'œuvre for the girls out in the patio, he burdened his arms all the way up, past the elbow, with plates filled with food, stuck a bunch of forks inside his cummerbund, and whisked a napkin under his arm with the technique, if not of a Habsburg, at least of a grandson of that other old Franz Josef, the one at the Bristol in Vienna.

Next to him at the explorers' table usually sat Captain Cyril Vigoroux, a stout man with a beard and a tropical helmet, a hat which is frowned upon in Quito. ("This is not Africa," the natives say.) Doctor Cyril Vigoroux was at one time a ship's sur-

geon on an obscure vessel, a small ship known as the suicide
boat. In the middle of the ocean, a woman squeezed herself out of
a porthole and was gone. . . . A few latitudes farther on, after
Neptune had come aboard as they passed the Equator, they found
among the débris and the pieces of decoration and costumes that
had come off during the celebration, at the bottom of the canvas
pool, the body of a Rhodes scholar . . . and the next day an old
lady was taken ill, Doctor Cyril Vigoroux diagnosed acute
appendicitis, had the steamer stopped and operated on her, and
to the surprise of the old lady, the ship, and even the doctor, she
lived, came up on deck awhile later, and walked off the boat in
New York. Years later she died and left all her money to the doctor. He exchanged the anonymity of a ship's surgeon for a membership in the Explorers' Club and the fame and glory that goes
with voyaging to places where no one has been before.

The third man at the table was a silent man, a man in whose
face were several animals: an Irish setter, a thoroughbred, affec-
tionate horse—and around the nose up near the bridge a good
deal of character. His forehead was usually corrugated with worry.
He was an explorer who had come to seek gold, the only depend-
able-looking man at the table. He sat in profound silence, smoked
a pipe and allowed his beard to grow, asked a few questions about
terrain and weather, and occasionally changed the way his legs
were crossed. He looked at the ceiling, out into the street, then
a long while at the waiter, and when the waiter looked at him, he
raised his eyebrows and so did the waiter, and brought him another gin and tonic. Ferguson was his name, Allan Ferguson; he
seemed to be an honest man and really wanted to look for gold.

During one of the great silences of Allan Ferguson I looked
with him out into the street. A woman passed, an Indian, barefoot, with twelve boards of wood strapped to her back. The
boards reached in a diagonal line from a few inches above the
street to perhaps three feet beyond her head: she moved quickly
in a trot and uphill, quieting the baby which was suspended from
her in a piece of cloth.

A beggar also passed—a statue of misery, in a well-thought-
out costume—in an overcoat that was as old as the man, made
of small patches of cloth, each one the size of a matchbox, a gar-

ment that forever renewed itself. He had hard dry feet, a cane, a white beard, and like all the other beggars sold lottery tickets and sang, *"Veinte mil sucres."* After he had passed the window, with a little black woman in black in front of him and a padre behind, a Rolls-Royce came along.

It was one of the used cars that one can buy for about a hundred dollars in New York. Gray and with a miniature tree of levers and throttles above its steering wheel, it had trouble turning corners, and filled the street from sidewalk to sidewalk. It was driven by a native chauffeur in a reversible leather coat. The radiator was covered with club emblems and its backside displayed "G.B." in thick letters on a square metal shield.

Ferguson remained silent, but Gerard de Kongaga, Minister of the Armenian Legation, who also sat at the explorers' table, leaned over and asked me whether I knew the owner of the car. "Thinks nothing of wearing suits like this"—Kongaga pulled his necktie out of his coat and showed its loud pattern—"hunting and fishing chap, lives right next to you"—I was staying in a small villa in the Mariscal section then—"fellow who owns that car."

"Englishman?" I asked.

"Ra-ther," said Kongaga, "remittance man, wonderful chap; here he comes."

THE MORALE OF THE NATIVES

He appeared before me every morning, across a three-foot garden wall, somewhere between an acacia tree in full bloom and some lotuses that grew close to his balcony. He was nude at about nine in the morning and a small monkey sat on his fist; he sang, and then lay down on a couch to take a sunbath.

A little black boy in a white coat brought him his breakfast, rubbed him with some lotion, and then stood by to chase the flies away. At ten he went into his house and then appeared after short interludes, first in his underwear, next stuffing his shirt into his trousers, and eventually fully dressed. He tied his cravat in the sun; his song had no melody, it was a formless tra-la-laa, a noise made of the pleasure of living, completely thoughtless, without beginning or end. For the rest of the day, when he was home, Captain Alastair Monibuy shouted at his servants, played with his animals, and took pictures with a Leica—pictures of anything and anybody.

He had arrived in Quito in the old Rolls-Royce, making the perilous journey from Babahoyo, driving himself, a high testimonial to the motor and the chassis of the old car.

In the back of the car he had stowed several Louis Vuitton suitcases and a dozen polo mallets, a rifle and fishing gear, a saddle and a case of gin—gin was his favorite drink. His eyes were like two round emeralds, and when he drank they shone with hypnotic brilliance. He stood always tense, one leg a little ahead of the other, the upper body erect, shoulders back, one hand in his trouser pocket, playing with keys or change, and the other holding the glass tightly.

The whole little man was closely packed into good clothes, so tight that one felt the buttons on his suit or shirt would pop off any minute.

He first lived at the Metropolitano, but later found a little villa in the Mariscal section of Quito, an inexpensive livable house with a large garden and a garage, and a place where he could keep his zoo. He had a monkey and two tigrillos. (A tigrillo is really an ocelot, but having no tigers of their own, the Ecuadorians have elevated that animal to the rank of tiger, using the diminutive.) He had also a macaw and two parrots. His ménage was sloppy, as was his person. There was a drawer full of bottles of Geneva gin in the living room; cigarette butts and matches accumulated in the washbasins of all the rooms, and somewhere there was always a stack of empty bottles. Broken glasses in the fireplace, and a long blond hair or dandruff on his coat. His hair was sticky and dirty.

He had trained an Indian boy as a servant, a very attractive mulatto as a cook, and the mulatto's twelve-year-old daughter to make the beds and clean the house. He smacked them all across the backside with his riding crop whenever they passed by him, and then laughed a hearty ha-ha-ha-ha-ha, a furious signal that also escaped him after every short, loud, and deliberate sentence. He did not speak, he telegraphed his ideas and observations, leaving out all unnecessary words—the telegram always came in faultless English. He had been to Sandhurst, he said.

After he had asked me for lunch one day, he showed me how he had decorated his house. Nailed on the wall in the living room hung a uniform in which he had flown for Franco, and next to it was a large frame in which, behind a glass, he had arranged an assortment of letterheads, with most distinguished addresses printed on them. There were about thirty of them and the best were: The Château de Gande, The Athenaeum, Chequers, Ten Downing Street, The Horse Guards, etc.

Each of these letters started with "Dear Bimbo," as he was known to his intimates; but the text in every case save one was hidden by the letter next to it. In the center of all these expensive papers, in cream and oyster hues, was a note from Hilaire Belloc, with text and signature showing, acknowledging the gift of a book. Once, when he added a new letter and had the whole correspondence laid out on the table, in order to arrange it anew, some of the other letters were laid bare. The one from the Athenaeum requested the return of a loan; two others were regrets.

On the opposite wall hung another frame, into which he had written "My Passions," and this contained photographs: a string of polo ponies, a Savoia-Marchetti seaplane, a yacht and a sailboat and several girls, all British and pretty and blond, with their hair lose on top of their heads; every one of them had signed herself "With love to Bimbo."

He knew everybody and he had several kinds of behavior and fitted himself into almost any group. He never said anything, but his loud ha-ha-ha-ha followed every word he said and was infectious. People laughed and did not know why. He was the only completely happy man I have ever known; he lacked the capacity to worry.

Bimbo rode well, was a generous host, made compliments to the old ladies, and hopped from table to table. The doors of all good houses were open to him; he had, when he was in need of them, passable manners, and he had so ingratiated himself that he was permitted to come late everywhere and even sit down to dinner in riding clothes and mud-caked boots. Many a father thought that at last a man worthy of his beautiful but still unmarried daughter had arrived in Quito; dressmakers worked, florists were busier, wine merchants, butchers, and even saddlemakers felt the presence of Captain Alastair Monibuy.

One day he gave a cocktail party at his villa. He stood at the entrance playing with the change in his trouser pocket, pounding guests on the shoulder as they arrived, and roaring cheer.

The villa was filled, every room loud with conversation, long past the time when people usually went home. A dinner was hastily put together, some extra drinks made. It lasted late into the night. When almost everyone had finally departed, there was a scream from above, and then a body fell down the stairs.

It was the Armenian Minister, Gerard de Kongaga. This diplomat of good family and most amiable disposition had clamped himself to the banister, after talking to himself in the corner of the corridor above for half an hour, and then he had let go.

Kongaga had spent most of his life in Schönbrunn in one of the famous retreats of Professor Lorand, a healer who believed in occupational therapy. Kongaga had built so much garden furniture and so many birdhouses that he had become an expert carpenter and painter.

Since his arrival in Ecuador, however, he had never been sober. When he came to parties it was in the manner of a blind man who has lost his dog: he saw people where none stood, and offered them his hand in greeting. That day, as he came up the stairs, he passed the host, mistook the Papal Nuncio for the French Minister, embraced him, and told him dirty stories. He recognized the host later on and went up to him, held on to Monibuy to steady himself for a while, and then turned and looked into the room full of people. One could see him calculate his moves; he narrowed his eyes and surveyed his chances. There was a table filled with glasses to the right; a few feet away, opposite that hazard, stood a statue on a taboret, and beyond this was a chair with a lady in it, the British Minister's wife. Wanting to say something nice to that lady, and observing that next to her was a vacant chair, he decided to sit down. He smiled at the Papal Nuncio, let go of Monibuy's hand, stood straight up, buttoned his coat, and then—one, two, three,—he started off. . . . The lady was not there; it was a tall vacant Jacobean chair, upholstered, that had looked occupied. The chair next to it was there, so he took the arm rests into his hands and, with the dolorous mechanism of a paralytic, sat down—between the two chairs—pulling both down over him. He was rescued with great effort and seated in the chair on the left, and then he was quiet until the people who had lifted him up turned away and began to talk again. Then he plotted again and thought up a new and perfected excursion—which ended up in the fireplace.

He never became violent, his gentle face expressed nothing but a mild disappointment; he liked everyone and everyone liked Gerard de Kongaga. The women openly regretted that the rich, good-looking, and gallant man had few sober moments. He fell loosely like an acrobat and seldom came to grief. At Monibuy's cocktail party he had fallen well again, and the host, the mulatto cook, and the Habsburg dragged him upstairs to the guest room and covered him up.

When the party finally began to break up, Bimbo decided that he could not sleep and wanted to go to the Ermitage, the El Morocco of Quito. The Ermitage was located in an old house. The policeman on duty in the street outside, the Carabinero Number 18, made himself useful opening and closing automobile doors, smiling at people, and acting as the doorman. In his faded greatcoat with the big saber at his side, he had gone better with the place when it was called Volga Volga. Like all the policemen in Quito, he was a half-breed. He had an old handkerchief tied around his face to protect nose and throat from the cold; but he kept this in his pocket on mild evenings and amused himself by imitating the songs of various birds, for he was an accomplished whistler. The rooms of the Ermitage were low and dim and so badly upholstered that when a patron sat down on one of the imitation leopard-skin banquettes, the patrons who sat to his left and right bounced up and down several inches. Cheap glass and crockery were on its tables, badly painted Russian murals with troikas and snow and the cathedral of Kazan painted on the walls, left over from the days when the place was under White Russian management. From that period also remained a large glass globe which showered the room with snow effects when the lights were turned low. The place was managed by two Frenchwomen, Lydia and Tamara, each with a friend in the Government and excellent business acumen. One smoked from a long cigarette holder; the other sat on a high stool, and twice an evening she played a guitar and sang such ballads as *"Ma femme est morte."* Champagne was compulsory, the prices were out of reason, the music was native, and when they tried to play such things as "St. Louis Blues" or "South of the Border," two of their favorites, it took awhile to recognize the tune; and then the flutes pulled your scalp tight and made your ears wiggle. But late at night, when they played their own music, their native music which is in somewhat the same beat as a two-step, they played with fine rhythm. The *crème de la crème* of Quito assembled here; it was particularly crowded on Fridays, the shoddy linoleum dance-floor half set with chairs and tables.

At midnight on the day of the cocktail party, when Bimbo and the Habsburg were driving to the Ermitage, after taking off a door of the car coming out of the gate of the villa, they heard a voice

from the back seat. It was Gerard de Kongaga and he said, "You
fellows aren't mad at me, I hope." They stopped the car and told
him that they were not mad at him, that they were very happy he
had come along. The old Rolls-Royce squeezed itself through
the streets of Quito with its loud special horn going tatitata all the
way to the Ermitage.

Kongaga crawled out of the car into the arms of his friends, and
the three of them entered the room and advanced to the bright
light where Tamara had just finished singing a couplet. Everyone
became wide-eyed, Lydia quickly rushed to dim the room and
turned on the snow effect, and the ladies looked the other way.
Gerard de Kongaga stood in the center of the dance-floor minus
his trousers. The room was darkened, the music started, and a
waiter ran out for the policeman-doorman.

When the Carabinero Number 18 came in, he laughed and
tried to be very friendly. He stood in front of Kongaga and tried
to hide him from the audience with his big coat. Kongaga was
busy twisting at the only button which was left on the policeman's
coat; little pieces of thread hung empty where the others had
been and the coat was held together by the belt from which the
saber was suspended. The policeman tried to make himself part
of the fun and hooked his arm into Kongaga's and said, *"Vamos!*
Come on, let's go! Let's go home—no?" and started to pull him
slowly from the room. This did not go well with Captain Monibuy. He looked hard at the policeman and then tore him away
from Kongaga. "Take your hands off that man instantly—let go
now! Do you know who that is? That is His Excellency the Armenian Minister"—but the little policeman said again, *"Vamos*
—let's go home," and pulled on Kongaga's sleeve once more.
Monibuy drew his shoulder back and hit the policeman so hard
that he fell, spun, and disappeared—all but his small feet—under
a ringside table. There was quiet again and the Habsburg dragged
Kongaga out to the Rolls-Royce and they drove him home.

The next day Monibuy was in his little summerhouse in the
garden. He came out in a bathrobe, and he shouted over the wall,
"You know, I wore out a suit last night; they ripped the sleeves
out of my dinner coat." His boy brought a bloater and he drank
some tea. He sat in the morning sun for a while and his

boy rubbed him down. At about eleven a car drove up, a police-- man appeared and announced that the Chief of Police was in the car, and asked whether he might come in. The Chief came and put his cap and saber away, took off his gloves, and had some tea. He leaned back in his seat and looked up at Pichincha and over at Cayambe and said, "What a lovely day. It was . . . you love my country? Ah, I am glad, is beautiful, no? And such lovely weather." He changed his tone and kept his hands busy snap- ping his gloves together and taking them apart again. Then he watched the labor of some ants on the garden wall and said wea- rily, "I am a very busy man, I am perhaps too serious. So many things happen, stupid things, and everybody comes to me with their troubles. I think there was some trouble last night—I do not go out much, I do not know much of these places—I hear in a place called the Ermitage, and somebody—I have not heard the name—I think with perhaps a little too much to drink, comes there, without proper dress . . . and there is a fight. Nothing important—it happens all the time, it happens everywhere—but I wish people would not hit our policemen; it is so bad for the morale of the natives."

THE BOOTS OF GENERAL ALTAMIR PEREIRA

I had lost a pair of English boots by leaving them too close to a campfire in Patagonia. I woke up the next morning and the soles fell off them, the soft part over the ankles was like lint, and I held the shafts in my hand. They were costly and very old, they had been on many rides, and ever since I had lost them I was sad whenever I thought of them, the shop where they were made, and the fine color they had turned.

I saw a pair of well-cut boots hanging out of a fauteuil in the lobby of the Club Pichincha one afternoon, and I asked my friend Manuel Pallares to tell me whom they belonged to. Manuel immediately introduced me to the man who wore them, General Altamir Acyr Pereira.

You must never admire anything too much in this hospitable land, because it becomes the immediate duty of most people to make you a present of it. The general regretted that he could not take off his boots there and then and give them to me, but he promised that the next day his personal bootmaker, one Leopoldo Sandoval, would present himself at my residence and bring with him a hide, a selected hide from the prize cattle of the General's own hacienda in Antisana. The bootmaker would then take my measure for a pair of boots exactly like the General's own.

He asked me what hour would be convenient, and then clapped his hands for the mayordomo of the Club Pichincha. This man came, stood at attention with his fingers glued to the seams of his trousers, and repeated to the General word for word that tomorrow at ten Leopoldo Sandoval would come to me with the hide of the prize cattle of Antisana and make me a pair of boots with the compliments of the General. He turned and gave this order to another servant, who took a cap and ran.

I sat in stocking feet in the patio of the house the next morning and waited. Monibuy dressed and sang. A man with a beard and golden spectacles came and wanted to sell me an interest in some caves that were filled with bat manure, a most wonderful fertilizer. And finally Kongaga came and said, "Don't tell me you are waiting for the cobbler, that you believe you will get those boots! Talk, talk, beautiful talk, that's all it is. They sing these things off like the national anthem. 'My house, my horses, my hacienda are yours.' But it doesn't mean a thing."

The cobbler was late, but he came. Leopoldo Sandoval appeared with the hide and a boy and a piece of brown paper. In the garden house he put my feet on the paper one after the other and drew around them with a pencil, taking measurements and dictating all the details to his son. He snapped out the numbers and retired backward out of the house, to turn around only when he was twenty feet away, after making a last compliment and bow, together with the small son.

The boots, comfortable and elegant, arrived a few days after a fitting, and with them an invitation from the General to visit him. He lived in a palace in the center of Quito, in a cool old Spanish baroque house, with a garden large enough to race horses in. The rooms in his house were on two floors, the apartments large enough to entertain two or three hundred people.

At the door was a heavy crocheted portiere whose lowest fringe struck me just under the nose. Bending under this, you entered the room. Four fountains made of marble stood on the edges of a flowered red carpet in an inner sanctum determined by a quadrangle of mother-of-pearl columns. In each of the fountains were two silver birds of paradise, one with his head down, the other up.

In the exact center of this carpet stood a circular sofa, such a one as stands in the first-class waiting room of the railroad station at Monte Carlo. People sit in a ring around it, legs outside, backs together, and over them is a jardiniere with ferns and a palm.

Between three high and wide windows, framed in heavy green velvet portieres with hundreds of pompons, stood Louis Seize chairs, authentic pieces. Hanging between the windows in large frames were sepia-tinted photographs of the Flatiron Building, the Roman Colosseum, and the Hotel Plaza in New York. The General told me he loved America.

One wall was dominated by a family group, the General and Doña Faviola, and around them their nine sons, reading from left to right: Alejandro–Aquilino–Alfonso–Arquimedes–Antonio–Arturo–Altamir–Anselmo–Antenor.

The space on the other wall was taken up almost entirely by a large painting, a Swiss landscape. It was not only high and wide, but also thick. The General took a key from a vitrine, and found a small keyhole in a door that was painted on a house in an Alpine village in the lower left corner of the picture. He inserted the key and turned it and music began to play. The painting became alive: a small train chuffed out of a tunnel and ran over a bridge, a Montgolfier balloon rose in the air, descended and went up again, and two blacksmiths hammered on an anvil. I was afraid to admire the picture too much, because the hospitable General might have given it to me. The music slowed, the train also, and the Montgolfier bag sank in its last descent as we sat down to eat.

The General said that he had heard that I wanted to go into the jungles of Oriente and up to the headwaters of the Amazon. He had a large hacienda in the jungle, he said, and three of his sons were in there, Altamir, Arquimedes, and Anselmo, very lonesome and happy to see anybody.

The way in started from Baños, and to Baños he would send me in a car. I would have to stay there awhile, and from there a truck would take me to the Río Negro, and then horses on into the jungle.

"My home, my servants, my horses are at your command—and I think you had better take a boy along to look after you."

He clapped his hands again and his mayordomo arrived. He asked him to call a boy named Aurelio.

"This is the boy you need. He usually rides with me. He speaks a little English. He will take care of you." The boy came and the General said to him, "Go with this man, he is your *patrón*," and to me, "Send him back when you are through with him."

Aurelio from then on was never more than six feet from me. Even in the dark, when I had completely forgotten that he was there, he stood silently in back of me. He always smiled, he never was tired, he picked things off the floor and chairs and hung them up. He had the curiosity of a young dog and he warmed the lonesomeness of the long rides with his simple English phrases. The first one he tried out on me was, "I love you, Mother."

He ran along to help me pack my things. Just then two planes roared over the Metropolitano. He went to the window and looked up, and then he said to me in Spanish, "One day they will come over, hundreds of them, and kill us all with them, with these machines, with bombs that come down."

"Who," I said, "will come and do that?"

"Oh, the damned Yanquis."

"And who told you that?"

"Oh, everybody knows that."

"But who told you?"

"Ah, it's real knowledge," he said. "My brother, who can read, has found this written many times in the magazine called *The Voice of the Worker*. My brother drives a bus, and he gets fifteen sucres a week for calling the bus 'Adolfo Hitler,' because it's a nice new bus. And other bus drivers get ten sucres for calling the bus 'Hindenburg' or 'Alemania' or 'Berlino' or 'Hamburgo' or 'Zeppelin.' The buses go through the city and to the villages. 'Adolfo Hitler' runs from here to Machachi."

We passed "Adolfo Hitler" on the road the next day. Aurelio waved to his brother, and in three hours' ride we came to the Pension Hilda in Ambato, again, like most pensions, run by Germans.

On the stretch between Pelileo and Baños we found a bus called "Zeppelin" with a broken wheel, its forty passengers standing around it. Farther on there was rain and a landslide. We had to climb over it and found "Napoleon I" waiting there. In this vehicle we rode on to Baños.

Near the old empty stone church in Baños, whose walls are shrill with the mettlesome complaints of sparrows, is a holy pool of copper-colored hot water. A stream of the heavy fluid breaks through the rock out of the side of a mountain. Cooling off in wooden gutters, it runs down into the pool in two streams, each one the thickness of a strong man's arm. It runs from a stone urn, then thins out, becomes a few shades lighter, and falls heavily

into the waters below. There are no bubbles. Outside of a gulping sound there is no disturbance. It is like hot sirup, hard to
wade and swim in.

The water is let out every night and two Indians scrape the
residue, a golden slime, from the walls of the stone pool. They
go to an icy waterfall that comes down the mountain ten feet to
the left of the pool, get buckets of water, and throw them into the
eight dressing rooms that the community of Baños has erected
for the convenience of visitors.

That is the only thing they have done, cut the stones for the
pool, built the cabins, and appointed the Indians to keep it clean
at night. All else has been left undisturbed—there is no sign, no
list of rules, no one to rent out bathing suits, and no tickets needed.
Early in the morning or late in the afternoon you can go there and
be alone, and it is as if you found the pool in a far-away field.

At the edge of the pool sheep and cattle graze, their hoofs
buried in Alpine plants and small flowers. The land descends in
terraces to the church, to another pool that is filled with dark
brown, icy mineral water, and to the far emerald-green fields of
sugar cane that fill the valley like a wide river.

All around soar mountains so steep, so rigid that the light
seems to tumble over them. The mountains remain opaque as if
dark green chalk were rubbed over a rough black paper. After
you look at them for a long time the shapes of trees and plants
appear, softly and loosely sketched.

In the early morning, in the first daylight, when the sun rises
high up near the glaciers, clouds like the bellies of a thousand
whales crowd themselves down over the valley. The sun shines
above them, and some light comes through. Then everything
swims in bluish milk; veils of gray gauze fall over trees and houses
and change all the distances. They stay awhile, lift again, sometimes dissolve, and when they come down too close, the air currents over the wild waters of the Pastaza tug on their edges, tear
them up, stretch them out, and drag them down toward the
jungle.

People come to the holy waters of Baños with twisted hands
and with rheumatic troubles, and some of them can hardly walk
when they arrive. The water is indeed miraculous. It cures most

of them, and the few that are not cured are better when they go than they were.

What is gained in the baths is undone in the hotels and pensions of Baños. Fortunately there are few, and all of them are small. The beds are damp, sagging, narrow cots, the legs unsteady. The food is abominable in all. I took a room in the most highly recommended and most comfortable of these places, the Gran Hotel Astor. It stood in front of an untidy yard facing the pool, looking as if a small child had designed it—a window in the center of the upper floor, and one, two, three irregular windows more to the left and right; a door under the center window and six more windows below; a roof, a chimney, some smoke, and, over the door, "Gran Hotel Astor" written in crude letters. In every one of its windows, instead of a curtain, hang the wet bathing suit and towel of a guest. Over the door is the date when this sorry edifice was finished. There is the screaming of children, and no one comes to receive you. In the lobby is a poster in Spanish: "Come to Germany, the land of music and culture."

Going through the house I found in one of the rooms a young Indian woman, barefoot, singing with a broom in her hand. She was the entire staff. She waited for me to speak. She then thought for a few seconds about whether a room was vacant. Ecuador is the paradise of hoteliers. No matter how bad, their hotels are always filled. She remembered after a while and after having looked at it that there was a room, but she said we must first go down and see the proprietress.

This woman is usually to be found in the doorway between the kitchen and the dining room, and she is German also. She frowns into the kitchen from habit, then turns and smiles into the dining room, because a guest is usually there.

She fell into a few pleasantries that day, and looking at the Indian, she said, *"Oh, diese Naturkinder,"* and explained that the girl, whose name was Luz María, "the Mary of Light," was fond of animals, and that she had discovered that she kept a nest of small birds in a silver drawer in the dining room. The silver Madame referred to was an assortment of greasy knives and battered spoons, and forks with half their prongs bent or missing.

"This way," said the woman, and I walked out of the kitchen

and around the edge of a loamy yard, red with water that ran off between the stones of the pool.

The room was on the second floor, close to a bath. The bath had a long narrow tub, and a tall stove was attached to it. The bed was still unmade, the doorhandle came off as the door was shut, and the only good thing about any of the thirty-five rooms of this hotel was the view from their windows. The Gran Hotel Astor is on a most enviable site, overlooking the pool and the village. Aurelio slept on the floor at the foot of my bed, and we waited for the mayordomo of the Hacienda El Triunfo to come with his truck and take us in toward the jungle.

BENITIN AND ENEAS

In this village, in Baños, is a small restaurant called the American Country Club. It used to be run by two men who were partners in this enterprise, one named Benitin and the other Eneas.

Benitin and Eneas are the Spanish names of Mutt and Jeff in the American comic strip which appears in translation in the newspaper *El Comercio* in Quito. The restaurateurs were known by these names because one was tall, the other short, and also because their real names—they signed themselves Vorkapitch and Sasslavsky on all official documents—were too difficult for the Castilian ears of their clientele.

The general equipment of a restaurant in this land demands no great amount of capital. The local painter makes a sign for it, and you need in addition a strong padlock for the door, four tables, twelve chairs, a few glasses and plates new or old, tinware and a corkscrew and two salt and pepper shakers and a bottle of imitation Worcestershire sauce—and the dining room is taken care of. At the bar is a box for the ice which the Indians bring down from the glaciers, a kind of hard, sooty snow, and the light comes from one weak bulb, without a shade, that hangs on a wire in the precise center of the room together with a sheet of flypaper. The flypaper acts as a sail, so that whenever the door is opened the light is carried to the left or right, and in a busy restaurant, in consequence of this, the shadows of every object are constantly in motion.

There is some kind of oven in the room and a pan to wash dishes. To divide kitchen from restaurant a curtain is hung, and with two pots and pans, the kitchen is ready.

What lifted the American Country Club into the rank of a *restaurant de grand luxe,* however, was that Benitin had invested in a music machine—a highly polished smooth cabinet with a slot

into which a sucre could be dropped. When this happened, the instrument began to hum for a while, lit itself up in brilliant rain-
bow hues, and then rendered six pieces of staccato music to
which people danced, while the Indians sat at a respectful distance outside the club and listened until the doors were closed.

Eneas, the other partner, had come through with an equally
elegant contribution: he had installed two waterclosets, one for
caballeros and the other for señoras. The advertisements of the
American Country Club featured both "dancing" and "confort
moderne."

The room was small and usually crowded, and warm. The ceiling was low. Benitin and his music machine were out in front. He
attended to the four tables there and kept watch over the two
dozen bottles of assorted spirits which comprised the cellar of
the club.   Eneas and his investment were in back of the curtain.
He crouched over a low inadequate oven, cooked, made ham
and chicken and club sandwiches, and talked to himself.

Eneas was not satisfied. The place was the only restaurant in
Baños, it was in an excellent position facing the plaza, and it did
good business for luncheon, dinner, and late into the night. He
stood behind the curtain all day long until closing time; he did
most of the work while the other one hung over the bar out front,
laughed and talked with the customers, poured himself drinks,
and listened to the music.

"Why," said Eneas to himself, and to anyone who came behind
and listened to him, "why should I work like a dog and split the
profits with him? This town can stand another restaurant."

The next time he found himself in bad humor, he took advantage of a routine dispute with his partner and declared in his native Czech that he was through being a poodle, that he wanted his
share of the business and also the waterclosets.

A watercloset in this remote valley is a rare convenience. It is
not only a testimonial to the initiative of its owner; it costs a good
deal of money. Once ordered, its arrival is problematic; land-
slides will delay it, bridges may be washed away, there is the
chance of breakage or of total loss. The time that passes between
the day it is ordered and that when a donkey finally brings it to
the door is one of chagrin and suspense.

It is easy to understand why Eneas insisted on taking his investment with him to his new restaurant. The new place, which was
immediately next door, was higher; it had once been a Government building, sported two Ionic columns and a coat of arms
over its door. It had fallen into neglect, but Eneas had painters
busy for a week, put a carpet on the floor, built a solid division
between dining room and kitchen, and hired an artist from Ambato to decorate the interior.

At the entrance next to the columns he placed two large palms,
and from the ceiling he hung Japanese paper lanterns with red
75-watt bulbs in them. He even entertained the idea of having an
electric sign made with "Salon Hollywood" flashing on and off.

After the "confort moderne" was properly installed to the left
and right, Eneas hired a native cook and he himself put on a chef's
hat and supervised the preparation of the specialties of the house.

His tables, in accusing contrast to the American Country Club,
were covered with clean checkered tablecloths. For most of the
day Eneas now stood out in front waiting for his guests, his new
waiters in a semi-circle around him, alert as pointing dogs.

It was all in vain.

Next door, without even whitewash on its walls, the American
Country Club was crowded; people laughed and danced to the
music of Xavier Cugat and Enrique Madriguera, corks were pulled
and glasses broken, the noise went on until dawn. But Eneas continued to stand alone among his empty tables and chairs. At long-
spaced intervals a hurried customer came running from next door,
ordered a drink, and asked Eneas to turn on the light in the back,
but the rest of the time his place yawned with emptiness and failure.

A month after he had opened it, Eneas closed the Salon Hollywood. The chairs and tables he sold to Benitin. The confort
moderne he decided to take with him.

Four donkeys inside the Salon Hollywood stood loaded with
the heavy porcelain, the fixtures, pipes, and water tanks. Eneas
gave his last instructions to the Indian who was to deliver the
cargo in Ambato, and then he sat down under a striped new
awning on one of his own chairs, in the midst of his tables and
palms, which now were all part of a sidewalk café in front of the

American Country Club. His former partner Benitin served him
some rice and mutton. Eneas took a half-hearted bite and then
pushed the plate away and stared out into the plaza.

This square is formed by three rows of houses half fallen
apart, maroon, yellow, green, and black. Two have no roofs and
moss grows on the tiles of the others. The doors, the balconies,
the stones at the entrances have all been shifted to conflicting
angles by earthquakes, and there is one balcony that makes the
heart stop beating. It is high up and has no railing, just three short
beams coming out of the house with two pieces of rotted gray
board laid over them; and out on this platform a baby crawls
every day to play and listen to the music of the American Country
Club.

A few feet north of the center of the square stands an immense,
fanciful tree. Its wide branches carry stout green leaves the shape
and color of laurel. The trunk of the tree is bent and twisted and
it is as if it were hammered out of dull silver. Most of the leaves
hang down over a fountain, a severe octagonal basin which, like
all the stone in this humid valley, is soft and enchanting under a
coverlet of fan-shaped miniature greenery. At the side where the
water spills over the stone hang long beards of dripping grass, and
from this grass the water flows down across the wide steps that
encircle the fountain. The water quietly enters a large puddle
that is in the exact center of the square. In this dark brown water
a white church reflects itself, making the fourth side of the
square. On days when the sun shines, shadows heavy and black,
like blankets of indigo, lie under the tree; the water in the fountain is black and the only light comes from a basket full of lemons
spread in front of an Indian woman sitting under the tree, and
from the ponchos of besotted customers over in the native tienda
across the square.

Into this scene Eneas looked for the last time. His donkeys,
loaded with the confort moderne, passed the tree and their gray
hides were reflected in the puddle. They drank from the fountain
and one of them raised his head, showed his teeth, and began his
peculiar song. The church bell clanked and a sudden wind shifted
the spray of the fountain. More water spilled and ran down over
the side.

The Salon Hollywood was boarded up, the shutters nailed together. Eneas, with an Indian carrying his belongings, walked to the bus for Ambato and soon was gone.

But the tragedy of Eneas repeated itself in Baños soon afterward, with disturbing similarity in details.

When one walks under the big tree on the plaza and looks into the water, one sees a small red flame burning in the water. It is the cloak of the Lord who sits outside the old church. He faces the square on a small table covered by his fiery velvet cloak and shaded by a small and broken black umbrella.

His face is cut out of polychrome wood; the agonized glass eyes are turned heavenward; his mouth is half open, showing a row of small real teeth behind his blue lips. His body is a ghastly mess of wounds and running blood. He is covered with them all the way down to the toes, which the Indians kiss all day long.

The statue is not without merit; it is Spanish baroque, vulgar, done in the spirit of butchery, but the modeling of the face, hands, and feet is exquisite work. It is very old.

On the poor head, above the crown of thorns, they have put a wig taken from a doll, a wig such as Shirley Temple dolls wear. Two long flaxen curls hang alongside the face, the rest down over the cloak in back. At the feet is a strong-box, and from the shoulders on a string dangles a sign which asks for alms: "Give me something for my temple."

The Indians bend the knee before him, give him their coppers and realitos; but they love much more the Madonna who sits inside the church. To her they pray and sing, "Santa María, Santa María, salve regina."

Even for the *misa de gallo,* the earliest mass, this church fills up. It is an adobe building with some stone here and there, ordinary windows, and a low roof. It is a church only because it is blessed and has a bell tower, otherwise it is just a long room divided into a place for the congregation and spaces for the altar, the confessional, and a small stone pulpit from which the padre preaches. It is lit by candles which the Indians buy, and they also bring from the surrounding fields the flowers which decorate the altar—mostly large white, sweet-smelling lilies.

Besides the padre there is a sacristan, a trembling, chalk-faced, ancient frater who never looks up and always prays so silently that one hears only "s—s—s—ps—ps—s—s—s" when he passes.

The Madonna between the altar and the confessional is the statue of a beautiful young girl, without sorrow. She is life-sized, painted in the ever-fresh tones of church statuary. She wears a forget-me-not-blue cloak over a snow-white dress, she is smiling, and all in all she looks as if she had just come out of a bath. The Indians have been told that she arrived in the middle of a very dark night, riding on a black donkey. The animal with its sacred burden pushed open the door of the church and walked in. Inside, it trotted up to the sacristan's bell, took the cord in its teeth, and—dingaling, dingaling—rang it until the sacristan and the padre were awakened. The Indians love the story and must hear it over and over; the old sacristan tells it to them once a week, standing in front of the Madonna. On the back of the statue, pressed into the stucco of which it is made, one can read that the Madonna came from very far; it says there: "Gebrüder Pustet, Fabrik Kirchlicher Geräte, Leipzig" and "Made in Germany N° 186432."

The old church in Baños was built by the Dominicans. They had rented it to the Franciscans and these brothers were not very happy with the arrangement. They said to each other that Baños could stand a second church, and that it was folly to pay rental to the Dominicans.

Not far from the old church they decided to build their own. The new edifice was high and entirely of stone. It was lit by electricity, had three altars and six confessionals. The pews were of costly woods, elaborately decorated; there was a runner down the center aisle for high holidays, and windows of stained glass. The main altar housed in its lower part a relic of Saint Francis, and in its tower hung three new bells.

The church was opened with processions and ringing of all the bells—with every ceremony known to the church. Hot-air balloons were sent up bearing the image of Saint Francis. It was lit not only with electric light but also with hundreds of candles. A new organ installed in a proper choir played in easy competition with the leaky antique instrument that is hidden behind the altar of the old church. The Indians came, wandered around in their bare feet, touched everything—with their hands and their eyes. They slowly took inventory of the new church, and then all of them ran back to their Madonna.

More resourceful and persevering than Eneas, the padres, who had noted the Indians' attachment to the holy Virgin, sent to Quito for one of the brothers who was a sculptor. He brought his tools and retired into the woods around Baños, where he began to carve a Madonna out of a seasoned piece of hardwood. One of the Indians, the one from whom he had obtained the wood, saw him and told the others, and when finally the Madonna was finished and set up in the new church, the Indians said, "Oh, no," and shook their heads; "that is not the real Madonna; our Madonna is in the old church. She came riding one night on a black donkey." Like children they remembered the story. Again they ran back to their church and asked the sacristan to tell it once more, and bought more candles than ever and decorated their Madonna with large bouquets of lilies and sang, "Santa María, Santa María, ora pro nobis!"

But even then the Franciscans did not give up. They reasoned that if Saint Francis, the Madonna, and Heaven did not help, perhaps the Devil would.

There arrived from Quito a large painting of Purgatory. It is one of numberless similar canvases that can be seen hanging in almost every large South American church. Baños until then had been without one.

Painted on panels which, when put together, form a picture twenty feet wide and eighteen high, it baffles the onlooker for a while with the maze of its figures. It is as obvious as a circus poster and painted in the same hues. Framed in fumes and flames and in the upraised arms of penitents, it depicts the Devil's holiday. He stands fanning flames with green batwings attached to his shoulders; his sweating assistants have the faces of black pigs from whose fangs issue blue and yellow flames like those from a plumber's torch. The catalogue of their amusements is a tiresome repetition of cooking people, sawing them in half, pinching and cutting up the rueful throng. Liars' lips are sewn together, thieves mutilated; and, to make it clear that this torture is not ended by death, one of the devils is shown driving spikes into a lecher's head, while the next one pulls them out again. In the center of the tableau is a most ingenious machine. The Devil himself is busy turning the crank. Attached with thorny twigs to a large, flaming wheel is a young, most carefully painted woman, altogether nude. She looks voluptuous and her sinful lips are half open; her flesh glares white in all the red, blue, and gaseous colors around her. The instrument to which she is tied is so built that as the Devil turns the crank, the girl's breasts and abdomen will sail into a crowded arrangement of spikes, hooks, small plowshares, and knives, which will disembowel her. The last victim, from whose blood the knives are still wet, is now at the bottom— an old bearded man, with the word "Adulterer" written across his body, roasting over an open fire.

Fortunately there is escape from all this. The sinners' eyes are hopefully lifted to a high, narrow bridge at the end of which stand two angels, one with a chalice in his hand, the other holding half open the door to Paradise. Beyond, half a mile inside Paradise, on a throne of silver clouds, sits the holy Virgin surrounded by Franciscan friars, with wings like angels, reading masses for the poor souls below and advising the Madonna for which of the sinners she is to intercede.

Hand in hand with the painting came a week of bell-ringing, processions, and exorcism. The Indians were there, all of them, and children were trampled as they crowded close to the picture. The padres explained it to them in detail—they asked to have the devils pointed out to them, and they listened to the story. The women sometimes left the church in tears, thinking of departed relatives and of their husbands' and children's future.

The padres granted reductions in the cost of indulgences, and lowered the prices of masses for the souls of the dead. It was possible to buy an amnesty of three hundred years in Purgatory for five realitos, and for a few days a thin stream of coins went into the treasury of the Franciscans.

All at once it stopped again, and the church was deserted. The sweet warm smell of the Indians, the revolting perfume of sweat and poverty, moved back to the Madonna. Soon afterward the new church closed. The doors and windows were bricked up, the old church inherited a bell and took a few of the pews. The great stone building stood forgotten; an avocado tree split its nave, and the fruits hang down over the altar. It echoes the cries of bats and of the small birds that are born in the electric light fixtures and in the tower.

The Franciscans left. Four donkeys, loaded with the eight panels of the picture of Purgatory, walked across the square and up toward Ambato.

THE RIDE WITH RAIN

On a Tuesday morning, shortly after the earliest mass, the truck from the Hacienda El Triunfo came up to the Gran Hotel Astor, and the mayordomo, Señor Rafael de Gangotena, sounded the horn several times. We drove off in a pink light, the sunrise reflected from a sky filled with small clouds. But first we had to stop at the Jefe Político's house to telephone our departure into the jungle.

Only a specialist can deal with the telephone here and send words over it. The local telefonista got out of bed and turned the little crank for a long while. With every feature strained he screamed into the apparatus, and then closed his eyes and held both earpieces to his head to listen. We sat down outside, and after a while the man came out exhausted and told the mayordomo that the message was delivered.

The telephone wire was with us as we went on. Beginning at the office in Baños, it runs over to the American Country Club, then to the side of the church, and along several telephone poles to the Gran Hotel Astor. Thence it is stretched over the pool to an avocado tree, next it swings loosely across the Pastaza, and from there on it follows the river, as the road does. The wire is old and camouflaged in greenery, and here at the beginning of the journey swallows are perched on it.

The road is wide and well built; the roar of water accompanies it to the right. This is the loudest river I have ever heard; it has the sound of a chorale played on tubas augmented by the sound of thin old wood breaking, of antique furniture being smashed.

Bridges are crossed, cars pass, the dust flies; and suddenly, after crossing three well-built bridges, the good part of the road comes to an end. Now it becomes narrow and hard to drive on, it crosses water again on a leaning wooden structure, and then it

239

ends completely and turns into a mule path. Here is the Río Negro, with a few houses standing to left and right. Today the river is not black but of a light shade of green, which turns into white foam wherever the water is parted by a rock.

As the green water falls here, it is blown to spray that fills the valley. Wet leaves nod in the strong current of air that descends with the river. There is a whir and a rattling as in a bad cabin on a tramp steamer, a tumult deep down in the earth like the turning of an engine. Everything is moist, a kind of upward rain hangs in the air, a glow of small opalescent soap-bubbles, and the rocks and leaves are rinsed in blue and red and violet as the light strikes them.

The mayordomo put a poncho on a rock and we sat and waited here. In the river a little below the falls there are boulders, put there by design or chance, so placed that a man can jump from one to another and cross over. I did not think that mules and donkeys could do it. They came out of the forest on the other side after we had waited three hours and had stared so long at the water that the falls seemed to be standing still. They jumped across the river one after another and then, wet with spray, they stopped near the truck and the rock on which we sat. The aroma of their cargo arrived ahead of them, a sticky sweet and alcoholic smell. Each of the animals carried on a packsaddle two rubber tanks of a distillate made from sugar cane. The black sacks were sewn into hemp bags and weighed about a hundred pounds apiece, one on each side of the animal. As the donkeys and mules were freed of their burden and the sacks stowed away in the truck, a hideous stench mingled with the odor of alcohol. It came from the packsaddles and the blankets that went across the animals' backs, and from the animals themselves.

From the shoulder to where the saddles ended, each animal was covered with shiny sores, and a part of the spine was laid bare. In red and yellow wounds, suppurating and immediately black with flies, small ends of white thread twisted, wriggled, and crawled—fine worms a few millimeters long. The filthy pieces of sacking that served as saddle-blankets were smeary with the discharge of the wounds.

As the animals were freed, they threw themselves on their

backs and rolled in the road. Then they tore at the grass and ate
it as quickly as they could. They went to drink water; and in
about two hours, when the cargo had all been stowed away, they
were saddled again. Now they carried bags of cement, machetes,
picks and shovels, and crates of stores. My baggage was wrapped
in oilcloth and tied to the right and left side of a donkey, and
then the first mule turned and started to cross the river.

In a long string the others followed, their ears up as they went
from rock to rock. But soon they were trotting along in stupor,
drunk with fatigue; there was no neighing from the few horses,
no donkey brayed, and only the drivers who ran alongside were
audible—forever singing the same string of curses.

The road swings up like a stairway alongside the Pastaza. It is
so high up in an hour, and so close to the river, that it becomes
intestinally disturbing—it is as if you were riding along the roof
of a building on a road made of soap, on a sleepy, stumbling
horse. In this acrobatic undertaking there is nothing to do but sit
still and trust to the four small hoofs. The river is so far below
that it is no louder than water turned on in the next room. There
comes a moment when the whole scene begins to wobble again,
when the aerial road turns suddenly upward and inward, in four
decisive turns. The horse reaches with his hoofs—and you wish
he had hands—to get a grip on the muddy stairs; he arches his
back, pulls upward, and you find yourself about five feet away
from the brink and going inland.

The horse on which I rode, an unkempt pony, folded his
front legs as in prayer when we went down the next mountain.
He took the curves of his own accord and all I had to do was to
sit still. The animal calculated, he knew exactly how far to lean
over to the right or the left; it is a breakneck descent and at the
bottom there is mud again. He was like a snake at one moment
and then like a frog; he crawled and hopped, and we were down
at the riverbed again and crossing the Pastaza. At the riverbank
the animals piled together and had a few minutes' rest. Crossing one after another, they became cats, feeling with outstretched
hoofs under the water until they found secure footing and tried
to look down through the green current; then they moved,
steadied themselves, looked, felt, and advanced again, always

standing diagonally in the strong current, the water up to their chests.

A donkey here costs two dollars, a mule three. These cheap, bad-looking, unkempt animals, all of them ill and many of them with fetlock joints, win all your attention, pity, and admiration. They are intelligent, resourceful, and brave, and they put you through a routine of fear, surprise, and gratitude that keeps eye and mind fixed on their hoofs and shoulders. There is nothing else you can look at on this first ride—a little patch of mud, water, a stone, or a bridge that appears around their ears just ahead.

In the next few kilometers a comparatively quiet passage followed, with only a few quebradas to climb down into and out of again. We came to a field with some banana plants and a few coffee bushes; alongside the road was a hut, and playing around it were several small black boars. It was the usual house, its walls made of split bamboo covered halfway with earth, an earthen floor and a cooking vessel, and the upper part black with smoke.

I observed what appeared from a distance to be a sweet domestic scene. Three people—a child, a woman, and a man—sat one behind the other and seemed to be arranging each other's hair. When I came near, I found that what they were doing was eating each other's lice. They searched for them with the manners and the industry of monkeys, parting the thick black hair, quickly taking the insects to lips and teeth and eating them. The group remained completely absorbed in their pursuits as the mules and donkeys passed them, and from far away at a turn in the road I still saw the three red ponchos close together.

We rode into the forest and then it began to rain. A lukewarm rain, dancing with gnats and mosquitoes; it doubled its pace a moment after it had begun and came in strings a few inches long. It changed the light, and everything became warm and moved closer together. It brought with it the stench from the galled backs of the animals, foul sweet air rising from the saddle as if it came from a heater, and above all else the smell of alcohol.

The water ran down from the sky as if a hose were being played on my hat; then it ran down over my nose; and after a while the inside of the hat got wet, and it ran to the shoulders, to the elbows, down to the horse and over the saddle. It weighed everything down and it was noisy. I wiped my face and shifted in my saddle and a new trickle went down inside my collar. The sound of the horses' hoofs was like pumps going, and all around water fell in sheets from the trees and flowed down over the large leaves. It bent strong flowers down until they emptied themselves and rose again. The saddle-leather stopped its twisting noises.

Sometimes the men whipped the donkeys and mules and they fought their way out of puddles and morasses into which they all but sank. We came to a swinging bridge, and here again they stuck their tired heads together and piled up, because only one at a time can cross. These bridges hang from wires that are fastened to rocks or trees or anchored into the ground and weighted down with stones. As the animal steps on the narrow slats of wood laid crosswise to form the floor, the bridge begins to sway and dance. Each new bridge has a different motion—some merely rotate, others follow the mechanics of a hairpin, with two periods of violent trembling before they come to a bend; some lurch upward and then slide off to the side and stand for a while like the roof of a house. Again the mules and donkeys were alert and had their ears up; they steadied themselves by bracing their front or back legs. According to the bridge, they would go forward with a rush on one, with a steady run on another, and creepingly on a third. Sometimes the bridges break and the animals drop into the river.

Toward late afternoon we climbed out of the low clouds. We passed some fields of sugar cane and for a long stretch the road was wide, smooth, and orderly as a park. There were waterfalls, and the perfume of plants and flowers, and a barefoot Indian passed, carrying on his back a large woven basket and a live giant ant-eater tied hand and foot.

In the wet green opening at the end of this part of the road stood a few houses, not enough to make a village. In front of one of the houses were some Indians and all the dogs of the settlement. I got off my horse and found them praying and standing around a chair, on which a child was sitting. The child was dressed in white, its hair decorated with silver wire and tinsel. It was a little girl, and she was dead. She must have been dead for a week; the face looked as if it had been rubbed in gray ashes. To make it sit up straight, a piece of the silver wire had been wound around the neck and attached to the back of the chair; the clay-like baby hands were folded together and tied with a rosary. There were vases of artificial roses, two candlesticks, and paper wings attached to the white dress. The dress, several sizes too large, was covered with lace and embroidery. The mayordomo explained it to me: the child, who is now an angel up in heaven, is kept as long as possible and rented out to relatives, and carried about in processions from house to house. This goes on until it is in such a state of decay that it can no longer be enjoyed. Then the child is finally placed in its coffin, with the words *"adiós, mamacita"* on the lid, and the properties are returned to the priest or the nuns from whom they were borrowed.

The parents and the relatives seemed completely happy with this arrangement. There was little wailing, the mother was again in a blessed state, the little brothers and sisters and the father had someone to pray for them up above—and it is a chance to celebrate, to drink, and to praise God and Santa María and the patron saint of the little angel.

The knotted telephone wire that had followed us all the way made a turn here, and there was a river to ford, and it became evening suddenly, without sunset. We rode on; a brace of small green parrots balanced themselves on the telephone wire; there was a new forest and beyond this a bridge made of logs close together with earth stuffed in between.

Beyond these logs was a way station, a hut called the Hacienda Mascota, where we were to stay overnight. It stands in a large fenced field which serves as a pasture for the animals, who must feed themselves during the night. Inside is a room for the master when he travels, a bed covered with mosquito netting, a clean pillow and sheets and a blanket, a gun, and a locker with a strong iron padlock to which I had a key. In the locker was a can of sardines, a candle, ammunition for the gun, and a box of soggy saltines full of ants. I gave the sardines to Aurelio, who took them to the cook to open the can.

Meanwhile the cargo had been stowed away under the porch, and the mule drivers had gone to the open-air kitchen and brewed

their yellow soup in a large pot—the national dish called "locro"
—corn soup with potatoes, eggs, and red pepper. The arrieros sat
in a long line around the porch; they fell asleep leaning against
one another and against the house. In their ponchos, with their
long, disorderly hair and beards, they might have been a tableau
of the Apostles on Mount Olivet, except that all of them looked
like murderers and stank of alcohol.

I walked out on the porch and saw my first jungle picture. Out
of the trees, moving jerkily as if on strings, came soft, black kites
with red ears. They directed their course to the pasture, toward
the grazing animals, and hovered over them. They were vampire
bats. They fluttered over the donkeys, mules, and horses un-
steadily for a while, and then they drank. The animals stood quite
still, without kicking or turning their heads: the operation must
have given them comfort. The bats flew off a way and vomited
the blood, and then returned for more.

I walked back to my room; I had to step over the mule drivers
to get inside. From out of the darkness around me came Aurelio's
voice. "The soup, patrón," he said. He had the table set and bread
laid out, and a small lamp which he lit. The cook had opened the
can and put the sardines into the soup along with the hard-boiled
eggs and the potatoes. "Is very good," said Aurelio.

THE RIDE WITH THE LONG NIGHT

I drank some orange juice for breakfast at the Hacienda Mascota, and waited until the horse was saddled. Aurelio had run up to get the oranges from an Indian.

The mule drivers, loading their animals, looked more romantic than ever. They never wash themselves or comb their hair; water does not touch them unless they fall into it or get caught in the rain.

There were some rabbits at the edge of the field with little ears like those of bats, and someone had shot a deer with an old musket. The Indian who took care of the Hacienda Mascota showed me the antlers and explained that they are turned inward so that the animal can move easily through the dense forest.

Two soldiers and a prisoner arrived—the soldiers in uniform, with guns and shoes, tired and disgusted; the prisoner with a loose, striped convict suit and barefoot, light and happy. One of the soldiers introduced the prisoner as Señor Hector Espinoza. He was a bad and dangerous fellow, the guards declared, and had to be watched carefully. Among his misdeeds was a spectacular escape. He had asked the kind warden of the Panóptico in Quito to let him attend the baptism of his last child and the warden had given him permission to go with a guard. The prisoner told the guard that he would like to buy a little flour to make a cake for the celebration, and the guard took him to a grocery store, where he asked for a kilo of flour. He took the bag without paying for it and exploded it in the guard's face. By the time the carabinero could see again, the bad man was gone. They caught him a year afterward; he was sentenced and sent to the penal colony in the jungle; and now he was being taken back to the Cárcel Municipal in Quito, as a witness in the trial of another felon.

At night they tied him up; in the daytime he ran ahead and sang, and the two soldiers ran after him.

The three shared the sardine soup of the day before and then went on.

Outside the stockade of the hacienda lay a dead donkey. The caretaker of the Mascota had cut the skin and the flesh from him, and left only his head and the ears. Inside the ribs was a dog who growled whenever anyone came near to disturb his meal.

From there on, the day was like the first. The road went up and down, the animals swayed on bridges and wound their way a day's ride farther into the jungle.

About five in the afternoon of that day, Aurelio came close and pointed up into a tree. I had to look long and hard in the direction in which he pointed; so protective is the design that I would never have seen it myself. Some shiny green became a serpent, a sliding mass in all the other green of leaves: in the light greens, the dark greens, the saw-toothed green, and the deceiving shadows of palm leaves, a solid, dangerous mass of coils, it moved, slid, braced itself as if it had invisible arms and legs. The foliage about it trembled; a group of parrots flew past and then all was still again.

Late that day I noticed an increase in the echoes as the leaves and trees were suddenly without shadow, and then quickly night set in. It is like turning down a lamp. The trees change their form and take on soft contours, the green becomes slate-colored, and within it the small red fires of the wild orchids glow and then die. Tree embraces tree, and the things that grow downward and upward lose their ends and beginnings. It is all tired and caressing, it hums and chats awhile before going to sleep; and then new noises, small shrieks, yells, and deep bass voices take over. It breathes with a loud breath and even in the dark you feel that it is green here. An air root that swings from the branch of a tree comes out of the darkness, another one, invisible, touches your shoulder farther on, and then all at once it is as if you sat in the cabinet of a spiritualist, hung about with large sheets of black velvet that drink up all the light. You sit helpless in a bath of night; the saddle below you moves up and down, and through it you feel the horse, warm and walking, and imagine its head and tail and ears, but they are not there; nor can you even see your hands, though you bring them up to your nose.

Aurelio sees and the horse sees. Aurelio comes alongside and says, "A tree, patrón—watch out in front of you," and then I lie down flat over the saddle and there is a tree, a low arch across the road; I think I am going to bump into it, but it brushes down my back like a moldy sack.

"Look out, patrón, a bridge"—and look out, a river; the bridge sways, the river is wet. Farther on there is a cool current of air on the right, and then comes the sound of water running in the next room and the horse goes slower and has his head all the way down. He has pulled the reins forward and I know that under my right stirrup, with the smallest margin between us, is the river far below.

The horse is drunk with fatigue; he makes a false step, stumbles over a root, and you almost hear the angels sing; but that also passes, and awhile later, farther on, at a point where we come out of the forest, all at once—as if someone had thrown a burning coal on the black velvet—there is red light, a glowing stove hung in the sky; and silhouetted against it is the outline of the volcano Sangay. The road is visible now, and the scenery reminds you of a tropical cabaret in which everything is lit by red lanterns; and so it continues to a small village with a church, a tailor with his Singer sewing machine and charcoal pressing iron, a small shop, and a hotel with a bar.

Here the jaded animals were dismissed again, to seek their food in the dark. The mule drivers had a place to sleep somewhere and the mayordomo waved to the hotel—it has just "Hotel" written on it, no name. The electric light here burns from six to nine. A Salesian padre was walking up and down with a man in riding boots, and the proprietor of the hotel received us with many compliments. I bought a box of saltines and a can of sardines, the only available food in the store, opened the can myself, and retired into a quiet corner in back of the house to eat them.

Aurelio carried the saddle and bridle upstairs, and I asked the Spanish proprietor for a room. He said with many fine words that he was delighted, and to take the room on the right upstairs, in which already two caballeros had put their belongings. The may-

ordomo was also put into this room. I asked him next for a washroom, and he ran to a door a few feet away, opened it, and gave
me a lamp: outside was a large field with trees around.

"Be not sad, patroncito," said Aurelio; "you must accustom
yourself to this comfort."

I drank some whisky and walked up and down, and Aurelio
walked a few feet in back of me; and then the electric light was
turned off in the street, and we decided to go to bed.

Upstairs we found the two caballeros asleep in one bed, and
the mayordomo and I were to take the other. "I like to sleep near
the wall," said the mayordomo. The bed was an arrangement of
boards with a thin, beaten, and filthy mattress over them. The
snoring caballeros had covered themselves with blankets; a smoking petroleum lamp stood on a box, and the windows were without screens. Señor Rafael de Gangotena closed the shutters, and
when I asked him why, he drew his finger across his throat and
told me that across the river was the penal colony and that sometimes the convicts escaped and murdered travelers.

He then barred the door with the chair, put his revolver next
to his head, spat out of the bed in a curve onto the floor, turned
over, and went to sleep. Immediately the air in the room was like
that of a crowded saloon; a soggy wet heat rose from the floor,
moved out from the bed and the walls, and came down from the
ceiling.

The walls of the room were papered, and after having quietly
opened a window, I took the lamp and sat down on a box to read.
The walls were papered with copies of the *Schweizer Hausfrau*.
The first article that I came to was one of a series on good manners. The author seemed to be troubled in that installment by
the problem of what to do with a lighted cigar. "What to do on
meeting a lady"—the article began—"while walking along the
street, wearing a hat, carrying an umbrella, and with a lighted
cigar in one's mouth:

"When one carries an umbrella in one hand, has a hat on one's
head and a lighted cigar in one's mouth, and meets a lady, one
naturally takes the lighted cigar into the right hand, moves the
umbrella up over the arm, then takes the cigar and puts in into
the hand that holds the umbrella, thus leaving the right hand

free to remove the hat. One can also stop and say a few friendly words to the lady. Under no circumstances does one leave the cigar in one's mouth while talking to the lady, even while removing the hat. Of course no one will be so rude as to come for a visit to a lady with a lighted cigar in his mouth."

An exchange of letters and several personal notices followed this useful advice.

" 'How can hemorrhoids be quickly and thoroughly cured?' asks a young woman, Mrs. S. H. of Rorschach. ANSWER: 'Hemorrhoids are cured quickly and thoroughly and most easily if for three or four weeks you eat two oranges a day. After a few days of this cure the hemorrhoids will begin to shrink and in fourteen days they disappear completely. Wishing you success [*Guten Erfolg wünschend*]'—Frau Lehrer Dubeli, Zürich."

"On account of death, for sale: 3 bird cages, 1 apparatus for perspiring in bed [*ein Bettschwitz Apparat*], a leather sofa in good condition, and twelve easy lessons in French."

The last article in this group was a melancholy announcement by Herr Lehrer Kläui in Brüggen, near St. Gallen, who offered to educate unruly boys and guaranteed success.

When I looked away from the last line, I saw a swarm of insects sitting around me. They came in through the open window and flew into the lamp. I closed the window again and killed the mosquitoes and beetles; the dead bugs lay on the table and the chair and on the floor. And then I fell asleep.

THE DAY WITH HUNGER

The two caballeros were still snoring at the Swiss wallpaper—
at a part where some poems by Hölderlin appeared in a Sunday
supplement—and the door was blocked by the tilted chair.
Through the cracks in the floor came smoke.

I went out to see if the hotel was on fire. The smoke rose in a
twisted smeary column from under the building. The hotel stood
on long poles, on which two monkeys on strings slid up and down,
and the kitchen was under our room. A woman cook was below,
barelegged in stockings of mud, a parrot on her shoulder and at
her feet an assistant who fanned the flames.

As usual Aurelio had slept on the floor outside my room. He
stood up in his poncho and disappeared to get out horses. An old
proverb here says that half the journey is getting out of the inn.

The mayordomo was next to appear and ordered breakfast
for us both.

A table was set on the veranda of the hotel. Out of a closet
came a tablecloth reserved for distinguished guests; it was egg-
stained and tomato-spotted. A handful of tinware, forks, and
spoons, were set down. The mayordomo put his revolver next to
his plate and looked in the direction of the oven. The cook
brought milk and coffee. Here in the land where some of
the world's best coffee grows, if you love coffee you must bring
your own and a percolator besides. In Ecuador and the rest of
South America, in good and bad hotels alike, they cook the coffee
long in advance, brewing a foul ink of it, which is cooled and kept
in a bottle. Half a cupful of this dye is poured out, the sugar bowl
emptied into it, and a little warm milk added on.

The mayordomo ate and drank and asked me why I did not eat.
I had an omelet with tomato in front of me, and although I was
very hungry and had not had a proper meal for days, I had no in-

tention of eating it. I had wiped my fork and spoon and was starting on the cleaner end of the plate, when I looked across the square
and saw a butcher stand. There under a big tree stood a wobbly
box. It was covered with tin, an old oil can cut in pieces and nailed
over it. An Indian woman with a baby tied to her back stood next
to the box with a leg of mutton in her dirty fingers. Overhead was
a cloud of flies, so thick that you could reach into it, squeeze a
fistful together, and throw them away. The woman had a machete
and with this she carved the meat, the way you sharpen the end
of a fence post. I sent Aurelio to buy two bananas for my breakfast.

For short intermissions we came out of the forest and then we
rode into it again. The jungle has doors—like entrances to green-
houses. Outside there is a wall of earth, thickly covered with a rug
of small leaves that resemble laurel. Sunk into these, solitary and
apparently stemless, are little flowers, gentians. Then you come
to an arrangement, bright as traffic lights, of pretty shrubs with
tubiform flowers, copious reddish blossoms; and the chalk-colored
blooms of geranium trees stand high in back. From a stagnant
pond, crowded with weeds and small fat plants that resemble
watercress, the black limbs of dead trees reach out, and on them
sits an army of flies, bugs, and beetles in the colors of sulphur,
arsenic, and copper.

There are rows of ferns on the green band of the wall, their
compound fleshy fronds stuck into the turf; and then you are
inside and a botanical monotony begins.

Against the flat green-gray curtain of the background soar
the trees, and the parasites that grow out of trees. In this steam
bath are acacias, odoriferous flowers, yellow with binate spines
three inches long, and fern trees with lacy leaves six feet in length.
Bushes also grow on the trees, and everywhere are orchids.

From under our horses' hoofs came clouds of butterflies, some
white and some with the pattern and color of mock turtle soup on
their wings. After a while the very large orchids took on the shape
of immense sauce-boats standing and hanging in the branches.
Under them were huge leaves that had decayed or been toasted
crisp brown; they began to resemble filets of sole cooked in butter—the very brown ones like pompano cooked in a paper bag

—and the orchids, which were a strong fine yellow, seemed like dishes of mayonnaise.

I smelled other cooking too. It seemed as if invisible cooks were hidden in the jungle, and with painful, accurate detail of shape, color, and taste—and, above all, smell—held dish after dish under my nose only to take it away for a better one. I dreamed an immense bill of fare for the next few miles, a nightmare that began with assorted hors d'œuvre: céleri rémoulade, saucissons d'Arles, the hams of Poland, of Virginia, of York, of Westphalia, of the Ardennes and Bayonne, the choucroute garnie, the Tiroler Bauernschmaus. Then the soups: vichyssoise, germiny à l'oseille, onion soup au gratin, and marmite with marrow dumplings. The fish course followed: swordfish steaks, shad and roe, clam pan roast, cold barbue, and cold salmon. Confusion set in after this: hashed brown potatoes mixed with ham and eggs appeared. Pâté de foie gras, mackerel in tomato sauce, Bismarck herring and other agreeable pickles, bouillabaisse and pilaff with chicken livers, curry and chutney and Bombay duck, canard à la presse, and a tray of assorted cheeses—Camembert, Brie, Pontl'Evêque, Roquefort.

After I had gone through all the bills of fare, I thought of restaurants and their proprietors, their décor, doormen, potted palms, white and gold interiors, cherubs, orchestras, coat-racks, and of their service good and bad.

Of the vulgar tubs of butter at the Reine Pédauque, of the Restaurant Numa back of the Madeleine and its stacks of escargot plates. Of the big places in Copenhagen and Rotterdam with the red carpets, the immense waiters, and the terrines of soup in which, under a lake of melted butter, asparaguses thick as thumbs swam around. The carpets were dark as oxblood, and the people with stiff napkins tied around their necks sat eating for three hours. And Tirol, and hunger from skiing, a different language spoken at every table in an inn as remote as the little Flexen in Zürrs; the Salontöchter in the Swiss hotels, the stew made with Steinpilze, the peasant women who brought the little strawberries down from the fields. The restaurant in the basement of the Grand Central Terminal in New York, the part with the counters on the right, where you are served by waiters who rank second in gruffness and bitter faces only to those of the Lafayette, but where you get the best ham and eggs in the world, and seafood and stews that are rare.

The Chinese restaurants; the Grotta Azzurra in downtown New York in a cellar with horrible murals, mostly frequented by political rabble, where they cook lobster with small Italian plum tomatoes and where a waiter who looks like d'Annunzio brings you half a dozen napkins with the lobster and three plates for the empty claws and shells; and then, a little farther uptown, Luchow's. . . .

When I am in New York I usually cross Fourteenth Street and revolve the door of Luchow's on Sunday evenings. It is then that a small private miracle takes place. I sit down and watch for the arrival of occasional and peculiar guests. Where they come from I do not know. From a museum down the street, I think, where they are prepared for this visit with infinite care, where the men's noses are painted red, and the thin blue veins of too good living are etched on their cheeks; where antique Prince Alberts are taken out of camphor and brushed.

Here I have seen a Schubert and two Brahmses, and on their arms lovely old Winterhalter ladies. One man who comes is a Lenbach portrait of Freiherr von Menzel the court painter, and another looks like my friend, the eighty-year-old K.K. Hofschauspieler of the Munich Theater, Konrad Dreher. For their entrances, the orchestra fiddles through forgotten Waldteufel music. It is sad and *hausgebacken;* it seems as if outside, instead of the bawdy street, there should be the stop for the green and white trolley-car to Nymphenburg. The years of hopelessness and disgrace that have changed all this seem but a cloud of cigar smoke, rheumatism, beer, and Kalbsbraten.

At about that part of the restaurant dream my horse stumbled; I woke up and began to smell cooking—real cooking. We came into a clearing again and I hoped that we might be near a small hacienda which perhaps belonged to someone who had a chicken on the fire, or that we were at least in the vicinity of the hut of a Salesian padre—these good men sometimes cook for themselves. Between two large walls of earth, we saw a native hut from whose neat chimney smoke was rising; there was also some promise in washing that hung in the sun to dry, and in a well-fed dog.

I slid off my horse and found an oven at the back of the house, where an Indian woman was busy with food. She had a friendly face and she was reasonably clean. There was soup on the fire and she was busy cleaning out a monkey. She cut him up, going inside him with her knife, turning over the blade as if stirring stomach, liver, lungs, and then emptying him out. She singed off the hair and cooked him over an open fire. Another woman and a man came and sat down, and they ate the monkey, the man taking an arm and starting by eating the inside of the palm. He nibbled at the fingers and spat out the nails. The woman bit into the ears first. It was like eating a baby. My hunger was gone—I got on my horse and rode away.

Rafael de Gangotena came galloping back to me and wondered where I had been, and he said that we would be at the Hacienda El Triunfo in half an hour. He warned that ahead was a deep ravine bridged by two trees with earth stuffed in between, and said not to worry, the horse knew the bridge and would walk across and just to let him go.

The bridge came, and after it the hacienda. We were met by Don Antonio, the oldest son of the owner.

What music there can be in the sound of bathwater running into a tub, in hearing a cocktail mixed; and what pleasure in a simple table laid, and a bottle of wine in a bucket. There was even a bathtowel, a clean one, and a cake of soap.

THIS IS ROMANCE

The Hacienda El Triunfo reaches over several mountains and up into two valleys. It is bordered by three rivers and most of its ground is cleared of jungle. The trees have been cut and left lying where they fell; a wide stretch of land is planted in sugar. It grows and then is cut. The sugar is taken to a shed where it is put through rollers that extract the juice. The juice runs into large vats where it ferments; into stills where it is turned into alcohol.

The alcohol is poured into rubber sacks. The sacks are carried by mules and donkeys to Río Verde. From Río Verde the truck takes them to Ambato, to the office of the Estanco de Alcoholes, where a Government inspector takes them over. It is bottled, flavored, and sold to the Indians. A very simple arrangement that leaves a nice profit to the state and to the owner of the hacienda.

Labor is cheap, mules are cheaper; the one costly item is the machinery. When the sugar press has to be replaced, most hacendados would buy an American one, but the Krupp works offer one just as good for half the price and worry about installation and replacements.

The motor that drives the rollers, however, is American. It is an ordinary Willys-Knight motor, taken out of a used car. Its owners speak of it with respect and affection as if it were a person. The motor was carried into the jungle in three weeks' time, the heavy parts by detachments of forty Indians. Since it was set up in a shack at the Hacienda El Triunfo, it has run five times around the world. Its speedometer is attached to it. It runs at an average speed of thirty miles an hour, day and night.

A group of boys, their hair, faces, clothes, and feet crusted and smelling like custards, feed the sugar cane into the rollers, and the sweet brook flows down a gutter through the roof of the house below. From this house comes the sweet alcoholic stench that fills the valley and attaches to everything that is here and trails out of the jungle with the mules all the way to Baños.

Some cacao, some coffee are grown here. There are a few banana forests, and experiments with California fruits—notably navel oranges and grapefuit—and with peach and apple trees are made here. This varies the green of the fields here and there; it is a private hobby of the owner. The money comes from sugar. It is extremely simple.

It all can be understood in ten minutes. At noon a siren blows. There is an eight-hour day, a paymaster, a doctor's shed, a breeding farm for donkeys and mules. The animals are fed the tender ends of the sugar cane, the juicy tops that are too small to press, and as long as they are young and not in service, the horses and donkeys are all fat and strong and healthy. Once they start working they wear out, and when they are through they are left whereever they fall and are replaced by new ones.

On a hill is the house where the owner and his sons live. One side of it overlooks the industrial part. On that side are the kitchen, the pantry, the store rooms, and the servants' quarters. The other side faces the jungle. The building is high up on stilts, and from the guests' rooms out over the land below hangs a wide veranda; leaning over it you have the sensation of looking from the bridge of a ship.

The walls, the partitions between the rooms, are made of split bamboo that is whitewashed. The beds are made of wood, the mattress supported by rawhide strips which are laced from one side of the bed to the other. In each room is a closet, a gun, ammunition.

A few yards from the house is a communal washstand with a shower bath. The shower is a barrel high up, filled by a boy who climbs a ladder. In this small house is also a bathtub. It smells of chlorine here and recalls the sanitary comforts of the barracks in army cantonments during the last war.

A cook and an assistant are busy around a small oven, and a boy waits on the table, wearing a white jacket when guests are present. The food is very good, with respectable French wines and an occasional bottle of champagne. Cocktails are served and whisky and soda.

In the afternoon the strip of the greenest green, that of the valley filled with sugar cane, is altogether like water, and then the illusion of being on shipboard is strongest. When it is evening, and the moon rises, a large improbable yellow signal, when Sangay colors one half of the sky red and the jungle exhales its peculiar and wondrous perfume, and the mists roll up against it, then it is theater.

On Altamir Pereira's shoulder at that moment usually sits his pet monkey. He holds onto his ears with his long cold fingers and repeatedly draws his cheeks back in short, fixed, and malicious grinning, and then he searches in the young man's thick black hair.

Altamir is dark and handsome, an aristocrat with a mole under the left eye, with enough brutality in his face to save him from being pretty. Into this musical-comedy backdrop he sings "You're the Cream in My Coffee," and then his favorite:

> This is romance,
> It's an omen of splendor,
> And you turn to surrender
> In a night such as this.

> This is romance,
> There's a sky to invite us,
> And a moon to excite us,
> Yet you turn from my kiss.

He goes through it stanza after stanza; he knows every word and pronounces it carefully. He has an old gramophone that is turned on most of the time, and he runs through all the Broadway moaning of the past ten years.

That night, after he had sung "She's a Latin from Manhattan," he turned and said, "Ah, American girls are standard—those legs, that skin. Ah, I don't know what it is, but no other woman on earth has it so much." He took a deep breath and sighed again and finished his song, his eyes half closed.

"Tell me about New York," he said. "Gee, the last time I was there, two years ago, someone introduced me to Joan Crawford at a party, in El Morocco, and to Franchot Tone. And here we are in this goddamn jungle. By God, couldn't you get me a job somewhere in New York? I'd do anything to get out of here."

The American songwriter, producer of musical shows and moving pictures, has nowhere more faithful followers than the youth of South America. Everything American is O.K. or swell or peachy. They have taken over all our slang words, some of them dated, and they love to speak in a Brooklyn jargon, talking out of the side of the mouth.

They know by experience that the beauty and the leniencies of the Parisienne are a fable, and they seem to think otherwise of New York. In nine out of ten cases, the locale of the small, transient ménages which they love to establish is in the neighborhood of Riverside Drive and the Seventies, around the Charles M. Schwab edifice.

Another favorite locality, dense with tender memories, is on the heights around Columbia University. The ladies in these episodes are always blond and beautiful beyond their power to say. They all are sweet, chic, completely unattached, and liberal-minded, and their names are handy, smart, easy to remember, like the roll-call of a musical comedy chorus.

The young men of wealth have access to the upper East Side, and to Long Island. They know the good restaurants, and their families stop in midtown hotels, usually in large suites together with their servants, whom they bring along. Two of the Pereira sons were born in New York, and they therefore refer to the Plaza as the Maternity Hotel.

The bamboo poles of the veranda vibrated all evening to the music of George Gershwin and Cole Porter. Into the night, like boys in a dormitory, they kept their conversation going through the airy walls. I had to listen to every word that Miss Crawford said that evening, to the details of a house party at Sands Point; and I had a clear picture of the charms and the anatomy of a dozen American girls.

Altamir was pale and wan the next morning. He said he couldn't sleep all night thinking about American girls. During breakfast an Indian came up and asked to see the patroncito. The Indians here are decently treated and come with their problems and requests direct to the master. There are no Great Danes to protect him from them.

The Indian whined in the manner of a small boy asking his mother for something he knows he will not get. He said that one of his friends had just returned from Quito, where he had worked at the British Legation, and that there at the Legation they had what is called the English weekend. He had talked it over with the other Indians and they all agreed that it would be very nice to have the English weekend at the Hacienda El Triunfo. He had come to ask the patroncito what he thought about the idea of having the English weekend. The patroncito asked him to repeat the story and then laughed, and the Indian laughed. The patroncito put his arm around the Indian's shoulder, and the Indian, laughing with all his teeth, said that he had just thought it might be a good idea, and left. The problem was solved—no English weekend.

We went into the jungle several times, on horseback and on foot, at my request, and also to visit the headhunters. We heard stories that they were very bad, and as many stories of how good they were. It was laborious portage. On the rides in the surrounding country we took a compass and a bugle. Even natives get lost here; but we always found the way home.

The jungle itself, once you are used to looking at parrots outside a cage, and at orchids without a florist near them, becomes fatiguing in its sameness—green, green, green—water green, moss green, tree with green orchids, green tree with parrots, fallen green tree—climb over it—monkeys and their repertoire, repeated a thousand times with no variation in scenery.

The Indians that live along the roads, the workers and Government people and the whites, are unhealthy-looking, flabby, with yellow in the whites of their eyes and yellow in their skins; even the Negroes seem chrome-yellow under the surface. The teeth of all of them are bad.

You come occasionally upon a small store. The stock consists of ammunition for antique firearms, of Chiclets (you find these throughout Ecuador), of patent medicines all trademarked Bayer, manufactured in Leverkusen, Germany; cheap padlocks with the Yale trademark, also made in Germany; candies wrapped

in tinfoil in very bright metallic colors in large glass jars; cans of
sardines and herring in tomato sauce; whisky, chiefly White Horse,
the seal broken and the whisky cut; and brandy, Marie Brizard
and Hennessy, also cut; pictures of saints; crosses and candles;
no newspapers, no magazines, no writing materials; a few pairs
of shoes for men, and cloth for women; machetes; and buckshot
in glass jars.

There are spare parts for sewing machines, for the American
Singer and the German Pfaff. "To know how to repair a broken
sewing machine is very important here," said Altamir. He could
take any one of them apart and put it together again. The natives
are as grateful for that as for the ministrations of a doctor.

We met a wandering photographer, a man with a box such as
one finds in public parks, and a piece of sleeve attached to his
box camera through which he reaches into it to develop the pictures while the subject waits. He had nailed photographs which
he had taken all over the outside of the large wooden camera.
Looking through them, I saw several girls who had had their picture taken with a sewing machine, in the fashion of people elsewhere who have themselves taken with a car or a horse.

On the longest of these trips we came to the settlement of some
Jivaros, the headhunters of the Amazon. They were hospitable
and friendly. We sat for a while on the floor of an elliptical house.
Altamir spoke a few words of their language. We had to drink
chicha. They seemed intelligent, their fields were in good order,
the house was cleaner than those of any of the Indians around
Quito. A boy performed miracles with a blowgun, shooting Altamir's hat full of holes. They allowed us to inspect their equipment,
and they were all healthy and very clean.

The poison, the famous curare, with which they hunt, Altamir
informed me, they no longer brewed, but bought from white
traders. It came most probably from a chemical firm in Germany,
he said. The only jungle note I could detect was the jaw of a
vicious little fish, the piranha, which hangs next to the vessel in
which they carry the poison. Before dipping the dart into the
semi-solid fluid, they notch it with the teeth of this fish, so that
the end is almost cut off. Monkeys, when hit, quickly pull the
missiles out of their skin, and the poison would have no effect.

As it is, the point breaks off, and the monkey drops down in a few minutes.

The women of the Indians we saw had surprisingly attractive and almost Castilian features; the men seemed amused, and continually smiled. I hoped to find a shrunken head, and I looked around everywhere, inside the house and in back, and under trees, as one would look for a forgotten canvas in a house recently occupied by a painter. But nowhere was there a sign of one, or the sign of blood, or of any preparations. The household was in order, a complete set of pots and pans, of bed and baby clothing. There was nowhere a man without a head. We said good-by to the Jivaros, and gracefully and politely as Chinese they let us go.

Back at the hacienda's donkey farm, I made the mistake of admiring a young animal, and it was given to me as a present. Filomena was her name. She was pretty as a majolica vase is pretty, or a Spanish shawl, or a Massenet elegy; and at first she aroused the protective dislike that such prettiness always evokes. This had to be overcome.

Filomena was three feet high, with another foot of ears, all in wool as soft as a new chinchilla coat, with four white stockings and ebony hoofs. She wore a black mask across the face, and out of this shone her large, intelligent, and stubborn female eyes. All in all it was a costume for *A Midsummer-Night's Dream,* made to the specifications of Walt Disney.

I took her along with me when I left the hacienda and started on the way back to Baños. She danced at the side of the road in and out of the forest, and amused everyone with her caprices, with her sudden stops, her nervous hops to left and right, with falling asleep and with inquisitiveness that often ended in fearful surprises. She slept with Aurelio, and sometimes she ran ahead and at other times she came along after us. Altamir and I and Aurelio rode our horses close together.

We left the Swiss Hotel the morning of the second day, and came to the swinging bridges, over which Filomena had to be carried. She was light as a bird. And then we came to the aerial road, where the horses go down the three dangerous steps to a ledge that hangs out over the Pastaza's bed a thousand feet below. Filomena danced out of the forest and jumped and then she was gone. She kicked and turned, becoming smaller and smaller. I saw her fall for a long while and then she was out of sight far below us. I remembered the headline in Guayaquil: "YOUNG GIRL DESCENDS THREE STORIES."

"I have no gun, only a revolver," said Altamir, "and if I could go to a place where I could see her, I might not hit her with a revolver, only wound her. To go back for a gun is out of the question. I know you are sentimental about animals," he said, and repeated, "I have no gun, only a revolver. I cannot get down there; I would not go down for a man, even. What I mean is, I can get down, but I would never come up again. Neither would the donkey. Perhaps she is dead. If she is not dead, all her legs are broken. Good—so what will happen? Tonight, when it is dark, two green eyes come out of the leaves, and one smack of the paw and a little hot breath, big white teeth, and not much pain, and it's all over. The tigrillo will eat her up, and tomorrow Filomena is part tiger, a proud fate for a donkey," he said.

> There was a young lady of Niger
> Who smiled as she rode on a tiger.
> They returned from the ride
> With the lady inside
> And the smile on the face of the tiger.

We rode on, and after a while he started a long description of a blonde, who loved him for five weeks in Saratoga, where his papa went to take the cure. "Brr," he said, "cold up there in September. . . . You know what you could send me when you get back—a pullover. A pullover is very useful down here. It gets cold so suddenly. I feel cold now. Feel my hands."

DREAM IN BROOKLYN

The road coming back from anywhere is always much shorter than in the first passage over it. Altamir Pereira rode alongside as far as the Hacienda Mascota, excused himself once more for inadequate hospitality and for the fiasco with Filomena, gave me a list on which he had written the names of gramophone records he wanted sent to him and the size of the pullover. Then he wheeled his horse and rode back.

I came to a grotto late that day, a hollow room in the side of a mountain large enough to put a cathedral inside it. Its walls were lined with mosses and ferns, all of them wet, dripping, green, and fresh. Bats, asleep, hung stored away on the ceiling, and a mute column of dark, leaden water flowed into basins of stone. Small lizards ran their fiery patterns along the walls. At the stone basins two donkeys were standing drinking, and an Indian was playing on a flute. The donkeys were loaded with equipment, and between them was a small one, as pretty and with the same coloring as Filomena; and except for the few hours of pain, the memory of the slow descent, it was a kind of resurrection.

It is one of the cursed things about owning a movie camera, or just a plain camera, that you cannot look at such scenes quietly and leave them alone and go away. They cry out to be filmed, particularly when they have color possibilities. It is then that you have to get off your horse, find the light-meter, measure the light, judge the distance, jump from left to right, look back at the sun, check the light again, measure the new distance, and then wonder whether it would not be a more interesting composition from the other side.

In the meantime, the donkeys have had enough water and wander away, the Indian has stopped playing his flute, become interested in the camera and come closer to inspect it. When finally he is arranged in an interesting group with his animals, his face is frozen and without quality, the donkeys are clumsy, and all freedom is gone from the scene.

Furthermore, whenever something rare has presented itself on the street, in a bullring, at the door of a prison, on a mountain, or in the water, I have always found that my camera was either in the top drawer of my wardrobe trunk at the hotel, that I had used up all the film, or forgotten to wind the motor. I have promised myself again and again not to take the machine along, but again and again I do; and it is a disturbing and unpleasant companion.

I asked the Indian in the grotto to drive his animals ahead of him down the road. He wore a deep purple poncho, the road was like a zebra skin, slashed with lights and shadows, and I wanted to follow him awhile with the lens. After ten feet of film had been run off, I came to a curve and saw in my finder, sitting on a rock, Allan Ferguson. He was burnt black, he wore a poncho, and he looked even more distinguished in it than when he sat at the explorers' table at the Metropolitano in Quito. He stood up and waved. He had lost weight.

He was just resting a little, he said, and the Indian and the donkeys were with him. He had been six months in the Oriente, and he added in the crushed tones of failure that he had been looking for gold. He pulled a small vial from the pocket of his shirt and poured some gold into the palm of his big hand, two irregular nuggets, almost round, three worn, blunt fishhooks, and a golden nail.

"That there is gold in there is certain," he said, as if to excuse his presence.

He said that everyone who had gone in had found some, but no one had yet found the Valverde treasure.

Of all the golden legends of South America, the legend of the Valverde treasure is perhaps the most plausible and the only one that has rewarded those who have gone after it. At least they have all come back with a few dollars' worth of souvenirs.

The treasure is the ransom which the Indians collected to free Atahuallpa. Among all the old and faded papers that are guides to buried treasures—texts which have the cozy gurgling sound of a roulette wheel, and are also as full of promise as a prayer— the Derrotero of Valverde is among the most convincing. The document was written by the Spaniard Valverde on his deathbed and illustrated with a carefully drawn map made by one Atanasio Guzman, an unfortunate man, a somnambulist, who one night walked out of his house and fell into a ravine, where he perished.

The original Guide was stolen from out of the archives of the city of Latunga, and no one knows precisely when it was written. It is known that the King of Spain instructed the Corregidors of Ambato to search most diligently for the treasure. They organized the first expedition, and they were the first to return without it, having lost the padre who accompanied them mysteriously just on the spot where the gold was supposed to be hidden.

Allan Ferguson said that the Guide was simple and direct, and almost photographically correct, until one came to the end of it. He sighed deeply, hunched over his mule as he talked, his long legs almost walking along with the four feet of the animal. We had to stop at the Río Verde. A bridge had been washed away, and repairs were being made that would take a few hours. A little way from the river is a small house that serves as an inn, and here we sat down to rest awhile.

Ferguson searched in his saddle-bags and came back with the copy of the "Guide to the Valverde Treasure" and the Guzman map. He unfolded both, moved his finger along the text, and read it aloud to me:

"Placed in the town of Pillaro, ask for the farm of Moya, and sleep (the first night) a good distance above it; and ask there for the mountain of Guapa, from whose top, if the day be fine, look to the east, so that thy back be toward the town of Ambato, and from thence thou shalt perceive the three Cerros Llanganati, in the form of a triangle, on whose declivity there is a lake, made by hand, into which the ancients threw the gold they had prepared for the ransom of the Inca when they heard of his death. From the same Cerro Guapa thou mayest see also the forest, and in it a clump of *sangurimas* standing out of the said forest, and another clump which they call *flechas* [arrows], and these clumps are the principal marks for the which thou shalt aim, leaving them a little on the left hand. Go forward from Guapa in the direction and with the signals indicated, and a good way ahead, having passed some cattle-farms, thou shalt come on a wide morass, over which thou must cross, and coming out on the other side thou shalt see on the left hand, a short way off, a *jucal* on a hillside, through which thou must pass. Having got through the *jucal,* thou wilt see two small lakes called 'Los Anteojos' [the spectacles] from having between them a point of land like to a nose,

"From this place thou mayest again descry the Cerros Llanganati, the same as thou sawest them from the top of Guapa, and I warn thee to leave the said lakes on the left, and that in front of the point or 'nose' there is a plain, which is the sleeping-place. There thou must leave thy horses, for they can go no further. Following now on foot in the same direction, thou shalt come on a great black lake, the which leave on thy left hand, and beyond it seek to descend along the hillside in such a way that thou mayest reach a ravine, down which comes a waterfall; and here thou shalt find a bridge of three poles, or if it do not still exist thou shalt put another in the most convenient place and pass over it. And having gone on a little way in the forest, seek out the hut which served to sleep in, or the remains of it. Having passed the night there, go on thy way the following day through the forest in the same direction, till thou reach another deep dry ravine, across which thou must throw a bridge and pass over it slowly and cautiously, for the ravine is very deep; that is, if thou succeed not in finding the pass which exists. Go forward and look for the signs of another sleeping-place, which, I assure thee, thou canst not fail to see in the fragments of pottery and other marks, because the Indians are continually passing along there. Go on thy way, and thou shalt see a mountain which is all of *margasitas* [pyrites], the which leave on the left hand, and I warn thee that thou must go round it in this fashion ℰ. On this side thou wilt find a *pajonál* [pasture] in a small plain which having crossed thou wilt come on a *cañon* between two hills, which is the way of the Inca. From thence as thou goest along thou shalt see the entrance of the *socabón* [tunnel], which is in the form of a church-porch. Having come through the *cañon,* and gone a good distance beyond, thou wilt perceive a cascade which descends from an offshoot of the Cerros Llanganati and runs into a quaking bog on the right hand; and without passing the stream in the said bog there is much gold, so that putting in thy hand what thou shalt gather at the bottom is grains of gold. To ascend the mountain, leave the bog and go along to the right, and pass above the cascade, going round the offshoot of the mountain. And if by chance the mouth of the *socabón* be closed with certain herbs which they call *'salvaje,'* remove them, and thou wilt find the entrance. And on the left-hand side of the mountain thou mayest see the *'Guayra'* (for thus the ancients called the furnace where they founded metals), which is nailed with golden nails. And to reach the third mountain, if thou canst not pass in front of the *socabón*, it is the same thing to pass behind it, for the water of the lake falls into it.

"If thou lose thyself in the forest, seek the river, follow it on the right bank; lower down take to the beach, and thou wilt reach the *cañon* in such sort that, although thou seek to pass it, thou wilt not find where; climb, therefore, the mountain on the right hand, and in this manner thou canst by no means miss thy way.

"But you can miss your way. It's as easy as following a policeman's direction down a set of streets to a jewelry shop, until you get there, to the end where the hieroglyph is. It directs you to go to the right, the map says to the left. I went left and right, and I tore out all the weed *'salvaje'* I could find. I put my hand in the stream, I waded in it, and there I found the golden fishhooks, the nail, and the pills. Of the tunnel with the church-porch I found no trace. For a while I had a fever, and one night I shot my underwear full of holes. I had it hung up to dry outside the hut in which I lived, and I lay there for two days more, but otherwise I lost no time. I was all alone—six months alone. But I didn't mind. I always wanted to be an explorer and a prospector. I mapped the whole territory.

"I did everything, I planned carefully, I took just this Indian. I thought the more I take the more they eat. They eat up all they carry. I arranged to be supplied in there once a month. The trouble with most expeditions is that they can't stay there. There's nothing to hunt, no fruits, no Indians to buy from. Six months I was in there, all alone."

He sat back, the corners of his mouth twitched, and he unpacked his gold again. He brought out the little glass bottle and spilled its contents on the table. It glowed in a green light; his fingers dwarfed the golden pills and the three golden fishhooks. He arranged and rearranged them according to size and put the golden nail on one side and sat and stared at them.

Men such as Allan Ferguson are terribly hard losers. You find them as railroad station-masters, as artillery or police captains, on the bridges of steamships and in pursers' offices. Their mustaches, when they wear them, are always neatly trimmed, their eyes clear and honest, and their souls in order. What they say is always true; they wear costumes and uniforms with pride, march in parades, lead cotillions, and join in singing. They have always wanted to be what they are, and when all is right they are enviably happy. But when the plan goes wrong, when their ships are taken from them, or the wheels on their little wagons break, they are lost and beyond help.

I thought that Ferguson would really cry. Hardly in control of his voice, he put the golden fishhooks one by one back in the bottle, and he said:

"He's a Greek; he sold his small place in Brooklyn to go into partnership with me when I told him about the Valerde treasure. He's waiting down in Guayaquil. I don't know how I'm going to tell him. He thinks I'm a swell guy. He trusted me, he gave me the ten thousand dollars."

With a parting look of sadness he put the bottle with a string tied around it back into his shirt.

"Next time I'll go up on this side," he said, and pointed to the side of the mountain on his own map.

The disease is incurable.

THE HEADHUNTERS OF THE AMAZON

On the fourth day out of the jungle, between the Río Negro and the Río Verde, we felt five distinct earthquake shocks.

We were sitting in a house to wait for a bridge to be repaired—another bridge. Our horses were tied to a fence outside. As the woman who was serving us poured two drinks into our glasses, a piece of the ceiling fell down on her hand, upset the glasses, and knocked down a bottle of whisky.

The floor trembled as if a herd of horses were running past outside; then, briefly, there was the sound of musicians plucking on the strings of violins. The woman ran out, her hands folded in prayer, whining "Santa María." Birds were in the air, the sun was shining, and the horses were gone.

Three telegraph poles weaved back and forth for a while; the wires swayed and then parted. The ends, like whips, snapped back to the poles to which they were attached. Two children had run up and were clinging to the woman, and all three of them were on their knees in prayer. The house did things one never would expect of a house. It moved like a person about to step out in a slow dance; like someone getting ready to take his leave, or making up his mind to sit down—undecided, half-finished gestures. After a while it settled down again. It held together, but all the perspectives of its doors and windows were changed. The show was over in about three minutes.

The men who had been working on the bridge were gone, and the bridge was now beyond quick repair. We found the horses scattered and trembling, and rode up along the river to look for a ford. Some distance above, we crossed through the white foam, and descended on the other side to the Pastaza road again.

In the light green fields of sugar cane ahead, there appeared an hour later the roofs of the Gran Hotel Astor, the Hotel Free Air, the Pension Suiza Alemán, and also the three steeples of the two churches of Baños, all intact.

Now, coming out of the jungle, the Gran Hotel Astor seemed beautiful and important to us. It stood exactly where it had been, white and simple. The screams of the proprietress sounded from the kitchen. With its electric lights and its two bathrooms, it was a very comfortable hotel, and while we were away it had undergone some changes.

Two boards had been placed across the copper-tinted morass that oozed from the swimming pool, and over these, carrying a breakfast tray in her hands, walked Luz María, the child of nature. She advanced in a new and difficult gait, and when I called her she turned the way soldiers do when they practice right- or left-about faces. I looked at her feet and saw that she had shoes on. She glanced down at them quickly and smiled, and walked on with the sound of someone nailing two planks together.

In sympathy with the hotel, nature also had changed. A benevolent upheaval had taken place. The waterfall that dins into the ears of everyone in this valley all night had moved some fifty feet to the right of where it originally came down. Its old bed remained as proof, a slimy band hanging down the mountainside.

Where the untidy yard of the hotel had been, a brook now flowed, bathing the roots of several rooted trees. These had been carefully festooned with lianas and orchids, and the blackness of their trunks was offset by large-leaved waterplants. A screen of twenty-foot palms cut off the road, the service entrance to the hotel, and the bathhouse that stood next to the hot-water pool.

Out from under a swinging bridge, carrying a maze of air roots in his arms and a hammer in his mouth, an Indian appeared followed by a second dragging the trunk of a palm tree, and a third man, dressed as a ship's carpenter, carrying the leaves that belonged to the tree.

I walked into the hotel and found at one of the doors a pair of short, fat, yellow boots, the kind that no one but Cyril Vigoroux would wear. Next to them stood a tripod and an old movie camera, two cases of whisky, and a trunk with "EXPLORA INC." stenciled on it.

Luz María clattered in, her face filled with responsibilities. She stopped an instant, doing another about-face, to explain that an explorer was here, and that he was making a moving picture of the Jivaro Indians.

"I think I'll call it 'The Land of Nadi Nadi' or 'Heads Off'; but the title is not important," said Cyril Vigoroux. He pinched his left cheek, quickly and several times. A fly had bitten him there: the red blotch looked as if he had rouged himself.

He sat cross-legged on a packing case in a pair of boots identical with the ones that stood outside his room. He had six pairs of them, he explained, made especially for him. He was fast as a carp, in an open shirt, an old man with large breasts and a beard. He excused himself, brushed some dirt from his sleeve, and rushed away in his sun-helmet, bush jacket, bulging khaki knickers, and awful boots.

"Julie," he cried into his jungle, "oh, Woodsie, do me a favor!"

From the green depths of his plants he turned, pushed a banana leaf out of his way, and shouted that luncheon was at one-thirty on the dot, and to bring his old friend Allan Ferguson along.

"Julie," he cried again, "oh, Woodsie, where are you?"

Cyril Vigoroux had taken possession of practically the whole hotel. He had divided it into store rooms, offices, living quarters. He had also had signs put up forbidding you to spit on the floor. I got the room I had occupied before going into the jungle. Ferguson went to the Pension Suiza Alemán.

I wanted to lie down and rest, but the bed was not made and rest was impossible. The hotel was in a fever. Luz María clumped up and down, the carpenters hammered and sawed, all the stairs creaked, and doors were continually being opened and closed.

I then thought of taking a bath, and Aurelio ran for some towels; but a bath was also impossible. The tub was occupied by a bird. He was very beautiful, tall and snowy white. His single blue-gray leg stood in three inches of water, and all around his foot lay dead shrimp. A few of them floated in the water. The bird showed no surprise or other emotion. He appeared to be stuffed, and I thought at first of taking him by his convenient neck and standing him outside in the corridor while I took a bath.

But then I saw life in him. It was in his eyes, though not in the eye itself. The eye was like a disk cut with a precise, hard tool—

several circles, one inside the other, the innermost the core of a target filled with blackness, and around it a wheel of luminous watercolor gray. At long intervals, with the brief efficiency of an optical instrument, he flicked the lid across his eye like the shutter on a speedy camera, the only sign that he lived.

Suddenly, and again mechanically, his white body had moved to the other end of the tub. From under the feathers a second leg had unfolded and with it he had spanned the length of the bath. Near the hot and cold faucets he stood still and wiped his glass eye with his lid. I left him there.

The corridor of the Gran Hotel Astor was crowded with groundsheets, eiderdown sleeping-bags, canvas buckets, guns, letterfiles, and several packing cases, all of them numbered and stenciled: "EXPLORA INC., CYRIL VIGOROUX." One large one was labeled "Tongue Depressors" under the doctor's name.

The child of nature came climbing up the stairs like a skier up a mountain. She turned painfully and then knocked on my door to say that luncheon was on the table. Allan Ferguson was already there. He was seated next to a blond girl. Cyril Vigoroux, who came running, introduced her as his discovery and star, Miss Claire Treat. It was the girl whom he also called Julie, and sometimes "Woodsie." Julie was her real name.

"I'm the outdoor type, 'woodsy,' you know," is how she explained it.

Miss Treat managed to look at the same time like a little girl and an experienced, easily accessible companion. Her face was divided into lovely details; after thorough searching for faults you found she was still beautiful, perhaps too beautiful. It sang all over her, and you only feared that when she got up there would be some painful compensation, the disappointment of a bad walk, a sway-back, or bandy legs.

She was, at the moment lunch began, displeased with her hairdresser, a youth from Quito.

"The minute he put the first pin in my hair, I knew I was stuck," she said. She turned her head slowly as if it were on a turntable and showed a perfect hairline, lovely ears, and curls hard and even as if glue had been poured over them.

Allan Ferguson sat quietly. In an hour's conversation, he said yes and no several times; that he loved to dance, that he had been in the Oriente for six months, that he had taken a warm bath at the Pension Suiza Alemán that had lasted for three hours, and that tonight he would walk around for another three to enjoy the sight of houses and electric lights.

No one paid much attention to the fourth man at the table, Lucien Tirlot, the young leading man. He played the role of a doctor, and had previously been a landscape gardener in Miami. He carried Miss Treat in and out of all the quebradas in the neighborhood of Baños. He rescued her from the jaws of crocodiles, and hung with her from precipices. He had been selected personally by Cyril Vigoroux on account of his faultless profile. He cut woodblocks of the Indians in his spare time, but disinfected himself thoroughly after every contact with them. For most of the time he sat in the shadow of a great tree, named after the famous Eucadorian poet Montalvo. He leaned there on his right hand and the left hung down out over his knee. He used up all the bathwater at the hotel. During luncheon his eyes were on his hands; occasionally they swung up to Allan Ferguson.

Doctor Vigoroux talked most of the time. He detailed the aims of his organization. The alert doctor's business affairs were most involved. Not only was there the film, which he directed and for which he had written the scenario. He was burdened with "tieups." He had, he said, a tieup with a cigarette concern, and one with some sleep-inducing coffee people. He was tied up with several publications, zoological, geographical, and of interest to travelers and explorers.

He was after the largest boa in the jungle and almost had his hands on it. As soon as the Indians produced this snake, he had it tied up with a lecture-tour management, nationwide in scope.

He had Claire Treat tied up, and also a tieup with a steamship company. But the greatest tieup was with the group of Jivaros who sat outside in the yard of the hotel. These he wanted to bring to America, to exhibit them shrinking heads. The heads of animals, of course—of dogs, cats, departed household pets.

The tieup with Miss Treat needed no explanation. She put two lumps of sugar into his coffee, broke the third in half, stirred the coffee, put the spoon beside the saucer. She did all this as

mechanically as he kissed her hand about a dozen times during
the meal. In between he pinched his cheek and looked around
for the waitress.

After the coffee, Cyril Vigoroux told several old stories, none
of them amusing enough. During this recital, Lucien Tirlot leaned
over to me and asked whether it was true, as he had read in the
Quito paper, that Allan Ferguson was really a Norwegian baron;
and then he said that he thought he was a very striking man.

"I think he's wonderful," he added and sat up straight again.
Claire Treat also examined Ferguson. She measured his hands
and arms, and looked at his hair, his lips, and his eyes.

Ferguson sat erect, heroic, silent, and listened politely; and
after Cyril Vigoroux had told his most ancient and most South
American joke—about a padre and why he has a tonsure at the
back of his head—we all got up.

Woodsie played the young girl. The long black lashes were
down over her eyes; she could blush at will and the color had
risen in her sunburnt cheeks.

Allan Ferguson pulled her chair as she got up. The big, brave
man, with the horsy honesty in his countenance better established
than ever, looked damp and clumsy.

Woodsie lit a cigarette—at least she brought out of her coat
pocket a packet of paper matches. They were brilliant red, and
printed with a large golden "21" and the names of the partners
who own this elaborate New York restaurant. This matchbox
served her as a small passport. It announced where she came from,
with whom she liked to go, and what her pleasures were. It also
lasted forever because before she could tear out a match someone
was always ahead of her. That and a Lilly Daché hatbox were
her proudest possessions.

Cyril Vigoroux led the way to his jungle, sat down on the stairs
of the hotel, and invited us to watch the shooting of some scenes.

The Indians sat about waiting to dance, to shrink heads, and
to be dangerous. Most of them were recruited from the
hills around Baños, three or four of them with their wives and
children. The ones that were always placed close to the camera
were real headhunters.

Like animals that are kept in cages, the Indians during their confinement in the backyard of the hotel had become disorderly and unclean. They left the remains of foodstuffs about; filthy clothes were draped over the fences; and they sat close together under a washline from which a sloth hung, blinking and groping along the rope ahead of him, his unfinished face turning slowly left and right.

The Jivaros seemed not overly eager to practice their ancient customs, to dance and sing. Their war cries were half-hearted and the doctor got the proper performance only from the chief, whose wife was soon to give birth to a baby.

With great authenticity and attention to the smallest detail, this Indian had retired into a little dream ranch which he had built for himself out of chonta palms and large leaves. There he sat brooding, bent over in a cowering posture, in the kind of couvade that is often reported of the ancients and of primitive races, and frequently of the headhunters of the Amazon.

This couvade is a state in which the father takes to bed and receives all the delicacies and careful attentions that other people properly regard as the mother's. The remains of the desserts of the Gran Hotel Astor, the left-overs of rice pudding, of custard, of ice cream, were carefully scraped together from the plates after lunch and taken out to the low house of leaves. To bring this important domestic detail within the swift and sure unreeling of his story was one of the problems of Dr. Cyril Vigoroux. Meanwhile he examined the mother, and hoped that the child would soon be born, as the chief was badly needed.

Production had advanced to that part of the film where the enemy is killed and the tsantsa—the trophy to be shrunken—is severed by two swift strokes from the trunk of the victim. The warrior sits down and receives the juice of tobacco mixed with saliva from the chief, who blows it in through his nose, a ceremony which protects the warrior against the vengeance of the dead enemy's spirit.

Everything had been very satisfactory thus far, explained Dr. Cyril Vigoroux. A head had been obtained with some difficulty. An attendant at the morgue of a hospice in Quito obliged, since the Jivaros refused to bring one of their own enemies' heads. The face had been properly peeled from the skull and it lay boiling in a ceremonial vessel. The doctor fished it out with a stick. It resembled a dirty washrag with holes for eyes and mouth; a wrinkled part was the nose, and the ears were still attached at the sides. In the kettle swam large eyes of fat, as in a soup. It smelled of ordinary cooking.

Before they could continue with the shrinking process, which reduces the head to the size of an orange, the important ceremonial was necessary. The chief did not want to come out. The warriors protested through their spokesman that they did not wish to have the tobacco juice blown in through the nose, that they had never heard of this ceremony.

The spokesman reported back to them that it would not be tobacco juice but chicha, and they accepted this amendment. The chief, however, remained in his house of leaves and insisted on awaiting the birth of his child before he would take part in the ceremony. Dr. Cyril Vigoroux examined the mother again and said that in another twenty-four hours he hoped they could proceed.

In the meantime, in another chapter of the film, Lucien Tirlot was dragging Claire Treat through the jungle, and they came to the lagoon in back of the Gran Hotel Astor. The doctor had them rush on and fall face forward into the water, and then he had them do it over again. He finally decided that Woodsie should come alone. She leaned down in the posture of the nymph in the White Rock mineral water advertisements; she wore a carefully torn shirt, her hair was loose again, and Cyril Vigoroux waded into the water to make closeups of her heavy breathing. He stretched her out on a jaguar pelt, and then completely lost the thread of the story. The rest of the afternoon was taken up with lovely still lifes and the shooting of a crocodile. He said he had tieups in mind.

Dinner was at seven, and afterward Cyril Vigoroux came along for a drink at the American Country Club. He was tired, and he wanted to work on the next day's continuity, he said; so he walked home, and I went with him. Woodsie and Allan Ferguson stayed to dance, and as we came to the hotel, we saw Tirlot through the window making woodcuts.

The doctor's room adjoined Miss Treat's. It was a frugal apartment: the same cot as in all the other rooms, a piece of native rug in front of it, and in the center the electric bulb hanging at the end of its wire without a shade. There was a radio, and also a gramophone standing on a specially constructed trunk that held records, all of them classical, Sunday evening program music.

On another trunk which he used as a bedside table was a small bar with half a dozen bottles of liqueurs, all sweet: chartreuse, kümmel, benedictine, and such stuff. For his particular guests Cyril Vigoroux went to the trouble of making a pousse-café, pouring it so that the colors of the spirits remained separate, one above the other. It took patience and a very steady hand, and it made a horrible combination.

On a shelf above the bed was a smeary jar half filled with vaseline. A sprig of blossoms was stuck in it.

He looked at his swollen cheek in the mirror over the washstand and yawned, and then he took his boots off and put them outside the door. He pinched his cheek and sat down on the bed, rubbing his thick legs. He had to write half the night, he said, and yawned again; and then he remembered that he also might have to deliver the Jivaro baby.

Someone outside was singing above the waterfall's tumult, the Indians and the animals were quiet, and all was otherwise silent in the thirty-five rooms of the Gran Hotel Astor in Baños.

The walls of the hotel were thin, neither the doors nor the windows fitted well, and the ceilings on the second floor were made of mats nailed to the rafters. At midnight there was a sound of metallic tapping. I wondered for a long while what it might be, and finally remembered the bird. He was eating his shrimp in the bathtub.

"I don't like mystery boys!" shouted Cyril Vigoroux at three in the morning. "All this bunk about his father being a Norwegian baron—Christ, I can't stand all these phonies that come around here! You, of course, think it's wonderful. . . . Oh, my God, the way you look at him when you dance with him."

"What do you mean?"

"I mean dancing—hanging from some son of a bitch and going around in circles. I suppose that's fun, great fun. . . . Leaning up against a leg—I'd rather do it in bed. My God, the fun women miss by not knowing anything about music, good music I mean!"

"It's funny," said Woodsie in a new and competent voice. "It's funny that you always say things that apply to yourself—all this blustering and bluffing, and when anything important comes up, you sit there in a corner and wag your tail, when you really should speak up."

"What are you talking about?"

"You know what I'm talking about."

There was silence and then a few loud slaps, a scream, and "oh! oh! oh!" and then all was quiet again. A palm swayed outside, the bell of the church tolled four times, and out in the new yard of the hotel the moon shone on a broken barrel of green dry paint that was spilled over an old Singer sewing machine.

Vigoroux came up to the pool the next morning and sat down in the water beside me, and Luz María brought breakfast.

After he had stirred his coffee and before he drank it, holding the cup in his hand, he said, "Good God, I hate to lay hands on a woman, but it does them good sometimes. The fit she threw the first time I smacked her. I hit pretty hard; I hit her the left side of her face with the palm of my hand. She turned her head and I hit her on the right, good and hard.

"You know how little girls act the first time you thrash them; they can't believe it, and they gasp in surprise, say 'oh! oh! oh!' and then break out in screams. Well, that made me really mad. I turned her over and beat her until my hand hurt. She'll boast about it. They love a hiding, you know."

He drank some coffee, swam about in the pool, and asked me to put a plaster on his cheek where the fly had bitten him. Then he put on a bathrobe, slipped off his bathing suit, and ran back to the hotel.

An hour later he was silent. He was sitting cross-legged on one of the rotten trees. In back of him lay the alligator, dead, that had been thrown there after filming the day before.

"She's gone," he said. "With what's-his-name. With Ferguson."

ADOLF IN QUITO

Luz María, in her new shoes, saddled a horse, and I set out from Baños with Aurelio. We rode to Pelileo and Ambato, to Lasso and Latacunga, and back in slow stages by way of Machachi to Quito.

Quito is a kind of penal colony for diplomats. In some cases they are banished to this high capital for minor indiscretions, alcoholism, badly conducted affairs of the heart or the state, or —as a typist at the American Legation remarked of his superior —"because he hasn't got all the marbles the Loh'd wants everyone to have."

This makes on the whole for a group of likable, outspoken, and refreshing people. Not being *persona grata* with their own governments, they get along well with their hosts, tell well-flavored stories, and are usually excellent companions.

The German Minister is a delightful gentleman. No one hisses him or tries to throw stones through the windows of his house. Although six carabineros are needed to guard the Italian Legation, no protection is needed at the German. The Minister is a devout Catholic and goes regularly to the cathedral, where he has to stoop to pass through the portal, because he is so tall. He tries to hide himself at the few parties he attends, and leaves before anyone has had more than two drinks. If, in this land of surprises, the German Minister is a kind and cultured gentleman, it might follow that a Jew here would endorse Hitler. As I discovered, he sometimes does.

I ran into Herr Doktor Gottschalk one day when he was sitting alone in the back room of a place that might well be the German Legation—a whitewashed and brightly lit restaurant called the Salon Berlin. This establishment is a succession of vaulted rooms, somewhat like a rathskeller. The air is heavy with the stench of pickles and stale beer. Over a counter on which there are stacks of smoked herring and pumpernickel, a good-natured proprietor leans between a cash register and a sausage-slicing apparatus. The clientele is chiefly young men, standing straight, most of them in knickers and belted jackets, their hair clipped short, heavy-muscled, loud, and healthy. They are a group who used to do their best to look like typical Heidelberg students but now make every effort to look like mechanics on their day off. They are for the most part employed by German import-and-export companies. There is no picture of Hitler in the restaurant and no Nazi flag, but "Deutschland über Alles" and the "Horst Wessel Song" and all the brutal hymns of the new Germany are as popular here as the barrel of sauerkraut that stands in the outer hall.

When I arrived, Doktor Gottschalk was eating a pair of small sausages and drinking a glass of blond beer. I had met him once at the Hotel Metropolitano, and had been surprised afterward when someone told me he was a refugee and a Jew. The Herr Doktor is straw-blond, blue-eyed, professorial, and somewhat arrogant in his walk and his gestures. As soon as I sat down, he brought the conversation around to Hitler. He swallowed the remnants of the pair of sausages, took a deep drink of the Vienna Export, and started to speak of Adolf. He said the name as one does that of an old friend.

"I don't know," he said, "what Adolf had against me—God alone knows. I am not like the others. You know, I was in the field from the first day on in the last war—captain in a line regiment, Austrian artillery, decorated with the Iron Cross, first and second class, and mentioned three times in army dispatches. I was being recommended for the Pour le Mérite just when the whole *Schweinerei* came to its disgraceful end. All that counted for nothing, for absolutely nothing." He said this in a tone of voice which seemed to mean that he admired the thoroughness with which the new government did away with everyone who was a Jew.

"My mother was an Aryan. Also, my wife is purely Aryan; we have a son named Kurt—you should see them. My grandmother was already *hoffähig* at the court of the old emperor, and my father, the old Doktor Gottschalk, personally treated

Adolf's mother. All that means absolutely nothing. Can you
understand what Adolf has against me?

"My Papa," he continued, starting in on another beer, "was in
Ischl when he treated Adolf's mother. My dear Papa was in the
habit of keeping all the letters that grateful patients wrote to him.
He had one from Adolf, a very nice letter, thanking Papa for the
care he had given his mother. It was a long and elaborate letter,
taking up two pages, written on both sides.

"Papa was quite an old man when Adolf came to power, and
he was a famous specialist in Vienna when Adolf marched in.
Then the trouble began. Many of the others, the old ones, committed suicide. We stayed home, and then Papa thought of the
letter—he thought of it when my brother, who is also a doctor,
and I were taken in protective custody and when my little boy
was forbidden to go to school. He thought that the letter would
do some good, and sent it to Adolf through the proper channels.
Adolf at the time was in Vienna, and some influential friends
who were in the new government saw to it that it came to Adolf's
attention. Papa waited and hoped that it would do some good.
It did.

"Adolf made it possible for us to get out of the country immediately. My brother and I were released, we could take our
furniture along, and while everybody else had to stay in line to
wait for various permits, we left in a matter of a few weeks. Our
other property, our money, and my father's and brother's and my
own practice, of course, were gone.

"Papa, who is here with me, is now eighty. My brother has
gone to Chile. He is a gynecologist and has found an appointment
at a hospital in Santiago. Papa was a famous man in Vienna, and
some time ago the Nazi Gauleiter of Quito called up and said that
he would send his wife over to have him examine her. Papa got
very mad, and he told him over the phone that, according to
National Socialist law, the examination of an Aryan woman by
a Jewish doctor was equal to having relations with her and punishable under the same law. She came anyway, and the Gauleiter,
a very nice man, came with her and laughed and said that the
law did not apply to Papa because he was over the age limit." The
Herr Doktor chuckled.

"But Adolf could have been a little kinder to us," he went on. "There are several half-Jews in the government over there, and even in the army. For example, Marshal Milch is a half-Jew. There is a way in which to get around the regulations. The Aryan mother goes and swears that while she was married to the Jew, the father of her child was another man, an Aryan, and in important cases that is accepted and no more is said about it. If he had wanted to, Adolf would have been able to make some such arrangement available to us, but in the tension, and burdened with all the details and all the worries he must have, one cannot expect him to bother with any one individual case."

He touched my arm and pointed to a man who had just come into the Salon Berlin and was being greeted with reverence all around. "That," he informed me, "is the secretary of the electric works and the local agent of the Gestapo."

The Gauleiter came over, shook the Herr Doktor's hand, and walked on. The Doktor was visibly proud. He pointed out other people to me, including one of the pilots of the air line to Guayaquil, a baron. "The air line has become an Ecuadorian company," he told me, "since all the trouble with the United States began, but only five percent of the capital is Ecuadorian. It's still a German company, and when there's any motor trouble we have parts here from Brazil like that." He snapped his fingers.

The Gauleiter passed us again and nodded. The Herr Doktor smiled and said to me, "You know, they have been very nice to us refugees since we are here. I went to the Consulate the other day about some papers, and the secretary there offered me a chair and said, 'Herr Doktor Gottschalk, if there is anything we can do for you, turn to us with confidence. We have instructions from Berlin to extend to you and other refugees any aid that is possible.' My son is even going to the Colegio Alemán, the best school here."

The Herr Doktor had a nice house in the center of Quito, and invited me to go home with him. On the way home, he bought the *Comercio* and quickly read the headlines. "You see," he said, "Adolf is no fool! Did you listen to that marvelous speech he made the other night about stopping the war?"

The house was orderly and the furnishings were those of a well-to-do German household. A picture of Hindenburg hung in the dining room, and a mediocre oil painting of an Austrain artillery battery hung over the Herr Doktor's bed, an immense featherbed which he had been allowed to bring over with him, along with all his books and the family silver and porcelain. The father, a white-haired and bearded gentleman who looked more or less like all great Viennese specialists, was in a wheelchair.

The Doktor's wife was the middle-aged, well-groomed German *Dame,* looking like a very young Queen Mary, German in the fashion in which many English appear German, a little rounder, a little more provincial, with a stiff high collar and a hard eye for the servants. The boy, Kurt, came in while I was there, clicked his heels, bent low and suddenly from the hips, as if about to kiss my hand, then stood at attention, a perfect specimen of the Hitler Jugend. He wore short trousers, for which he was already too old. They left exposed a good deal of sunburnt leg, covered by yellow down.

The Frau Doktor told me that a play was going to be put on by the students and teachers at the Colegio Alemán. It was a Nazi play, so Kurt, for obvious reasons, had not been asked to take part. However, he and his parents were invited to attend a dress rehearsal that afternoon, and the Frau Doktor suggested I come along. That evening, when the real performance would be given, only members of the Nazi group would be admitted. After the performance in the evening, the Nazis would have tea and cakes together at the school, the Frau Doktor explained. "We, of course, are not asked to that party," she added, with a look at her husband, "and what goes on there, and what is said and decided, one can only guess."

Driving out to the Colegio Alemán, the Frau Doktor told me that she was glad her boy would be here in Ecuador until things became a little different over there. Today he would be in a very peculiar position in Germany. There, it would be better if he were a half-Jew instead of being what he is, a quarter-Jew. If he were a half-Jew, he could obtain permission at least to marry a Jewish girl, but being a quarter-Jew, he would be, according to the Party, too good to marry a Jewish girl and not good enough to marry an Aryan, and in consequence would belong to the unfortunate group that is not permitted to marry anybody. "But that," said the Herr Doktor, "might eventually be changed."

We arrived at the Colegio Alemán, which consists of a clump of buildings standing in a large garden. There was a Nazi flag, large as a bedsheet, flying at one end of a football field. A kindergarten mistress, her hair pulled into a tight knot, passed with some children, half of them Ecuadorian, the other half German. They wore the small aprons that one sees in French nurseries. The buildings were immaculate. Over the door of each classroom was inscribed the purpose to which the room was assigned— "Arbeitszimmer," "Lesezimmer," "Spielzimmer," "Speisezimmer." In the kindergarten, a sun-flooded room containing very little furniture, a life-size, full-length picture of Hitler hung under a frieze of geese and rabbits. I asked the Herr Doktor whether this school, which was a public institute of learning in Quito, was a Nazi institution. "Not very much," he said. "The Herr Direktor is a very broad-minded man."

I was not permitted to attend the dress rehearsal, but I met the Herr Doktor the next day at the Salon Berlin, and he told me that the play was about an old Jew and that he was glad his papa had not been strong enough to go along. He and his wife and Kurt had sat through the whole business. He talked and talked, and then I went and talked to some others—half-Jews, quarter-Jews, full Jews—and I found in a number of instances more or less the same unbelievable and pathetic attitude. Out of all I heard, I gathered that many of the Jews in Quito—a city where nothing expected happens—feel like this:

"He'll rule the world, or at least Europe. In my case an error has been made. In the haste and hurry, the laws were made too strict. They had to be strict; you can't do things half-way. Too bad, but I shall be among those who will perhaps be called back. When it's over, he'll need every man—every doctor, every engineer, every scientist, every able executive. The soup is never eaten as hot as it is cooked. And then my Iron Cross, and the fact that I have kept quiet here, where I might have talked, and the fact that I have an Aryan wife and a child who is only a quarter-Jew—all this will make it possible for me to go back to the most beautiful, the best, the greatest land in the world. That's the reason I send the boy to the Colegio Alemán, so that he does not lose touch with the *Vaterland.*"

And audibly my Herr Doktor added, in his soft Viennese German, *"Damit der Bua wenigstens was anständigs lernt.*—At least in this school a boy can learn something respectable."

PRISON VISIT

Atop one of the foothills of Pichincha, high above the city of Quito, bathed in sunlight, stands a white building with a cupola. It is the Panóptico, and it has an evil name. Don Juan Palacios in Guayaquil had recited its horrors to me, and wherever I asked permission to visit the prison I was told with politeness and much regret that this one wish could not be granted. Diplomats in cautious conversation told me again that its cells were subterranean and wet, that the prisoners were chained to the walls, underfed, without proper clothing. Bony, feverish victims of political miscalculation, who died slowly, without consolation, and stank to high heaven. Lucky were they who were sent to exile in the Galápagos Islands or marched into the jungles of the Oriente; there death was quick and in the daylight.

The magnificent name of the prison and its story drew me up the hill, which I climbed in short stages of thirty paces at a time. For a while, when you return from the low lands, it is difficult to breathe in Quito, and you proceed by resting on a streetcorner, advancing thirty paces, leaning against a house and then a tree. Thus I arrived at the Panóptico.

Outside, propped against the building, were two sentries in khaki uniforms, with legs crossed, resting their hands on the barrels of their guns. They were talking and laughing; one turned, when the other pointed at me, and raised his eyebrows.

"I would like to see the Director of the prison."

Ah, he said, but that was not so easy; there had to be arrangements made for this ahead of time, a letter, an introduction, a pass, or else one had to arrive in the company of an official of the Government, or at least of a policeman.

I told him that I knew all that, but that my visit was an exception, that I was a prison official myself, from the United States of North America, that I was the secretary of the warden of a prison.

The soldier's eyes grew respectful and obedient, he leaned away from the building, saluted, and dragging his gun behind him he almost ran up the portico to the door, where he told the story to the man who sat on guard there. The guard stood up and said, "But certainly, come in, come in, the Director will be happy to see you."

Door after door opened. By the time I arrived in the reception room of the Director's apartment I had shaken hands with several officials and rapidly answered questions.

What prison?

A prison in the State of New York.

Ahhh!

A man motioned to a red leather couch in the comfortably furnished room. There were white curtains, a few cages with birds singing in them, and under my feet a green carpet. Much light came in at a high window.

A small man entered. He wore a long, tightly buttoned black coat. One of his hands was in a black glove; he held this hand in back of him. He had a small white spade beard, a distinguished face. He stood away about ten feet from me, and bowed. I got up.

He said, "Sing Sing?" I answered, "Sing Sing." The door opened again and a young man was shown in. The little old man turned to him and said with raised eyebrows, "Warden Lawes, Sing Sing."

The Director bowed deeply. He was followed by a retinue of secretaries and assistants and guards. As he sat down on the couch beside me and pumped my hand, he repeated "Sing Sing" as if it were the name of his first love. He picked a stray hair off the collar of my coat, and then, standing up, I was introduced to the staff, and someone was quickly sent for something to drink. An order was given for luncheon, and then from a drawer of his desk the Director slipped a worn Colt .25 into his pocket and said, "Permit me," and went ahead.

"I will go ahead," he said. "You do not know the way."

He was athletic, of good bearing; I think partly Indian. His clothes were simple; he used his chest and lips at times as Mussolini does, the body swaying with both hands at the hips, the lower lip rolled out as in pouting.

We passed two heavy gates, went through a long tunnel, turned to the right, and entered one of the cellblocks in the star-shaped building.

"Our population in this prison is five hundred and five men, and twenty-four women. Most of them are here for crimes of passion. The population of Ecuador is about three million."

"Where does the music come from?"

"From the political prisoners. We have three of them. They are not forced to work, so they sing and play guitars; here they are."

Without stopping their song, the three young men nodded to the Warden. They were in a cell with flowers at the window and a small parrot in a cage; two sat on the bed, the third on a three-legged stool.

"Now we go to the shops." We crossed a wide square and entered a house filled with the noises of hammering, sawing, the smell of wood and leather, and above that the smell of lilies from the prison yard. The prisoners sang here also; the windows were high and without bars. They stood up as the Warden came in; their faces remained at ease. Shoes were made here and some furniture, small trunks lined with paper on which flower designs were printed. In another part of the room men were carving small skulls out of ivory nuts, and one was arranging a miniature of the Crucifixion scene inside a small bottle. Some of the men smoked, some rested, all smiled as the Warden spoke to them. They all very proudly showed their work. The Warden told them all, "Warden Lawes—Sing Sing," and in a few words described my famous prison to them. He stopped and spoke to several men and told me what crimes they had committed. Some of the men asked him questions, and he answered with interest, thinking awhile before he spoke. He usually touched the men or held them by the arm; he bowed and smiled when he had finished with them, and he told his assistant to note several things the men requested.

From this room we climbed the stone steps up to the roof of the prison. Lilies were blooming in the gardens below; on the south side there was a swimming pool into which a stream of water poured from the mouth of a stone lion. A sentry lay on the roof. He got up and kicked the magazine under his pill-box and reached for the rifle which lay on the blanket on which he had been reading; he pulled down his coat and started pacing up and down, the gun over his shoulder.

"Does anyone ever escape from here?"

"Yes, sometimes," said the Warden. "Here, right here, is where they escape." He pointed to the roof of the cellblock that was nearest to the mountain. To clear a wall that is eighteen feet high, a man had to run and then jump out and down a distance of some thirty-four feet; he landed in a thicket of candelabra cacti on the other side of the fence. I asked the Warden how they punished the men when they caught them. "If he jumps well," said the Warden, "he's gone. It's not easy; he must want to be free very badly, and I would not like to risk it, would you? His friends will hide him and we have one less prisoner. If he jumps badly, he falls down into the yard here and is perhaps dead—at least he will break both his legs. He will never jump again; the pain, that is enough punishment. And you, Señor; in Sing Sing, what you do?"

"Oh, we lock them up in a dungeon, with bread and water and no light, for a week, two weeks, a month."

"I do not believe in that," he said with the Mussolini gesture. "I do not believe in vengeance. Look here, down over the edge; this man is a bad fellow, I had to do something. I have put him alone by himself on half-rations. But I gave him the dog and cats and I come to see him and talk to him. I am troubled with his stupidity."

I crept to the edge of the roof and looked down. In a court by himself sat a young, wild-haired fellow. His half-ration consisted of a big bowl of soup, a small pail half full of rice, and a loaf of black bread. The dog and cats were sitting close to him waiting for the remnants of his meal.

"You know," continued the Warden, "he is my only problem prisoner; before, it was full of them. The military ran this institution; the military mind is stupid—boom, huuuump, march, one, two, three, four, eyes right—shouting, marching is all they know. I am an advocate; I try to be humanitarian; not soft, please do not mistake me, I mean economic with life; that is my idea. I look at my prisoner when he comes in, I have studied the science of criminology, I have a knowledge of the system Bertillon. I am sorry when a man is brought in and I can see by his nose, his eyes, his jaw, and his skull, that he is a bad fellow for whom I can do nothing. That one I send away, to the Galápagos. It's not bad for them there; they can sleep and fish. Here he would do terrible damage.

"Here I keep the men and women who have perhaps even killed somebody, who have done something in one moment of their life that was wrong; they know it, I know it, we're both sorry; let us make the best of it. First of all I tell them to forget it and work. I know each man here. I hope they all like me as much as I like them.

"We have no death penalty here in Ecuador. The maximum sentence is for sixteen years; that is for cold murder.

"All prisoners receive wages, the current wages that would be paid if the man worked outside. The wages are divided in three parts. One-third goes to the prison, and by this the institution supports itself; one-third goes to the man for pocket money; and one-third is saved for him, with interest, for the day when he is freed. If he has a family, the pocket money and the savings account are split according to the needs of his wife and children, but he must receive some money for himself and a small sum for his freedom; he may not want to go back to his family. Any of them can go out, if I say yes. A prisoner's wife can visit him; she can go out into the garden with him, and bring his children. He can sometimes go home with her. And I like it when they paint. Here, look into this cell."

We had come down from the roof. Almost every cell had pictures in watercolors or crayons—simple pictures of landscapes, saints, animals, in flat poster effects; some in brilliant colors, some uncertain and shaky. They were painted on the walls of the cells and sometimes along the corridors.

The Warden knew all the rare ones. He showed them to me with pride, and particular pride at the absence of pornographic ones.

"I would let them alone if there were any," he said. "A man's cell is his private room here. He can do what he wants. I am just glad I have never found any.

"Now let us go to the women."

The twenty-four women live in a prison within the prison. Here there are more flowers, three tangerine trees, and clouds of linen hanging over them.

These women have stabbed cheating lovers; one of them did away with her baby. They spend their days washing and ironing the drawers, undershirts, and socks of the cadets at the military academy. Their children are with them. Little boys and girls run and sing in the yard. They go out to school and come back to eat with Mama. The little houses, of one room each, are orderly, and all the women were smiling. One was nursing her baby.

"Born here," said the Warden with pride, and pinched its cheeks.

We said our good-bys and walked back to the reception room. While we waited for luncheon he pouted again in the Mussolini manner, crossed his legs, and looked out of the window over Quito. He turned abruptly to pose a question which apparently had difficulty in forming itself into words.

"Señor Lawes," he blurted, "I have heard so much of you. I have read so much in magazines. Your stories are published in our Spanish journals very often. I have seen a moving picture that you have written. You are such an intelligent man and so— what is the word?—efficient, and also—what is it?—versatile. How you do it? Here I have a little prison with five hundred people. I am busy all day and half the night and every Sunday—I have not had a vacation for a year. How can you do it? I think it's wonderful."

POOR ANIMAL

The Arena de Toros in Quito seats about a thousand people, one leaning out over the shoulders of another. On Sunday afternoons it fills to the battered brass music of the municipal band fortified by the players from a regimental band.

The boxes are cement cubicles which form the base of the structure. Those on the shady side of the ring are occupied by Society and the diplomats. From the boxes well-dressed five- and six-year-olds dangle their legs into a narrow corridor, which provides a haven for the fighters. It receives them out of the dangers of the ring as they leap with grace, when time allows, over the wooden balustrade. This protective fence is strong, worn, and splintered. It carries a few advertisements and is about five and a half feet high. Here in Quito, the bulls also jump over it and are booed for it.

Bullfighting, I am told, is a very expensive sport. The local impresarios are not rich enough to endow it properly. Outside of the opera *Carmen* I know little or nothing of what a real bullfight should be. I have never read Mr. Hemingway's book on it, nor had I ever seen a fight in Spain or anywhere else when I went to my first in Quito.

Bullfighting cannot possibly be anything like the vicious, slow butchery that is performed here.

All over the town are flamboyant posters: in the upper right corner a lithograph of a giant bull, under it the portraits of the two fighters, and at the bottom the heavy-lettered announcement that the "BRAVISSIMOS TOROS DE ANTISANO"—the most brave bulls of Antisano—will be fought.

I had not seen the bulls, but the fighters live at my hotel; their room is two doors away from mine, they eat a few tables away from me in the dining room. They are men with ordinary faces,

hard to classify: not sportsmen, not mugs, not businessmen; perhaps rather the nondescript young man who just works at a grocery, who comes to fix the telephone, or hangs around a billiard
academy—the Latin edition of such a young man. They eat
hunched over with their faces almost on the plate, they drink
with moderation. One of them stares at a full-bosomed woman
during most of his meals. They seem without bravado, and here
in the hotel no one pays any attention to them.

On Sunday, they don't appear for luncheon. About two in the
afternoon they come into the lobby, clad in tight, gold-embroi-
dered costumes, one white, the other a patched, faded old rose.
Then they wait in front of the hotel and a friend drives up in an
old Lincoln touring car with the top down. The porter places the
two embossed sword cases and the capes on the front seat next to
the driver. The fighters climb in, their pants almost splitting as
they bend over; seated, they wave their hands at a small group of
admirers. Little boys hang on the door handles and ride on the
running board. They drive off to the arena.

Marching into the ring, they have grown in stature: the music,
the bright sunlight on the yellow sand, the ritual, and the cheer-
ing crowd lend them height and power.

The municipal band fills the arena with a tune from a Fred
Astaire film; it's the song, "Dancing Cheek to Cheek." They play
this over and over. I don't know the proper names for the entire
retinue, but they all disappear in the shelter of the wooden balustrade. A bolt is taken from a heavy door, it opens, and out of
its shadow trots the bull. Black, lithe, alert, he dances almost to
the center, head held high, then he reaches for the spike that has
been stuck into his side under a blue rosette. He licks at it with his
tongue.

The bull is the son of little cattle. The high altitude is given as
reason for his smallness, and also for the absence of horses.

The game starts. It is interrupted by trumpet signals, by
changes in formation and various ceremonials. The animal
charges sometimes, and there are brief moments when he angrily
passes close to a man and comes out from under the cape in bewildered surprise. Salvos of applause greet the fighter's turns in
these maneuvers, his form, his timing. This goes on and on; the

animal is winded and stops for air, his tongue out, like a panting dog.

Not until after the banderillas are stuck into him does the little bull sense the purpose of his presence. It is then that he loses his water, that he soils his hind legs and trembles. He looks around for help at the closed door through which he came, at the wide ring of faces, and at the one means of escape, over which he has chased several of his tormentors—the wooden ring. He runs, clears it with his front legs, and awkwardly clambers over, pulling his hind legs after him.

It is at this part of the performance that shock and disgust begin. It would seem as if at this point, in the name of sport, or simply because of a dull performance, the animal should be dismissed. He has shown that he is scared, that he does not choose to fight, that he has mistaken the whole thing for play in the fields. The time allowed for his killing has already been stretched to the limit and beyond. But he remains.

The crowd boos. The torero is in the center of the ring. He raises both shoulders and tilts his head in the gesture of "What can I do with such a bull?" He walks over to the partition, his sword in his right hand, and stabs it into the animal's haunches to drive him to an opening twenty feet ahead which leads back into the arena. The animal cannot turn. Its back, torn by the banderilla harpoon ends, is a dripping shawl of dark blood. The long rods above his shoulders sway and tear his wounds at every motion. The little boys reach down to twist the banderillas out of him to take home as souvenirs.

To make him go back, the torero and his crew keep stabbing harder, cursing louder. Step by step they succeed.

Slowly the bull steps out into the arena. He sways, he is weak, blood rains from him. The fighter confronts him with a gesture that might be beautiful and exciting, if it were opposite an angered, dangerous, and fearless animal. He measures along his sword, whips up on his toes, levers his body over the sunken head of the animal, high between the horns, and—to the applause of the whole audience—rams the blade into the shoulders of the bull. He misses his aim; he has stuck the sword into bone.

A mute, distant moan comes from the animal. It is a sickening sound and a sickening picture. The sword shakes. With pitiful, inadequate despair the little bull charges his attacker. The torero disappears behind the fence; two other men dance in with capes and turn the animal from him. This gory act repeats itself until three swords are stuck into the bull, not one of them having found its target.

The bull is in a small quarter-moon-shaped strip of afternoon shadow. There he sinks onto his knees, close to the door which he hoped would open for him. It does, and out of it comes the only mercy of that afternoon, a man in a red shirt with a short dagger. He ends the disgrace with two quick stabs behind the animal's head.

This is a reconciling thing, relief, and quite the nicest part. With an acquiescent nod, like a child falling asleep, the animal turns its head and sinks down on its knees, quite naturally, as in prayer. A chain is put around the horns and three horses drag the limp body out, scraping a wide path across the arena.

The band plays "Dancing Cheek to Cheek" once more; the torero drinks a glass of water, to be refreshed for the next bull. Everybody is applauding him; no one is leaving.

THE PROMISED LAND

"The green hut in which we lived stood in a lagoon of turquoise water. To the left and right of it soared high curtains of greenery, and between these and beyond a beach of coral sand was the sky, liquid, yellow as chartreuse in a thin glass.

"The sun came up and birds spread their wings and sank down to the lagoon. Flamingos made pink question marks with their necks and then searched the water for sardines and small frogs.

"Down out of the high bamboo structure of the roof, where he sat motionless and hunted flies and mosquitoes all night, climbed Tala, the pet chameleon. He changed to the color of the sky, to the blue of the water. As Waha's soft, small hands caressed him, he made short flute-like sounds and the comb on his head began to glow, first like the dying fire in an iron stove, then more intensely like a fiery lance; and on his body's sides, on the gills, and in the soft, loose folds of skin under his throat appeared brilliant orange flames.

"A barbaric ornament, he sat on the girl's shoulder, and the two points of the blood-red whip of his tongue danced into her hair, to her neck, and shot through her slender fingers.

"No woman's body on the whole island was softer. Of the three women that Womo, the Headman of Tago Tago, had given me, she was the tallest and so young that her teeth had not been filed. A wreath of camellias went from her shoulders to her abdomen, the largest and most beautiful of the flowers lay over the softly pulsating groove between her firm bosoms. She folded the mat on which we had slept. A small red bug was hidden under the mat. She crushed it between her white teeth and with the red liquid painted the eyes of a faded turtle carved into the side of the hut. I had obtained all this, together with an outrigger canoe and several miles of beach, from the chief, in return for an umbrella, an old opera hat, and a pair of spectacles without lenses. . . ."

This Gauguin idyl was the opening effusion of a serial of 50,-000 labored words, my first exercise in fiction on a typewriter, composed before I had ever seen a palm tree outside of a hotel. It was written mostly at night, many years ago, and sent by registered mail to the *Ladies' Home Journal*. It came back with the magazine's editorial regrets. I have put it away in my trunk, the trunk in which publishers find unpublished manuscripts shortly after the author dies. It is up in the attic, where this trunk is always discovered. The beach in Tago Tago, the hut, and the sunrise remained a blue dream tent in which I sat for a few years; and I forgot all about it until I came to Ecuador. For those who still dream, the jungles, the seacoast, the tropic isles, and the mountains of Ecuador offer all the scenery, every variety of climate, and they are the ideal proving ground for adventure and escape; but the dreams seldom seem to come true, and the people who are happy here would also be happy in Scranton or Tallahassee. There are spectacular failures, mild, resigned ends, and unhappy finales in fever or return home—and there are also compromises in the form of jobs as sewing-machine salesmen or as agents for condensed-milk companies and Crisco.

The two outstanding examples of yes and no that I met in Ecuador are André Roosevelt and a retired German major of infantry who was an amateur zoologist. Neither has chosen to live in as unbuttoned a paradise as I imagined on the beach of Tago Tago. Both are married, have a complete wardrobe, live with their lawfully wedded wives, and even brought their dogs along.

The German major has a place along the River Pastaza. His house is a neat mountain chalet with window boxes and a small brass plate on the door, with the major's name and title neatly engraved on it. Next to the name plate, and the only one in the jungle, is a doorbell. Underneath is a scraper for dirty boots, and inside is a mat with *"Willkommen"* written on it.

The property stands in overwhelming scenery, with mountains all around it, and faces the long silver ribbon of a waterfall. Monkeys fly from limb to limb of tall trees, parrots chatter everywhere. One of them is domesticated; it walks around and speaks German and Spanish. *"Gott im Himmel,"* he says, and *"Guten Tag," "Buenos días"* and *"Mamacita."* In the garden along sanded walks that are neatly raked stand benches made of lignum vitae. There is a tame tapir, an animal half-pig, half-elephant; and a very serious and ancient Galápagos turtle feeds on cacti. The turtle is the color of rock; his eyes are dull, and he stands on heavy legs like those of a rhino and crunches thorny cactus leaves as a cow chews grass. There is an egret that follows the major like a dog, and there are two dogs, Great Danes, that lie under huge avocado trees. The dogs' eyes are on the foliage above, their heads lie between outstretched paws, and when they hear the rustling of leaves or the sound of a breaking twig they come to attention and bump into each other trying to catch the pears that fall from the trees. They carry the fruit to a corner of the patio, and with their lips drawn back from the teeth they gnaw away the soapy skin, eat the meat, and then play with the stone until the major's wife comes out of the kitchen and tells them to stop and get out of her garden, where German vegetables grow in orderly rows: kohlrabi, soup greens, black radishes, root celery, and red cabbages.

Major Timmel sat with me under an arbor that rained its sweet blossoms over tables and chairs and into the soft wind that carried them across to the house. We had walked to the waterfall and visited the cages in which he kept various animals and birds. The major had brought back several orchids of immoral design, astounding flowers, like hats invented by a lewd modiste. He held one of them in his hand, and as he spoke dismembered it carelessly, dropping the petals down into the soft sand. He sighed, *"Ja—Frühling giebt es für mich nur in Deutschland."* Spring, the month of May, existed for him only in Germany. He spoke of the beauty of pine trees in winter, of the gurgling of melted water running under the snow, of the first crocuses, of the unfolding of the horse chestnut's leaves and of its blossoms, of thaw and violets, and of a little geranium carefully nursed through the winter in a red clay pot on a window. Outside the window, a cobbled tidy street, small houses on both sides, little women going to church. "Do you know anyone—who would buy this godforsaken place?

"I have installed electric light, all sanitary conveniences. I have forty devoted Indians who work my land. I plant sugar, cacao, coffee. I hunt and fish. There are no taxes, no interference from the Government. The sun rises at six and sets at six every day. In back of my house is a natural pool with hot, healing water that is excellent to drink when you cool it—it tastes like Vichy. My wife came here with arthritis—couldn't move a finger. Now she's completely cured.

"The Government is most generous: you get free three times as much land as you cultivate—a marvelous opportunity for a young man. I will sell for anything and go back to Pomerania," he said, with a sweeping gesture. The major's wife served coffee, knitted with the arthritic hands, and sat in silence, only occasionally nodding in agreement when he spoke.

As everyone does here, the major attached himself immediately to me with all his hopes, fears, and troubles. They poured out of him in an unhalting stream. He showed me books and photographs, explained his circumstances and, with an air of the greatest confidence, he began to speak of Franklin Delano Roosevelt.

"I have no use for a man who almost always smiles; I am suspicious of that sort of humor." He leaned closer and said, "Neutrality—ha—hahaha!" The parrot echoed the laugh and added, *"Gott im Himmel."*

"Wait a minute," said the major. He disappeared into the house, with the egret at his heels, and came back with two folios, made out of wrapping paper and stitched together. He explained to me that a friend in the States mailed him the *New York Herald Tribune* regularly, and that since even before the beginning of the war he had clipped all items relating to Germany out of the *Tribune* and pasted them into the two books. In one he pasted the good, in the other the bad—one book was thick and the other thin. In the thick one were essays by Miss Thompson, underlined in part with red ink, and accompanied on the margins with exclamation marks and the words, "Lies, lies, nothing but lies," also in red ink. The other volume was thin and its pages blank except for a statement from Poultney Bigelow, a speech of Charles Lindbergh's, and a report of the Quakers' committee from their Berlin correspondent.

He showed me next, in the bad book, a picture of the Sixth Avenue elevated railroad being torn down, and explained to me that this was one of Roosevelt's undertakings to help the Allies. The elevated railroad, he told me, was shipped directly to Liverpool, to be made into munitions. He had heard this in a German broadcast, and now, he informed me, Roosevelt was busy trying to tear down also the Ninth, the Third, and the Second and First Avenue elevateds, also to send to the Allies. No, he did not like, he said once more, a man who always smiled.

When I rode back to town, his wife gave me some sausage and cheese and a bottle of good coffee to take along. He rode with me a good distance and outlined the future. He told me what would become of India, of the Dutch East Indies, and of England. He left me when we came to a swinging bridge and shouted that he hoped I would find someone to buy his place; now that Germany would become a fit land to live in again, he wanted to return, he shouted, across the turbulent water.

André Roosevelt has always found it easy to live in tropical places. He spent years in Bali and is now happy in Ecuador. Half an hour out of Quito at the foot of Mount Pichincha is his small house in a large garden.

The reason I think that André Roosevelt is happy here is that he has taken with him most of the troubles of civilization; with less pressure, and much less hurry and noise, he has access to our griefs: visits from unpleasant people, bills to pay, disputes with tradesmen, overdrawn bank accounts, callers from the telephone company, Christmas shopping, plumbing out of order, and doctor, lawyer, dentist; and for Ruth, his wife, there are hats and dresses, either to envy or to laugh at. There are also the many cares of running a house, which is no more exempt than one in Scarsdale from the need of being painted, and the large garden that must be kept in order. . . .

"Look at my garden. Ruth planted these forget-me-nots only last week, and now look at them." The flowers, innocently blue as the cloak of the Virgin of Quinché, are up to children's elbows; the daisies are as big as the faces of alarm clocks; the garden hums with colibri, bright and expensive as a Cartier window.

The garden sings, the bushes say good-morning to you as you walk past them. It is not out of a René Clair scenario but a sensible garden: the voices come from the children of the servants who stand among bushes, plucking dead leaves, loosening earth, watering flowers. *"Buenos días, patrón,"* they sing, and, *"Buenos días, patroncita."* Two of them belong to the cook, others to the gardener, the most beautiful to Cirilio, the butler.

This Cirilio at first meeting is a fearful man. He is as wide as he is high. His thick black hair grows from his eyebrows back down to his shoulder-blades. He can pick up things from the floor without bending, and André Roosevelt says that he spends the night sitting in a tree. The children's dresses are made of old Roosevelt curtains and Cirilio's wardrobe also comes from his master. His wife cuts the pants off in the middle; then she takes the two lower parts and sews them together, and a few buttons make them into a second pair of trousers.

The economics of the Roosevelt ménage are very simple. A hundred dollars a month covers all expenses, including rent, auto hire, entertaining, and the salaries and food for the servants and their children's food. Cirilio gets $2.50 a month; and the cooks get $2.00 each. The cooks are not very good in Ecuador, but then you have two of them.

Roosevelt has two cooks. One day we shot a rabbit up near the summit of Mount Pichincha and brought it home. The cooks had never cooked a rabbit before, and with Indian patience they sat for hours by the side of the duck pond and plucked the rabbit.

Ruth Roosevelt takes the fashion magazine to which she subscribes to a tailor in Quito, buys cloth which the Indians weave and dye, and is well dressed.

There is some difficulty with servants. All the servants are Indians. They are very sensitive, easily offended. They usually leave in the middle of a dinner party. When they are scolded for something they become sad, take their gloves off, and go home to their mountains and sit under a tree and eat bananas for a few days. Unannounced, and without explanation, they return, kiss your hand, and say that they have missed you.

Cirilio is more than sensitive. He must never be reprimanded when he forgets anything. If André says to him, "Cirilio, you must remember not to serve on the right side of the guests, but on the left," the damage is done. The reflection of the candles in his large black eyes becomes hazy, he puts the dish down, beats himself on the chest, and makes a long speech. "Oh, I am so stupid!" he starts out. "I have the head of a cow—on the right—no, on the left. Oh, you have told me so often, patrón!" Nothing can stop him. The food gets cold and Cirilio is gone to the hills with his children, insulting himself all the way.

When all goes well, he is happy and sings, and he is very much attached to the patroncita. He follows her throughout the house with paintpots, brushes, canvas gloves, and a ladder. Ruth loves to paint. The house always smells of fresh paint, mostly a terrible shade of blue. In overalls, brushing her blond hair out of her face with her forearm, she paints floors, garden furniture, tables, benches, doors, and window shutters. Cirilio holds the ladder and points to corners that have been forgotten, and apologizes. He knows that the patroncita likes to have everything painted new. That is one of the few things he is certain about.

To give a party is a nervous, dangerous obligation in Quito, largely on account of the servant problem. André gave a cocktail party. We went to Quito to buy wine and whisky and food. Spirits and imported wines—champagnes and brandy—are the only expensive items for entertaining in Ecuador. We were returning loaded with packages when André saw some pâté de foie gras in the window of a small shop. He is very fond of pâté de foie gras, and we bought all the cans the man had. They were dusty, and the proprietor of the shop blew on them and wiped them off with his sleeve.

After we came home and started a white wine punch, André got a box of crackers and we went out to the garden to a newly painted table and benches with the six cans of pâté de foie gras. Each of them sucked in air with a "Fhhhssss" as it was opened. The pâté had shriveled up. It seemed very old and looked like chewing gum. André moved away from the cans and smeared the pâté on the crackers at arm's length, and he said nothing. But there was a tin of anchovies, and he put on each cracker two filets of anchovies, laying them crisscross on top of the pâté. There was also a tube of some very sharp-tasting paste, and out of this tube André squeezed a rosette, just in the center where the anchovies crossed. We finally stuck a stuffed olive on the whole business. We made about forty of these canapés, and when they were done, Mr. Roosevelt took one and ate it. "Much better," he said, and handed one to me. "In fact, it tastes damn good. Have one." It was terrible.

André went to dress. He goes about most of the day in a long robe, a vegetable-dyed purple piece of hair cloth designed by his wife. Cirilio lit the candles, straightened out the silver, buttoned his white jacket, and was constantly asking the patroncita if he was doing everything right. The patroncita went to dress, and then all at once Cirilio disappeared. He had remembered that the patroncita loved to have everything painted fresh.

When the first guests arrived, Cirilio was standing alone in the lobby, his kind eyes shining. He passed the tray of canapés to them, but they could not take them. They held their hands far away from themselves. The hands were blue. Cirilio had just painted the doors, the doorknobs, the railings. "Oh, I am the head of a cow!" he said, when he saw what had happened— and then he was gone, and he did not come back for a long time.

BUENOS DÍAS, GRAN HOTEL

The train from Quito down to Esmeraldas on the northern coast is somewhat smaller than the one that comes up from Guayaquil, and it does not go to Esmeraldas, but that is planned. The engine and the coaches are already marked "Ferrocarril Quito—Esmeraldas."

There are three coaches, the first for baggage, the second for Indians. This one is insufficient, and most of the Indian passengers, together with their chickens, sit on the roof. Occasionally they bring one of their saints along, a statue decked out with flowers, and then it becomes a gay train, filled with color and music—it looks like a gondola coming down the Grand Canal. The third car is divided into two parts; the half that is toward the Indians is plain first class, the end toward the landscape is the observation car.

In this last part are six wicker chairs, upholstered in a stout, faded kind of billiard cloth. On the seats are rings such as the bottoms of wet beer glasses leave on a table. They come from the steel springs that have wormed their way up through the horsehair. You sit on them unless you have brought a pillow along or a blanket.

But you have ample chance to change your mind about the ride. From the moment you arrive at the depot until the train leaves you are surrounded by chauffeurs who plead with you to let them drive you to Otavalo, the last station. It's more comfortable, faster, and it won't cost much more, they tell you. As train time approaches, their advice becomes anguished. They run after you and take hold of your arm. "Don't take the train, go by car." They pull the corners of their mouths down and point at the engine, the train, or the conductor. "Don't go! Don't take it! It's terrible!" They say this under the nose of the station-master.

It is seven-thirty by the sun, a quarter to seven by the bells on the cathedral, and ten minutes to seven by the station clock. (There is an observatory in Quito which has the right time, but it cannot be seen from here.) The train leaves at seven sharp; that is, when the station-master whistles and the engineer waves good by to him.

As you pull away, you see the city first below you, then above. You ride through a wild garden without fences. Everywhere grow white lilies, geranium trees stand in all the gardens, costly birds fly through the air, and in the early hours when the clouds hang low in the valleys the landscape is as clear and luminous as if it were painted on the side of a very thin porcelain cup. It is, moreover, neat in its wildness; all the leaves, the plants, and the grass are washed and combed. Wherever you look, it is a picture out of the Bible, and the sparrows have little combs on their heads, like small roosters. I believe this is the most beautiful and the most varied landscape I have seen in all my life.

On several sharp curves the conductor will point out to you places where the engine has jumped the track and rolled over. The engineer and the fireman jumped to safety. They were going too fast, explains the conductor. Midway between Quito and Otavalo, he comes and offers you a tray with dusty sandwiches and lukewarm beer.

The train stops at a small village about every half-hour. The village surrounds it—small earthen houses with walls on which cubaya plants grow, little black boars, Indian children who ride on the train out of the village while the conductor stays behind and embraces a friend. When the train is already under way, the conductor runs after it, and swings himself to the rear platform. He smiles. Everyone smiles. This is really new, all of it.

Sometime during the journey the conductor comes with a little board to which is attached a paper. He has a pencil stub which he wets with his lips; then he asks you for your name, nationality, and profession, where you are going, where you come from, and why. You can give him any answer you choose. He writes it down politely in the letters of a six-year-old. If you are asleep, he waits. He whispers the questions to you if anyone else is asleep in the car. If you are a political menace, then, a rebel, a fugitive, or an assassin, just stay asleep until you reach your destination. No one will know that you have left Quito for Ibarra, Tulcán, or Alaosi.

On the day I went to Otavalo a man sat opposite me, asleep. At a sudden stop for water he woke up, unpacked some food, offered me half of it, and then started a conversation. "Madame Alvarez and I have wanted to be a father for many years," he said. "We have tried everything to be a father, Madame Alvarez and I, for about sixteen years, ever since we were married. But it is of no consequence; we are not a father. Madame Alvarez has even burned candles to her saint, all for nothing.

"Then, one time, Madame Alvarez goes to visit a sister in Chile, for one months"—he held up his right index finger and repeated—"for one months." The finger again—"In one months, Señor, I am a father. That is why I am on this train, I am visiting my niño, I am visiting as a father once a month. And you, señor?"

"I am also visiting a niño. I am writing a children's book, and I am looking for a child, an Indian child, to find out how he lives and what he looks like."

He then gave me the name and address of the schoolmaster in Otavalo, and offered to take me to a good hotel there, and he told me that he also had been a literary man, a publisher in Santiago, Chile.

He scratched the outside of one fat hand with the fingers of the other and then told me that his paper had failed because it was an afternoon paper.

"My paper had a small circulation, about twelve thousand. That is not enough. The circulation was so bad, my friend, because it was an afternoon paper. We have an alcoholic problem down there. Everybody drinks, and at five o'clock when my paper comes out nobody cares about anything, nobody can read any more. We have tried to print it in very large, easily readable type, but the same results. Now I have a small hotel in Quito."

The train dipped down into a valley that looked like the badlands of North Dakota. The Indians sang on the roof of the train and my companion began to snore. When he woke again he peeled a banana, and as the conductor passed and held out his hand for the ticket, he gave him the banana peel. The conductor took it and opened the door to throw it out. Then the brakes screeched and we were in Otavalo.

Otavalo is like all other mountain cities—marketplace with cathedral and Government house, municipal band, Indians in white clothes and ponchos, more beautiful than any other Indians; donkeys everywhere, and a large shop filled with coffins. (The death rate, the infant mortality, is appalling here. The little coffins are like cigar boxes, unpainted, and cost thirty cents apiece.)

Before Señor Alvarez went to visit his niño he took me to the principal of the school, Señor Andrade. This earnest man lived in one room and a kitchen. Every object in the room wore a little black necktie: four such cravats were tied on the four feet of the couch, one black bow across each picture on the wall, one across the neck of the Virgin, one on each cooking pot, and one across a small statue of Harlequin and Columbine. The teacher explained to me that six months ago his wife had died in childbirth, that she had been fond of all these things and had held them in her lovely hands, and that they were in mourning for her. He put on a black hat and we went to his school. The school was large, with light rooms. There was a basketball net in the yard.

The teacher told me that the Ministry of Education was very advanced in its ideas and that as soon as it was at all possible they instructed children in the matter of sex. He waved to his honor pupil, a little boy, and asked him to bring his homework. He handed me a homemade blank book. Just as our children at that age make their first designs of houses and people, here there was a picture in colors, and very modernistic, of a man in profile with "El Estómago" written under it. The man seemed to have just eaten; the estómago was filled with small pencil dots. The next page showed teeth and the digestive system, and then came a page on which the title was decorated like a Christmas card, with sunrays, little stars, scrolls, and illumination surrounding the words "La Sífilis." Equally beautiful and fetching was the next title, "La Gonorrea." This was done in green, with darts. The teacher explained that such instruction prevents shock later on.

We went back to my hotel, the Hotel Sucre. The waiter's name was Francisco. He was an Indian and barefooted, and he was also the cook. Francisco also helps clean the rooms and water the lilies. The hotel has one story and is square. The seven rooms face out on the courtyard. The rooms have no windows—the door is left open. The food is terrible and very cheap. You eat out in the courtyard. It is one of the most beautiful hotels I have ever been in. Francisco, walking silently, is always near; you can't complain about the service.

As I ate some boiled eggs, a man came out of room No. 4 and introduced himself. He was the chancellor of the Belgian Legation in Quito. His car had broken down and he was waiting for it to be fixed.

He held his head and said, "Have you ever seen anything like the hotels in this country? Oooooooh! I don't mind this one so much, but in Guayaquil, the first day I arrive, I say, 'Portez-moi un journal.'

"The telephone answers, 'Good, Señor.'

"Half an hour later I telephone again, and as the paper has not arrived, I say once more, 'Send me a paper.' Half an hour later a boy arrives and asks me what I want. 'A paper, where is the paper? The paper that I asked for half an hour and an hour ago, where is it?'

"He answers me nothing.

" 'Ah,' I said, 'that means you have no confidence in me. You want to have the money first, the twenty centavos!'

" 'Oh, no, patrón,' he said. 'That is not so.'

"But he held out his hand. I gave him the twenty centavos and he brought the paper.

"A few days later on, I find outside my neighbor's door a paper on which is written 'Buenos días, Gran Hotel.'

"I call the boy. I show him the paper. I say to him, 'What does that mean?'

"He says, 'It means, "Bon jour, Grand Hotel. Good day, Grand Hotel." '

"I said to him, 'Don't take me for an idiot! I know what it means, Buenos días, Gran Hotel.'

"And I said once more, 'Why is "Buenos días, Gran Hotel" written on this paper?' And he answered, the stupid, 'It is written there because it is the paper which is brought to the guests.'

"I said, 'Why don't you write "Buenos días, Gran Hotel" on the paper you bring for me?'

"To that he had no answer. And then I said, 'Good, I will give you the explanation. You are, all of you, *une bande de dégoûtants*. I know very well that the papers with "Buenos días, Gran Hotel" are offered to the clients with the compliments of the hotel, and only because I occupy the most expensive suite here and because I am a foreigner, you take me for a fool and make me pay. That is why; now go.'

"Cher Bemelmans," he said, "write that in your journal."

I asked Francisco, who had listened to all this with big Indian eyes, standing in the shadow of the door, for pen and ink, and then I wrote it down word for word as he said it. Francisco stood in back of me and read over my shoulder. When I had finished, as the ink was wet, he took some earth from the wall of the hotel, rubbed it to dust between his hands, and shook it over the paper to dry the ink.

The wine was rancid here. The proprietor brought his horse in from the street, a white horse, and it lay down in the center of the courtyard among the lilies. Francisco washed a shirt and hung it between the pillars that held up the roof. The moon rose, and a bird came and sang in the courtyard. The lilies and the white horse drank up the light. Francisco brought a lamp into my room, and then he looked through my trunk, examined the camera, looked through pictures, took the razor apart, and asked what was in the bottle. He sprinkled the eau de cologne on his head and asked me what the Belgian had said about "Buenos días, Gran Hotel."

He raked his thick black hair with my comb; then he became sleepy. The bed was large—boards and the usual beaten old mattress. He fell asleep at the foot of it, and I covered him up. He was about ten years old.

The next morning he brought me a newspaper. It was old and had lain in the hotel for about a month, but on it he had written in crude letters, "Buenos días, Gran Hotel."

THE PAINTED GRAPES

The proprietor was snoring in his room, and the beds creaked in the rooms of all the guests whenever they turned in their sleep. I lay for a long while with my arms crossed in back of my head and watched the sunrise through the open door. There was no window in my room. None of the rooms of this hotel has windows. The doors all face the courtyard.

The donkeys sang in the mountains outside, and in the room next to mine I heard the noises of a man getting up. He poured water into a basin, walked in slippers across the floor, stropped his razor, and yawned. A Saint Bernard dog with matted fur and feet as big as a lion's, his face unhappy and great loose bags under his hopeless, bloodshot eyes, walked out into the patio and rubbed his pelt against the wooden column.

His master, in a nightshirt, a glass of water and a toothbrush in hand, came after him. The man looked up into the sky,

scratched himself, and then gargled and brushed his teeth and
spat the water into the gutter of the patio. He then bent over the
plot of lilies, smelled them, and disappeared again in his room,
where I heard him sit down on the bed.

In the frame of the green door the picture that I had watched
for two hours was again undisturbed: a few feet away, between
the legs of a metal washstand, two lilies and a few cobblestones,
and on the wall across the yard a free chalk-colored fresco showing a stag hunted by hounds. Over the picture hung a piece of old
roofing with grass growing between faded tiles and above these
tiles far away was the volcano Tunguragua. It looked like a cone
made of ground coffee; an hour ago, before the sun rose, it was
indigo, then for a little while it was the color of an eggplant.

Attached to the door that led from the street into the hotel was
one of the bells whose lament is heard when one walks into a
small shop in France. It clanged at about seven.

Two barefooted Indians and a small black boar came in. Silently, but for the tinkle of three silver Maltese crosses that hung
from the woman's shoulder, they sat down, and the man helped
his wife to take a baby from her back. She reached up into her
hat and took clean linen from it and changed the baby's clothes.
They then sat down under the painting of the stag and the
hounds, and the small boar rooted in the soil among the lilies.

The Indians of Otavalo own their land and their houses; they
work the ground with wooden plows, raise animals, and bring
produce to market. Some of them weave cloth, others are
potters. Their linen is spotless. They walk, sit, and stand with
exquisite grace.

The men wear black pigtails; they have historic, decided faces,
and the women look like the patronesses at a very elegant ball. It
is baffling that they achieve this effect just sitting in rows along
the sidewalk, their bare feet in the gutter.

The Indian who sat under the deer became impatient; he got
up and walked into a room which had one wall lined with rows
of bottles of Mallorca and chicha. He helped himself to a bottle
and sat down. The two smiled.

The Indians always seem sweet to one another. They talk
quietly, and they have a sage arrangement—only one of them,

either the husband or the wife, may drink. They take turns. The sober one sees to it that the other gets home safely. You meet them on all the roads that lead to Otavalo, their fine faces beaming with majestic friendship. The children run alongside, everybody sings, a man leads a woman, a woman pulls a man, no anger, much laughing and the music of an instrument. They greet you with a sweep of the beautiful five-pound hat that almost throws them off the road. They seem a fortunate and happy people.

The Indian in front of me put the bottle away and then Señor Pilar, the proprietor, came out of his room and bought the black pig between the spokes at the foot of my bed, and in the same frame the money changed hands.

The distant volcano Tunguragua was alone again, its color much lighter now. The sun was half-way up its side. A coronet of white clouds was near the summit, and at its base were two rows of eucalyptus trees. From here they looked like miniature poplars leading up to a château. Between them red spots, the ponchos of Indians far away and high up, crawled down and disappeared among the blades of grass on the roof in front of me.

The man next door came again, now in a pair of badly cut dark gray breeches, not riding breeches and not plus-fours, but a style half-way between. With these he wore green woolen golf stockings and high laced black boots. While he was tying a knot in his cravat a butterfly went past his face and he ran after it and tried to catch it on the rim of one of the lilies. The butterfly sailed away and came through the green doorway into my room, with the man after it. He caught it, excused himself, and took it to his room.

After a while he came back and explained to me that the butterfly was an extraordinary specimen, and, excusing himself again, he stepped on the foot of my bed, reached to the ceiling, and collected two cocoons and a large moth. He delivered a brief lecture on these discoveries, and then introduced himself as a native of Switzerland, Herr Vogeli, from Tribschen, on the Vierwaldstättersee, Lake Lucerne.

The dog had come into the room also, and Herr Vogeli told me how glad he was that he had brought the animal along to Ecuador. It was, he said, the only good thing that had happened to him. The dog was of great help; he made things very comfortable. Whenever they came to stay at a hacienda or a hotel, he locked the dog into his room for an hour before retiring. The Saint Bernard acted like a magnet. From all the cracks in the floor and the walls, from closets and out of beds and carpets he drew the hungry fleas. After an hour he was taken out, doused with a shower of "la loción Flit," and then Herr Vogeli retired in peace.

He patted his faithful friend. The dog was busy scratching himself. He tried to reach a spot in back of his ear, lost his balance, rolled on his side, and violently clicked his teeth on some evasive fleas in the hair at the tip of his tail.

On the evening of the same day I sat down on a bench in the Plaza Sucre. A beggar passed first, carrying his old mother on his back. She held a fan of lottery tickets in her hand, waved her withered arms, and called, "Twenty thousand sucres next Sunday."

When these two were gone, a group of little people appeared, cretins, Mongoloid children, idiots in a group, guarded and led by an old man in a wide Panama hat and a blue linen coat. They huddled together in the camaraderie of infirmity, their large heads lolling, their limbs in grotesque poses. They bent down over the street with garden tools, and removed the grass and small plants that grew between the stones. With great effort, they brought the bouquets of weeds to their guardian, who opened a large sack into which they slowly deposited them—watching the old man's face for approval, a smile and nod of the head with which he receipted for the grasses.

From the sack they hopped back to search for more. They laughed, slyly, inwardly, as if in possession of a great and happy secret. They wandered slowly around the plaza. Before the door of the cathedral they knelt down, removed their caps, lifted their faces, and made the sign of the cross.

They looked again for the old man's approval, and went back to the grass, and moved on with their silent smiles, disappearing into the City Hall. There they have a room for their belongings, and another with two rows of small institutional beds, and a large one for the overseer, who is with them day and night.

Outside of the public building stands the Jefe Político, the foreman of a group of citizens whose principal purpose is to keep themselves warm under their ponchos. They stand staring into the square, and, like the cathedral, they are part of every South American plaza. The sight of a young woman, of a cockfight, or of a good horse awakens them and makes them turn their heads. For the rest they stand or sit and gossip. Occasionally one raises an arm to push a necktie to the left or right. He reaches with two fingers into the folds of his skin for a flea. This done, he sinks back into his stupor. If he is a policeman, he blows a little short whistle every half-hour to announce that he is still there.

From the far end of the plaza, between two palm trees, appeared the Swiss, with a cigar box under his arm and followed by his dog. In the box he had new butterflies and cocoons, safely bedded in cotton. The big dog tried to make himself small enough to squeeze under the bench, and his master sat down above him.

With a hand that smelled of ether, Herr Vogeli pointed at the lampposts which stood on the four corners of the plaza and said that exactly at six-twenty the night before he had observed a group of butterflies that appeared from the direction of the volcano. They were all gone in another ten minutes, after flying from lamppost to lamppost. He told me that if he could measure the degree of humidity, then he could make a graph and tell precisely when the butterflies would be here again.

Herr Vogeli seemed to know a good deal about butterflies and insects. I told him how surprising it was to meet a Swiss who was not an innkeeper or the proprietor of a sanitorium.

He said he was very sorry, but that butterflies were only his hobby. He really was a hotelman, and while keeping his eyes on the lampposts, he made me acquainted with his story.

"I am here," he began, "on account of that swine Goldoni. Goldoni is a man who is building a railroad through the jungle down to Esmeraldas. He has been working on it for four years, and in all this time he has finished exactly eight kilometers. He is under arrest now, but that is all beside the point. I came here to open a hotel in Ibarra, a few miles from here, in back of the volcano."

The lamps were lit, there were fluttering wings about them,

and Herr Vogeli in his bicycle pants, with the straps sticking out in back of his boots, ran quickly off. He came back, disappointed; the butterflies had not arrived yet, he had found nothing but fairly common moths.

This man Goldoni, he said, sitting down, came to Vogeli's inn one day in Tribschen on the Vierwaldstättersee. It was on that part of this complicated lake that Richard Wagner composed the music for the *Meistersinger* and most of *Siegfried* and *Götterdämmerung,* the place where he spent the happiest years with Frau Cosima—a hallowed spot. A garden restaurant with iron chairs and tables under shade trees reflected itself in the lake. On sunny days it filled up with guests, and above them was the top of the Rigi; it was lovely and peaceful.

When Goldoni came, the garden, the inn, the chairs and tables were dripping; the season was ruined by a month of rain. Vogeli had trouble with his employees, with his wife, and with the three guests who were staying at the inn. They complained about the steam heat being out of order. Goldoni listened to Vogeli's troubles, and then suddenly slapped him on the back and said, "Vogeli, you are my man. Vogeli, you come with me."

He took Vogeli along to the Kursaal in Lucerne, and sat him behind a glass of wine; he pushed the vase of flowers that stood between them out of the way, and while an Italian orchestra played, he told him about Ibarra, about Ecuador.

"Ha," laughed Goldoni, "imagine a land where every vegetable and flower grows wild, where you can get all the help for ten francs a month, and where there is no such thing as a strike or rain." (It rained a little, he said, but only during the night.) Ecuador, the Land of the Future, where it is spring the year round. In the most beautiful part of that land is a lake, bluer than this one here, and on that lake, he told the wide-eyed Vogeli, was Ibarra, a city of ten thousand inhabitants.

There, with one side fronting on the lake and the other on the newly built railroad station, Goldoni would build him a hotel, modern, complete from cellar to roof. It would have no competition, since there was no other hotel, restaurant, or café in the whole town. And he would never have to worry about the steam heat—there was no need for any. It was always pleasantly warm, not hot, not cold. It was, as he had said before, the land of eternal spring.

Besides this, Goldoni explained, Vogeli would be a god. "If you drive in a car," he told him, "and your hat blows off, the policeman runs after it, and if he does not bring it back quickly, you call him down and report him to his superiors."

Vogeli then asked about butterflies. It was very late and they went to the Café Saint Gotthard, because the Kursaal closed at eleven, and there Goldoni continued his story and ended by proposing a contract. Vogeli signed some papers, sold his inn, packed, and left his wife, to go ahead to Ibarra.

"I found everything the way Goldoni had described it; I must say that, I can't say different. The hotel was not started yet, but the lake was there, a very beautiful lake. The provisions are cheap here, and I can get all the employees I want for less than ten francs a month. No one strikes in this country, and it rains very little. There isn't another hotel or inn—that is true also. Ibarra has ten thousand inhabitants, yes, but eight thousand of them are children; the rest are Indians and have no money. There are two white men, but they drive to Quito every week to eat and drink.

"But I like it here, I think I'll stay; I will look for a small place in Quito, and start with a pension. The butterflies amuse me, and they are a profitable hobby. I sell most of them.

"Besides, I can't go back. Everybody would hear about this, and the sparrows in Lucerne and Tribschen would whistle from the rooftops that Vogeli is a fool."

We walked back to the hotel. Painted over its door were a vine and some grapes. Vogeli pointed to them.

"Poor bird deceived with painted grapes," he sighed. In spite of his fine dog he wore a bracelet of fleabites; he scratched himself, and told me that the quotation was from Shakespeare.

THE FRIENDS OF ECUADOR

Herr Vogeli, dressed in a green suit and a green hat, was standing first on one foot then on the other, looking around in all directions and saying that he could not wait any longer. "In this country you might as well throw your watch away. Nobody, not even the police are on time."

We had engaged a car for half-past seven, to take us back from Otavalo to Quito. It was now half-past eight. We walked through the town to look for it and it was nowhere to be seen.

At nine-thirty it appeared, an ancient Hupmobile. The driver explained that as soon as we had picked up another passenger, we could start, and he hoped that we had no objection to having somebody else ride along. The new passenger, he said, was a Government official. We sat down on a bench and waited, and for the next half-hour the Government official did not appear, so we asked the driver to take us to his house. It was half-past ten.

We drove to a little house and the driver honked his horn. The official came to the window in shirt and suspenders, and bowed and smiled, and lifted a finger as a signal. He disappeared between heavy white curtains, came back to the window a few seconds later, and held up a baby. Next the curtains were pushed aside by a fat round hand: a candy-colored satin bedjacket appeared, and Madame also nodded and smiled. There is nothing you can do when a baby is shown but nod and smile, and so Herr Vogeli smiled, the driver and his friend smiled, and I smiled.

The curtains closed, to open again in a little while; the Government official continued the pantomime of the good life by showing us a coffee cup. He also signaled the fact that he was hurrying by gulping down a piece of bread. He bowed himself out, backing into the white curtains, and for the next ten minutes the window was dead. The door of the house opened about eleven and the official in black appeared, followed by wife and baby and a half-grown Indian girl who carried bottles, pillows, a rubber sheet, and a bag. All of them smiled and nodded; the baby cried and tried to swallow its small fist.

Herr Vogeli looked angry. The places were divided. It was a large car, with old upholstery, artificial flowers in small glass vases to left and right, and a rosary above the steering wheel.

It was eleven-thirty and we all sat up like sacks. The windows were half open but it smelled of nursery, of rubber sheet and boudoir, and of dog—the Saint Bernard was invisible, but unmistakably present, among the feet.

The chauffeur and his friend—drivers here always have a companion—were reasonably comfortable in front. The car started off and an animated conversation began in the front seat. The driver turned around, laughed, tried out a few English phrases, and pointed at the scenery. Only occasionally were both his hands on the wheel; sometimes he needed both of them to illustrate his conversation.

A few miles out of Otavalo, we came to the first blind and terrifying curve. It is a spot where you keep your mouth continually open to find words for the beauty of this land. We drove as fast as the car would go and on the wrong side of the road. Half a foot from the running board down to a mountain stream far below, stretched a prickly thicket of candelabra cacti and bayonet-leaved plants. To the right of the road was the base of another mountain that went straight up. On that side, in a small earthen niche, stood a statue of the Virgin. At her feet was an empty can that once had held tennis balls, now filled with field flowers, and the lower half of a beer bottle stuffed with a bouquet of forget-me-nots.

Just ahead in the middle of the road a four-year-old Indian girl in a blue poncho walked behind her sheep, and, squeezed against the bank, an Indian rode on his donkey. There was also a jet-black bull with wide horns, full grown, grazing on a thin strip of dusty grass.

Into this arrangement of animals and people, all so close that they touched each other, our car charged at full speed. The driver kept on laughing and talking to his friend even when an enormous bus appeared from the opposite direction. "Mamacita" was written on the sides of it. In the bus were some forty singing Indians, and on its roof, among clusters of bananas and chicken crates and sacks of corn, sat six more.

It was all over very quickly. Our driver took his hat off to the Madonna, the bus disappeared in a cloud of its own dust (it, too, had fortunately been on the wrong side of the road), the Virgin in her niche trembled a little, the bull cropped his grass, the little girl and her sheep went wandering on, the Indian on the donkey smiled and waved his hat. And it happened all over again on a curve a few miles farther on. God has not only made this country beautiful; He seems to close an eye very often in love for its people.

The mother, the baby, the nurse, and the dog were asleep. Herr Vogeli told the story of his experiences to the Government official and then he also fell asleep.

The official turned to me and observed that, while occasionally the immigrant is deceived, the Government has also had its share of painted grapes. He spoke of a group of Austrians that had come to Ecuador in 1928, a party of fifty men and fifty women. The opinion was then current, said the official, that foreigners had more business acumen, were braver, more resourceful, and enduring than the natives; and great concessions were made them.

The man who had organized the immigrants, a German, was well known in Quito. He was an adventurer who had lived several years in the jungles of the Oriente, and he had written many articles for an Austrian magazine called *Die Übersee Post*. In this paper he sang the usual praises of the rare woods, of gold and emeralds, the eternal spring and the flowers, and he mentioned the fact that eggs cost only one centavo apiece.

His articles got so much attention that he went to Vienna and organized a Society of the Friends of Ecuador. He issued membership pins and certificates, collected weekly dues, and accepted the savings of barbers, plumbers, chauffeurs, and store clerks. One farmer joined, too; and he sent them all to Ecuador.

He put one man in charge and he himself stayed behind to organize a second group.

On a cold and windy day in November, the first part of the

Society of the Friends of Ecuador left Hamburg. They were miserable at first, and seasick, but after a while the cold wind stopped howling, the clouds moved away, the waters suddenly were blue and green. They had enough to eat and drink, and for the first time in their lives they were warm in winter. They lay on deck and let the sun shine on their pale stomachs, and all at once they were in Guayaquil.

They went to a small hotel. The one who was their spokesman wondered why no one had come to receive them. . . . They stayed in the small hotel until their money ran out; then they sat in the parks of Guayaquil. The authorities were up in Quito and knew nothing about them. The six policemen of Guayaquil looked upon white men as lords; they had never arrested a white man, and so they left them sitting in the parks unmolested.

The Government finally heard of them and took them to Riobamba and then to Quito. The fifty families were temporarily housed in the presidential quinta and a man was deputized to look after them. Every day they wrote on a piece of paper what they needed, including wine and beer, and it was given to them.

The Government then asked them to look around for land to settle on, and meanwhile granted them a pension of sixty sucres a month per person. The sucre at that time was four to the dollar.

It was arranged that the families should stay in Quito while the men went out to find farms. An additional grant was arranged to buy implements and seeds for them, once they had chosen their land.

The barbers, store clerks, and chauffeurs—and the one farmer —headed for the jungle, of which they had heard such wondrous tales. They found the orchids; the wild pigs came close to their camps; the forests were filled with game and the rivers with fish. The only unpleasant and disturbing thing was the song of the ocelot at night: a noise like that of a bow drawn slowly across a double bass. The men hunted all day long and occasionally waded in the shallow waters of the river to look for gold; each of them had a horse, a saddle, a gun, a young Indian woman, and sixty sucres for drink, and the eggs were really one centavo apiece. They never wanted to go back.

There was loud howling from the wives and children left in
Quito, and finally the Government cut the pension; it had had
enough of them. The one farmer had cleared some land and
planted bananas, but the others went back. A few left for Chile,
others stayed in Quito to become barbers, mechanics, and plumbers again; and one of them still works in a butcher shop.—And
that, said the Government official, was the end of the Friends of
Ecuador.

The silence that followed the story awakened the baby and it
was fed. Then all at once the car stopped, and the radiator cap
went up in a column of steam. The assistant driver ran to a
near-by brook and came back with water, the car started and
stopped again, and this time there was no gas. . . .

The Government official looked at his watch and took the
baby, the Indian girl took the bottles and the rubber sheet, and
Herr Vogeli took the bag. We ran a little way to where the track
of the Quito–Esmeraldas Railroad crossed the road and waited
for the train. It stopped for the blue handkerchief which the Government official waved. Soon we were all arranged in a first-class
compartment, baby, rubber sheet, dog, and all.

Herr Vogeli had put the official's bag in the baggage net above
his seat and had fallen asleep. For a while I debated with myself
whether I should wake him up or get up myself to push the little
bag back. It slowly wobbled closer and closer to the edge of the
baggage net and then began to lean over; it had almost gone too
far when the train went up a steep incline that made it slide back
again into its proper place. Thus it advanced and retired several
times, turning little by little, until it was flat against the wall and
secure.

TO A WHITE ROSE

Back at the Hotel Metropolitano in Quito, I told the bellboys to have the trunk sent to the railroad station and the bag to the plane. Two boys carried the trunk out of the room. I had never waited less than an hour for a car, half an hour for a train, and I wondered whether the plane would leave on time.

"They are gross and dull, these Germans, at times—God, how dull they can be; but they are always orderly, and always on time," said André Roosevelt. "Look at Frau Hagen: her house is in order, her husband is in order, and her business is in order, and when we drive out to the flying field you will see the motor going, gas and oil on board, and the pilot ready."

We had to check the trunk through to Guayaquil first, and we drove to the station. We overtook the trunk a few blocks before we got there and saw that the bellboys had farmed out the job. They were walking to the left and right of the heavy trunk, and an Indian woman, quite an old one, was carrying it on her back. The boys came along to collect the tip.

The man in the baggage department was tired; he did not weigh the trunk, he just walked around it. It was a large wardrobe trunk and he pushed it a little, stood to one side and crossed his arms, and then said, "Twenty sucres."

I said, "Oh, no, ten sucres."

Seventeen sucres it cost finally.

The plane was ready. It goes to Guayaquil in three-quarters of an hour, the same distance which takes two days in the train. There is no radio beam. Motor failure would be fatal. Two German pilots are at the controls. They can't carry much cargo, have to limit the number of passengers, and take off with the gas tanks half full. The air up in Quito is thin. The plane is an old Jun-

324

kers Transport, but they also have several smaller machines which are used for charter flying and for surveying.

The pilots were young men; one of them had just arrived from Germany, and the other was showing him the landmarks along the route.

The plane, after rising from the field and circling it, loses altitude until it is over the Guayas River. There it banks and, tracing a half-circle over the cemetery, settles on the field at Guayaquil. The field is surrounded by fences and low wooden houses, with tall palm trees rising above them and everywhere, on fences and roofs, no longer disturbed by the roar of the engines, sit rows of black turkey buzzards, silent and ominous.

I met Don Juan Palacios, my historian, in the lobby of the Gran Hotel that evening. He sat next to an empty teacup, under a sign that said, "Five o'clock tea, at all hours," and he almost burned his fingernails holding the stub of a black, sweet-smelling Ecuadorian cigarette. He looked more decayed than ever.

It was the beginning of the rainy season. The cloth of my suit, the newspaper, my hat, everything was moist. Sheets of water fell in the streets, small waterfalls ran off the corners of buildings. And as soon as it stops raining a plague of bugs arrives, and all at once they are everywhere; their number is estimated in the millions. The bomberos are called out sometimes with all their fire engines; they have to wash the bugs off the sides of buildings, clear the telegraph poles, and flood them down the streets.

In the rest of the world they live out in the pantry, under the sink, and in the plumbing, and they are called cockroaches; but here they fly. They fly like swallows and they are worse than vultures, and on top of that they sing "Pyiiiiii, pyiiiiiiiii." Their name is "grillos." They love to eat cotton and wool. If they can't get either of these, they will take silk. I think that they know how to open doors and unlock trunks. Two of them can do away with a sweater in a few hours.

A grillo came gliding through the high portals of the hotel and —smack, bam!—landed on the glass-topped table in front of me. He folded his wings neatly under two covers and disappeared. Another one landed on my shoulder with the impact of someone slapping me.

"Sit still," said Don Juan, "the boy will take care of it."

A bellboy stationed there for this purpose came, and deftly threw the grillo to the tiled floor, where he spattered.

A whole group of them came flying in together. They settled on the floor, turned about as mechanical toys do, ran rapidly in this direction and that, feeling and tapping ahead continuously with long antennas. Six of them ran under a wicker chair and chased out a small, hysterical dachshund who had just arrived in Ecuador. His eyes glassy and his tail between his legs, he trembled and tried to get out of his collar. Don Juan Palacios bent down to the dog and assured him that the "cafards" would not eat him up.

"Oh, dear," said a woman at the left to her husband, introducing another woman, "I've just found out that we're both from Mason City, Iowa. I want you to meet her. This is Rose White——"

"Rose White"—Count de Ampurias turned in his chair, looked at Rose White and translated the name, Rosa Blanca—Rosa Blanca—Rosa Blanca. He played with the words, and after a while he said, "Let's go along. I want you to meet someone I am very fond of, an old friend of mine. I want to take you to a very interesting place that you must see before you leave Ecuador."

We took a car and drove to the old city, and then we walked for a while. Majestic palms stood swaying among rows of badly lit hovels. We walked through a melancholy street with a sidewalk, without drainage; and I had to grit my teeth because we slid along on a carpet of grillos.

The houses were of wood, and their doors of split bamboo. The only pieces of furniture in them were hammocks. Through the open doors, in the rhythm of pendulums on dozens of clocks, the feet of women were swinging from the hammocks.

Stray donkeys and goats grazed on patches of grass between buildings and in the road; radios blared; there was wild yelling, and the high hard voices of women. In front of one house a man in a poncho was washing his hands in a brook of water that ran down off the roof. At the end of the slippery promenade, Don Juan Palacios loosened the grip on my arm, pointed ahead, and said that this was where his friend lived, the Villa Delicia.

"*Ah, mes belles années,*" he sighed. "She was as beautiful as
the Devil. Ah, when I was a young man, I wrote, I danced, I
played polo and piano. I don't shine at anything much now."

We arrived at the gate of what was for this neighborhood a
reasonably permanent house. Every shutter was closed. It stood in
a garden with large trees, such as one finds in the old cemetery in
Guayaquil, and it must at one time have been a good address.

For the last steps approaching the house, Don Juan Palacios let
go of my arm. He knocked loudly. A young colored woman in a
white apron opened the door, and when we were inside, Don
Juan said, "I wonder whether this is the right house. I have not
been here for years."

Just then a voice upstairs sang: "Amelia, *de l'eau chaude—*"
and the Count said, "Ah, yes, this is the place."

We walked into the parlor. Three chairs stood around a table,
and a buffet against the wall. As my eyes grew accustomed
to the dim light in the room, I thought that I saw a man looking
up from under the buffet. I went and knelt down, and saw the
fat face of Charles Laughton. I looked around the room then and
discovered that it was papered with a large poster for *Mutiny on
the Bounty*.

The maid, who came in with some drinks, explained that
Doña Rosa was exceedingly fond of Clark Gable, and that the
local distributor for the films of several American companies, a
friend of hers, had brought her the poster as a gift. They had had
much trouble finding a place where Mr. Gable, full size, could be
posted up to his best advantage. The room was small and it was
on this account that Charles Laughton fared so badly. They had
had to cut him in half to fit the paper around a window. His head
was near the floor on one side of the room, and his legs and torso
came down from the ceiling opposite.

The agent had also sent a poster of the quintuplets, but the
maid informed us that Ecuador does not like quintuplets. There
are too many children in Ecuador—children in Ecuador are nothing remarkable; to have five of them at once would be a catastrophe. Rosa Blanca, however, liked them, and she had cut
them out and pasted them over the bed in the room where she
slept. The maid opened another door, and we saw a brass bed in

a blue room, with the quintuplets laughing down from the wall.

As the maid left the room, she was pushed aside by Rosa Blanca. Don Juan Palacios arose, and spread his arms, and muttered. There followed a vast exchange of caresses and mutual assurances of love and esteem. He kissed her hand and brought her across the room to introduce me.

She wore a yellow dress, tight and shiny like a wet lollipop. She was a comfortable bed of soft white flesh, her shoulders and bosoms the pillows and bolsters, her plump middle a plumeau. She had thick ears and a thick tongue and green eyes, and her hair, which was white at the roots for a sixteenth of an inch above her scalp, was a dead canary-yellow down to her shoulders.

She sat down and spoke of troubles with her hairdresser and of general ennui with the world. The Count moved close to her and kneaded her arm. With her free hand she toyed with a cross of garnets.

Don Juan shouted to the Negro girl for more beer, and he smoked several black cigarettes.

The cold wind that blows down into Guayaquil at night made the room uncomfortable, and Rosa Blanca sent the maid for her furs. A smeary silver-fox jacket was put across her shoulders.

The Count began to talk about the past. "Tw-tw-twenty years ago," he started—and then he fell into a fit of coughing, gulped like a fish, and suddenly looked like a corpse.

Rosa Blanca carried him onto the bed in the blue room, and called to the maid to bring cold water. Then she telephoned someone to come and fetch him home. She sat down in the Mutiny on the Bounty room, looking warm and moist and not without attraction. She belonged half in a salon and half in a stable. She was a polyglot woman, speaking in four languages at once. She did not like Ecuador, she said—no concerts, no theater, nothing. The city she liked was Shanghai.

"In Shanghai, my friend in bed is also my friend on the street. Here, if I meet him tomorrow on the street"—she motioned with her head toward the blue room—"he will pass me without seeing me. That is what I am going to have put on my tombstone," she said. *"Vous qui passez sans me voir*— I have to think up something to rhyme with that."

The Count sat up in bed and protested that it was not true, what she had said; that he would not only recognize her, but speak to her.

"Bah," she said, "go to sleep, lie down, quiet, sh!" But Don Juan came to the door, like a child that refuses to go to bed, and called her, "Rosa Blanca, Rosa Blanca, mon enfant, come here, come to me, my sweetheart."

He was in his stocking feet and his hair was disordered, and he sagged at the knees. When he stood up straight, he was about five feet two; now he was like a very old child.

"Go to bed, sh!" she said. Don Juan took out a diamond stick-pin and held it into the room under the lamp. Rosa Blanca only said, "Go back to bed," and she went and kissed him on the cheek. He jumped into bed with an unexpected leap. In the dark room he talked quietly to himself for a while until he fell asleep.

Rosa Blanca spoke of a son who was studying law in Santiago, Chile. She folded her large hands, which were not as clean as one might wish, in a peculiar fashion, a kind of interlocking of gears. Her fingers were covered with diamond rings as large as pieces of butter, all of them false. She talked of her husband, in the States, an impresario whose band was called the "Katz Embassy Grenadiers."

The housebell rang. A little man came for Don Juan Palacios, an earnest, insignificant, thin man, pale and worried, with a large nose. He was accompanied by a policeman, and he said neither "Good evening" as he came in, nor "Good night" as he left with his tired little brother.

THE S.S. *SANTA LUCIA*

"We were not very serious last night," said Montegazza, when he came to the hotel to see me off. He had a white rose in the lapel of his *pet-en-l'air*. We crawled down the main street of Guayaquil past the shops and had our shoes shined and bought two lottery tickets.

When we came to a bookshop Don Juan remembered that he had promised to give me his history of Quito and a set of his books on Ecuador. He lifted one foot and stepped in and accosted a clerk with one of his imperial gestures. He took the clerk aside and talked to him very earnestly.

The owner himself came out from under a stairway. He bowed his greetings, and the three went into a corner where there were many shelves of books.

Count de Ampurias took several thick leather-bound volumes from the shelves and began stacking them together. He opened one and commenced to read it. While the clerk stayed beside him, the owner came and took me by the arm and led me quietly over to the store's rear door. The Count gave a quick look in my direction, a sudden signal of alarm and suspicion, and returned to his book.

The owner said that it would be best if I left, or I would never get rid of the old man. Don Juan Palacios, Count de Ampurias y Montegazza, he explained, was not a count at all. His real name was Cristóbal Calderón. He came of an eminently respectable old family, was well-to-do, owned a large hacienda—but had trouble inside his poor head.

He was not dangerous—"Oh, no, just peculiar." He struck up friendships with visitors who interested him, and appeared in curious outfits. When the exchange had been better, he had lived all year in Paris; but now he was back home.

The owner of the bookstore held the door open for me, and said that the whole thing dated from very long ago, an unhappy love affair. People said it had something to do with roses. He bought roses, he wore roses, he looked up every book on roses, and he raised them and sent them to everybody he liked—white roses.

The proprietor opened the door a little wider and smiled good-by. I said that I thought Count de Ampurias was a very charming man. The proprietor closed the door.

"Ah, yes," he said, "and that is not all. He is noble, esteemed, very cultured and illustrious, and not sufficiently celebrated—*nunco bien ponderado."*

With this threefold compliment we were back in the aisle beside the Count, who took my arm and assured me that all the books were ordered and would be sent to me directly to New York. He turned and gave the bookseller some very explicit shipping directions.

"C'est ça," he said.

The man bowed deeply and promised everything.

In slow advances, as if in oversized slippers, we walked down to the Guayas River, and found the blue launch *Gloria*—"the swiftest, the most commode, the most secure." Her captain steered with his bare feet. A string of pelicans came along in even beat, and they lifted themselves over the roof of the small launch.

"Municipal councilors, we call them," said Montegazza, "on account of the large mouth, the folds at the throat, and the big belly."

He mounted the steps to the steamship one by one; to lift either of his legs some forty times was torture for him, and up on deck he sank into a chair in complete exhaustion. The last bananas were loaded below, the last passengers came aboard, two monkeys were sold and a lot of Panama hats. The Count had a drink with me, and when the whistle droned again, he left. The owner of the *Gloria* helped him down the ladder.

The little man became smaller and smaller and mixed into the people below. The blue launch *Gloria* pushed away. White cranes and blue herons sat in the trees along the riverbanks, and the drone of the *Santa Lucía's* steam whistle sent them up into the sky. The sailors on the battleship *C* waved good-by.

The land on both sides of the ship slipped away. Below in the launch Montegazza, his face the size and color of a walnut, waved his cane and his handkerchief, and over me came again the emotional sloppiness I feel when I go away from anywhere.

The *Santa Lucía* is like a big comfortable nurse. It is also like a country house. Everything is large and clean and orderly. The Captain's uniform is white and fits, and all the clocks are right. The pink ham and eggs look bright and clean and appetizing in the morning, and for dinner the ceiling rolls back and you can eat under the sky as on the roof of the Waldorf—with only the stars to show that the boat is moving.

Young girls in yellow dresses wait on you; there is no great formality. A slow and careful adjustment back to where trains run on time and bills are collected, to the sharp and serious life—an adjustment that is made very nicely.

The next morning, while we were still in Ecuadorian waters, I found near the swimming pool, beside a cup of coffee, an artificial leg. It was dressed in a tennis shoe, a white stocking, and a blue garter, and it remained there until lunch time. It was the last remnant of the beautiful madness of this lovely land.

AUTHOR'S NOTE

The Donkey Inside is the notebook or sketch-pad of several voyages through South America.

In a sense it is a portrait of that continent, from Chile to the Panama Canal, but it is focused on Ecuador, because there I found, in stronger outline than anywhere else, the things peculiar to South America.

Shielded by inadequate transportation (a small, baroque red train serves Quito three times a week, and it was not touched by airlines when I arrived), Ecuador has been left sleeping on, undisturbed by tourists.

The terrain, the architecture, and the landscape—the light that lies over it and the animals that walk about in it—are rendered as they are. As for the people, with the exception of André Roosevelt and his wife, the Indian boy Aurelio and all minor characters are wholly fictitious. Whenever character and person had to be painted in broad, immediate color, I have taken license to use the devices of the fiction writer. And to spare the reader the fatigue of meeting too many people, I have, whenever I found it right, put together several and of this amalgam made one person, such as Allan Ferguson. Cyril Vigoroux, for example, is a portrait of all the explorers I have met—at least of all the explorers of that type. I have taken the feet of one and the ears of another, and I hope it comes out all right.

Thus, too, it was actually three o'clock in the chapter where I make a boat arrive in the morning. The conversation with the Swiss hotelkeeper, on the train from Esmeraldas to Otavalo, really took place over the railing of a small steamer on the Lago de Todos Santos, in Chile.

It fitted so, it made a good picture.

Club Pichincha, Quito, Ecuador

333

I Love You, I Love You, I Love You

SOUVENIR

Every time I pass, along the West Side Highway, a spot just above Forty-sixth Street, there comes over me the feeling that I experience at the dentist's as I wait for him to get through putting the little drill in his machine, the sorrow of saying good-by, and the sadness of a band playing far away, all rolled into one. It's the stretch where you can look down on the *Normandie*. I am glad to report that workers are busy righting her. The superstructure is gone and on the side over the de luxe cabins are planks and lamp posts. It looks as if a street stretched over the water, over the ship—a strange thing to contemplate, a fantastic scene.

I have always given more affection to the *Normandie* than to any other ship. I loved her for her gaiety, for her color, for that familiarity with all the world that was her passenger list. In her décor she leaned toward excess; there was something of the *femme fatale* about her. She assumed a seigneur's privilege of frowning on the lesser, fatter, slower, and more solid boats. Like all aristocrats, she had abominable moods. I think she was more female than all the other ships that I have known. I think that's why I loved her so.

We traveled on her once under extraordinary circumstances. We intended to spend a year in Europe. I had booked passage on her and was ready to sail when an eager young man with an extensive vocabulary came to see me. He told me that the French Line was delighted to have us cross on the *Normandie,* that its directors wished to make everything very comfortable for us, and that instead of giving us just an ordinary cabin, they were glad to be able to offer us a *suite de luxe.* I am not one to sleep on a hard mattress when I can have a soft one, so the young man and I bowed to each other and had three Martinis each. I went to Mark Cross and bought a set of new trunks to go with the better accommodations and had my tie pressed. We also invited a lot of people to see us off.

It seemed that at the last moment all the ordinary cabins *de luxe* had been taken and the only thing left to do with us was to put us into one of the *Suites de Grand Luxe.* We went into a palace called Trouville—private terrace, servants' dining room, feudal furniture. Everybody was satisfied, particularly with the Lalique ashtrays.

The next morning I sat in my *dodine* rocking on my private terrace and regarding the morning sun and the sea. After five minutes of the most profound rocking, and of the most profound silence, except for the rocking, I thought I would burst with rage when a man appeared on my private terrace and stood there, looking out to sea.

I shouted, "Excuse me, but I don't think we have met."

"Oh, I'm so sorry. I just came out," said the man.

"Do you happen to know that this is my private terrace *alors?*" I said to him.

"Oh, I'm so sorry. I'm just admiring the view," he said and turned away. I kept on rocking. He walked over to his own pri-

vate terrace. He was introduced to me later as the banker Jules
Bache.

The day after sailing, the great hall, crowded the night before
with good-by sayers, messenger boys, pickpockets, and weeping
relatives, was now swept clean. The runners had been taken up,
the furniture put back in place. The room of silver, gold, and
glass, large as a theater, floated through the ever clean, endless
ocean outside the high windows. In a corner, a steward who
looked like Sacha Guitry was arranging French stamps in boxes
and straightening out the writing paper. Up on the sun deck,
children were riding the merry-go-round that was built inside of
the first funnel. On the outside of that funnel was a small plaque.
It was like the charm on a bracelet, elegant and tight. On it was
inscribed: *Normandie—Chantiers Penhoet, Saint-Nazaire*—and
the date she was built. *Chantiers* is a lovely name for a shipyard.
It sounds like a song, like the name of a beautiful song-bird.

There was a dark fortress of a woman on board that voyage,
an old countess with a face made of Roquefort and eyes like
marbles, the kind of marbles that boys call "aggies." She sat
wrapped in her sables in the front row of three lines of deck
chairs outside the main salon. On her lap, covered by a small
hound's-tooth blanket, asthmatic and dribbly, sat a Pekinese with
thyroid trouble; his eyes were completely outside of his head.
Whenever my daughter Barbara passed by her chair, the old
countess lifted the blanket, gave the dog, whose name was Piche,
a little push, and said to him, *"Piche, regardez donc la petite
fille qu'elle est mignonne!"* One day she reached out her hand,
but Barbara ducked and ran all the way to the Trouville Suite
nursery, where she burst into tears.

The other outstanding figure on that trip was a young widow.
She was dressed in long, glamour-girl blond hair and black satin.
I think she rubbed herself with a lotion every morning, and then
pasted her clothes on her body; there wasn't a wrinkle in them.
A doctor could have examined her as she was. Her arms were
weighed down with bracelets, all of them genuine, and of course
she had a silver fox jacket. An icebox full of orchids helped her
bear up throughout the voyage. She appeared with fresh flowers
at every meal, and she had with her a sad pale little girl, who was

not allowed to play with other children. She wore a little mink coat on deck—the only junior mink I have ever seen.

The way the young widow managed her entrances into the dining room reminded me of Easter at the Music Hall. She waited until the orchestra played Ravel's *Bolero* and then she came, surrounded by expensive vapors, heavy-lidded, the play of every muscle visible as a python's. At the first landing of the long stairs she bent down, while everyone held his breath, until she succeeded in picking up the train of her dress. Then a faultless ten inches of calf and ankle came into view and, with industrious little steps, she climbed down the rest of the stairs to the restaurant. Once seated, she smeared caviar on pieces of toast and garnished them with whites of eggs until they looked like the cards one sends to the bereaved; with this she drank champagne and looked out over the ocean. The sad little girl said nothing the whole day long.

The last night on board, the widow fell out of her role. A beautiful, exquisitely modeled, long, slim, gartered leg came dangling down from a high-held knee, out of black satin and lingerie. She danced like Jane Avril and let out a wild cowboy "Whoopee," blowing kisses to everyone.

I think the tips on that voyage amounted to more than the whole price of the passage. I have never enjoyed such service. The elevator had not only one operator but a second man who squeezed himself into the cab, pushing the first one against the wall. Then he asked the passengers for their destination and handed this information on to the operator. He also opened the door and rushed ahead to guide us to whatever room we had asked for. The service was perfect, altogether too perfect. I ran into trouble because of its perfection several times. Once, when I went to arrange for railroad tickets, the bearded man standing inside the kiosk bowed, rubbed his hands, and asked me where I wanted to go after the ship docked. I said, "First to Paris, and then to Zuerrs in the Tirol." I ordered three tickets to Zuerrs. I said to him that Zuerrs was on top of the Arlberg between—but I got no further. He stopped me and explained, "It is I, monsieur, who will tell you where Zuerrs is found!"

Was there ever anything more real, more certain, than the

appearance of the Scilly Islands and Bishop's Rock when, at the end of the voyage, the mists began to take on a greenish tinge and slowly, out of them, came the cliffs and green hills of the English landscape?

Later, off Southampton, the *Normandie* turned into the wind, her propellers trembling as the engines idled. Baskets of Dover sole were brought on board, and a few people with ruddy complexions and sports clothes came up from the tender, to make the crossing over the Channel to France.

As we steamed slowly into Le Havre, the Sacha Guitry steward in the lounge put his stamps away and locked up the writing paper. Then came the most lenient customs inspection imaginable, and we found ourselves about to board the blue boat train for Paris. Instead of an engineer, the chef leaned out of the train, his white cap floating in the smoke of the engine.

When we arrived in Paris, we had to wait until they carried Danielle Darrieux off the train. The frugal French taxicab drivers almost threw their caps in the air when they saw her. They waved them with the greatest degree of abandon and enthusiasm, but they did not let them fly. We finally persuaded one to take us and our baggage. It was impossible to go from the Trouville Suite of the *Normandie* to the old Hotel de Nice on the Boulevard Montparnasse, or even to the respectable anonymity of the Saint-Georges-et-D'Albany. So we went to my favorite hotel in Europe, the Ritz, on the Place Vendôme. This rare mansion has the quality of making one feel it has been one's home for centuries. Its elegance is effortless. It might be the residence of an archbishop or a first-class *maison close*. Its chief decorative features were the women's hats in its corridors, the garden, the porters, the waiters, the professional beauties, the young dancing men; the good and the bad made its pulses beat, its doors swing with *élan* and music. It had an imposing entrance on the Place Vendôme and a quiet one on the Rue Cambon. It had, of course, hand-churned butter, an excellent cellar, and the model of all maîtres d'hôtel in the person of Olivier. It also had a nice set of prices.

One day in the third month that we stayed there, I sat looking out over the elegant tops of the fat cars below in the square while on my fingers I counted the money I had left. It seemed that most of it had simply disappeared, that the year in Europe would shrink to a short vacation, and we would never see Zuerrs in the Tirol.

That afternoon, after I had counted my money three times more, and during the process it had not increased, I went over to the French Line office.

"Look here," I said to the man at the counter, "I would like to have a return passage on the *Normandie*—a cabin for three people in the third class—somewhere near the linen room; an inside cabin, all the way down near the bottom of the ship, at the minimum rate."

He took my name and disappeared. I had seen him on board several times on the way over. He came back looking extremely worried. It is hard to overdo an imitation of a Frenchman when he is excited. The young man acted like Lou Holtz telling a French joke, with gestures.

"Non, non, mais non, non, Monsieur Bemelmans—ça–ne–va–pas!" He emphasized the last syllables separately, exercising his eyebrows in double-quick time. Then he spread out a first-class cabin plan. "We have orders, monsieur, to extend to you every courtesy. The suite in which you came over happens to be free on the return trip, and it is"—here he made a blue pencil mark, and a princely gesture with his right hand—"hereby reserved for you again, and at the same price you paid for your passage from New York, the price of an ordinary first-class cabin."

"Look," I said—while he had his hands folded and both eyes closed—"I am a writer—"

"I know," he interrupted, flashing the palms of both hands, like two searchlights, "that is just why we wish you to write something very nice—*ah, la publicité, la publicité*—is very important. That is why we are glad to be of—"

"I am a writer," I continued, "but I do not write only about the *beau monde*. I also write about the simple life. I have found out how beautiful it is upstairs. Now I wish to go downstairs, you understand, and find out how it is down there."

He focused his attention on me by glaring at a red spot on the left side of my nose, where a French bee had stung me in the Jardin d'Acclimatation. He made a lance of his pencil, and pointing at me, he opened his mouth—but I got ahead of him.

"I now want to experience," I said, "how a man feels who has no money, or very little, and who has to eat and live in the third class."

"Ah," he replied, "Victor Hugo did not become a hunchback in order to write *Notre Dame de Paris,* and if Balzac had lived like Père Goriot . . ." I stopped him with an icy look, and he returned to a contemplation of my nose, folding his arms and waiting. When I had said my piece, he pushed the cabin plan so that the suite lay in front of me, and pointed at it with his pencil.

"It is all arranged," he said; "you will live in the suite, and every day someone will escort you to the third class, where you may observe life. For your repasts you will, of course, come back upstairs. Madame and the *bébé* will stay upstairs. It will mean a lot of writing and paper work, explanation and confusion, but that is what I am here for."

"Look," I began once more, "you must be very patient with me. I am a very simple person. My mind has chronic limitations. Furthermore, I belong to the ultra-realist school of writers. I want to experience the feelings of a man who is *obliged* to travel in the third class with his wife and child."

"Enfin"—he shrugged his shoulders—"I have nothing to say." Hopelessly, he shoved the plan around and made the reservation. We sailed back in the third class later that summer.

I saw this man again, a short while ago. He was bent over another book of reservations, in a New York hotel.

"Tell me," he said, searching for the spot on my nose, "what did you find out on that trip? How was the third class?"

"Oh," I said, "I found that a glass of *vin ordinaire* is good, and the *cuisine bourgeoise* is excellent; that the vibration and the pitching are bad. But there was a sharp-faced youngster who tasted ice cream for the first time, and ate himself sick on it. There was a man at our table with a wife and child and dirty fingernails, who appeared on the Passenger List as Mr. and Mrs. Ginsberg and Infant Condé; and at the next table was a return-

ing missionary who brought his own savages with him in the form
of three children who had to be put out of the dining room at
almost every meal. There was also a beautiful girl and a young
man who loved her. They were coming back from a trip, the
promenade obligatoire through all the chateaux, cathedrals, ruins
and galleries of France. They believed in themselves and in the
little book in which they had the names and dates of everything.
They could never let each other alone. There was a man in a
sweater and cap who had left his home, his business, and a fortune of several million marks behind when he was dragged out
of bed one night by the Gestapo. He still hid himself behind
ventilators and sneaked along the corridors. He was a sick man
when he came on board. He sat alone and ate alone, his eyes
always looking down. He was still followed by ghosts. He clung
to the side of the deck house, when he walked outside, or stood
alone on the deck. He seemed to apologize for his own presence.
He was afraid that it would all end and from somewhere a hand
would seize him and drag him back into his misery. Slowly, he
began to heal. . . . The last day, I saw him look up. He smiled.

"We also had the honor of having at our table a detective from
the uniformed force of the New York Police Department. He was
a wonderful man, as big as a house, with a heart of gold and a
handshake that hurt for three hours. He had been on a real bus-
man's holiday, inspected jails, police stations, crime bureaus, and
disorderly houses. He spoke like a radio program. He was like
a book that opened at the beginning of every meal and closed
again when he left the table. He lived his life more successfully
than any man I have ever met. I think he was really a happy
man, the happiest man I have ever known. He lacked the mechanism for being otherwise.

"This enviable functionary must be allowed to express himself. I took down his dinner conversation of Friday. Listen:

" 'Well, this goil I was telling you about, Virginia di Milo,
traded the love and security of a good home to become a glamour
actress in Holywood. She ran away with a rat named Max, who
promised to make a star out of her. He just posed as a director.
In real life, the poor goil was Goitrude Schmitt from Brooklyn.

" 'I was born in Brooklyn too, and I was raised in Brooklyn, went through kindergarten and grammar school there and right up through Adelphi Academy. My father was a Republican, but he believed in Wilson. He was like a fish out of water, and I guess that's where I get my idealism from. Take Roosevelt! If something happened to that man I think I'd have a real crying spell, I feel about him the way I did about my father. He's a gentleman. My old man was kind too, but when somebody didn't do the right thing he could slug, just like Roosevelt. . . .

" 'Well, Goitrude Schmitt was dead of malnutrition in a cheap rooming house when she met her end, and the last scene was in the home of a broken-hearted mother in Brooklyn, who had come down looking for her, running through the Missing Persons Bureau, but it was too late. . . . That rat, Max, who was responsible for all this, who lured her away and brought her to a life of shame, landed in jail, and we, the detectives of this department which has brought him to justice, hope they'll throw away the key. . . .

" 'Now I hope you'll understand this story and take it to heart. Don't disappear, don't be a vanishing American. Good evening.'

"There was hardly a dry eye in the room as he got up and went, with six Catholic priests, to see Betty Boop in the third-class movies.

"I remember, too, half a dozen athletic young Americans who used the ship as a gymnasium, despite the purposes of its builders and all the restraining efforts of the crew. They managed to appear one night in dinner clothes, with their girls, up in the first class. . . . Oh, it was all a lot of fun on the *Normandie,* upstairs and down."

"Be careful, be careful," said the clerk, beginning to breathe like a Yogi. "Don't talk about her any more, or I'll cry."

I LOVE YOU, I LOVE YOU, I LOVE YOU

She came over and into my bed and leaned her ash-blond head on my new *framboise*-colored twelve-fifty Saks-Fifth Avenue pajamas, and then in the cadences of Leslie Howard, with her eyes on my lips, in three distinct shadings, soft, softer, and the last words in an almost inaudible whispered tone, she said, "I love you, I love you, I will always love you." And she added, "I hope you will take me back to Paris when the trouble is over and when the *Normandie* is painted new again."

I said that I hoped I could soon, that I hoped all the boats would be painted new again soon, and to myself I said that I hoped also that she would be able to say "I love you, I love you, I will always love you" exactly as she had said it, on the stage, because then she would be a great actress. But I am afraid that, instead, my daughter Barbara will be the pen pal of some future desperado, or, if we're very lucky, the chatelaine of Alcatraz or Sing Sing.

Barbara was then three and a half years old; most of her life has been spent in Europe; she has also been in Chile, Peru, Ecuador, and Cuba. She knows the captains of at least half a dozen liners. Everywhere she has met nice people and left them nicely alone—and everywhere, with the nose of a retriever, she has found out and attached herself immediately to some socially maladjusted individual.

In Paris, Barbara formed an underworld friendship with a backstairs Villon whose name was Georges. We had two friends by that name. One was bon Georges, the other bad Georges. Bon Georges is Georges Reyer, the novelist and writer for *Paris-Soir;* he had introduced me to bad Georges, who was in the words of bon Georges, *"un chef de bande sinistre."* Bad Georges was my guide to Paris at night, and he assisted me in some reportage.

Once, after a long all-night tour, we were sitting in my room about nine o'clock when there was a knock at the door. Barbara was up and came in and said that two men were outside looking for Georges. Georges' hand closed around my wrist, and he said, "Remember, I have been with you all night." The men came in, and I told them truthfully that Georges had been with me all night.

They were surprised and said to me to be very certain of that; then they said, *"C'est une affaire extrêmement grave."* The one with the beard who said that seemed to love this phrase—he repeated it several times. They left without taking Georges with them. Georges said a prayer after they were gone and offered me back my watch, a watch which I had missed since the first day I met him. He said he had been sorry about it all along. I thanked him. Barbara said that it was *"une affaire extrêmement grave,"* and Georges said, "Ah, you are so right, most *extrêmement grave."*

I wanted at the time to get a nurse for Barbara, to take her to the park and to watch out for her. Several applicants came, but Barbara did not want a nurse. Georges, who was always with us, could be her nurse, she said. I told her that men were not nurses, but she said they were; she had seen the little daughter of an Indian maharaja who lived in the hotel go out with a nurse who was a man, wore a turban and a beard, and played with the little dark-skinned child in the Champs Elysées. Georges said he loved no one better than Barbara, but I said no.

We walked out of the Ritz on the Rue Cambon side, up toward the Madeleine. On the right-hand side there is a toy shop. In this shop Barbara saw a small statue of Napoleon on horseback, brightly painted in the manner of a toy soldier. Immediately she wanted it.

Barbara has methods of stating a claim that put the propaganda of Doktor Goebbels to shame. Here is the work she did on Napoleon: "Papa promised Barbara a toy—please buy a toy for Barbara, Barbara wants a toy, a toy for Barbara, Barbara wants the little soldier on the horse, please buy the soldier—Mamma said Barbara could have a toy, please buy a toy for Barbara."

This nasal singsong text, wailed off-key like reedy, Oriental beggar music, is repeated for three hours. It is like having two peanut whistles tied to your ears; after a while one does not hear the words any more, just the music, but there is also a grip on the trousers, pushing and pulling, and tears are in readiness for the final effect.

"All right, Barbara, we'll go back and buy the little soldier if you only stop this, if you promise to be quiet."

"Don't be a fool," says Georges. "Don't be a fool and buy it. I will steal it for her."

We had arrived near the Madeleine, and I asked whether we could sit down and have a drink and an ice cream before we went back to buy the Napoleon. Barbara weighed this for a moment and then agreed. Georges said he had to go somewhere and excused himself. He was back by the time I paid the bill, and sat down and ordered another drink. He gave the Napoleon to Barbara under the table, and, with both hands and tilted head, cut my protest short. "It is nothing," he said.

Georges was thin and small, he wore a cigarette on his right ear and a cap, his jacket was tight as a brassière and rode up over his hips when he walked. He was continually pulling it down. He looked like an advertisement for a *bal musette*. The arrangement for taking Barbara out was made at the end of a three-and-a-half-hour filibuster that went something like this: "Barbara wants to go with Georges, Papa promised that Barbara could go with Georges, Georges wants to take Barbara to the park—"

Georges reported every day, and he was an ideal nurse. He took Barbara to the Luxembourg, walked around with her while she rode the little donkeys, sailed boats for her in the Tuileries, took her to the Jardin d'Acclimatation, and out to the Restaurant Robinson in the trees.

The first time they came back from a Punch and Judy show I was not there, and they both sat in that long corridor of the Ritz which is lined with showcases. Georges' eyes were on the rings, bracelets, pendants, and wristwatches in the showcases.

Olivier, the maître d'hôtel, passed and saw him, and he called the doorman and the reception clerk and asked everyone, *"Qui est ce phénomène-là?"* Somebody had seen Barbara before, so they asked her, and she said that Georges was a friend of Papa.

"And who is Papa?"

"Papa has no hair," said Barbara by way of explanation, and then she added, *"C'est une affaire extrêmement grave."*

"Ah—oui, ah oui, alors," said Olivier, *"extrêmement grave."*

Even the maid was worried and said it would end very badly and I would be sorry the rest of my life for letting Barbara go out with this creature. There is, she said, such a thing as *"le kidnap."*

The next day, after they had gone, I was a little worried. I looked down out of the window. The Place Vendôme was filled with chauffeurs and the municipal shade of green that was on its freshly painted lamp posts and autobuses. Usually buses do not run here, but the Rue Royale was being torn up to be recobbled, and the buses that usually go to the Madeleine passed in front of the hotel. A Senegalese Negro, with feet like two *pains de ménage,* climbed across the square.

On one corner stood two men, one carrying a big easy-chair, the other a bouquet of pink and white tulips stuck in mimosa. They waited for the traffic to pass; and when this got tiresome, one put down the chair and the other sat down on it and smelled his bouquet. A sailor, with some teeth missing, was making love to a girl leaning on a lamp post; a couple crossed the center of the square with three black poodles.

In front of the Palais de Justice stood a German tourist in shirt-sleeves and *Lederhosen,* held up by embroidered suspenders. He had a green hat with *Gemsbart* on it, a cigar, and a Baedeker. The greatest charm of Paris is that here in this bright light no one paid any attention to a couple with three black poodles, to the man in the easy-chair with his bouquet, or to the man in a Tirolian costume. The view from a Paris window is never monotonous.

After a while Georges and Barbara came out of the hotel right under my window; they walked to Schiaparelli's store. Barbara stopped and looked at the stuffed white doves that hung in it, suspended from thin wires, and Georges lifted her little white dog Fifi so that the dog could see them too. Then they walked on to Cartier's. I was afraid—they had a gold-and-pearl elephant clock in the window which Barbara wanted. I thought for a moment that she would ask Georges for it. I could just hear her say to him, "Papa promised an elephant for Barbara, please buy the elephant for Barbara, Barbara wants an elephant—"

She did. Georges ground a few centimeters of cigarette under his heel, pulled down his jacket, looked around, and then shook his head. I looked around too, and was greatly relieved—there were three *agents de la Sûreté,* with their eyes on Georges. Two of them followed him and Barbara down to the park. There was no need to worry—Barbara was the best-guarded child in Paris.

STAR OF HOPE

Three infantrymen, their arms interlocked, came up the Boulevard Raspail. My friend Georges leaned over the marble-topped red table and said, "I am ashamed whenever I see such soldiers! Look at them, walking arm in arm like girls! When they are far away they look blue, then they slowly get dirty, and when they are close to you, you can observe that their uniforms never, never fit. They are like horse blankets with a bandage wrapped around the middle.

"Look at them—how they wear the cap, and the cigarette hanging out of one corner of the mouth! And the shoes! Too big! And not shined! And the uniform always dirty! The Germans are too clean, and the English walk with their hands in their pockets, but the American soldiers—that is something else. I love America!"

The three soldiers, now hanging together with their elbows around each other's necks, had turned the corner and were going down the Boulevard Montparnasse. They sang, and one looked back at the legs of a woman who was emptying a pail of water into the street.

A waiter came and spoke a few words to Georges, using his hand as a screen between his mouth and Georges' ear. Georges got up and walked to the rear of the café and spoke to a girl. She had a young, obedient face and raven hair. She gave him something, or he gave something to her. Georges sat down at the table again, and the girl passed by without stopping and went out on the sidewalk.

"I must be very careful," said Georges, and looked around. "I must be very careful. One can never tell, because if they recognize me and catch me, it is good-by. I will go to prison for long, stupid years—and in France prison is not a club like in America.

"But I don't think they will catch me. The French police are very dull. They make their round-up always at the same time, always the same police. I know them from far away. Every child knows them. It is not fun to elude them—just tiresome and a matter of watching the clock."

A stout policeman with a Hitler mustache, his cloak draped over one shoulder, the thumbs of his round hands stuck in his belt, slowly passed in front of the sidewalk café.

"Look!" said Georges. "Look at him! Look at the face! You have police like that in America? I don't think so. You have G-men, not police to laugh at!"

Georges drank some black coffee, then he turned and watched two women who had sat down a few tables away from ours. They were large and well dressed. One of them talked very loudly. "My cousin Jaqueneau," she said, "owns the property. It's an original grant from the king of—"

"Fake!" said Georges. "Fake jewelry. Yes, the jewelry is certainly fake. I can see that from here even without glasses.

"The ring and the brooch are fake too," he added, leaning forward.

"And so are the earrings," he concluded, and turned away.

"Of course, there are always the traveler's checks. Don't look now, but her bag, on the chair, is open. Inside, in the little black folder, there are the traveler's checks.

"They are a nuisance, traveler's checks. Lately they come in very small amounts—five dollars, ten dollars, seldom higher. You have to sit up all night and practice the signature or, what is worse, teach a girl to sign them. Then you must run to some night club in Montmartre, sit and drink a while, and, when it is late enough, cash them and get out. I prefer money, or jewels.

"Paris has changed," he sighed. "Oh, how Paris has changed! I lie awake at night trying to think about new ideas, but it is all for nothing, everything has been tried.

"It is almost impossible to live here any more, and I am one who is alert and willing to work hard, but—" He snapped the sentence shut, shrugged his lean shoulders, and with his hands said, "What is the use!"

"In America you have at least the hold-up to count on. But the French people, they don't believe in it, they don't believe in it at all. They don't think that the gun can be loaded! They don't believe it can be dangerous because nobody in France has ever been shot in a hold-up. You can go in, anywhere, ask for the proprietor, and, when he comes, point a gun at his stomach. You know what happens? You know what he will do? He will argue with you!

"If some intelligent people would only get together here, hold up fifty or sixty people and shoot them, then perhaps they would begin to take it seriously. But we have no cooperation here. That is why I love America.

"Of course there are other things. There is the casino. For a while I made a little money playing roulette, but I became very nervous. I placed my bets on the colors. When the color was right, I left my bet. But when I lost, I quickly snatched it back, in a split second's time. Sometimes the croupier would start a scandal, but then I would say, 'Ah, sorry, I thought I still had time.' Sometimes they made me march to the director's office, and the director tore up my card of admission and the casino telephoned to all the other casinos not to let me in. I had to change my name and get a new card. But eventually they begin to remember the face, and then the game is over.

"Once I had a little business, in the Gare St.-Lazare. It was a telephone business, and it was good as long as the calls cost one franc. I had twelve telephones in this station. I went every morning and put a little cotton in each one of them. When people want to get their money back after calling a wrong number, and move the hook up and down, the franc falls down, but it does not come out. During the afternoon hours I returned and collected, sometimes eighteen francs, sometimes twenty—not much, but it was a steady income. I wanted to include the Gare du Nord too, but just then they changed the telephones.

"In the quiet months, when there are no tourists, when things are very bad, when I am altogether broke, then I have to work very hard to make twenty francs.

"As a last resort, I go to a rooming house, late at night. I look very respectable and serious in a dark suit, and I ask for a room with a wide bed, because it is much easier to get rid of double-size sheets. I pay for the room in advance, for one night's lodging. I notice immediately, as I walk in, whether or not there is a little carpet. If there is none, then I explain to the woman that I am a peculiar fellow and that I like a little rug in front of my bed; also that I cannot stand towels with holes or frayed edges. In the middle of the night I get up, pack the little rug, the sheets, the pillowcases, mirror, towels, and curtains in my bag, and leave quietly.

"I go directly to a place where the complete outfit is bought at the regular price of thirty francs. Deduct from that the ten francs paid in advance, and you have left twenty francs for one night's work! Oh, I am so tired of this country!"

Georges ordered another glass of coffee. The girl who had spoken to him earlier in the rear of the restaurant passed in front of the tables with a man. Georges went on, "The mentality of the French people is awful. They mistrust everybody. You could lie here in the street like a dog and they would leave you there. No one will turn a hand to help you, and if they find out that you have done something bad, then they will kick you on top of it!

"In America, in the United States, do the people there have a nice mentality and not think that everybody is a thief and a crook? Do they behave nicely? Do they give you hospitality? Do you think if I arrived there with two or more nice girls—you know, *goût américain*—that I could do a little business?

"Not on the sidewalk like here, of course. I mean a *salon,* on Fifth Avenue, with a maid in a white cap and a little apron, a few bottles of champagne, everything very nice, and the right connection with the government. It would take a lot of money of course, the passage, the furniture, the government, and the girls.

"I could have made a good deal of money here last night," he said, "enough for all the expenses and more for a small reserve capital. Last night they sold sixteen thousand francs' worth of heroin, right here.

"Turn around and look at the bar. Over the bar you see some light fixtures, glass tubes with light in them, neon lights. One of the tubes you see is without light. That is where they keep it, inside the tube. The maître d'hôtel here is in this business also.

"I don't like to deal in it regularly. It's too dangerous. But once in a while, for a good supper, a nice present for someone, for a vacation in Deauville, or to help out a friend—then it's all right.

"The price changes. Now we sell it to the girls on the street for fifty francs the gram. They sell it again for perhaps seventy-five.

"The profit is in the Americans. They pay more—at least a hundred and fifty francs and for that they get just a little bit of heroin. We mix it for them—seventy-five per cent bicarbonate of soda and twenty-five per cent heroin.

"They love it, but they are good for only one sale. The next day they go to Versailles. But no matter what price you ask, *O.K., Georgie,* they say, and pay. Oh, I love America!"

PALE HANDS

On one of the bright days of the spring of 1940, when the Maginot Line still held, Hippolyte de Glenzer gazed up into the untroubled Paris sky. His face, which normally looked as if it just had been slapped, looked less so for a little while as he calculated the neat profits from two small old masters that had been sold for him in New York and thought of the sum that had been deposited for him in a New York bank. The high heels on which he walked, attached to patent-leather pumps (he was only five feet three without them), clattered down the Rue des Gobelins, and he whistled and turned over in his mind the pleasant idea of running out on the misery that no one here saw coming. Although his right hand was bandaged, he rubbed both hands together gently. At the end of the street he stood still for a moment and then, with his bandaged hand, waved for a taxi and got in it. He said good-by to everything as he looked out of the window of the moving cab; he smiled indulgently at a poster that advertised armament bonds and, as he passed a *succursale* of the Crédit Lyonnais, he closed his eyes and spelled to himself the name of the New York bank where his money was secure and waiting.

He got out of the taxi at the Café du Dôme and sat down at a sidewalk table to wait for his friend Georges. Georges was his sometime secretary, valet, friend, chauffeur, and mechanic. M. de Glenzer had with him a small green envelope with some money in it for Georges—a bonus on a transaction a few months old. From his corner table, de Glenzer looked up and down the Boulevards Raspail and Montparnasse, but did not see Georges. At the table next to him someone said that Hitler was only bluffing, that the war was a fake.

Just before the trouble began, a few weeks before the German-French frontier was closed, Georges had driven de Glenzer across the border in an open car into whose double canvas top two van Goghs, a Hieronymus Bosch, and three Holbeins had been sewn. They had got into France a few hours ahead of the agents of the *Kulturministerium* and the Gestapo, who had caught the poor fellow who had sold them the paintings. Everything went quietly, professionally, without excitement or trouble until they had safely passed the border; then Georges drove like a madman, and at Nancy, the first place they stopped on the way to Paris, he poured drink after drink into himself to celebrate the deed, and then he said to de Glenzer, "Ah! I like you. I like you very much," and slapped him between the shoulders. De Glenzer swayed on his bar stool, coughed, and fell, and a brandy glass broke in his hand and almost severed his thumb. He had had the cut attended to immediately, but the wound had become infected, and in Paris he had had to go to a hospital; now it was properly sewed up with six stitches, and healing.

De Glenzer looked at the restaurant's clock for the seventh time; he had waited for half an hour. He decided to go, but just as he was paying his bill Georges arrived. He had come from around the corner, where the Cinéma Raspail was, had walked from there to the newspaper kiosk, proceeded to the flower wagon, and quickly run into the Dôme. He had entered it through the side door where the cigarette stand is, from there had crossed through the bar, and had surprised de Glenzer, who was looking into the street, expecting him to come from there.

De Glenzer offered his unbandaged hand and then gave Georges the green envelope. Georges counted the contents and said that the sum was acceptable, in fact most generous, and while he put the money in a black wallet and stowed the wallet away in his inside coat pocket, de Glenzer informed him that he hoped to go to America.

"You are right. Good God, here it's no longer fun! It's misery; it's a rotten life. If I could only get out of here too! *La Belle France*—bah!" said Georges. "I would love to go with you to America. I think I would like it there. A nice woman, you know —not poor. She does not have to be young, not very young, and she does not need to own a Château de Sans-Souci. What I want is comfort. I'm a homebody. I love a nice home, furniture. I would do the marketing myself. I would attend to her, make her happy. I know how to do this. Do you know anyone like that in America? Do they understand an arrangement like that?" He looked down at his hands, which were gloved.

"I love soft gloves," he went on. "Yellow gloves." He took them off and de Glenezr saw that his hands were pale. He had never seen Georges' hands before. "It is a habit with me. I seldom work without gloves. One leaves no fingerprints that way. I am so used to them that my hands feel uncomfortable when I have no gloves on them. It's like dreaming you are without your trousers in a large room filled with people. I even wore them when I sat in front of the hotel in Noirmoutier, and everyone took me for an English lord. I should have stayed there longer. It is dangerous for me here; the police are still on the alert. It was much nicer in Noirmoutier—the sand, the sun, and only one policeman, an idiot. That is why I would like to be in America, away from the police—start a new life. I think I have come back too soon. It is not safe for me here."

Georges' sharp face was sunburned to a dark-brown olive shade; only his hands were pale. He told de Glenzer that he had got tanned hiding out on the Ile de Noirmoutier. He had sat day after day on a bench in back of the orphan asylum without a hat; his had been blown into the water crossing over to the island. He had kept his hands in his pockets or in his gloves.

Georges looked up and down the legs of a young woman who passed the tables of the Café du Dôme and then said, "What were we talking about? Oh, yes, we were talking about the police. I have come back too soon. I sense this. I get a feeling somewhere here in back of my head, between the ears; my collar gets warm and then hot, and I know there is danger. I feel this now. I know I must make myself scarce for a while longer. I should have stayed another month—it was nice in Noirmoutier. I will have to make another trip. I must go away again. I think I will go to Basle; I have an aunt there. I know Basle well—a lovely city. Have you ever been in Basle? There, to the right—don't look now. Two tables away from us, the man who pretends to read the paper, the one with a copy of *Paris-Soir* in his paws—look at him."

De Glenzer looked.

"I think I am speaking the truth," Georges went on, "when I say that only an agent of the police can have a physiognomy so blank, so gross, so stupid. Let's go. Follow me, this way."

Georges went ahead, turned, and scurried down the circular stairway inside the Café du Dôme, where the men's washroom is. Just before one goes into the washroom there is another door. This door Georges opened. They went through it to the kitchen and into the back street. Georges threw the butt of his cigarette away and pressed against the houses. He moved so fast that de Glenzer had to run and was out of breath when they came to the end of the street. He jumped after Georges to the rear platform of a passing bus. Georges bought the tickets, folded them, and stuck them under a wedding ring which he wore on the index finger of his pale left hand.

"My gloves," Georges said, "I forgot my gloves!" He shrugged his shoulders and put his hands in his pockets. "I must go tonight," he said. "I will find out when a train leaves. I have to make some arrangements before I go. I have a good friend who is the headwaiter at the Café des Deux Magots. You know the place. I must speak to him. He is my banker and does some business for me. Here we are," he said, and jumped off when the bus turned the corner facing the Deux Magots.

They sat down at a small table in front of the café. In the square there was a great commotion—a taxi had rammed a baker's delivery tricycle, and a bus, trying to avoid a further collision, had swerved, mounted the sidewalk, and crashed through the iron gate of the little park next to the Church of St.-Germain-des-Prés. Three gendarmes were busy restraining the various characters in the drama.

Each of the gendarmes, his short blue cape thrown back over both shoulders, gestured with a pencil stub with which he wanted to write a report of the accident in his notebook. They waved these notebooks while the drivers of the vehicles shouted at each other, *"Andouille!" "Tête de lard!" "Chauffeur du dimanche!" "Tordu!"*

A trembling little man sat on the steps of the rectory holding a handkerchief to his face; the curé's housekeeper brought him a glass of water and helped him inside. The headwaiter friend of Georges explained that the little man had just missed being crushed against the iron gate when the bus mounted the sidewalk, and had nearly collapsed from fright.

The headwaiter then shouted for his waiters. They were all in the street, waving their napkins and giving eyewitness accounts of the accident. One of them held up the front wheel of the tricycle, which was in the shape of a figure eight, and pointed at the driver of the taxi. The headwaiter went out into the square and chased them all back to the café.

Unconcerned with all this excitement, a Hindu passed through the crowd with dignity. He walked very erect, in native garb, and clinging to him, hobbling along noiselessly on feet stuck into small high-heeled shoes, was a short, dark, East Indian woman. The Hindu and his companion headed for the jewelry shop at the left of the café.

Georges looked after them and remarked how wonderful it was that in Paris one could dress up in any fashion one pleased and no one bothered about it. "Yes, yes," said Georges. "It is very nice, very, very nice." His eyes roved over every visible part of the streets, the square, in and out of the restaurant. His eyes were like gulls that ride the air; they never rested.

A little while after the Hindu and the little woman had gone into the jewelry shop, they came out. The woman trotted along, holding on to the Hindu's robe, and she tinkled now.

"I don't believe it," said Georges. "Look!" He pointed at the woman's feet. De Glenzer looked down and saw that she wore bracelets on her right ankle, six golden bracelets which the Hindu must have just bought for her. They tinkled as she walked.

The Hindu sat down at a table in back of de Glenzer and Georges and called for a waiter by clapping his hands. He wanted to order something. He repeated the order three times, but the waiter shrugged his shoulders. He could not seem to understand the Hindu. The waiter went to get the headwaiter. The Hindu repeated his order with gestures, but the headwaiter did not understand him either. Georges leaned back and listened, then said to de Glenzer, "I believe this gentleman is trying to speak English." He listened again and then said, "I believe this gentleman cannot speak French. It sounds like some kind of English to me. Yes, he is trying to speak English; it's very bad English, but I think I know what he wants. I think he wants a gin and tonic for himself and a chocolate and vanilla ice for the lady, and some pastry." Georges then smiled and turned to the Hindu and said, "Excuse me. My name is Georges Duval. Allow me to order for you." He called the headwaiter and told him what they wanted. The Hindu was very grateful. He rose and crossed his arms over his chest, saying, "Thank you, thank you, thank you very much." Bowing solemnly, he sat down.

Georges then spoke to his headwaiter friend and gave him a small package. He had hardly done this when he took de Glenzer's arm and said, "I must go now. I must leave you immediately. But you will hear from me. I will write you a note. I am taking the train for Basle tonight." He looked out into the square while he talked, and de Glenzer saw that the man who had sat close to their table at the Dôme reading *Paris-Soir* now talked to one of the gendarmes, who was writing in his notebook. Then Georges was gone.

There was a knock at de Glenzer's door late that night. Georges came in; he was cold and he had no hat. "I can't go home for anything," he said. "They are there already."

De Glenzer asked him whether he wanted more money, but Georges said he had enough. He pulled out his wallet and showed de Glenzer two of the four five-hundred-franc Swiss banknotes which de Glenzer had given him that afternoon, and some change; he also had his ticket to Basle. He had given the rest to the headwaiter to keep for him.

He needed clothes; he wanted to borrow a coat and a hat. There were a bowler and a raincoat in the closet of the room and he took them, then said, "Gloves. Quickly, gloves. I almost forgot the gloves. I am certain that by now my *signalement* is broadcast—pale hands, dark complexion. I must have gloves." De Glenzer had several pairs of new English gloves; he picked out a yellow pair and gave them to Georges. Georges shook hands and said, while putting on the gloves, that his friend would hear from him soon. He waved good-by with a yellow-gloved hand and was gone. He waved with his left hand. Georges was left-handed.

Some ten days later de Glenzer sat, as he did every day at around five, at the leftmost marble-topped table in front of the Café des Deux Magots, and next to his table sat the man with the physiognomy of the *agents de la Sûreté.*

He was almost always there. He had started a nodding acquaintance, and de Glenzer had always nodded back to him, but they never spoke. The *agent* read, as usual, his copy of *Paris-Soir* and then sat for a while, finishing a cigar. He put the paper down, yawned several times, and wearily looked for the waiter. The waiter came and counted the saucers; the man paid, got up, and went away, leaving his paper on the chair. De Glenzer picked it up and started to read it. It was folded down the middle of the second page, and at the top of the page was the report of a murder. The headlines told the story:

TRAGIC NIGHT ON THE
BOULEVARD MAGENTA

AFTER HAVING KILLED HIS AUNT,
A YOUNG HAIRDRESSER
DISAPPEARS

"SHE DID NOT WANT TO FOLLOW ME TO
AFRICA," SAYS THE MURDERER

Right under this was another item of crime, with headlines in large type:

NOTHING IN HIS HANDS
BUT THE BANKNOTES
IN HIS POCKET

A Crook Disguised as a Hindu
Makes Disappear $2,300
from a Bank Teller

The story had come by telephone from the paper's special envoy in Basle. Translated, it read as follows:

Yesterday afternoon there presented himself at the window of a large bank in Basle a younge man of exotic allure, his hair in a turban, his hands in bright-lemon-yellow gloves, and speaking with a frightful English jargon.

From his gestures and words, the clerk deduced that he wanted to change a Swiss banknote of five hundred francs against dollars. The cashier brought out of his strongbox a little package of American banknotes and showed them to the Hindu. That one took them an instant into his hands to examine them from nearby, but he gave them back immediately to the cashier, not without manifesting his most lively disappointment for having been misunderstood. The cashier excused himself and the difficult palaver began again. After a new and very expressive pantomime, the man in the turban succeeded finally in making himself understood—it was not at all dollars that he desired to receive but pounds sterling. The cashier, now much relieved, hastened to change the five hundred Swiss francs of the Hindu against English bills.

Our Hindu bowed solemnly, the arms crossed on his breast, before the cashier who had served him so well, and left the bank with measured step.

It was only in the evening, after the closing of the door, that our cashier, while verifying his cash, established, not without bitterness, that he lacked thirty-five bills of various denominations, which represented in total the *coquette* sum of 130,000 francs.

The Hindu, in examining the package of American banknotes, had, it appears, made the thirty-five bills disappear. The cashier observed that the Hindu was left-handed.

It is now the turn of the police of Basle to search for a young man with dark *teint,* lemon-yellow gloves, the hair dressed in a turban, and to decide whether he is really a Hindu or quite simply a professional crook disguised as a man of that race.

De Glenzer left Paris soon after. He had not heard from Georges. He worried about him and often thought of him, and consoled himself with the knowledge that in times of turmoil such characters as Georges usually fare well. De Glenzer arrived in New York with trunk and baggage on the *Excambion* and took up residence in a smart and quiet hotel between Park and Lexington Avenues, in the Fifties. He felt at home there; it had the smells and sounds of the Meurice or the Plaza-Athénée. In the elevators, in the corridors and lobbies, English was rarely spoken, French and German predominated, and there was some Hungarian, Polish, and Rumanian; it sounded like Maxim's at noon and, particularly at 5 p.m., it was crowded with overperfumed women, pomaded men, and monocles.

On a Friday afternoon, about a month after he had arrived in New York, de Glenzer called for the manager of the hotel. He wanted to give a party and wondered whether, instead of paying for a private dining room, he could use the sitting room of his suite. He wanted to have the grand piano moved out and a small one put in. On the grand piano stood a row of pictures of wonderful girls. He had obtained these from a refugee fashion photographer who also promised to bring some of the girls themselves to the party. When the manager, Mr. Kalbfuss, came in, de Glenzer was busy opening a bottle of Chilean champagne. It had been recommended to him by a South American diplomat; it was supposed to be excellent and cheap.

Mr. Kalbfuss looked around the room, at the piano, at the beautiful girls in silver frames, and said, "Certainly, certainly. Of course, of course, Monsieur de Glenzer. With pleasure."

De Glenzer thanked the manager and offered him a glass of the greenish champagne. He asked for his frank opinion about the wine. The manager rolled the champagne on his tongue and said he thought it was so-so, just so-so; nothing for a dinner but all right for champagne cocktails, with a napkin wrapped around the bottle. He asked whether he could sit down for a minute. "No one can find me here," he said. "I'll get a moment's rest."

De Glenzer poured him another glass of the champagne and said how very nice it was of him, the manager, to have the pian moved out. "Bah!" said Mr. Kalbfuss. "That is nothing, nothing at all, no trouble. You should know some of the things one has to do in this business, Monsieur de Glenzer," he said slowly, and wagged a finger. "You have no idea what we have to go through sometimes. It is unthinkable. There is not even a dream like it. You should thank God, Monsieur de Glenzer, that you are an art dealer and not a hotel man. Yes, you have really to thank God for that every day."

M. de Glenzer clucked sympathetically and started to take the girls off the piano.

"As for pianos, hear what happened to me two days ago, Monsieur de Glenzer," said the manager. "You would not believe such a thing could happen. I don't know how I could have fallen for it. It's the oldest trick in the business, and it wouldn't have happened to me if he had not asked me to break down a wall. A man comes in here; he looks about thirty, a refugee. He had lunch in the restaurant with an elderly woman, very well dressed —fox scarf, dog, diamonds. First they did not like the table they got, and after they were seated they looked at the menu and complained about our assortment of dishes. The man continually snapped his fingers at the waiter; the best was not good enough. They ordered a quart of Krug '28. Half of the food they sent back to the kitchen, saying that this and that was wrong with it. Then they called the headwaiter and complained about the service, and at the end the man signed the bill. He left a very poor tip, just like a really rich man. Then he sent for me.

"He said he wanted to look at some rooms. I took him upstairs myself, and showed him 98, the suite right above this one. He remarked that he liked the hotel—the furniture and everything was all right. The only thing he objected to was the sitting room —it was too small. He tapped on the wall with his cane and asked what was next door, so I showed him 99, the adjoining suite; he wanted to rent the two suites, he said, and break the wall through. He said he needed the space so that he could have his two grand pianos in this room, one facing this way and the other that way. He tapped some more on the wall and I telephoned for the engineer.

"The engineer came up and said yes, it could be done. We telephoned the renting agents, who have the final say about this, and they said that it was all right to knock down the wall.

"The man said to send a truck for his trunks and gave one of the best hotels in the city as his address. So just to play safe, just as a matter of routine, you know, I had someone call up, and they said yes, he's registered there and he's all right.

"On the way down he asked me to cash a check; he needed a hundred and twenty-five dollars. Here is the check. It is a false signature. He had given me the name of someone he knew was staying at that other hotel.

"The police were here. They asked me what he looks like. The only thing I remember about him is that he's about five feet six and he wore yellow gloves, and he wrote out the check with his left hand."

Hippolyte de Glenzer looked up as if far away he heard a familiar tune being played. The manager said, "I never would have fallen for it if he hadn't asked me to break through the wall. Nobody ever asked for that before."

De Glenzer went to the Colony for lunch to discuss terms for a Gauguin sketch. He looked through the crowd assembled at the good and bad tables as he sat down to wait for his client. Time and again, he had a feeling that Georges might be somewhere in the room, but he did not see him. A few nights later he thought he saw Georges jump out of a cab as he crossed Madison Avenue after dining at Voisin's. He knew Georges' motions well, but the man was too far away for him to be sure. Whoever he was, he disappeared through the door of a night club. A woman was with him. In silhouette they looked like Jimmy Walker and Louella Parsons.

De Glenzer followed them into the night club and was seated. The man who looked like Georges was across the room on a banquette near the circular bar. His head was turned away, for he was talking to his companion, a white-haired *grande dame,* with face and arms like asbestos, whose head was constantly in motion. The body, in black velvet, sat straight up, the neck was wrapped in a choker of diamonds. The occupants of the table suggested Goya, the Gestapo, the fall of France, the foyer of the

Meurice, an altar in a Spanish church, a sepulcher with the be-jeweled relics of an old saint. The man turned and looked at de Glenzer. He recognized his friend. He sent a small, sad smile across to de Glenzer and raised his hand—the left one. It was as pale as the woman's throat. De Glenzer waved back to Georges with his own right, the one with the cut and the six stitches.

WATCH THE BIRDIE

During that soft, green, May-wine-and-guitar-music period when Mozart, von Hofmannsthal, and Salzburg were the fashion and Queen Marie of Rumania came to the Passion Play at Oberammergau in a Schiaparelli dirndl, the young Polish photographer Zygmunt Pisik arrived in Salzburg, let his hair grow long over his ears, and changed his name to Johann von Schönberg.

He photographed everything in Salzburg, and he loved an ample, pink woman who was like a peasant commode with wide drawers that were filled with kindness, honesty, and submission —the cold Mamsell of the Hotel zum Frommen Brunnen. She was called the cold Mamsell because she supervised the buffet where salami, ham, and other cold delicatessen were served. She too wore a dirndl. Her hair was braided. She walked and stood in solid footgear. With a clop, clop, clop, gallop, she came out every evening and met Johann von Schönberg at a certain bench under a linden tree, and there was always a roll in her handbag, buttered and weighed down with a considerable slice of tender ham. "Here, darling"—she handed him the roll and gave him a kiss that was like the butter on the roll.

After one Salzburg season von Schönberg went to Berlin and worked for *Die Dame,* a German imitation of *Vogue.* He also contributed photographs to other magazines, and his art flourished when he began to photograph the nude.

The pictures he took of unclad young women in the snow, on skis, of two of them playing with a pushball, of one kneeling in dejection, of one with eyes half-closed under a thin black veil, of one on a polar-bear rug and labeled "Baroness X," found their way through the editorial room to the press with miraculous ease.

Von Schönberg was known among his colleagues as the worm photographer. He took most of his pictures lying flat on his stomach, with the camera tilted up. Girls photographed from that angle became his trademark. It was inevitable that such talent should take him to Paris. He wrapped up the polar-bear rug, packed in a leisurely fashion, and was boarding the train at the moment when an agent of the Goebbels Ministry appeared at *Die Dame* to request a list of the personnel. Schönberg was a certified Aryan with all his grandparents in order, but he disliked Nazis and on several occasions had said so, quite loudly. He was, besides, a Pole, with burnt-sienna skin and thick, shiny black hair, and there were a good many golden-haired and blue-eyed youths around who also could take pictures.

He arrived in Paris in German pants that rode high over his shoes. His hat suggested an excursion into the Black Forest and his shirt choked him.

He found a girl to pose for him and to clean his studio. Her name was Denise and she wore colored ribbons in her hair and she was always cold. They went out to eat together and she sat with a heavy sweater on, listening to him across one of the tables of the Restaurant Cécile, where the *choucroute à l'ancienne,* with napkin and bread and butter included, was seven francs. She didn't mind his German clothes. She loved him as he was.

His life changed when he met Roxanne Colombo and photographed her glossy Italian beauty backstage at the Bal Tabarin. She had him change his name to Henri de Beaumont. She saw to it that his hair was cut. He became thinner. He walked with elegance. Roxanne went with him to the tailor and the shoe-maker. A thin mustache bloomed under his nose. Denise disap-peared from his life.

Besides photographing pretty women, de Beaumont invented an editorial game which consisted of printing, side by side, pic-tures that complemented each other. There would be, for exam-ple, on the left-hand page a photograph of an old sea lion who looked like an ancient mariner, and on the opposite page a pho-tograph of an ancient mariner who looked like an old sea lion. In his new habitat, a studio on the fifth floor of a modern build-ing near the Observatoire, he pasted up a layout in which a pig and Julius Streicher were juxtaposed.

De Beaumont got several assignments after the layout ap-peared, together with a group of his nudes, in a French imitation of *Vogue*. He was sent to take photographs of a circus party given by Lady Mendl. He took snaps at Auteuil and at the various fêtes that were arranged by the Syndicat d'Initiative of the City of Paris, and in between these routine jobs he lay on his stomach in the sands of Le Touquet and Deauville and in the early, un-policed morning mists of the Bois de Boulogne. He moved to Clichy, and went to the Tabarin every evening in a midnight-blue dinner jacket with a blood-red carnation in his lapel. The maître d'hôtel sat him at a table while he waited for Roxanne to sing the quatrain that ended the show:

> *Princesses, duchesses, et marquises,*
> *Féerie lumière, oubli décor,*
> *Plus de cafard, à bas la crise;*
> *On peut rire de tout encore.*

Roxanne appeared in the nude on one negative after another until there were stacks of them. She did her turn on the polar-bear rug and she was shown holding up a balloon. She was the veiled nymph in the Bois and also was photographed with her clothes on. A boy who did de Beaumont's errands and helped him in the darkroom sometimes was worked into the composi-tions, the most successful of which showed the Left Bank arch of the Pont Royal. Roxanne, in a shabby coat, leaned on a lamp post and the apprentice leaned on her. De Beaumont screwed the lens out of focus to obtain the mood of waterfront and despair. He called it *Sous les Ponts de Paris,* and it won the first prize at an exhibition and made him famous. He raised his prices, had his sofa newly covered, and bought Roxanne a silver-fox jacket.

Into this idyll came a fashion model from Cleveland, Ohio, whom everyone greeted with *"Allo,* Toots." She had been re-cruited, together with six other girls, to pose in Paris when the great French couturiers had their shows for American buyers. The young women lived together in three rooms at an eminently respectable *pension de famille* in the environs of the Eiffel Tower. Toots had taken French in high school and did her best to converse in that language, although most of the people she found herself with were polyglots, like de Beaumont, and spoke some English.

Backgrounds against which to photograph Toots immediately suggested themselves to de Beaumont—the great stairway at Versailles, the Madeleine, the fountains on the Place de la Con-corde, marble horses, onyx columns, silvery trees. He looked at her professionally, optically, through a square made of his two hands, studying all her possibilities.

He stopped taking pictures of Roxanne, indeed forgot about her entirely, and lay on the grass in the Tuileries and on the pavement of the Champs Elysées and looked up at Toots in sports clothes leaning on Daimler cabriolets, sitting at sidewalk tables. After a week the lines of her body were as familiar to him as those of the Arc de Triomphe.

On a lovely morning in May, after photographing Toots in a governess cart in the Bois, de Beaumont suggested that she come to his studio that afternoon. He gave himself time to prepare lights, he sent the apprentice away, and then he called for her in his Citroën. When they got to the studio he opened a bottle of Sauternes and arranged some blue grapes on a plate. He asked her not to eat the grapes until he was through taking pictures. He brought out a large portfolio and from it spilled an assortment of fashion shots, the best of his life's work. He also casually drew from his files a picture of a classic Greek statue. He said that he would like to use that in a magazine layout on the left-hand page and opposite, in the same pose, Toots. He said that up to now he had not found anyone worthy of that arrangement.

"Je n'aime pas de poser dans le nude," said Toots.

"What are you—Snow White or something?" said de Beaumont. "What is the matter with you? Look, darling, it is only for the pleasure of the eye. There is a lot of precedent. Here, in this dossier—"

Toots shook her head.

"What an extraordinary child!" said de Beaumont. He put his face close to hers. "We still can do it. We will do it like the Venus de Milo—half nude, dressed from the waist down."

"I told you, *je n'aime pas du tout—du tout—de poser* that way. *C'est tout,"* she said.

While Toots straightened herself out and arranged her hair, de Beaumont poured out two glasses of the wine. He sat silent, with clouded eyes; then he said, "I wish you wouldn't be such a silly child. This has never happened to me before. This is not what you think it is. You must imagine that I am like a doctor—"

"Ha-ha," said Toots, and then, "What are you looking so sad for?"

"Oh, nothing," said de Beaumont.

"All right," she said, "I'll let you take one."

De Beaumont fished around the back of her dress until he found the locket of the zipper, but Toots shook herself and said that she'd rather do it herself. She undid the back and the tight sleeves of the black blouse and slipped it over her head. De Beaumont ran into his darkroom to get his plates. He whistled in there and knocked about and said to himself, "God, what a sweet business!" When he came out, Toots was standing in the middle of the room fully dressed. She had her hat on and she was pulling on a glove. De Beaumont made a mental note never to leave a model alone again.

"Does this furniture belong to you?" asked Toots.

"No," he said. "It goes with the apartment. Only the sofa there belongs to me. It's French Provincial. Do you like it?"

"Ah, oui! I had a grandmother on my mother's side who was French."

"I'm hungry," de Beaumont said.

They let themselves down in the automatic elevator.

"Après vous," said de Beaumont, and held open the outside door. He had never been that gallant to the others.

They drove to one of the large *brasseries* along the Champs Elysées, went down to the basement, and sat in a corner.

"We must speak French," Toots said while he studied the menu. "I, *moi*"—pointing at herself—*"je aime beaucoup le théâtre. Vous savez?* Sarah Bernhardt, Sacha Guitry, the Comédie-Française. *Tous les soirs,* when I can, *quand je peux,* I go to the theater, you understand. I, *moi, je veux être grande artiste—du théâtre,* or moving picture—"

"Ça c'est très intéressant," said de Beaumont.

She suggested that they go to the theater together, to see a performance of *Oscar Wilde* in English. *"Vous allez apprendre* English," Toots said, "and I will improve my French by translating the hard parts for you." A tight squeeze of his arm sealed this *entente cordiale,* and de Beaumont said to himself, "Time. Patience. Perhaps the next time, if I don't go out of the room. Perhaps then."

He drove her to a little theater he had never heard of. It turned out to be only one street away from the Bal Tabarin. De Beaumont bought two tickets in an upstairs loge. The curtain was painted to resemble a tapestry. It went up on a set showing the terrace of a hotel in Algiers—two broken-down wicker chairs, a tabouret on which stood an ashtray advertising the Galeries Lafayette, and a potted palm.

Lord Alfred Douglas, in a platinum-blond wig, his thin-fingered hands hanging on one hip, danced toward the place from which Oscar was to make his entrance. Toots started to translate the dialogue.

After the second act she sighed. "I have learned so much," she said. *"Avez-vous remarqué le* business *avec les* gloves?"

She had tears in her eyes when the final curtain came down. She shouted "Bravo!" and applauded to six curtain calls. They stopped in a bar for a drink, and afterward de Beaumont said good night to her on the steps of the *pension de famille* near the Eiffel Tower.

For the next two weeks he did fashion shots of Toots during the day and in the evenings they met, ate, and ended up in that little island of people who huddled together in the emptiness of the Odéon Theatre and sat through dreary performances of Racine and Molière. Neither the statue of Venus de Milo nor the polar-bear rug was brought up again.

In the summer of 1939, when the political horizon grew dark with storm clouds, Toots took the S.S. *Manhattan* back to America. De Beaumont drove her down to Boulogne-sur-Mer and waved good-by from the pier. Then he turned his Citroën around and went back to Paris. Toward midnight he was in the neighborhood of the Tabarin. He dropped in. Roxanne was still singing the same quatrain:

Princesses, duchesses, et marquises . . .

The next spring, a few weeks before the invasion of the Low Countries, de Beaumont aroused himself sufficiently from the melancholia which the American girl had imposed on him to do a montage of Winston Churchill and a bulldog. This was an instant and international success. A New York magazine cabled for de Beaumont, and again, just in time, he packed and left.

His table companions aboard the ship on which he left Boulogne-sur-Mer were two Poles. One was an author's agent, Sylvan Pogoda, who had just sold the American motion-picture rights of a play and two novels. He had once spent two years in America and was returning there now for the filming of a new story. The other was the son of a painter, who was taking his father's work across. He had also been to America before. The three agreed on the character of American women.

"You will rarely see a woman in America who is bad-looking," said Pogoda. "Some of them are ravishingly beautiful. They call them long-stemmed American Beauties, and, you know, they are. The long legs, the beautiful, slim long legs. They talk with them."

"I know," said de Beaumont. "I have had experience with them."

"But it is all a *trompe-l'œil* proposition," said Pogoda. "They are wonderful to look at and they have the soul of a tennis player, or a cash register. You could cry blood over the beauty of their eyes and hair and faces, but it is all false. They do not love the dog, neither the grandfather, neither the child, least of all the husband—not even the lover. The climate also is abominable."

Day after day, usually when they walked the deck after meals, the three men continued to discuss in bad French the unalluring prospects of life in the United States.

"Where does one eat in New York?" de Beaumont asked the day before they landed.

"Ah, that too is hopeless," the others said.

"There are good restaurants in New York," Pogoda explained. "But you must be a millionaire, an American millionaire, to go there. They are out of the question for people like you and me. If you are lucky, after a while, when you meet a friend, he may take you to his *bistro*. They are hidden away in side streets, or on the avenues where the high trains run, upstairs in apartments that are fixed up as small restaurants."

"My contract runs for a year," de Beaumont said. "I will live in a cheap little room and eat in the *bistro*. I will not buy a hat, a shirt, shoes, or clothes. I will save every penny and hurry back to France."

The editor of the American publication was delighted with the fearless approaches of his new photographer. He found that the girls in college clothes taken on the lids of sandboxes along Fifth Avenue, straddling the stairs at Vassar or the bulwarks surrounding the base of the Statue of Liberty, had great appeal for his readers. At the end of a year, de Beaumont's contract with the American publication was renewed and his visa extended.

One day he met the agent, Pogoda, who also had managed to stay in America, in the office of a publisher who wanted to bring out a photographic manual for which he, de Beaumont, was to supply the material. Pogoda and de Beaumont went to lunch together at an expensive restaurant in the Fifties. As they followed the headwaiter, Pogoda waved to a girl in a large felt hat and said, *"Allo,* Toots."

"It's Toots!" cried de Beaumont. "I know Toots."

They went over to her table. Toots introduced de Beaumont to the man lunching with her. His name was Horace. He was a dramatic critic. Horace seemed to know Pogoda. He nodded briefly and then studied the color of his beer while the others talked with Toots. She had just returned from Hollywood, she said, and was about to start rehearsals in a play Horace had picked for her.

"I didn't know you knew her," de Beaumont said when he and Pogoda were seated at their own table. "I knew her in Paris a couple of years ago. I didn't know she was in Hollywood."

"Oh, she's been out there two years. Her name is now Sandra Watteau. I went out there with her," said Pogoda. "It's a funny story."

As they sat down they waved once more to Toots, and she waved back.

"Ah, she's lovely," said Pogoda, with his finger pointing at the oysters-and-hors-d'œuvres part of the menu. To the waiter he said, *"Donnez-moi des* bluepoints. You know, I love oysters now. I used to detest them. It's a matter of getting over the first plate. Bluepoints and *stchi à la russe."*

"And for me, some *escargots* to start with," said de Beaumont.

"But coming back to Toots. Ah, what a darling! What a body!"

While Pogoda ate the oysters, he gave a short account of a very satisfactory stretch of life with Toots.

"Entendez," he said. "I worked on her with flowers, bonbons, tickets, and restaurants," he said. "Absolutely nothing happens. Kiss. Good night. Thank you for a lovely time. Good-by. I went almost crazy. Do you know where their weakness lies, Henri? They are sentimental. They are sentimental, like dogs. I will explain to you—where were we? Oh, yes. I tried everything. I tried to make her jealous. I keep away. I come back. Nothing happens. So one day I met her here in this restaurant. She was with that same fellow. I tell her that I am flying to Hollywood on the eleven-o'clock plane the next day to see about the filming

of *Le Moulin de la Galette*. 'I'll see you there,' she says. 'I'm taking the train for Hollywood myself tomorrow. I'm going out for a part in a picture.' I said to her, 'Oh, I can't take the plane if you go by train. Never. I will go by train also.' 'All right,' she said. And I thought perhaps on a train it will be easier. You know how easy and relaxed women are on shipboard.

"She told me what train she was taking. I wanted to engage a compartment, but it was fifty-four eighty-five for the compartment and the fare was ninety-one fifty. So I thought, one always can make arrangements with the conductor. I was glad I didn't get the compartment when I arrived at the train. Who is there? Horace. I thought that he had come to say good-by, but he stayed. He had a compartment for two, and when she came she put her things in with his. . . . The soup is for me," Pogoda said to the waiter, and then he continued. "I thought it was again all for nothing, but then something *épatant* happened, something glorious. Horace got off to go to a place called Central City. That is where they hold an annual festival, a sort of cowboy celebration. Ah, Toots is on the train alone. She had the compartment all the way to Los Angeles. It happened in Salt Lake City. I will always love that name, SALT-LAKE-CITY. It was morning, and while the train stopped in the station, Toots went out to walk up and down, and she bought a paper. All at once she came running back to the car. She held up the front page for me to look at, and through the window I read: PLANE CRASHES WEST OF ALBUQUERQUE. ALL ABOARD DEAD.

" 'I am so glad,' she said as she climbed aboard. I didn't understand right away what she meant, but when the train was under way again, while we stood on one of those drafty passages between our car and the diner, wobbling in that canvas tunnel that looks like the inside of a concertina, she embraced and kissed me, and she said, 'The plane that crashed was most probably the plane you would have been on if I'd let you go, darling.'

"I put my things in with hers all the way to Hollywood, from Salt Lake City on, *cher ami,* it was as easy"—he fiddled about in the air with his soupspoon, searching for the proper words—"it was as easy as putting a letter through the mail."

BRIDE OF BERCHTESGADEN

At every hotel and inn we stopped at that summer in Bavaria we were put into the bridal suite, because I always wrote on the register, "Bemelmans and Bride." It was good for a laugh; Bride was an old mountain guide and he would come into the place after I had registered, carrying our baggage and followed by his two dogs.

Bride had a carrot-red beard, wore buckskin breeches and hobnailed boots, and carried a guitar under his arm when he wasn't climbing mountains. He looked like a souvenir-postcard picture of a Tirolian. He was a famous guide and usually hung around the crags of the Ortler, Grossglockner, and Watzmann Mountains. He was my friend, and one of God's outstanding creatures. The last time I was with him we climbed for a week and then came down to Berchtesgaden, where I intended to try to arrange an interview with Mr. Hitler the next time he came to his mountain hideaway. We stopped at the inn, in the bridal suite.

It rained for three days and three nights. We stayed indoors all the time, read over and over the two magazines the clerk had, and looked out of the windows at the water that fell everywhere. Drifting fogs obscured the mountains and the roofs of the houses. Raindrops danced in the puddles, small rivers ran down the streets, and Mr. Hitler stayed in Berlin.

The fourth day, we watched the proprietor of the inn play cards for an hour with the teacher, the local pharmacist, and the stationmaster. Then we looked out of every door and window at the rain, and then we began to drink beer. We had some in the dining room and some in the lobby, where the card game was going on, and some in our room. We had a good deal before it was anywhere near time for lunch. In our room, Bride ransacked all the drawers in the bureaus, looking for anything, and found an almost empty bottle of American nail polish. He asked me its use. I explained it and then took off my shoes and fell asleep on the couch. When I woke up, Bride had just finished painting my toenails and was sitting on the floor in a corner, humming and accompanying himself on his guitar. I turned over and slept until two o'clock.

It was gray and cold, and we went down to the dining room again. That room was an immense, vaulted hall on the side facing the street. Raised a few feet from the floor was a balcony. On a nice day, we could have sat there and looked out of the wide windows, over the valley and toward the high mountains. Now we turned the other way and looked at all the empty chairs and tables. Zenzi, the waitress, brought us *Glühwein,* a good drink for such a day. It is red wine served heated in a big goblet, with some herbs in it. We drank slowly, dipping pieces of bread into it. Later we just drank it and smoked cigars. We did this for hours. Bride's two wet dogs slept under the table all the while, and stank.

Toward nightfall a porter came in and dusted and straightened a picture of Hitler which hung at the far end of the hall, and then went out and came back with two large Nazi flags. He draped these around the picture. Another porter came in and together they carried out most of the tables and arranged all the chairs facing the picture, as if for a lecture or an entertainment of some kind. Then two young men came in pushing a wheel-barrow stacked with wreaths and garlands made of pine branches, and with these they decorated the room. It began to smell like Christmas. Finally a radio and a loudspeaker were brought in and connected up. The loudspeaker was placed under the picture of Mr. Hitler.

The proprietor of the inn came to look things over and we called him to our table on the balcony. He told us that all this was in celebration of a National Socialist holiday, that Herr Hitler was arriving in Berchtesgaden that afternoon, and would make an address from his mountain villa at eight o'clock. "To-morrow will be a beautiful day," he said. *"Der Führer* always brings good weather with him when he comes to Berchtesgaden."

Around seven-thirty the hall began to fill with men. We had each had our seventh *Glühwein,* and I could not see them very clearly, but I heard the sound of their heels coming together in sharp greetings, the scraping of chair legs on the wooden floor as they sat down, and a sound of conversation—a deep murmur that came to my ears like the word "Rhubarb, rhubarb," repeated over and over. Bride seemed to be asleep. A song started the festivities, and I asked some men sitting a few yards from us if we should leave, but they said no, very cordially, and invited us to stay.

The Führer's address came over the loudspeaker and lasted for an hour and a half. Then the "Horst Wessel Lied" was sung, and when the men sat down again the local head of the Nazi party stood before Hitler's picture and addressed the assembly.

His address was shorter than Hitler's. Toward the end of it he told how proud all of them were to be privileged to breathe the same clean German mountain air as the Führer himself, how honored they felt at being here in beautiful Berchtesgaden, so close to their Adolf Hitler, "who is right up there behind us." At these words, the speaker pointed in the general direction of Hitler's mountain villa. It seemed to me at the time that he was pointing directly at Bride and myself. As he did so, the members of the assembly turned around in their chairs, looked at us, and applauded.

In an ashtray on our table was a cold cigar butt about the

size and shape of a small mustache. I stuck it under my nose, rose to my feet with great effort, and gave the Nazi salute. I also made a short speech. I can't remember what I said, but I screamed some words of encouragement in that hysterical tone, that falsetto pitch familiar to radio listeners all over the world.

There was a moment of silence when I sat down again; then the leader shouted, *"Schmeissen Sie das Schwein 'raus!"* and a beer glass sailed past my right ear. The next one must have hit me, for the rafters in the ceiling, the table, the uniforms, and Zenzi's big white apron all became an uncertain black-and-brown picture. I remember that both of Bride's dogs barked and that Bride was carrying me somewhere, like a baby. I woke up the next morning in the bridal suite. Bride and his dogs and his guitar were gone.

It was, as the proprietor had promised, a lovely, sunny mountain morning. I put a cold towel on my head and walked out on the balcony. Down the street, behind an immense flag, came little girls marching in military formation and singing. At the far end of the street a rheumatic old prelate hobbled in haste to reach a side street to avoid having to salute the flag. I felt a hand on my shoulder, and when I turned around I saw two young men in civilian clothes. One of them identified himself as a member of the Gestapo and said, "Herr Bemelmans, come with us—very quietly and without attracting any attention whatever."

We walked through the town as friends would, without attracting any attention. We went straight to the railroad station, where one of the young men bought two tickets, second class, to Munich; the other stayed behind, I learned later, to call up Munich and tell somebody we were on our way. After the train was rolling, the young man with me pulled a small notebook from his pocket and asked me to help him with his English. He was studying English, he said, to help advance himself in the service of the Gestapo. I helped him with it.

In Munich we went to the headquarters of the Gestapo, which was in what used to be the Wittelsbach Palace. Here I had to surrender my American passport. I was asked some questions, and after an hour's wait was taken to a prison in the center of the city by another young man in civilian clothes. Again we walked like friends and attracted no attention. He carried in his hand a large envelope on which was written in red ink, "Foreigner—Urgent." He seemed to know about my case. "I am ashamed on your behalf, Herr Bemelmans," he said to me on the way. "Why don't you like Germany? Don't you see how fine everything is? Have you seen one single beggar? Have you seen anyone badly dressed or in want? Have you seen anyone hungry or idle? Has a train been late for you? Other foreigners who come here and look around are full of praises for the Third Reich, and for its Leader. You should be ashamed, Herr Bemelmans!"

At the prison I was handed over to an official in uniform, who took me to a cell in which sat a small, pale fellow who introduced himself to me as the former editor of a Catholic publication. He told me he had been in solitary confinement for six months. He was very eager and jumpy and talked fast. "You are, dear sir," he said, sitting close to me and taking hold of my hand, "the first person I have spoken to in all this time. I have been in this nice bright cell only since yesterday—I think my case has come up for trial. Up to now I have not been informed of the charges against me. I have no lawyer; I don't even know what has become of my wife and my three children, but I am thankful to have someone to talk to."

He asked me why I was there. I told him my story and he said, "You won't be here long. An American citizen—how enviable, how fortunate for you! They will not dare to lock you up for long. You will walk on the streets this evening, or tomorrow evening, and hear the bells of the tramways and see people and eat in a restaurant and listen to the music playing. Of course you will get out—by seven o'clock tonight, I should think.

"But if anything should go wrong," he went on, gripping my shoulder with his hand, "and they lock you up alone as they did with me, then make yourself sit still, for heaven's sake. Don't start walking up and down, for you will walk around the earth in your cell; you will never be able to rest again. Another thing I will tell you that will help you: somewhere in your cell, on a wall, on the ceiling, perhaps on the floor, in some corner, at some time of the day or night when the light casts just the right shadows, you will find a place where an irregularity in the cement or the paint, a patch on the repair work, will outline for you the face of someone you love—your wife, your child, someone. It will take some imagination in the beginning, but after a while it will be there for you, strong and clear whenever you want it, to help you when the trembling starts, when the terror comes."

He seemed embarrassed by his own vehemence and stopped talking suddenly. I wanted to walk up and down but sat still out of deference to his advice. After a while a key turned in the lock and he whispered, "You see? I told you—they have come for you."

The keeper had my envelope under his arm. He took me to a waiting car and we drove to another prison of the Gestapo in a suburb of Munich—a dirty old building with sweaty walls. I was handed over to the warden and he ordered a keeper to examine me.

An examination in a German prison is most thorough. The room in which it took place was as bright as a photographer's studio, with floodlights around the ceiling. There was a glass-covered table in the room, with a powerful light under the glass, and as I took off coat, vest, and trousers the keeper stretched them out on the table and examined the cloth, the lapels, every seam and pocket with the light shining through them. He asked for my shoes and almost took them apart. With a flashlight, next, he looked into my mouth, at the roof, then under the tongue, and into the spaces between the cheeks and the teeth. Then he asked for my underclothes. Finally he asked for my socks; I took them off and stood in front of him and the warden with my painted toenails.

The warden looked at me intently and then laughed. He pinched my cheek, called me "darling," and ordered that for the other prisoners' protection I be locked in a solitary cell. Doing a lopsided fandango, with one hand on his hip, the fingers spread fanwise, the warden danced out, shouting "Yoo-hoo!"

I was locked in a solitary cell.

In an hour I got something to eat. Through a small opening in the iron door came a ladle; I turned, and from it a heavy lentil soup, with small disks of sausage in it, poured into a battered tin bowl which I held under it. A hand reached in and gave me a large slice of black bread. Both the soup and the bread were good.

The light began to change after an hour or two more and I began to look for a patch on the wall, an irregularity in the floor or ceiling. Against the Catholic editor's advice, I had walked up and down several miles. Then the door opened and the warden told me that he would have to release me, that the American consul was downstairs in his quarters with an official from the Gestapo.

I was released, and the consul advised me that I was to report to the State's Attorney the next morning. I got there promptly at nine. The State's Attorney was an affable, academic young man with a left cheek divided into six irregular fields by saber cuts. He received me in the outer room of a suite of offices under the inevitable picture of the Führer, but instead of the obligatory *"Heil Hitler!"* he said comfortably *"Grüss Gott!"* and offered me his hand in greeting. A one-armed secretary, a veteran with many decorations, brought my envelope and laid it on a desk. The State's Attorney pulled two chairs up to the desk, gave me a cigarette and lighted it for me, and waved the secretary out of the room. He began to speak, punctuating his sentences with a short, explosive, nasal "Ah-eh!"

"Ah-eh!" he said. "Disagreeable business, regrettable incident, Herr Bemelmans. Understandable, of course. A glass too many. Can happen to any of us. Ah-eh! Your—shall we call it panto-mime?—should have been ignored, of course. Some of our peo-ple, Herr Bemelmans, in a sincere effort to—ah-eh!—serve the party, are sometimes overzealous. You chose, however, a particu-larly awkward spot, Herr Bemelmans. Berchtesgaden is—ah-eh! —is the last place for such a—but let that pass.

"This affair has, however, gone too far simply to dismiss it. The party—that is, the state—cannot let you go—ah-eh!—un-punished. The police cannot admit having made—ah-eh!—a mis-take. In order to put this matter out of the way, I have permitted myself to make some calculations with which I hope you will find yourself in—ah-eh!—agreement. There is a very good train for Berchtesgaden, leaving Munich Hauptbahnhof at seven-forty to-morrow morning. They've reported the first snowfall in Berchtesgaden; there's some excellent skiing around there; Berchtesgaden is enchanting in late September. Ah-eh! While you are there, Herr Bemelmans, I suggest that you go to the District Court—I have written the address on this slip of paper for you. It is only a few steps from the station. In return for a small fee you will receive your passport there.

"Ah-eh! As for the amount of the fine, what do you think of, say, a hundred marks, Herr Bemelmans? Not too much—very little. Ah-eh! A bagatelle for an American, what?"

I went back to Berchtesgaden, paid my fine at the District Court, and got back my passport. Coming out of the building, I saw Bride and his two dogs walking up the street. They were a block or so away and I stuck my fingers in my mouth and whistled. Bride turned and the dogs stopped in their tracks. He had his guitar under his arm and, standing against the background of snow, he looked, as always, like a souvenir-postcard picture of a Tirolian. It was my last glimpse of him. Bride's arm began to rise involuntarily as if in greeting, and then all at once he had turned and was running up into his mountains, his dogs after him, as if they had seen the devil.

CHAGRIN D'AMOUR

Elegant, small, and endowed with all modern comforts, the Hotel Frankel in Port-au-Prince stands on the slope of a hill. The building has the appearance of a provincial baroque theater turned inside out. Its facade is an arrangement of foyers, balconies, boxes, and loggias which are decorated with flowers and palms; all over it hangs a drapery of bougainvillea whose blood-colored blossoms seem to be made of tissue paper. The beds are neat and comfortable, the food and the service are excellent.

Two Frenchmen who lived in the room next to mine, and wore unpressed linen suits, were leaning over the balcony which we shared and looking at something below. When I walked out of my room they straightened up for a moment and said good morning to me, and as I joined them they bent forward again.

The one close to me said in a hoarse whisper, pointing below with his chin, "What a magnificent woman!—Look at her—she isn't at her best in street clothes. In that sort of nurse's uniform she's wearing now she's extremely handsome, but you should see her in the water. I was bathing with her yesterday. She had on an old-fashioned suit, but she's all there; and when she comes out of the water, and the bathing suit clings to her—" He put the tips of the fingers of his right hand together and kissed them, closed his eyes for an instant and then looked up into the sky.

"I'd give anything," he said; "it's all firm and white—white shoulders, white arms and soft snow-white knees—and where the bathing suit ends, over the knees, there was a faint pink ring—"

"Where the garter was," explained the other Frenchman.

They almost fell down to the floor below as they leaned out over the balcony rail again, and one of them plucked and dropped a bougainvillea blossom. It spiraled down slowly, floating past the beautiful nurse, companion, or maid—whatever she was—who was playing chinka cheeks with a stout elderly lady. Mostly in white, with a very pink face; white hair, white lace, white shoes, white shawl—she was like the icing on a cake or the whitewashed front of the hotel.

By the time dinner was served, I had been introduced. The white lady was Mrs. Hamilton B. Hartford, American, from Rhode Island; the maid's name was Marie.

The tables at the Frankel stand out on the terrace in one straight line, and at dinner I sat at the one to the right of Mrs. Hartford. Mrs. Hartford ate alone.

Shortly after the soup was on the table a man in uniform appeared. He clicked his heels, bent over Madame Hartford's hand, and said a well-spoken French good evening.

"Camille Blanchetaille," said Mrs. Hartford, by way of introduction. "Lieutenant Camille Blanchetaille."

Lieutenant Blanchetaille was dark and tall and smiled with a row of teeth so good that they looked unreal.

"Madame," he said, sitting down, "verily loves my country."

"Ah, oui," said Mrs. Hartford, "yes, indeed I do—c'est for-mi-dable, cette île."

"It's very lovely of you to say that, Madame Hartford," said the officer.

The waiter brought a dish and lifted a large cloche from it. Manipulating a spoon and fork in his right hand like a pair of pliers, he took a shell and placed it on the plate in front of Madame.

"Ah, *les coquilles Saint-Jacques,*" said Madame Hartford. "*J'adore les coquilles Saint-Jacques. C'est formidable.*"

The lieutenant observed, "One eats very well here . . ." And after a pause he added, "Are you going to visit the *Citadelle* this time, Madame?"

"*Ah, oui, toujours je visite la Citadelle, chaque fois que je viens ici je la visite. C'est for-mi-dable—la Citadelle.*"

"*Ah, oui, Madame, pour ça, vous avez raison, la Citadelle c'est vraiment formidable.*"

Madame turned to me and said, "I love Haiti. You know, this is my fifth winter here."

And the lieutenant said in very broken English that he had the pleasure and honor to testify to that.

After the *coquille Saint-Jacques* was removed, the lieutenant asked Madame whether as a tourist and faithful visitor to Haiti she found it completely satisfying. "I mean," he said, "as far as our poor efforts at making people happy here can go."

"*Ah, oui,*" said Madame. She was completely happy. After a while of musing, arranging her hair, and fanning herself, Madame Hartford said that there was only one thing that might be improved. "Just one thing . . ."

"And that is?" said the lieutenant, sliding forward in his chair and waiting politely.

"The donkeys," said Madame, "the treatment of animals in general—and of donkeys in particular. The peasants sometimes hit the donkeys savagely with their sticks. I do not like that at all. We visitors do not like that; we do not enjoy seeing that at all; we don't approve of cruelty to animals."

The lieutenant looked sympathetic, wrinkled his forehead, and said, "Madame, I am distressed to hear that, and we can do something about it; no doubt a way can be found, a plan, something must be devised. We cannot have that go on, certainly not."

"I have thought about it," said Madame Hartford. "I have thought about it a good deal. First of all, the police should take away from the people any donkey that has been maltreated, and these poor pitiful beasts could then be taken to a secluded spot, put into a sort of sanitarium for donkeys, on a small island perhaps, where they can rest and graze, where they can be properly fed, their wounds taken care of. The donkeys could stay there for a length of time that is commensurate with their condition."

"Ah, yes, certainly," said the lieutenant.

"If the animal is very thin and has been abused he will stay for a few months. If he has just been struck a few blows and is only a little tired and overworked—well, then he will stay for about a week. The proprietor of the donkey, in the meantime, will be put in jail for the same length of time, and will also pay a fine. These fines will be used to support the donkeys."

"Ah, Madame Hartford," said the official, "this is a most excellent and sensible idea. But we are very poor here, we have not the money to build this sanitarium for the poor animals."

"Oh—that part," Madame Hartford said, looking down at her hands. "I think we might perhaps arrange—I'm so fond of those little gray beasts that I might persuade myself to do something about it."

The lieutenant asked on what day Madame would visit the *Citadelle,* and suggested that the next week-end would be ideal because he was free then and would be glad to accompany her.

Madame Hartford was delighted to have him come and she hoped they would get well-fed and strong donkeys to ride upon.

Lieutenant Blanchetaille got up, bowed, and walked to the back of the hotel.

After he was out of sight and hearing Madame Hartford leaned over toward the next table and said to its occupant, "He doesn't come here to see me at all, he comes on account of my Irish maid. Marie is a lovely girl, she is very beautiful, as perhaps you have seen—and she is a very fine type of girl—deeply religious, a Catholic of course."

At that moment one of the Frenchmen came down the stairs with a camera in his hand.

"She's out in the garden somewhere," Madame Hartford said to the Frenchman and waved toward the back of the hotel where the lieutenant had disappeared. "Frenchmen," she said to her neighbor, "have a horrible time these days, and this one is the very finest type.

"But to get back to Marie—she has established an *entente cordiale* with Lieutenant Blanchetaille. I don't know what to do about it. You see them talking together; she's gone completely overboard for him. Last winter he came to New York to visit her. It was very difficult for the poor lad. They had to go and sit in the balcony of the opera together, and I lost a good cook on account of it. She wouldn't eat at the same table with them in the servants' dining room. The lieutenant is Catholic too. I've tried to reason with them but you know what love is, and it's true love in this case, on both sides. I hate to lose her, but I will lose her, like cook. Marie wants to live here, and she's studying French— there's her dictionary. She carries it everywhere, and the trip up to the *Citadelle* is just going to be a French lesson.

"These poor gray donkeys—or the *Citadelle*—or Christophe —do you think that young man cares anything about all that? It's only so he can come to see Marie. He's not interested in talking to an old woman. Here they come!"

Marie asked for permission to go for a walk with him. They would be back before dark, she said. Together, they made a handsome picture, completely in order on this tropic isle.

"They are certainly proper," said Madame Hartford. "They will be back at nine, precisely. It's all very decent. They observe all the niceties. In fact if the lieutenant were white, or Marie were black, everything would be perfect and no one would be happier than myself.

"Ah!" said Madame Hartford touching up her coiffure and fanning herself, *"Le chagrin d'amour c'est for-mi-dable."*

HEADHUNTERS OF THE QUITO HILLS

The day before we landed, the purser of the *Santa Lucia* gave all the passengers who were getting off at Guayaquil a manifesto, prepared and issued by the Department of Immigration of Ecuador. Printed on good paper, decorated with a crest and written in four languages, it was a most polite invitation to visit upon arrival, or within the first twenty-four hours, the Chief of Immigration. His office, it said, was a few feet from the pier where we landed, right across the street from the Customs House. The purpose of the visit, the paper explained, was to allow the traveler to present his passport to the Chief and obtain from him advice and suggestions as to how to make his stay agreeable. The letter bore a magnificent signature under the words *"Honor y Patria."*

The next day, when we were to land, the doctor, a maroon-colored man with very small feet, came on board. The steward asked all passengers getting off at Guayaquil to assemble in the saloon. There were about forty of them, and among those I was the only non-Ecuadorian.

The doctor lifted his chin and his hands in a plea for silence, then in purest Castilian, his words arranged as carefully as his delicate hands, he informed the group that they all looked so well that he saw no need to examine anyone. He signed the ship's papers, closed his bag with a snap, and accepted half a Hershey bar from a small boy. Holding it in one hand and putting his horn-rimmed glasses into the pocket of his coat with the other, he bowed and made his exit, backing out of the room. This was the first instance in which I experienced the great leniency of this wonderful land.

It was very early. Some of the passengers went back to bed, and others waited for breakfast in the foyer of the dining room. I was sitting alone in the lounge when a native appeared, one of the first to come on board to sell Panama hats and other souvenirs. He floated suddenly, soundlessly, and barefoot into the room. He looked around, and then from a woven basket produced a smaller woven basket, and out of an inner nest of sacking took out a dark round object. He stroked a mane of blue-black, oily hair to one side, and there was a face. The native offered the shrunken head to me for three hundred and fifty sucres. I thanked him but said I did not want it, and he wrapped it up again. A Panama hat I did not want either. Panama hats are not made in Panama but in Ecuador. I had bought three of them because they are so cheap. None of them fits; two are too small and one is too big. I told him I had a Panama hat, and he disappeared.

At about nine I went down the steep stairs that hung on the side of the boat, to go ashore. I took a launch named *Gloria*. It was painted blue. We soon passed a battleship which was moored in the Guayas River. While we were in the shadow of this vessel, the man who was steering the launch took hold of the wheel with his bare, right foot, leaned forward, and removed a pillow from the seat. He opened a small locker and out of it he took a box in which lay a shrunken head. He wanted two hundred sucres, then a hundred and eighty sucres, and finally one hundred and fifty sucres for it. He brushed the black, dry hair with his hand, wrapped it around the face again, and put the head back in the box with the pillow over it. He took the wheel in his hands and brought his launch up against the pier. I went to the Grand Hotel, left my bags there, and then repaired to the office of the Chief of Immigration.

The building in which he officiates is the most ambitious in Guayaquil. It stands next to a statue of General Sucre, and the Department of Immigration is at the end of a long corridor paved with polished tiles. The visitor is reflected in them as he walks along and every step he makes echoes three times. As I approached, a clerk rose from his desk at the end of the passage. I carried the manifesto in my hand. He ran into a room and came back with another man; both of them smiled, and the better dressed of the two advanced toward me and opened his arms wide. "I am happy to see you. You have come to see me, no? You know I send out these papers to everybody, but no one, nobody, pays any attention to them, you are the first one"—he held up a finger—"in one month to come here. Take a seat." He spoke then of the beauty of Ecuador, recommended various trains and hotels, suggested excursions, alligator hunts, mineral baths, safaris into the jungle, and finally asked me to go along with him to a luncheon for a newly arrived diplomat, a man from another South American country.

He excused himself for a moment and went to get his hat. As soon as the Chief was out of the room, his assistant opened a drawer in his desk, that drawer in which people in American offices usually keep a cake of soap and a towel, and I thought he would bring out a shrunken head, but he only gave me a card on which was the address of a store where shrunken heads, Panama hats, and rings carved out of ivory were for sale. "Go there with confidence," he said, "you will get a very fine one, reasonably. Tell them I sent you—here, I will put my name down."

We arrived at the hotel where a flower-laden table awaited us. I lifted my Panama hat, and the Chief, in Spanish, offered a greeting difficult to match. He and the diplomat embraced each other as two people starting to dance—first to the right side, then to the left, and finally as if bumping into each other face on, while they continually patted each other's shoulders. The official then stood away a foot and a half and sang, "Most distinguished and estimated, cultured and noble and not-sufficiently-celebrated sir and friend, welcome to Ecuador." We sat down.

The menu was written in Spanish and in violet ink. It said:

MENU

CREMA SAN GERMAN

CALDO AL NATURAL

CORVINA COCIDO CON SALSA DE ALCAPARRAS

PAPAS FRITAS

PASTELITOS DE YUCA

SALÓN EN SALSA DE TOMATE

ENSALADA MIXTA DE LEGUMBRES

ARROZ   MENESTRA

PASTEL DE COCO

CAFE   Julio 1/1940

I understand Spanish well enough but speak it badly. The food was indifferent and the wine bad; the headwaiter, a half-breed, had hands like a baker and a shirtfront with tomato spots on it. His hair hung over his collar and into his face; he looked out of the window most of the time.

I called him for a match; I had no match or lighter. Ecuador has a match law; one cannot bring any matches or lighters into the country without special permission. The diplomat had a lighter but there was no alcohol in it. After a while the head-waiter called a waiter who brought some Ecuadorian matches, manufactured by the government plant, the *Estanco de Fosforos*. The waiter opened the box. The matches were of a dark wood, some of them split and others bent. The first one he tried to light broke in his fingers; the second he threw away; the third lit up with a sudden explosion—a small torch-like flame appeared, made a "Ffffhhhssss," and then, leaving a ribbon of thick, milky smoke, went out. Out of six more matches, two gave light. In the explosion of one of them, small fragments from the head of the match shot away, one on my cheek and another on my hand, where they burned with brief intensity, like the sting of a wasp. Finally my cigarette, labeled *Welcome* and made of dark, sweet tobacco, was lit. The waiter bowed down once more, waving the dead match, and muttered something. "No," I said. "Thank you very much. I have a Panama hat and I don't want a shrunken head either." He reached for the mineral water, which comes here in Perrier-shaped bottles and costs five cents a quart, and said that he had a very curious shrunken head, one with white hair and white eyebrows, very rare. I brushed the breadcrumbs from my trousers and got up and thanked him again. I said I had to go to the barber.

The Chief of Immigration had recommended a very good one. This barber, in a very aseptic shop on one of the main streets of Guayaquil, was fortunate in having a most beautiful manicurist, a young tropical woman with fatal allure. The barber stuck a finger in my mouth to be able to scrape better over my cheeks. He pushed my nose up, and made agonized faces while he shaved me. After stropping his razor for a second attack, he suddenly left me soaped in and under the sheet. In a few moments he came back with a shrunken head. He held it so that I could see it in the mirror which was suspended diagonally over my chair. I shook my head. He raised his eyebrows first, then one shoulder, and put the head away. All this time a dark brown boy, not more than six years old, had been shining my shoes.

I left the barbershop and walked back to the hotel. The boy who had shined my shoes ran after me, shouting, *"Patrón, patrón."* When he caught up with me, he pulled my sleeve. I told him that I did not want to buy a shrunken head. "No, *patrón*, no shrunken head," he said, "the girl, the manicurist, she loves you. You want to buy the key? Is only twenty sucres." Half a dozen children stood around now, some selling lottery tickets, others wanting to shine my shoes once more, and I said, "No, thank you." They all followed me to the hotel.

"Is only ten sucres now, the key," whined the little boy. "She love you very much."

The diplomat and I left on the train for Quito, the capital, the next morning. Our seats were reserved in the observation car. The diplomat said that his reception at Guayaquil had been very nice but he had had a much more elaborate and festive one in the last South American republic he had served. There, he said, they had sent the president's personal railroad car for him. He described this as an eighteenth-century drawing room on wheels, with carmine upholstery, brass beds, and large brass spittoons. It was supplemented with every modern comfort; it had not only a bathtub, but also a *bidet* and a shaving mirror on a movable arm.

He had sat in it, among the bouquets and telegrams which had been sent to greet him, for about two hours. Then he grew restive, looked out of the window, and asked the Chief of Protocol, who had been sent to travel with him, when the train would leave. The Chief of Protocol was embarrassed. He said he should have explained it all long ago and he regretted very much that it was such a stupid arrangement, but, although they had a presidential car, they did not have a presidential locomotive. The car would not move till it could be attached to the regular train which left the next morning.

Outside of the conductor, no one tried to sell us a shrunken head until the train stopped at Alausi. A railroad employee came into the car and offered a Zanza head again. The diplomat took it, turned it around, brushed the hair apart at the back of the head, and explained to me that it was a fake. One can always tell that they are fakes when they are sewn up in back of the skull. Furthermore, he told me that having been stationed both in Colombia and Peru, he knew about shrunken heads and had a fine collection of them which he would show me in Quito. "Don't buy one until you can recognize the real ones," he said. "Be very careful when buying shrunken heads, there are some good imitations made." For the rest of the trip he told me about head shrinking. He had made frequent trips into the jungles of the Oriente, been among the Jivaro Indians, and while he himself had never been fortunate enough to witness the ceremony by which these heads were obtained, scientists who had studied the Indians and their customs agreed that the procedure was something like the following:

If a warrior wants a shrunken head, he must bring home the body of an enemy whom he has killed in battle. The chief of the tribe and everyone in the camp gather around. After long and elaborate rites, the warrior cuts the head off the body with two sharp incisions below the jaws, leaving the neck on the body. The head is then placed on a *pingi nuka* leaf, a second *pingi nuka* leaf is placed on top, and the warrior sits down on the head, while the chief of the tribe blows tobacco juice up his nostrils to make him immune from any evil that the spirit of the dead man may be planning. After this, the skin is carefully peeled from the skull and parboiled in a tea brewed from various herbs. The face, at this stage, looks like a dirty washrag with ears, two slits where the eyes were, a mouth and a wrinkled part that was the nose. The hair is still left on the scalp. The inside of the face is then carefully scraped, and the head filled with hot pebbles which are allowed to cool. This operation is repeated several times until the head gradually shrinks to about the size of an orange. When it is small enough it is parboiled again and once more filled with hot pebbles. While it is drying, the warrior models the face, like a sculptor, and sets the features right. When it is quite dry and hard, the pebbles are shaken out of it and it is dyed black with charcoal. The eyes and lips are sewn up with the fiber of the *chonta* palm. It is then stuck on a lance and the Indians dance around it, shout at it, and strike it, while the warrior tells the story of the battle in which he killed the owner of the head. If the warrior has been lucky enough to capture the wives of his enemy as well, he takes them to himself, and they now sit through all the ceremony, wailing in chorus. If he has not captured any widows, he appoints his own wives to wail as proxies. The head itself is eventually forgotten or sold to traders.

When we arrived in Quito, I found that the best hotel in that city, the Metropolitano, was filled, so I went to the other, the Savoy. The light switches in this hotel are outside the guests' rooms in the corridor, a neat and clever invention, I thought; the guest turns the light on inside his room while he is still outside, and walks into a bright apartment. The invention has one drawback, however. When the guest is in bed, he finds he must get up and walk outside to turn the switch off again and then light a match to find his way back to bed. I had just got back to my bed the first night when the light was turned on again from outside. The door opened slightly and a bellboy crept in. He brought some towels and clean water and then came close to my bed. He pulled out a package from under his white jacket, undid a lot of white paper, and out of it brought a Panama hat. As he unfolded it, he almost dropped the inevitable shrunken head. He wanted a hundred sucres for it. I looked at it, and it was sewn up the back. He left and came back with a real one. For that he wanted three hundred sucres; it was yellowish, with an agonized expression, and short hair. I did not buy that one either.

In the rear of the Hotel Metropolitano is a small kiosk dedicated to the sale of souvenirs. The next shrunken heads I saw were there, on a string, a dozen of them hanging in a row behind the window. They seemed related to each other, and happy, almost laughing. They hung over some gourds decorated with landscapes, pictures of Indians, several plaques with the profile of an Indian chief, and paintings of volcanoes, stuffed toucans, and souvenir postcards. Some of the heads were gray-haired, and two of them were women. The price was one hundred sucres, and upon examination I found that they all were sewn up in back of the skull. When the owner of this shop saw me turn from them, he confided that he had real ones too. In back of his establishment, out of the drawer of a desk, he took two real heads, both of them pale and with the same miserable mien as that of the one the bellboy had shown me the night before. When I declined these, he said that he had a very real one, and after more hide-and-seek among his wares and souvenirs he brought out an excellent specimen, truly beautiful, wild and authentic, with thick hair, the Indian face in perfect miniature. He asked five hundred sucres for it.

I met the diplomat a while after, and he showed me his collection of genuine heads and he told me that he would take me to see a place where the fakes came from. We drove to the outskirts of Quito and then left the car in an impassable alley halfway up the mountain, Pichincha. There we found a little earthen house. It was surrounded by a wall on which plants and flowers and grasses grew in profusion.

In the courtyard stood a little man, half-Indian, half-white. He wore a blue smock and was surrounded by his works, his wife, and ten children. The whole family stopped working to greet us. They had been busy on some of the plaques that were for sale below. The manufacture of these was geared to an almost North American tempo; on two long shelves that reached from one end of the garden to the other, disks, pressed out of plaster, lay in rows. On every disk was the profile of an Otavalo Indian playing the pipes of Pan. The father had a brush in his hand. He sharpened the end of the brush, twisting it between his lips, and then started down the line. In one passage he put eyebrows on all the Indian profiles. He came back, hopping from plaque to plaque and stopping a second in front of each, and when he was done all the chiefs had an eye. His wife, more phlegmatic, wandered along the line putting carmine on the cheeks. The children were busy with other things; one mixed paints, another sawed coconuts carefully into slices, a third removed the white meat from the rings thus obtained, and a fourth fitted the coconut ring as a frame around the already finished plaques. Last, a little girl tied on ribbons to hang them up by.

"I am sorry my eldest are not here; my sons, Alfonso and Arquimedes, are out hunting," said the father. He offered us some *pisco,* and the diplomat said nice things to the baby. It was tied to the back of a girl of about five who was stacking up coconuts. Then he asked the busy man to show us how he made shrunken heads. He was reluctant for a while but, on taking another drink, eventually agreed to take us to his inner sanctum. This was another workshop which gave proof to the order and efficiency of this enterprising artisan. Here were rows of shelves again, and on them shrunken heads. He showed us three clay faces that wore the contented and smiling expressions of the Indians that hung in the window of the kiosk. He explained how he modeled pieces of goatskin over these. He left the hair of the goatskin on the part which was to cover the heads and shaved the parts that were to be faces; two little bars of hair were also left over the eyes. These he trimmed with manicure scissors so that they formed eyebrows; one can detect fakes immediately by this, because the hair on both eyebrows grows in the same direction and not away from the nose as on real faces. He said that he made about ten heads out of one goat. He marked the skin off with chalk the way a tailor divides cloth. The mouth and eyes he cut out with a razorblade. Madame or his oldest daughter, Carmen, then sewed them up with real *chonta* fiber; the whole thing is then dyed black, except for the ones he leaves white, a rarity of his own invention. He admitted that they went very well with tourists. The heads are sold in Quito and in other places for one hundred sucres, of which he gets fifty; the Indian profiles for twenty-five, landscapes of Quito, of Otavalo, of Pichincha, and Chimborasso anywhere from fifty to a hundred. We bought some landscapes. They were not without charm, flat primitives whose coloring with much blue and white in them is reminiscent of the murals in Italian restaurants.

He was proud of the sale and offered us more *pisco*, drinking out of the bottle himself because there was only one glass. Then he told us that he had been able to cut down the expense of making these heads somewhat by a surprising discovery, by using the pelt of an animal that was less expensive than a goat—a pelt out of which he also got ten heads, but with hair much softer than a goat's, almost human. He reached into a hammock and brought out a black fur. He said it was from a totally unknown animal and that he obtained the skin directly from the Indians of the upper Amazon. He let me feel it, and I spread the skin on the floor.

We said good-by. Night sets in quickly in Quito; it is almost dark at about 7 p.m. the year round. As we left, two young men came up out of the city. They were panting from the steep climb and one had a sack slung over his shoulder. "Ah, my eldest are here," said the little man. "Come, Alfonso, and you, Arquimedes." He introduced them, and the younger one put down the sack. A dog fell out of it, one of those mongrels with long, soft hair that one sees running with the Indians through the streets of Quito.

We said good-by once more to Señor Pazmino. On the way down to Quito the diplomat told me that the unhappy, yellowish heads one sees occasionally were heads obtained out of graves, with the aid of attendants in the morgues. Most of them were the heads of infants. This practice had ceased, he told me, partly because the shrinking is a good deal of trouble but chiefly because the tourists prefer the pretty ones.

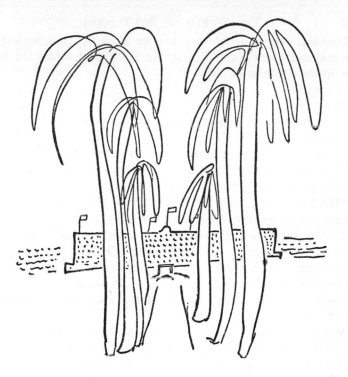

VACATION

In the fat, dead days of tires and gasoline I always tried to leave New York about four, in order to get out of the Holland Tunnel close to five. The ride over the Pulaski Skyway at that hour is one of the most exciting parts of a trip to the South. In the gaseous stretches of the Jersey landscape, half of it gone in shadows, stand drawbridges, factories, electric plants, and immense tanks. They have the beauty of the devil, with green and yellow flames leaping from chimneys, with trains smearing black smoke over a gray horizon. The landscape is framed in a loop of light, an endless gleaming necklace, rolling over the hills and bridges, that is made up of headlights of oncoming cars. In snow or rain it is doubly enchanting. It is not all gas and oil and stink. We even saw a rabbit.

Barbara, who sat beside me, had her nose flattened against the window and saw the rabbit first. He scampered across the highway in the direction of Newark.

"Pappy!"

"Yes, darling."

"Tell me a story about a rabbit. A story about a rabbit, a rabbit, a rabbit."

Once upon a time, a monkey and a rabbit met. The monkey said to the rabbit that it was a pity that he, the rabbit, could never sit still, but always had to look in back of him.

"Ha!" said the rabbit, "how about yourself? You can't sit still either, you always have to scratch yourself."

Both of them then agreed that for one whole day, from sunrise to sunset, they would sit side by side, and the rabbit would not look around, and the monkey would not scratch himself.

The day on which they were going to do this arrived, and at the moment the sun rose the rabbit and the monkey met and sat down side by side.

Without batting a lid, the rabbit quietly looked down at the grass in front of him. The monkey sat still, his hands folded in his lap. They remained in this position for hours. The time passed very slowly, and it was midday when the monkey, who knew he could no longer sit still, said to the rabbit, "When I was a soldier, bullets hit me here, and here, and there, and there—" and wherever he pointed, at that spot on his body he quickly scratched himself.

The rabbit was no better off. He felt that he could not look another second at the grass in front of him, and he also began telling a story. "When I was a soldier," he said, "the enemy was hard after me. To escape him I had to jump like this, and like that, to the left and to the right." Like lightning, his eyes followed the motions of his limbs, and every time he jumped he looked back.

Barbara, who was four years old, was asleep when I explained the moral of the story.

Before I fell asleep myself, we stopped at the Anglers' Rest in Seaford, Delaware. I tried to persuade the waitress who served us to bring Barbara some milk and vegetables, but Barbara didn't want any milk and vegetables.

"Well, honey, you can have spaghetti and meat balls," said the girl. "But why don't you order a submarine sandwich? My, that's good! Mmm."

"What is a submarine sandwich?"

"Well, a submarine sandwich comes two ways, the fifteen-cent one is seven inches long, and the quarter one is twelve—"

"What's it made of?"

"It's made of Italian cheese, salami, Italian seasoning, hot peppers, lettuce, and spiced ham; the cheese is put down first and then olive oil is put over it—it comes in a specially baked loaf of Italian bread."

Barbara ordered it, and ate it, all of it, all of the fifteen-cent one, and drank some of my beer with it.

I wanted a cigar with my coffee. The girl brought me a cigar almost as long as the sandwich, mustard-colored, with large ribs running through the wrapper. It lit up like a torch, and when I asked her whether she had any other kind she said, "No, honey, just a five-cent one."

I asked for the bill. She wrote it on a piece of paper called "Guest Check." She stuck a pencil in her hair and turned a knob on the radio.

A voice wailed, "Like a fool I didn't believe him and all the time I had a couple of detectives follow him. Why do I always have to hurt the people I love, and why, why do the worst things always happen to the swellest people?"

"Good night, honey," said the waitress, and we left and drove to the Norfolk ferry.

Someone told me that you could go aboard the ferry boat at about eleven, get a room and bath, and cross during the night, arriving in Norfolk at 7 a.m. The cabin looked like an illustration out of Dickens, the cast-iron bathtub was just large enough for Barbara, and the beds were two-story army bunks. However, the ferry saves time.

The next day, I followed the Ocean Highway, and turned inland as soon as it got warmer.

In New Orleans, Barbara was fascinated by another sandwich. This one was called "Martin's poorboy sandwich." She saw it in a little shop—outside of which hangs a sign showing a small boy who eats a sandwich larger than himself. A twenty-eight-inch loaf of bread is cut in half, loaded with sliced roast beef, lettuce, and tomato, and the whole is soaked in gravy and costs ten cents. The sandwiches, which are sold in several establishments, were invented during the Depression, and have made their inventor, a legless man, so rich that a colored chauffeur carries him from one "poorboy" place to the other. I refused, however, to go in there and buy two "poorboys," and so we arrived in tears at Antoine's Restaurant.

This exquisite and sufficiently esteemed restaurant is all that one expects of it. It is blessed with a proprietor who honors his profession and worships his ancestors (I have counted fifty-three photographs of them on menus, on souvenirs, on postcards, and in frames). He has a maître d'hôtel who is one of the few in that difficult calling who is free of all pomp. We ate in the 1820 Room, a private apartment in which hangs a large oil painting of Madame Antoine, a kind of Frau Sacher. Barbara was particularly elated because in a glass case along the wall of the room, among various personal belongings of Antoine Alciatore, the founder (1840-1885), there are a pair of baby shoes, the first pair he wore, kept right next to his shaving mug.

M. Isidor Cassou, the good headwaiter, an Adolphe Menjou type, supervised the dinner, and I had a terrible time because I had to eat the *spécialité de la Maison, les huîtres Rockefeller.* I detest nothing so much as oysters when they are cooked, and these were covered with a green mud and done *au gratin.* During the ordeal, M. Roy L. Alciatore, the grandson of Antoine, showed me a photograph in which he was shown eating the millionth order of this dish. I ate them quickly, almost swallowing the shell. M. Alciatore beamed and had a second order brought in.

The rest of the menu was superb cooking, particularly the pompano. It's an honest restaurant—the lights go out every time someone orders crêpes Suzette. The kitchen is badly lit; the chef stands in front of an old coal stove and cooks in heavy casseroles; everything is as it should be, and I hope it will forever stay that

way, including the cedar sawdust that is sprinkled on the floor.
It fills the rooms with an appetizing perfume. It smells like pencils being sharpened.

The road from New Orleans to Marco Island, where we went
to go fishing, runs along the Gulf of Mexico and is in excellent
condition. It will remain in Barbara's memory as a long line of
dead black pigs. She counted fourteen of them. These pigs roam
the country, half wild, and then, crossing the road, they are run
over by the fast-moving cars. I had to tell several pig stories.

The captain of the fishing boat on Marco Island was very co-
operative. He said, "I used to go barefoot, but now the place is
getting fashionable, and out of consideration for the lady of the
house I wear shoes." We ran into a lot of fish, and I observed
how much they resemble people.

Pulling them in became tiresome labor, and at the end of it
my arms hurt and the fishbox overflowed with them—all of them
silently gulping. I wanted to let them go, but the captain said he
could make something of them—fertilizer, I think.

Miami is Miami, and by no other name is there a city such as
this. The hotel employees were as efficient and quick as dentists,
and fingerprinted besides. Everything is to be had here from caviar to a Goodyear blimp. From a point of design and efficiency
the new hotels in Miami Beach are models.

The main highway to Palm Beach was now an unending, open-
all-night string of tourist cabins, orange-and-papaya-juice pavil-
ions, sea shells, carved coconuts, and cypress-knee souvenir
stands. There is another, quiet road along the ocean, one of the
finest drives in the world.

An unforgettable picture presented itself to me at a turn in
that road. It was past the S curve that leads to the Hutton castle
in Palm Beach. This edifice always reminds me of an advertisement for breakfast food. I am certain that at night gnomes work
there under the stairs of the baronial halls and in the vaulted
cellars, wrapping crunchy crackies, full of golden goodness, into
bright packages and mailing them out in Josef Urban boxes.

The castle's garden faces the unceasing sound of the waves;
the moon shone through the long, thin fins of palm leaves, and
on a bulkhead near the sea sat a black gardener and a maid, en-

gaged in ardent courtship. Beyond them, two tugs tried to get a steamer off a sandbank.

In Charleston, we stopped at a frequently and highly recommended restaurant. It is down near the slave market, and called Henry's. It is a restaurant of indifferent décor, which is often the sign of a very good place. On the tiled floor stood old Viennese bentwood chairs. The lighting fixtures are like those used in barbershops, and in the right rear corner of the restaurant's main dining room was a group of darkies—waiters arranged according in size, the small ones in front, the tallest in back leaning against the sideboard. I thought they were about to sing some spirituals, but they were asleep with eyes wide open.

One of them exiled himself from the group and slouched over to our table. "There is two kinds of chowder on the menu," he said, "a blackfish chowder and a special one, a Charleston chowder." We ordered one of each, and when they were served they looked and tasted exactly alike, a white, sloppy paste, flavorless and lukewarm.

The next thing, some seafood which was recommended as a native dish, and the *spécialité de la Maison,* turned out to be another stew, a kind of *rijstafel* with small fish scales that got between your teeth, and other foreign substances thrown in.

On this trip we stayed at several hotels that belong to a chain which is owned by a man named Dinkler. They are a kind of traveling-salesman hotel, very clean and satisfactory. In each of them, in the center of immense lobbies, stands a statue of the founder—a grim-visaged executive. On everything is printed "This is a Dinkler Hotel," and the doorman sends you to the next Dinkler.

On the highway that leads to Newcastle and back to New York is a hill. When I was halfway down it a green traffic light shone ahead. A car approached from the left over a crossroad and got stuck in the snow. Under the light, the hill was solid ice and it was too late to do anything. I pushed Barbara, who sat next to me, down on the floor, and then the crash came. The driver of the truck and his helper, two natives of Dover, were shaken up. The driver had a cut over his left eye, and we all had to go to a magistrate.

The driver and his helper were greeted by the magistrate as John and Charlie, and everyone told the story of the accident. The magistrate listened carefully to all three versions and then he leaned back and asked a few questions. He seemed an honest man and he looked out of the window somewhat bewildered. It was a difficult case to decide. He asked a state trooper to drive him to the spot where the accident had taken place, and when he came back he lit a pipe and looked out of the window some more.

The driver sat on a bench in front of us, near an iron pot-belly stove. He adjusted a small bandage over his eye. A little blood ran down over his face, and he wiped it away. The room was silent.

Barbara watched the man wipe the blood away. Then she said, "Pappy, why did you try to kill that poor man?"

The magistrate smiled gratefully. Nodding to me, he knocked on the table and said, "Guilty!"

CHER AMI

To work for me, to live with me, is hard. I am composed of disorderly habits. I live the way William Saroyan thinks people live,
and it's not so funny off the stage. Normally, I am filled with the
greatest good will toward my fellow men, and I manifest this with
generous gestures in all directions. I stop and smile at children,
and I spread breadcrumbs for the pigeons on the stairs of Saint
Patrick's, but the next day I would like to kick them all in the
shins.

My habitat is mostly bars and restaurants, hotels and depots, and the lobbies and entrances thereof. In normal times I am found on the decks of steamships, and on the shores of tropic isles. I arrive suddenly, somewhere far away, and once there I haunt the piers and terminals and curse if there isn't a boat or plane to take me back immediately. I get homesick as soon as I am away from where I've gone—going it's for New York, coming back it's for where I've left. To share such a life, one needs a mobile servant, adaptable as a chameleon, shock- and surprise-proof, a person who gazes into your face as into a crystal ball and then knows whether to come close or stay away from you the rest of the day. The coin is not too good, either.

The ideal servant for me is a kind of Sancho Panza, a companion and friend with the melancholy kinship of an Irish setter. The run-of-the-mill retainer won't do at all; no Treacher type, no Admirable Crichton for me. I'd rather have him inept as far as service goes, but let him make it up with perfection in all the other departments. Above all, let him be someone curious and different. My ideal would be an ex-sergeant of the Foreign Legion, or a bankrupt banker, a retired road-company leading man who could mug Hamlet and Shylock, or a third-rate Karloff. Give me a burglar, or even a dismissed G-man, anything, but not the meek soul to whose life a million polished teapots are a monument.

My wishes are usually fulfilled with miraculous promptness, sometimes with such dispatch that I get scared at the prompt benevolence that hovers over me.

For example, I wished for this fol-de-rol butler, and not very hard either. I did not go to any employment agency to look for him; I did not even put an ad in the paper, nor did I ask anyone if they knew of such a man. I just wished, and he came.

I met him in Haiti last winter. For a while I lived in the *dépendance* of a small hotel, the rooms of which were like the cells in an exquisitely run insane asylum. Every compartment had its own precise garden of tropical greenery. Planted in the exact center of each of these eight-by-twelve-foot gardens was a tree, not large enough for anyone to use it for climbing in or out of the garden, but with enough leaves to shade a rattan chaise longue, and with four branches for birds to sing on in the twilights of morning and evening. Each of the gardens was enclosed by a white high wall.

The floor of the bedroom was a mosaic of black and white tile, and in its center stood a bed with tortured cast-iron ornaments, small knobs, and buns, spirals and little brass blossoms stuck and twisted on its head- and foot-boards. During the day, the design of the bed was somewhat diffused under a tent made of mosquito netting, which was attached to the ceiling by a rope and pulley. At night, one was under the tent, and then the fancy ironwork was beautifully clear.

The morning after the night when I wished for the companion, I beheld on awakening the outline of a man outside the mosquito tent. It seemed that he had stood there for a long while. He was in a state of repose, leaning on the wall, and he threw the butt of a cigarette out into the garden when he saw me sit up. On his head was a Chevalier straw hat. I lifted the netting, and, leaning out of bed, I observed that my visitor was barefoot and sunburned, and that his hat was honored with the bright colors of a Racquet Club band. He had a lean, generous face, and looked somewhat like a skiing teacher or a derelict tennis pro. Over his lips lay a black mustache, and his shirt was without buttons. The sleeves were torn off halfway between the elbow and the shoulders, offering ventilation to his chest.

He sat down at the foot of the bed and told me that he was my friend. He told me his name and informed me that he was one of a group of escaped prisoners from Devil's Island, and that he was taken care of, with his companions, by the good *Sœurs de la Sagesse*. He and the boys lived at the convent . . .

He corrected himself and explained that he and the others were not escaped criminals in the strict sense of the word, but that since the Vichy government was unable or unwilling to pay the upkeep of the prison or the salaries of the administrators and guards at Guiana, the prison doors had simply been left open, and whoever wanted to left.

"I," he continued, "was a *doubleur;* that is, I had served my sentence but had to stay on the Island. We left French Guiana, my friends and I, in a sixteen-foot *canot*. No one tried to stop us.

We were twelve when we started. The hardest part was to get straight out to sea past the reef which is called the Frenchmen's Grave. To pass this, you have to go over sandbars in a straight line for about thirty-five kilometers, and then you turn left.

"That takes courage. We did it all with the aid of a map, which we had copied, and with the aid of a Creole, a seaman who knew the stars. We also had a small compass with us, and we got as far as Trinidad. It was easy. A captain of a ship must find a port; we only tried to find the land. The Governor of Trinidad gave us eighty dollars to buy a bigger boat, and with that we got as far as Jamaica. Now we are here and thinking of going on to Cuba. We have a tolerably good life here. Twice a week we watch the plane come in—that is where I saw you arrive. We sit in the convent garden or along the water most of the time, and the *bonnes Sœurs de la Sagesse* take care of us as if we were little birds, but it's not a life for a man.

"*Cher ami,*" he said, "do something for me. I am a pastry-cook, I have been a hotel director. I know how to drive a car and how to fix it. I can write on the machine. I can steer a boat. I am ready to go anywhere, and I am afraid of nothing. Give me a little food and pocket money, and I am your man, your servant, your friend for life."

He lounged back on the bed, lit a cigarette, spread his toes fan-wise, folded his hands in back of his head, and looked up at the ceiling, waiting for my answer.

"I wanted to talk to you last night," he added after a while. "I followed you from the cinema up to your hotel, but I thought you might get scared or nervous, so I came this morning."

He broke the few moments of silence, in which I thanked that particular department of Providence that concerns itself with me, by remarking that if I was worried about his past he could put me completely at ease. He confessed that when he was young he had made a mistake—he had disemboweled his mistress. Ah, Simone was a very beautiful girl, but she had been unfaithful, and he was not sorry.

I told him he could start in right away. He could pack my trunk and take it to the ship; and as soon as he got to New York, there were several people I would like to have disemboweled, but nicely, and I would give him a list every Monday. I gave him a small advance, and then I said that the only thing I was worried about was how he would get to New York, past the immigration authorities, the police, and J. Edgar Hoover's sharp-eyed and resourceful young men.

"Bah! Leave that to me," he said. "I shall be in New York— let me see—it's the middle of August now; give me until the end of September. It's child's play. About the twenty-fifth of September, I would say. Where do you live?" I gave him my address, and that afternoon he arrived with a boy to carry my trunk, which he had neatly packed. On the way to the boat he stopped the car at the *Magasin de Mille Cent Choses* and bought a pack of razorblades, which he said I needed; and then he said good-by and *au revoir.* He slowly shook my hand and lifted the Chevalier straw hat. He waved it so hard when the ship pulled out that the Racquet Club band came off and fell into the bay. A native boy dove after it, and he gave him a coin.

"Wonderful, wonderful," I said to myself and missed him immediately. Stretched out in my deck chair, I thought how very fortunate I was. When I got home, I was still gloating over the fact that I had found the perfect man.

One morning soon after my return I found a letter. It started: "La Havane, Cuba. *Cher ami,* I have the honor to address these few words to you, to inform you that, after a sudden departure from Haiti in a boat which I and a few of the others who shared my idea procured along the waterfront, we proceeded for Cuba. The beginning of the voyage was without incident. One night, however, we had some difficulty holding our direction, as a violent wind caused our leaking shell to dance an infernal sarabande on the waves.

"Without the sail and the mast, and also without the man who steered the boat at the outset, without a rudder even, the wind delivered us to the eastern shore of Cuba, and, to make our *misére* perfect, into a nest of waiting gendarmes from whom we were too wet and exhausted to flee. My companions and I find ourselves detained at the *Centre d'Emigration,* and I regret to inform you that my departure from here can only be effected by

the immediately sent sum of one hundred dollars. I will consider
the hundred dollars in lieu of six months of service."

I sent him the money. I have faith in such characters, and they
have never failed me. Neither did *Cher Ami.*

In the middle of one night when I lay awake, I had one of my
rare moments of worry again. Suppose, when he turns up, I said
to myself, he's the perfect servant, butler, and companion, and
besides, a good pastrycook. Suppose he's out in the pantry one
day squeezing many happy returns on my birthday cake when
there is a knock at the door, and it's the police. Then follows the
story of the body of a young woman, partly decomposed, found
crammed into the luggage compartment of my convertible coupé.
O.K., take him away; but he won't come quietly . . . smack,
smack, *klunk;* I hold the door open while they carry him out.
Then I have to get hold of Leibowitz, but Leibowitz has turned
judge, and Arthur Garfield Hays is out of town. And then the
trial and the conviction and the pictures in the paper, and then
the visit up the river, and the last mile. It's all absorbing, stirring,
and excellently done, but it's not much fun, riding back alone
from Ossining with a cold friend up there.

The morning after the night that I wished he wouldn't come,
he didn't come, but there was a letter from him, one of the nicest
documents I have ever received and certainly worth a hundred
dollars.

"*Cher ami,*" it said, "I have the honor to address these few
words to you, wishing to keep you informed of my condition. I
have the honor to inform you with my deep personal regret that
I will not come to America. Dishonesty is not my game. The
money you so generously sent to me is paid out in the most
splendid of causes. I have used it to obtain for myself and for a
friend who shares my idea, passage to Jamaica, from which isle
this communication is addressed to you. We have come here to
enlist in the forces of General de Gaulle. This is attested by our
pictures and the text which you will find under them in the accompanying clipping from the Kingston *Star.* It's not patriotism,
cher ami. France has not been a good mother to me. But it's the
quickest way to become a man again. Please accept my respectful
salutations. André Pigueron."

CAMP NOMOPO

After the first walk through the city, Barbara came back to the Hotel Metropolitano in Quito with her lips blue and her little fists clenched. Mimi put her to bed and I went out to look for a garment that would shield her against the cold wind that blows down from Pichincha. There was no snow suit to be had; it's not cold enough for that, and the coats for little girls which I found and brought back to the hotel Barbara waved away. Four and a half years old, she knew exactly what she wanted. She sat up in bed with the first measles spots on her chest and said she would rather freeze to death than wear anything like the samples she had seen.

During the next weeks while she was in bed, I had to design coats for her. I exhausted myself making a stack of fashion drawings, designs of dramatic coats and hats to go with them, and I cut paper dolls out of old fashion magazines and pasted my coats on them. The design that found favor with Barbara was a three-storied kind of pelerine, a garment such as Viennese fiacre drivers of the time of Franz Josef used to wear.

"This is it," she said. "That's the bestest good one."

As soon as Barbara was well, we went to a tailor with the design. The shop of Señor Pablo Duque Arias faces the square of San Francisco. It is like an indoor farm. Chickens run around among the sewing machines and over the low podium on which Mr. Arias's chief cutter sits with crossed legs; a cat, a dog with offspring, and a parrot complete the fauna; the flora consist of artificial paper roses stuck in a dry vase that stands on a small shelf between an oil print of the Madonna and a picture of the Temptation of St. Anthony.

Barbara eyed this *salon de couture* with alarm and suspicion, but she let Señor Arias measure her. He studied my design and then we went to the store of Don Alfonso Perez Pallares to buy the cloth—the tailor, Barbara, Madame, and myself. We found something that looked like the lining of a good English traveling bag. It was made in Ecuador and it was agreeable to everyone.

The coat was in work for a week, and on each day we inspected progress of the garment. At the end, Barbara looked into a mirror and was delighted with the results. It cost $7.50, not counting my time and talent. The coat was a very warm and useful garment on the return trip to New York in February.

Barbara is one of the seventy-five or a hundred overprivileged children who are allowed to play inside the cast-iron confines of Gramercy Park. Another little girl, equally well fixed, is an earnest, dark-haired, five-year-old whose name is Ruthie. Ruthie played with Barbara one day and they became friends—and at their third meeting, on a day in March, when Barbara was dressed in my creation, little Ruthie said to Barbara, "You look like Oliver Twister in that coat. That's a coat like orphans wear. I think it's terrible. I don't see how you can wear it."

On a visit to Ruthie's house that afternoon, Barbara inspected Ruthie's wardrobe. She did not wear the "Oliver Twister" coat when she came back, but carried it in her arms and hid it in the closet of her room.

She succeeded by a week of ceaseless cajolery and little-girl appeal in wangling a new winter outfit from me when it was already spring and all the Gramercy Park trees were breaking out with small green buds. Of course, it was an outfit exactly like something that Ruthie had, only newer.

Barbara and Ruthie were now bosom friends. They sat together on a bench facing a stone urn, to the left of the statue of Mr. Booth, and there they hatched another plot. The plan was to go to a summer camp together. Little Ruthie had been at this camp the year before and she described the sylvan, rugged beauty of that life to Barbara. Barbara said to Ruthie that she'd love to go but that she was afraid she would be lonesome, that she never had gone anywhere without her parents.

"Oh," said Ruthie, "after the third day you forget you ever had a father or mother."

Barbara came home with this bit of grim wisdom.

The camp we chose took care of a hundred girls. It was in the upper Adirondacks. The water came from artesian wells, the children slept in semi-bungalows and washed themselves at ten taps that spouted cold artesian water. The taps were conveniently located in front of the bungalows, the prospectus said, and the children got up to the sound of a bugle at 7:30 a.m. and did their own housework.

When I came to this part of the booklet I was convinced that nothing was better for our darling than to rise in the upper Adirondacks at seven-thirty and scrub herself at a cold-water tap.

Barbara hopped on one foot and on the other and clasped her hands with joy when I told her that she would be one of the lucky members of Camp Nomopo, which in the language of the Indians means Land That Is Bright.

The equipment needed for this simple life had to be marked with the name of the child and was as follows:

Bathing suits, 2	Bathrobe, 1
Bathing sandals, 1 pair	Tennis sneakers, 1 pair
Heavy bathing caps, 2	Handkerchiefs, 6
Cotton ankle socks, 4 pairs	Play suits, 2
Cotton underwear, 4 suits	Bedroom slippers, 1 pair
Pajamas, 3 pairs	Rubbers, 1 pair

Tennis racquet, 1

Tennis balls, 3

Toilet articles

Poncho, 1

Rain hat, 1

Riding breeches, 1 pair

Bed sheets, 3

Pillow cases, 3

Dark blankets, 3

Bath towels, 3

Face towels, 3

Mattress protector, 1

Laundry bag, 1

Duffel bag, 1

Folding knife and spoon, 1 each

Drinking cup with handle, 1

Sewing material

Bible, 1

In addition, there was this special equipment:

1 pair Nomopo gabardine shorts

1 pair Nomopo brown oxfords

2 white Nomopo shirts

2 Nomopo suits

1 Nomopo green tie

1 Nomopo green sweater

2 pairs Nomopo ankle socks

The whole thing went into a green army trunk and was stowed in the back seat of the car.

The cost of going to the camp for two months was a healthy figure, about what it would take to stay at a good hotel for that time. There was a canteen. There were, besides, provisions for pocket money to buy extra things at the canteen and an additional charge for the materials used in the arts and crafts building of Camp Nomopo.

The camp was full of cheer and gladness when we arrived. The Madame who ran it received her guests with the intense charm and cordiality of a Howard Johnson hostess; the counselors hopped around, and little Ruthie, who had arrived the day before, took Barbara by the hand and led her down to their semi-bungalow, Number 5. I checked on the waterspout which was right next to it. The cabin was a loose shelter built on stilts, open to the north and south, with no windows but large shutters that were held up by pieces of wood. In it stood six little cast-iron cots such as you see in orphanages; birds sang outside and the branches of the trees were the curtains.

In this room the floor was a row of unpainted boards through which, here and there, you could see the good earth. We also inspected the mess hall and the infirmary. The counselor that had Barbara in charge showed her how to make her bed, how to sweep the floor, and how to empty the rubbish bin—three duties that were her part of the housekeeping. Barbara did it all with gusto.

The Madame came around at about 3 p.m. and said, "Please leave before it gets dark. It's easier for the child that way."

So we said good-by to Barbara. She was brave. She said, "Good-by," and walked away with her back to the car, waving as she walked. Halfway down to shack Number 5, at the cold-water tap, she suddenly turned. The small face was streaked with tears and she came back and got a grip on her mother and announced that she would not stay in the camp.

I don't know where I got the courage because my heart was breaking, but I took Barbara, handed her to the Madame, who pressed her to her ample bosom. I got Mimi into the car, and drove off. We called the camp an hour later on the phone and the Madame announced that Barbara's grief had lasted for a quarter of an hour. "Now she's in the recreation hall having the time of her life, the little darling. She's sitting in front of the big fire with little Ruthie, listening to 'Peter and the Wolf.' Don't you worry a minute about her—and please, please don't come visiting her until ten days from now."

The next day, while staying at a hotel, I reflected what a wonderful racket a children's camp is, how much better it is than owning a hotel, for example.

Imagine if the guests of a hotel like the Savoy-Plaza arrived bringing their own three dark blankets and sheets, towels and pillow cases, made their own beds, emptied their garbage, went down to the cold-water taps in Central Park to scrub themselves, and without murmur ate the healthy, strength-giving diet you put before them! If instead of going out in the evening and spending their money in rival establishments, they would quietly sit around the bar listening to "Peter and the Wolf" or do arty-crafty things in the ballroom—all of them dressed in hats, shoes, and sweaters marked Savoy-Plaza!

We came back after ten days in which we wrote nine letters and received four cards written by Barbara's counselor. After a glowing report on how glad and happy and what a fine girl she was, the Madame sent for her.

She came in the rain, between the wet, dripping trees, in the

Nomopo rain hat, the Nomopo green sweater and poncho, alone and much sadder-looking than "Oliver Twister" ever was. She broke out in streams of tears when she saw us, and she kept crying even after it stopped raining outside. She blinked red-eyed in the sun that shone above rays of floating mist.

We went out to a playfield, and, at one moment when we stepped aside to discuss what to do, Barbara found herself surrounded by her comrades. Madame looked down at her with reproach, and her counselor, a maiden from whose Nomopo sweater I could hardly take my eyes, said, "You're not going to be a sissy now, are you, and run away from us?"

Barbara was the most complete portrait of misery I have ever seen, not excepting the work of El Greco. She cried, "I don't like it here. I want to go home with Mummy and Pappy. I want to go home; I don't like it here. I want to go home."

We took her into the car with us, and I said in French to Mimi that I thought under the circumstances it would be the best thing to take her home with us. While I spoke, she took hold of the leather straps that are attached to the convertible top of the car as if to anchor herself, and said, "You don't have to speak French, I know what you were saying. You said, 'Let's start the car and push Barbara out and drive away like the last time' "— and then she continued, "I dream about you at night and when I wake up you're not there, and in the morning another little girl next to me cries, and that makes me cry too.

"Ruthie said she cried too the first time last year, but her mother just left her there and never came to see her and now she's used to it, but I won't get used to it because I dream of you every night. And it's so cold in the morning, and I have to empty the pail and sweep."

The washing at the tap she had got around, apparently. She was streaked with dirt and her hair was a mess. She said, "We take a bath twice a week, down at the lake, and the water is cold. I want to go home. I don't like it here. I want to go home with Mummy and Pappy."

A man came to the car and smiled and said, "I'm only the husband of Mrs. Van Cortland who runs the camp, and I can assure you that Barbara's the happiest little girl when you're not here.

She sings and plays all day long. I think it would be a great mistake for you to take her away."

I told him that we would take her away. Barbara let go of the straps and the man said, "Well, all I can say is that in my twenty-seven years this has happened only once before."

Barbara smelled of garlic and unwashed hair. They had had meat loaf for lunch. It was dark by the time we had made the decision and we stayed for supper. It began to rain again, and there is nothing more wet and desolate than Adirondack camps in the rain. The meal was served on a drafty porch, a piece of canvas blew in with every gust of wind. The menu consisted of melted cheese poured over toast and a lukewarm rice pudding that tasted like glue; a glass of milk was served to each diner.

We left poor Ruthie behind, and the Madame and her husband assured us again that it was only the second time in twenty-seven years that such a thing had happened.

SWEET DEATH IN THE ELECTRIC CHAIR

Many years ago when I worked in a famous New York hotel, I lived in one of its unoccupied apartments.

I had with me a man I had picked up on a ferryboat. He was out of a job and by profession a tailor. He pressed my suits and sometimes picked up extra money by working at odd jobs in the hotel. For a hobby he played the violin; he played it quite nicely. His name was Lustgarten.

On one of the evenings when there were no parties at the Splendide and the ballroom remained dark and empty, Lustgarten and I went to the theater.

We went to see *Lysistrata*. During the second act a loud rain began to fall outside in the street, and after the curtain went down people jumped over puddles and ran, bent over, to the opened doors of taxicabs.

In a niche of the theater building, to the right of the door, pressed against the wall, stood a small boy and a larger one, who held him by the neck of a torn sweater.

The little one's face was wet and smudged. He looked up at the older boy. Under his arm, tightly squeezed, were several mussed copies of the *Daily Mirror*.

The rain came down in a curtain of strings and splashed on the sidewalk. Lustgarten unfurled an umbrella and stood on his heels, and when the umbrella was opened the larger boy moved under it, letting go of the small one. The little fellow sold me a paper. Immediately after he had received a nickel, he jumped out into the water and ran across the street to the second-balcony entrance of another theater. Lustgarten was pushed out into the rain as the larger boy chased after the little one. It all happened very quickly, and when we got to the other side of the street Lustgarten was almost thrown into the gutter as the bigger boy came rushing out of the balcony entrance and raced down toward Eighth Avenue.

We found the little one with two unsold copies of the *Mirror* sitting on the stairs with one shoe off. He told us that the other boy had stolen his money: the nickel he had had in his hand and, besides, the day's earnings of sixty-five cents which he had hidden in his left shoe. The thief had slashed down the front of the shoe where it was laced, pulled the shoe off, taken the money, and run.

"The dirty lousy bum," growled the little boy and picked the stubs of his shoelaces out of their eyelets. He said, with a nod in the direction of Eighth Avenue, that now he could not even go home, as a beating awaited him if he returned without money. He said that in a casual, tired fashion, and when I asked him where he would sleep, he shoved his filthy cap back, pushed his lower lip out, and shrugged his shoulders.

I decided then to take him home to the hotel.

Lustgarten pulled at my sleeve and shook his head. He whispered, "Give him some money, fifty cents or a dollar, and send him off—send him home in a cab if you must, but don't bring him into the hotel. Look at him. No joy will come out of this, and besides I wouldn't be surprised if the boy isn't covered with lice . . ."

A cab came along and I told the driver to take us to the hotel. Lustgarten sat in a corner and the boy, with his two copies of the *Mirror,* sat on the floor. I asked him how old he was and he said that he was eight. He answered my questions in a voice too old for a child, too young for a man; a soft husky talk like that of a young streetwalker. He smelled like an animal, like a dog. His face was a mixture of fatigue and impertinence.

Whenever we had reason to enter or leave the hotel unobserved, we used, instead of the front-entrance door or the employees' entrance, an auxiliary ballroom door at the side of the hotel on a street where the least traffic was.

It was, like all the Splendide's doors, a revolving door, cumbersome to open. Revolving doors are locked with two long plunger-like rods that go up into the ceiling. The locks are high up, near the top of the door. While I lit a match, Lustgarten had to reach up and find the keyholes, turn the door, let us in, and then lock the door twice from the inside. He was annoyed that he had to do all this on account of the boy.

Teddy came into the ballroom with no manifestation of awe. He held on to his newspapers and sat in the ballroom office waiting for Lustgarten to bring him a glass of milk and a sandwich. He drank the milk, ate the sandwich, wiped his mouth with the napkin, and then we took the service elevator up to the apartment.

After he entered the living room he walked to a large sofa, put his papers on it, placed his face on them, and then he fell instantly asleep.

Lustgarten wanted to get him to take a bath but I said to leave him alone. The boy slept all night.

"You must listen to reason, Herr Graf," said Lustgarten the next morning, sitting at the side of my bed. "Who is this boy? Where does he come from? Who is going to take care of him? What if anything happens to him? What about his parents? What about if the management finds out that he is here? We'll all be thrown out. I had a brother once who took a boy like this off the street—the trouble he had! I don't even want to tell you. Give him his breakfast, give him money, give him anything you like, but send him away, or you'll be sorry. No good ever comes of this kind of charity."

Teddy told me that his name was Iswolsky, that he was of Polish parentage, that he lived on Tenth Avenue and Forty-fourth Street, and that he attended a Polish parochial school in which English was taught two days a week and Polish the rest.

The boy who took his money, he said, regularly waylaid him but never had come as close to Broadway as last night. He usually waited for him down near the river.

Teddy was silent whenever Lustgarten came into the room. When I asked him whether he would like to stay with me he said, "Sure."

He was still wild and hungry-looking after he was washed. His face was old, he had a certainty to all his motions. In standing, sitting, running, there was never any play, any foolish posture in his limbs, no repetition of meaningless phrases or nonsense in his talk, no loud laughter and no song. He had a bitter logical mind, and he never cried.

There was some trouble with the Polish principal when I took him out of the parochial school and placed him in a public school. The teacher came out into the street with some neighbors and shouted after the car in which I drove away with Teddy.

There was more trouble when Lustgarten had to go to a store with Teddy and buy him shoes, a turtleneck sweater, some clothes and linen. Lustgarten did not want to go with Teddy and Teddy did not want to go with Lustgarten.

A week after he was in the new school I received a card, and the teacher said that she regretted to have to inform me that Teddy had appeared only twice. At the hotel he came and went very freely. He sometimes arrived at two in the morning, and several times he did not come home at all.

He had a pocketknife and besides always carried a string with a piece of lead attached to the end of it. With this apparatus he fished coins out of subway gratings. To pick up the coins he attached chewing gum to the lead. He traveled all over New York on the rear bumpers of automobiles and on the ends of trolley cars, and once he pushed some bricks from the roof of the hotel down into the street. There was a commotion but nobody was hurt. He denied doing it, but one of the maids, who was drying her hair on the roof of the hotel, told the engineer and the house detective who came up to investigate that she had seen a little boy with black hair on the roof just before the brick fell down. He spent most of his time in cheap movies, seeing the features twice. I took him along to better pictures occasionally, but he hated Chevalier, and of *Nanook of the North* he said, "Nothing but snow and whiskers." He did not enjoy the hotel's cooking and subsisted on hot dogs and hamburgers which he bought outside the Splendide.

"He is going to end up in jail," said Lustgarten. "On the gallows that boy is going to end. Just wait, your pet will make you a lot of trouble. I would like to be in charge of him. First thing every day, a good licking, whether he deserved it or not, and instead of pocket money I'd give him a slice of black bread and a smack on the head. Wait and see, you're going to be sorry."

Lustgarten wouldn't listen to any explanations or understand that to beat children is a completely European fashion of education.

Lustgarten came into the room with a triumphant face when he could at last report that a pair of studs were missing, golden ones. He said that Teddy must have stolen them. He came next with stories that small change was missing out of a box where he kept it.

The week after that report I was short a five-dollar bill. Next, two bottles of wine disappeared and a bottle of excellent scotch. We did not know exactly when it was stolen because we had not checked up on our stock for a while.

Lustgarten came and made a speech and begged to throw Teddy out, but I told him to have patience. I explained to him that a child that has led a life like Teddy's can't be cured with a lecture or a thrashing. "First we must get his affection," I said, "then we can work on him."

Lustgarten folded his hands and shook his head, and once when he buttoned Teddy's shirt he shook and choked him. And he looked at the bottles every day.

"Aha," he said the week after we had discovered the first series of thefts, and again with pleasure he announced, "Look, two more quarts of champagne, Krug 1928, extra dry, are gone. They were here yesterday."

"What interests me," I said to Lustgarten, "what I would like to know is, how does he get them out of the hotel? He's such a small boy; the bottles are heavy and awkward to hide—"

"He doesn't have to take it out," said Lustgarten. "Most probably he sells it down in the basement. Your pet is all over the house like a mouse. You can see him in the cellar, on the roof, in every elevator. He's the butcher's and cook's friend. They make hamburgers for him. As for the wine, he sells it perhaps to a bus boy or a waiter, who in turn sells it to a captain, who sells it finally to a customer for twenty dollars a bottle. That's why we have Prohibition."

"Why can't we put a lock on the closet where the champagne is kept?" I said.

"Because the closet is a very antique and shaky Sheraton sideboard."

"Then why can't we move the champagne to a closet which can be locked?"

That is where the argument ended. Lustgarten walked away, mumbling. He retired into himself for a week and he never looked at Teddy.

Toward the end of Lustgarten's silence, a man in a cheap overcoat and a derby came into the hotel and was shown to the ballroom office. He sat in a chair when I went to see him, opened his mouth and closed his eyes like a bird.

In a hotel, people like this usually have a cigar between their fingers and start their conversation with, "How much do you want for the use of the Hall?" but after the rental figure is quoted them, they get up and ask for the address of the Hotel Commodore or the Pennsylvania.

But this one announced that he was a detective. He asked me whether a small boy by the name of Tommy Iswolsky lived with me. He opened his mouth again, made an effort to speak, and then said, "Where's the boy? Where is he now, I mean?"

I told him that I did not know where he was, that perhaps he was upstairs. We took an elevator to the top floor and walked down to the apartment. Teddy was not there.

"In case he comes in while I am here," said the detective with closed eyes, "in case he comes, you just sit there and listen. I don't want you to do any talking or make any signs to him, you understand? You just sit here, and I'll be here, you understand that? I'll ask all the questions."

I gave the detective a drink and talked with him and after about ten minutes Teddy came into the room.

The detective called him, placed him in front of himself so that the boy's back was turned in my direction. He took hold of both the boy's arms and he closed his eyes again and after a while he said, "What's your name?"

"Teddy Iswolsky."

"What's this man's name?"

The boy told him my name.

"What do you call him when you talk to him?"

"I call him Chief."

"What does he call you?"

"He calls me Teddy."

"Where does he sleep?"

"In there."

"And where do you sleep?"

"In here on the sofa."

He asked a few more questions and then he said, "All right, sonny, run along now and play."

The detective picked up the phone and called a number. He gave his name and said with closed eyes, "I'm here on case number so and so, and this man doesn't seem to be either a criminal or a pervert. I'll hand in my report tomorrow."

He hung up. "Sorry, Mister. I think you'll hear from the Society," he said to me. "You know you can't just pick up a stray boy and keep him. There are formalities, papers to sign, but if I were you I'd get rid of the kid. I've never seen it work out. Good day, sir, and thanks for the drink."

Lustgarten said, "For God's sake, send that boy away. If the management hears of this—a little boy who is already a bootlegger, a thief, and you think you can do anything with him. Before anything serious happens, send him away." I walked out into the foyer on my way down to the ballroom. Teddy stood next to a portière, his cap in hand, the little old face pale, the mouth clamped into a straight line. I think I wanted to say something to him, and he wanted to say something to me. I had the doorknob in my hand for a while longer than it was necessary, but then I went to take the elevator to the first floor of the hotel to see that the plates for five hundred people were in their places and the waiters' fingernails clean.

I thought during the serving of the dinner that it was best to send him home. I thought that when the banquet was over, if it were not too late, I'd take him home myself. I thought about this after the soup was served. I walked out into the pantry.

Teddy stood on top of the service stairs, as he always stood at entrances, afraid to come into the room, and he sent his hungry look down at me.

The guests went home early, and when I got up to the apartment Teddy was waiting again.

I asked him to sit down next to me, and I asked him about his father and mother. He did not answer. He sat staring, and then he said that his father was in prison. He said that his father was in Sing Sing.

His father, Thomas Iswolsky, he said, had killed a man. He said that he had wanted to ask me for some money so that his mother could visit him. It would take five dollars he said. He confessed that he had taken some money to help his mother. She needed it, he said, for lawyers and to visit his father. His face was pale, his eyes large and fixed on a place he had picked to look at while he talked to me, a point somewhere between the half-open doors that led to Lustgarten's pantry.

He ran home with the money about eleven o'clock.

The next evening I had to see a man who wanted to give a dinner at the hotel and who had very definite ideas about the decorations of the room and the menu. He had an office downtown and worked late. I drove down to see him at 111 Broadway. Lustgarten and Teddy waited in the car. It was about eleven at night when I got through and we drove uptown again.

We passed Madison Square at the moment when the clock on the Metropolitan Building struck eleven. Teddy sat between Lustgarten and me. Suddenly he clawed himself into my coat and screamed, "Now they're cutting his trouser leg, now they're taking him in, now they're turning on the juice. It's all over," he whimpered.

It is difficult to console anyone, and more so to help a child. After Lustgarten understood that Teddy's father had been executed in the electric chair, he felt sorry that he had ever disliked the boy. He talked to him, took him on his lap, and when we got to the hotel he cheerfully unlocked the revolving door and took Teddy upstairs. He put him to bed and afterward walked around half the night, accusing himself. He apologized and said he was sorry to have been so mean and that God would reward me for my goodness of heart. He suffered a complete emotional reverse.

Teddy was gone most of the next day, and he came back and said that his mother needed a little more help. She had a small amount of insurance money coming to her, but bringing the body down from Sing Sing cost a lot of money. There were burial expenses and she needed money to put the children into proper dark clothes. He needed another twenty-five dollars, to which Lustgarten contributed an extra five.

Two days after, he came and told us that the dead father had arrived. He smelled, he said, of burns. When one stood at the head of the coffin, the hair, what was left of it and not completely singed away, smelled of vinegar. He explained that they use a sponge with vinegar on it to insure quick execution.

He was dressed in a cheap suit, the dead father, a cheap suit made in prison. He described the candles and the flowers in detail.

I told Teddy that I would take the afternoon off and go home with him and see what I could do for his poor mother. At this he suddenly protested.

"Oh—please, Chief—please—don't do that. You won't like it. It's terrible," he said. "The burns, the smell, and all the people crying . . ."

I held him by the hand because he wanted to run away. I had to hold on to him all the way to the address he had given the investigator. He wanted to jump out of the taxi, and while I paid he tried to pull himself free.

It was a windy day. Open newspapers floated down the street and ashcan covers banged.

In the hall of the house where he lived he kicked and bit, but I took him along up three flights of stairs.

There was a kitchen with laundry hanging from the ceiling, a leaden children's bathtub hung on the wall. A box filled with old shoes stood under a table and two dirty little girls searched in it for a pair to wear.

In the living room of the flat, very happy, big and alive, an honest enough man, with a black curly mustache that supported two red cheeks, sat Mr. Thomas Iswolsky, Teddy's father, eating sausages with his fingers and drinking beer. On the mantel in back of him was a kewpie doll, an American flag, a papier-mâché shepherd dog with rhinestone eyes, and several empty bottles of our wine.

In an adjoining room, graced with a crêpe-paper altar, and in bed, was Teddy's mother. The father explained happily that they were soon to be parents again.

Teddy was very quiet and well behaved and I left him there.

New Stories

"THE GOLDEN OPPORTUNITY"

At the Bavarian Press Club in Munich I took a jeep, which you can hire at the reasonable rate of a dollar and a half an hour, and drove to Regensburg. Along the route in this agricultural latitude I saw fine horses and immense pigs, choice cows in the fields, and had continually to avoid hitting fat geese. These are again force-fed here as they were in olden times. The peasant women hold the geese between their knees and—feeding good-sized dumplings, about thirty of them, into the birds, first forcing their beaks open—insert the food and then, by forming a ring with in-dex finger and thumb, slide down the bird's long neck, forcing the meal clot down its throat. The children too, in the small vil-lages along this route, seem well fed and have fat rosy cheeks.

There is no evidence of destruction in the small towns and villages that you pass on the way. While the Autobahnen are bombed, the less important roads are undamaged. The tiny, hard apples that hang in the trees planted alongside them, and that would make a kind of crabapple jelly, were left on the branches, although they were ripe. There are a good deal of hops grown, also barley and potatoes. Regensburg itself suffered little damage, except on the outskirts. After I arrived I took a city directory and looked under *P*, for the name of my old friend Pappelmeier, with whom I spent some unprofitable and dreary times on the hard benches and in the lockup of the local Lyceum. The professors of this institute tortured us in vain for three years. We repeated the same form, again and again, and were both held up as bad examples to the rest of three classes of pupils that passed us by.

My schoolmate Josef Pappelmeier, I found out on my arrival, had passed away during the first months of the war. The pieces of the story that follows were told me in a small garden along the Danube, by Pappelmeier's wife and daughter-in-law, and also later by his son Pepperl, who was in a camp.

My late friend had been of such extraordinary appearance that people who saw him for the first time turned their faces away, hid behind handkerchiefs or pocketbooks, or tried to turn into side streets. Caricature could only flatter him.

His face was like a Picasso drawing, where the model is seen from two sides at once. His crossed eyes sat so close together on the bridge of his nose that both could be seen when looking at his profile. It was like the arrangement of eyes on the face of a flounder. He had hair of the most improbable shades of red, and exposure to the summer sun and also to the cold winters of Regensburg turned the skin on his face to flaming patches of orange, carrot, purple, and old rose, all of it illuminated with a coppery sheen of the peach fuzz that covered his features. As he grew to manhood the comfortable cooking at his home and an unquenchable thirst for the rich local brews fitted him into the oval outline of the funny-paper-type German of happier days. He completed the caricature with two dachshunds and a green hat, to which was attached the usual bobbing chamois brush. The undertaker told me that, mercifully, he kept the lid on his coffin. He was mirth-provoking, even in death.

Because he found himself always surrounded by laughing people, Josef Pappelmeier was well adjusted and became a successful and happy man, learning his father's trade after he was, together with mo, thrown out of the Lyceum. He was envied later for the courage with which he wooed one of the nicest girls in Regensburg, who to the great surprise of all straight-eyed people agreed to marry him, and everyone in the old town breathed easier when the child of that union looked like a normal citizen at birth.

His proud father named him "Pepperl," which is the Bavarian dimunitive of Josef. He grew up, a healthy boy, impeded only by a slight speech defect, a liquid kind of stammering, which forced him to issue a few inarticulate, explosive sounds before he could express himself properly. He was, in school and on the street, called "Pappelmeier Pepperl," and, according to a teacher at a clinic for speech defects, this foolish appellation was responsible for his stammering. "You just try and say it," said Dr. Küssmaul. "Try and say 'Pappelmeier Pepperl.' How would you like to go through life with a name like that? Of course you'd stammer, and feel insecure, and fail in school, and want to run away."

Pappelmeier Pepperl's father was a Regensburg bon vivant, reveling in dishes cooked with red cabbage and sauerkraut, spotting his waistcoat with goose grease and the sauces that dripped off the various kinds of dumplings and *Spaetzles* that are the regional specialties.

When Pepperl was a baby my friend always took him along to restaurants and fed him on his knee. Pappelmeier was the only German I know who was unashamed to push a baby carriage through the streets of the old city, or carry his baby wrapped in flannels into the park—a job strictly assigned to women. He also refused to punish Pepperl in the good old-fashioned way, which recommends beating boys regularly like sacks of walnuts to make men of them, and that, many people said, and still say, was responsible for the tragedy of Pappelmeier Pepperl.

Old Pappelmeier had in years of hard work established himself as an independent manufacturer. He owned his own house, which stood on a square called "The Golden Opportunity." The façade of this building was so wide that on a black band, three feet high, between the windows of the second and the third floors, there was room to spell out in letters that were broad and golden "Josef Pappelmeier—Atelier für Präzisions Mechanik." On the two ground floors were the drafting and work rooms, and above them the living quarters of the family. Frau Pappelmeier led the detached life of the women of her kind. She lived a silent, obedient existence in the back of the house, more wishless than that of the one girl they employed to help her. On Sunday she followed her husband, who wheeled Pepperl in his carriage along the Danube to a piece of property on which the precision mechanic eventually hoped to build a villa, such as all the better people of Regensburg owned. The practical family man hoped to construct its solid foundations with the heavy boulders that formed the remnants of a tower, once part of the defenses of Regensburg. He wanted to call the place, which was on a hill overlooking the valley of the Danube, "Belvedere." His wife now remembers with sadness and remorse, as if it had been a prophecy, that she had said to him, "Leave it, Josef, as it is—ruins are so beautiful [*Ruinen sind doch so schön*]. Now we have lots of them," she says.

He followed her advice, and in the romantic weeks of his life he erected an arbor on this property and planted a grapevine, the fruit of which never ripened in the raw climate of that latitude. The grapes stayed green and hard, like those made of glass and used for decoration. Asparagus grew, and some pears, hard and sour apples—there was no idle time in Pappelmeier's day. Pepperl as a baby showed promise of equal amounts of energy. His mother remembers how he perpetually headed on all fours toward the fence that enclosed the property. She did not suspect then that it was the first manifestation of his wanderlust, which was eventually to be his undoing.

In this garden, some years later, on one of my previous visits to Bavaria, Pepperl's father told me of his worries about the boy. He had said then: "I don't know what's to become of Pepperl. He's not like my own flesh and blood at all. He's all thumbs, he has fingers like sausages—but that wouldn't matter if only he took an interest in the business—but he doesn't listen to a word

I say—he leans on a drawing table with his chin in his hand, and
when I'm through talking to him he looks like somebody that just
wakes up out of a dream. 'What?' he says, or sometimes he doesn't
answer me at all. I say to him, 'Look, Pepperl, it's all right with
me if you don't want to be a precision mechanic, if you think it's
beneath you, I understand. If you want to go into something else,
and become a doctor, or into another trade, and be an aviator, or
a brewer, or something else, I understand—I'll look around and

see what I can do. Look at me,' I say—then he looks at me like
a dead calf, and then he stutters, 'N-no, Papa,' and then I say,
'All right, you tell me what you want to do, Pepperl.' Then he
leans over the table again and looks out through the window and
he says he doesn't know what he wants and his mother talks to
him. She says, 'Pepperl, look at this beautiful business, your papa
worked so hard to build it up for you—look at this golden opportunity. Why don't you learn to be a good precision mechanic
like Papa? We can leave you money, but money gets lost, or there
is an inflation, but here you've got something that nobody can
take from you, no matter what happens.' But that's all for
nothing—he stands there and looks and I don't know what to do.
They say beat him until he is soft as a wet diaper and break him
—and make him do it—but I can't see that it would do any good,
and anyway I can't do it. The worst thing is, I need somebody
next to me, in my business. I've got a few things on the board, a
new injection pump for Diesel motors, and some clasps and

mountings that I have designed, and I don't want an outsider to have to hand it to, but I need somebody, and why should I have to take in a stranger when I've got my boy?"

The period of indecision lasted several years. Josef Pappelmeier wrote me that he finally had to take in somebody, a poor relative, a young man by the name of Franz Hinterwimmer, who had served his apprenticeship under a respected and well-known master mechanic in Nuremberg. I saw this young man the next time I came to Regensburg. He had the ideal elongated fingers for his delicate work, a face as sharp as if it were laid out with a triangle, and eyes deep in their sockets, just right for gripping the black, tubular magnifying glasses with which precision mechanics and jewelers do their work.

"I thought," said Pappelmeier to me at that time, "that perhaps this boy, this relative, Franz, who is ambitious and quick as lightning, would shame Pepperl into going to work, or make him jealous, but the boy has no pride at all. He stood there and watched the other, the one who worked at the bench that was rightfully Pepperl's, and he looked at him as if the other one were an idiot, and after a while he just turned his back on him and walked away. I said to Pepperl, 'Hinterwimmer will be at the head of this business one day,' but Pepperl just pulled up his shoulders and walked out, and promenaded along the Danube—and I say, how much longer can this go on? And his mother talks to him every day—'Look at this beautiful business lying here, waiting for you,' she says. 'Why don't you become sensible, Pepperl, why don't you go and learn the business just to make Papa happy?' But he doesn't seem to hear anything you say to him."

The poor relative, Franz Hinterwimmer, advanced from the workbench to the drafting table and the inner office. The uncertain dreamer Pepperl eventually changed. He came out of his shell and revealed himself at first in the halting words of the inhibited and oppressed and later in fluent speech. One day he said to his parents that he wanted just one thing and that was to travel, mainly to get away from Regensburg, from the house in The Golden Opportunity, and from the ambitious relative Franz Hinterwimmer.

His father took a long walk with Pepperl, and they came out

to the ruin in the garden along the Danube and sat down on the
weathered bench and table in the arbor. Pappelmeier Pepperl
became articulate again while his father was speechless at the
son's queer logic and un-German outlook. The boy had thought a
long while, he said, and taken everything into account. He said,
"Look, Papa, if you make any more money than you are making
now, we only have to hand it to the government in taxes. Now
you had a hard life building up this business and I am properly
grateful, but you never had any fun, never any real fun, because
you had to worry all the time and think about your work—and
what have you now?—still worry. Now why don't you give me the
kind of youth that you would like to have had? I don't ask for
much—I just want to live my own life and get a little happiness
out of it."

Papa was surprised. He had a funeral oration all ready for
his son's plan, but when he looked at Pepperl's face he buried it,
for he truly loved his son. He sat back and watched a paddle
steamer splash in the Danube, and then he got up and led the
way back home. He went to his favorite brewery and sat down
in the restaurant thereof, at his usual table. He was so upset that
he did not discuss the problem with either the jaundiced municipal
councilor or with the canon who came there to meet him and play
cards nightly.

The next day he went to his house and he said to Pepperl,
"How much do you think you'll need?" And Pepperl had his
calculations made to the penny and ready for him. The father
then arranged for the necessary funds and reached into the till
to supplement the sum with some petty cash. Several days later,
after the mother had counted his linen over and over again and
added to his purse from her own household savings, the traveler
bid good-by to the old house, and with the curious eyes of the
poor relative on him he walked out with his parents to the railroad station. After a bitter time during the buying of the ticket,
and a last meal in the restaurant of the terminal, during which his
mother stared at her plate and the old man was unable to swallow
his beer with any degree of pleasure, at last the train was announced, the signal bell rang, and, seated in a compartment third
class (he wanted to travel in plainest fashion and cost his parents

as little as possible) Pappelmeier Pepperl left aboard the local train for Munich on his first journey.

In the Bavarian capital he was like Goethe in Italy. His first journey was reported in four letters that found space in Regensburg's newspaper. They reflect the mood that once was in that romantic old town whose token signs are the twin towers of the Church of Our Lady—steeples that do not stab at the sky but rather look like two old green umbrellas held up into the sky by pilgrims in russet-colored cloaks.

Free of all worry, young and in a new suit, Pappelmeier Pepperl roamed happily through beer halls, museums, royal palaces, and the English Gardens, drank tea at the Chinese Tower, and watched flowers being painted on royal Nymphenburg porcelain. He made excursions to the castles of the Bavarian Kings, listened from the medium-priced seats to Wagner and Mozart, read the story of Lola Montez, watched the peasants in the fields, and observed the customs of people who lived in small villages in the mountains. If Pappelmeier hoped that his son would return to him saying that he had found the world dull and had enough of wandering and wanted to settle down and learn to be a precision mechanic, he was sadly disappointed. Pepperl returned only to entertain the silent dinner table with anecdote and travelogue. He supplemented his meager wardrobe with a gray suit, arranged his finances, and he was off again, this fateful day in the other direction, toward Nuremberg.

The traveler of today may tear out the pages of his guidebook that concern themselves with the treasures of this city, but at the time Pappelmeier Pepperl came there it was rich. He was privileged still to promenade along the mysterious slow waters of the two rivers that join there, see the city's gilded fountains, and stand in the churches, whose ancient stones had the texture of Roquefort. In these hushed retreats stood wondrous carved wood altars, in gilt and faded colors, dusty and worm-eaten, cut by Riemenschneider, whose every angel's face, saint, bird, leaf on small tree, dog, and drapery was executed with religious devotion, high artistry, and patience. In the footsteps of the many English and the Americans, who loved this comfortable patrician town, Pappelmeier Pepperl tramped past all these wonders.

One day, crammed with much emotion, he started to visit the famous Albrecht Dürer House, feeling pride.

From there he went to the old fortress, and with awful thrills stood fascinated as a guide demonstrated the workings of the Iron Maiden which stood inside the tower and cried out with her rusty hinges, as the heavy figure was opened, disclosing her spike-studded interior and the sieve through which the victims' blood was drained off. Pale as the other tourists, Pappelmeier Pepperl came out of the tower and wanted to get to his hotel, where he lived under an arrangement that included his meals, at five marks a day. He never got inside of it. He found himself in a thickening mass of people, which enfolded him, so that he gradually lost the freedom of his arms, and did not have to walk, being pushed along through flag-draped streets. Stuck in a vast sea of faces, he was washed along and came to rest after having been carried past his own hotel, to the front of another, which was called "Deutscher Hof," and there the crowd shouted and cried and sang, until Adolf Hitler appeared on the balcony. The hysteria of the mass transferred itself to him, on that first of the *Parteitage*. He shouted himself hoarse and was pushed out to the stadium, and he came home to the hotel walking over the dead and trampled flowers with which children had covered those streets of Nuremberg through which the Führer had passed.

Pappelmeier Pepperl, who usually was of good appetite, had missed his midday meal and he now let his evening soup get cold. The patriotic exercises to which he had been exposed continued within him; there was shouting and marching in his head as he lay back on his pillow. He heard the Führer's words over and over again: "Germany shall live in all eternity." He felt hot tears flowing down his cheeks and saw himself, with the talent for melancholy that is in the make-up of most Germans, in a faraway soldier's grave, but covered by a wreath that would never wither.

Early the next morning Pappelmeier Pepperl presented himself at the headquarters of the party; he was referred to the proper authorities; his answers to a questionnaire that had been handed him were satisfactory and his spirit admirable. He was told, however, after a physical examination, that he would be a soldier of the head rather than of the heart, and he was told to wait, pending the investigation of his person and record.

In the meantime he was to return to Regensburg and wait. At his father's house the returning Pepperl found the poor relative seated at the family table. There had always been an undeclared war between them, but this suddenly ended as Pepperl spoke of his last journey, of the Führer and the *Parteitag,* of Göring's address and of the jubilation and the crowds. During this exciting recital the poor relative Franz Hinterwimmer sat stiffly in his chair, his deep eyes steadily on the speaker's face. At the end Pepperl turned to his father and announced that he had applied for membership in the party.

At this the father left his mouth open, but the usually silent Hinterwimmer turned over the lapel of his gray jacket, showing a button with the emblem of the S.S. Jumping up and coming to stiff attention, he greeted Pepperl as a blood brother, gave him the party salute, and became agitated. He appeared to be an altogether new person. He repeatedly jumped to his feet and often hit the table as he engaged in a loud political confession of faith and drank the health of the new-found Nazi.

Old Pappelmeier shook his head when they told him that he too should join the party. "I'm already a member of all the things I want to belong to," he said mildly. His wife now remembers and admits, sadly, that she advised him to join. "Everybody is doing it," she said. "Just wear the uniform occasionally, Papa, to show where you stand, and all you have to do is attend a meeting now and then, and once a month collect on street corners for the party."

He shook his head and said no, but Pepperl's party membership, and the ability and energy of Franz Hinterwimmer, brought untold benefits to the firm. As time passed a large building was put up outside Regensburg, which manufactured the products of the firm of Josef Pappelmeier, and it was proper and beneficial that preliminary talks concerning the contracts for this undertaking took place in Munich and Nuremberg with the S.S. Lieutenant of the Reserve Franz Hinterwimmer, now no longer the poor relative but a member of the firm, who appeared in a long, dark cloak at S.S. Headquarters. The final papers were signed by Parteigenosse Pappelmeier Pepperl, who for these purposes slipped into the gray greatcoat of a lesser branch of the service, that of an ordinary party member, but one with a relatively low number, entitled to special privileges, because he had joined early.

His mother again says with self-accusation that she was proud when she saw him walking through Regensburg in his uniform coat. "He was so elegant," she says, "with gloves always, just like an aristocrat. And everybody in Regensburg who looked at Pappelmeier's new factory and its big smokestack and its wire-enclosed entrance for its two hundred employees now envied him his smart son.

"*Ja, ja,*" says Frau Pappelmeier, "it was all too wonderful and all on account of Pepperl's journey to Nuremberg."

Pepperl himself became tired of praise and success, and he also found the uniform too stiff. He left the glory to Hinterwimmer, and everything might have been all right if he had not gone traveling again. He went to Munich and went to one of the best tailors there, the firm of Kielleuthner and Cie, and ordered himself an extensive civilian wardrobe. He also went to Budapest, and he changed to first-class compartments and sleepers, and, returning to Regensburg, he astounded the city with his elegance. He became engaged to the only daughter of the richest brewer there, not because of her riches, but because she had the allure of the women he had admired on his recent first-class travels, whose slim calves he had watched as they hopped the steep steps of the fast trains he rode. She was the only one that was as languid as the beauties he had seen at the Walterspiel Restaurant in Munich and at the Bristol in Vienna. Sylvia had style.

She had been christened Liesel, but she changed it almost as soon as she could speak. She pouted into all the shop windows of the Regensburg couturières and, protesting their offerings, she walked about covered by a white, severe, tailored raincoat and a small sport hat. Her heavy ginger-colored hair was not braided

but rolled down over her shoulders, and, in spite of the Führer's dictum, she painted her lips and rouged her cheeks. Sylvia and Pepperl had recognized each other immediately; she pleased him, although she was disapproved of by his parents and even her own father, who told her that she looked like a streetwalker. After a hasty marriage, which everyone in Regensburg prophesied would end in disaster, the happy and elegant couple provided again a bitter farewell for their parents, for after the wedding breakfast at the Hotel Maximilian they drove away in a new pale-gray Mercedes Benz cabriolet; the honeymoon was to be spent in Berlin.

At this part of the story Frau Pappelmeier, who told it, sitting in the arbor along the Danube, patted the hand of the beautiful woman who sat next to her, and who was Sylvia, her daughter-in-law. Pepperl's wife then walked away to the fence, where her own little girl stood, rooted with fascination, watching two colored soldiers of the American occupation forces swimming in the Danube.

Frau Pappelmeier continued then, "I was wrong—we all were, I must admit. I didn't have any hope for the marriage, but it turned out good. I don't know what I would do without her now. She has eyes for no one but for Pepperl."

As I said, they went to Berlin, and in a cabaret they were seated next to a man who was also with a young woman who was smartly dressed, and this man also wore the party emblem in the lapel of his coat, and he had the manners of a man of the world. He smiled across to Pepperl and his wife and he started to talk— first about Berlin, and life, and his travels. He seemed to have been everywhere, and Pepperl became very interested. The stranger then asked him about this and that, and Pepperl told him about his own travels, and about how they were just married and how he had joined the party after seeing the Führer in Nuremberg and how beneficial it had been to his father's business. Pepperl did not put his light under the table, but spoke about his philosophy of life, and the man admired his spirit, and told him how lucky he was, and how rarely one found anyone so young, and from a provincial town like Regensburg, with so wide a horizon, so sure a grasp of the meaning of things. He also said that he had great connections and that he might be of help to Pepperl in advancing him further into a position where his talents could find their proper sphere, and he suggested another meeting. The two men had found themselves in complete harmony on every question, and they left the restaurant together as friends.

The stranger and his companion then called on Pepperl and his wife at their hotel and took them on a tour of the city's most elegant places, and over wine and liqueurs the men discussed the Fatherland's needs. It was in the week of the crucial decision over Poland. The stranger came to the point quickly and said it meant war, and he asked about the capacity of the Pappelmeier factory in Regensburg.

Pepperl set his forehead in wrinkles and in strictest confidence gave his new-found friend the latest statistics on production in the Pappelmeier factory for precision instruments. He told him about the number of gauges that were manufactured for the Messerschmitt factory, whose huge new plant had been built right next to the Pappelmeier works, as well as the number of precision instruments for submarines. He gave his estimate of the number of planes that were flown away from Regensburg and offered to find out the latest figures as soon as he got back. The man said that he would come to Regensburg and visit Pepperl and

have a look at things himself. As they got up he gave a proper and stiff party salute and a "Heil Hitler." As they stood in the lobby of the Femina night club, while the girls were getting their cloaks, he quickly checked the information once more. After a second martial good-by he left with his companion.

There were elaborate presents of flowers and perfume for Sylvia the next day, and then the stranger vanished. Pepperl saw him again several months later, when he appeared in Regensburg. Soon after that he saw him for the last time in a Nuremberg courtroom, after the friend from Berlin had been arrested as a spy. Under order from a Nazi judge the man identified Pepperl, and

somebody read the information Pappelmeier had given to the
debonair man in Berlin, and which that one had put down in a
small book, in a code that the efficient Gestapo broke as quickly
as they had the accused. The accused pleaded for Pepperl; he
remarked, without being asked, that Pepperl had been his victim,
that he was a good follower of the party, and that at any rate he
was too stupid to have had evil intent.

Pepperl's mother told me that part of the story with a trace of
annoyance. "He's not stupid," she said.

After the trial Pepperl was allowed to go home and told to
wait. The poor relative came into the room which the son of the
house never left and without a word placed his service gun on
the table, indicating thereby that Pepperl should shoot himself.
What followed then we hear from Pappelmeier Pepperl's own
lips:

I was lying with my wife on the sofa in my old room, and I
spoke to her. I knew that something was in the air, because one
day before I had a kind of warning. I spoke to her about what
we should do with the child that she expected if I were to be sent
away and if all our property were to be taken from us, and she
cried quietly. Then the bell rang, and there were two men in civilian clothes outside, and one of them said, "Good afternoon,
Herr Pappelmeier. We are here to check papers and passports.
You travel a good deal; give us your pass if you please, and may
I have a look at your papers." I had all my papers in the best
possible order. "Good," said the one who spoke, while the other
one looked around the room. "Have you any books or papers
here that concern the activities of the party?"

"Yes," I said, "I have various books. It is among my duties
to read them."

"Yes," said the one.

The other went to a bookshelf and looked at the books I had
indicated. "Have you weapons of any kind?"

"No weapons," I said.

"Good," he said, while the other replaced the books.

"We regret very much," said the spokesman, "but we have to
search the apartment."

"That is perfectly all right," I said, "go ahead, allow me to show you the rooms."

I must say that they were very polite and correct. When they were finished looking around they said, "We have one more request to make of you, Herr Pappelmeier. Your superior at headquarters would like to have a word with you this afternoon."

"Certainly," I said. "I shall take a streetcar and hurry to see him right away."

"*Ja,* Herr Pappelmeier, there is no need of that, because we have a car downstairs; we shall drive you there," said the man, and at that moment my knees were weak. The men suddenly stood at my sides.

"Come, Herr Pappelmeier," they said.

"I would like to say good-by to my wife, if I may."

They were again polite, I must say, and let us say good-by. I had a ray of hope. One always hopes that there is a mistake, and I went down to the car. There was a chauffeur in uniform. It was a closed car without insignia, and again I had hope. One of the men got in, and the next one motioned to me to follow, and then the other got in, so that I sat between them, and the car started off. And I said, "We are going in the wrong direction, the headquarters building is that way."

The car drove awhile. Then the one who had been silent said to the other, "Have you told Herr Pappelmeier already?"

"No, I haven't told him yet," said the other.

"I regret," said the second one, "to inform you, Herr Pappelmeier, that you are under arrest."

"I thought you said that my superior wanted to speak to me," I said.

"*Ja,*" said the one. "I said that, but now we're going to the depot to take a train."

Then I said to myself, "Oh, God. Now things are suddenly different."

At the railroad station the car stopped not at the regular entrance, where I had always bought my ticket, but at the end where it's deserted toward evening and where freight is loaded. It was getting dark and there was an enclosure. The two men walked me to the gate.

"Oh, one more of those swine," said the guard at the door and
let me in, and with a group of others I found myself waiting in a
shed. After an hour we were marching out on the platform and
then assigned to a car. In every one of its small compartments
were about ten men and one guard. There were two benches facing each other on which we sat down, and the guard sat on a chair
at the end, almost in the corridor. Five and five of us sat facing
each other in front of him. None of us knew how to behave ourselves, but we gradually learned that. He was an expert at striking
anything with the butt of his gun. He balanced it precisely and
used it like a javelin. We sat for a while, and we heard some crying and whimpering in adjoining compartments. The journey
started. The man next to me had a cold and reached into his
pocket for a handkerchief, to blow his nose. That is where the
butt of the guard's gun came flying the first time and stunned him;
it smacked him square on the side of his face. He bled, and the
prisoner who sat opposite him said to the guard, "Excuse me,
but he only wanted to blow his nose." The gun butt sailed in
again, this time to the head of the one who had made the excuse,
and he cried out in pain.

"You are much too friendly toward each other," said the guard.
"We don't encourage friendship. You on the left there," he said
to the prisoner who had spoken, "smack that man, opposite you,
the one you worry so much about. Hard. Harder. Go on." The
man had hit his opposite twice, halfheartedly. He hesitated and
the guard lifted his gun again. Then the prisoner did as he was
told. "Now you there on the right, smack him back, the one that
hit you." The other man obeyed. "Don't be afraid, don't protect
one another [schont euch nicht] or I'll teach you how to smack,"
said the guard. "I want to hear it, keep it up until I say stop,"
and so the two with the blood streaming from them smacked each
other until the guard said, "Halt."

"We're not traveling for pleasure," he announced. "They
won't like it if I turn you in without a little damage showing. But
I am not like other guards. You may not think so, but for a
Dachauer I have a heart. You're supposed to stay awake until we
get to Dachau. I would let you sleep except that I think you are
stupid. You don't know how to sleep yet. And I'll have to teach

you, and I'll teach you, also, how to wake up; that's because if the controlling officer comes in here and sees that my prisoners sleep, I'm in trouble."

Now he said, "Listen carefully. You sit at attention, absolutely still, you have your hands on your knees, and keep your head up. You look straight ahead."

He watched us, and then he said, "Now let me see how quickly you can go to sleep. Upon the command 'Schlafen' I want you to close your eyes, and get down with your heads, because that's how you sleep the very best way, and when I say 'Wake up,' then you wake up, but immediately, because the one who wakes up last gets a reward from me." He balanced his gun again and held it ready.

He must have played this game often, because after he gave the command "Sleep" he quickly banged his gun on the heads of all those who did not bend quickly enough. At the command "Wake up" he hit two. At the next command of "Go to sleep" everyone ducked his head so quickly that he bumped it against that of the man sitting opposite him. It was of no consequence whether a man went to sleep fast or slowly; if he did not crack his skull against a fellow prisoner he was hit with the gun butt of the guard.

The guard amused himself with issuing commands until he finally was satisfied and tired of playing with us. "Sleep," he commanded once more and made himself comfortable. "Now that I have taught you how to sleep, God help those of you that don't wake up properly," he said and closed his eyes.

We left Regensburg about eight in the evening and we arrived in Dachau at ten o'clock the next day.

We marched in through the gate of the camp and came to the place where you give your name and profession, and there was one who asked me my trade. I hesitated for a moment because I was confused about what I should say, what was best—precision mechanic, party member, traveler, or what. At any rate, while I was thinking what to say, a guard hit me in the stomach and then swung his fist into my face so that I spat out teeth and blood, and I had to write down the answer. I wrote "precision mechanic."

"Get out!" he screamed then, and before I could turn I was hit

again, by somebody I did not see, and then I fell and I heard a
humming sound like that of bumblebees in the summer, and it
felt like a very hot summer day, and I landed on the floor, softly
and with unimportance, as if I had decided to lie down under a
shady tree. It was quiet and I was comfortable. They must have
dragged me out. I was wet, and there was a voice that woke me
up, and it came near. A man took shape. He stood in front of me.
I was one of a row of men. I was standing up and I felt blood running from my mouth and nose, but I had already learned how to
behave and did not lift my hand to wipe it away.

"I want to be able to hear a needle fall," said the man in charge
of us who talked. He was our superior. I learned later that he was
an habitual criminal, as were all the block eldest who were responsible for the bunkers in which we lived. They had been
transferred from regular prisons to concentration camps and been
given charge of the barracks in the capacity of noncommissioned
officers. They were to be addressed as "Herr Unterscharführer."
Unter means under, *schar* is a small group, and an *Unterscharführer* is the leader of a small group.

These civilian criminals were feared and called "capos."

"I am going to tell you now in few words," he said, "how you
are to behave yourselves. In the morning, first thing, the cells are
cleaned. Then we stand at attention and each man reports. First
he says his name and number, then his cell number, and then
he says why he is here.

"You understand, we stand against the wall, hands down, at
attention. We sing out the information, loud and precisely, the
head up, or else there's unpleasantness, you understand."

"Yes," said the men. "Yes."

"Yes what?"

"Yes, Herr Unterscharführer."

"Yes, Herr Unterscharführer," said the group.

"Next we take the night bucket. And with that we advance, in
double time, to the latrine. We do everything here in double
time, you understand, or else there is again unpleasantness, you
understand?"

"Yes, Herr Unterscharführer."

"In the latrine we empty the bucket, and then we let water into it and then we rinse it out, and then we run back and we put the bucket on the floor in the corner of the cell and go to the wash-basins, and there we wash ourselves, but all that is done like light-ning because if any of that takes as long as it takes me to tell it, then there is unpleasantness.

"There isn't any talking at all here, ever.

"Have you heard of me, any of you? Have any of you ever heard of Gneissl?" He looked up and down the line, and there was one face he didn't like, that of a fat priest. He went to the man and put his fingers around his throat. "I want to know whether you have heard of me," he screamed. The man opened his mouth, and the capo used his fist on him. I looked away. There was a moan, and then a series of slaps and punches, and a sucking sound as if the last of the water were running out of a bathtub. We all stood and looked straight ahead.

When the capo was through he said, "We'll leave him here. He needs fresh air." And then he wanted to see how quickly we could run, and then he told us that he was famous for his discipline, and then we were put into our solitary cells.

I remained there in the same shirt and trousers in which I had arrived, and only once did anyone talk to me. The capo, Gneissl, came in, and he had a piece of paper in his hand, a small brown piece of paper, with something written on it with a pencil.

I stood at attention as commanded, flat against the wall of the cell, the hands at the sides, and the head up, and announced the number of the cell, my name, and that I was here on account of being a traitor.

"How long are you here now?" said the capo.

"Four months, Herr Unterscharführer."

"Look at this carefully," he said and held up the little piece of brown paper. "I found this in the cell next to yours. Now if you were me, what would you do about that?"

"I would punish the prisoner, Herr Unterscharführer."

"Good, and what kind of punishment would you give him?"

I thought for a while. We were fed every sixth day, so I could not say, Cut his rations. We had only one blanket, so I could not say, Take that from him. And we slept on a wooden bunk, so there was no mattress to withhold.

The capo came near me. "Well, how would you punish him?" he yelled and reached for my throat, just as he had done it the first day with the priest.

My knees were weak. "I would," I said, "take his exercise away from him, Herr Unterscharführer."

"You are crazy," said the capo. "You seem to think that this is a sanatorium. First I'm going to give him a thrashing, and then he will stand, he will stand day and night with the window open. He will not sit down or lie down. He is going to stand twelve days."

He took his fingers off my throat and left the cell, and I held my ears then, because it started again, next door, just as before, the punching bag and the sucking sound. He had left me alone to save his strength for the man in the next cell.

I came out of solitary confinement one day and was given the striped uniform of the regular prisoners, who are called "Ka-Zettlers," a term that is derived from *Konzentrazionslager,* meaning concentration camp.

I was assigned to a barracks with several other men, and it seemed unreal that when the new capo had left the room for a moment we all bowed and introduced ourselves to each other. There was a traveling salesman for the Eberhard Faber Pencil Company, an administrator of a charitable institution, a manufacturer of woolen goods and a man who had been active in the repertory theater, a Catholic chaplain and an architect for tunnel construction.

We all had said "formerly" when speaking of our professions, but there was somebody here who, even at this low tide, tried to impress and used the present tense. He bowed stiffly and said, "Von Domhoff—I'm the chairman of South German Electric." He continued as far as saying, "I'm the director of thirty-six—" when the theater man shut him up, saying, "O.K., my lord." The term "O.K." had then already been taken over into the German language. The old von Domhoff disappeared soon after, and most probably went to the crematorium; he was no good at digging in the peat bogs, and he had a lot of gold in his teeth.

There is much that I can't remember any more, because it was so terrible. The barracks were immaculate, and around them were plots of grass, and this grass was not allowed to be shorter or longer than ten centimeters. It was carefully watched. There were the most exquisite flower beds everywhere; there was the strictest order. The various prisoners were marked with different identification tags; political prisoners had red triangles, pederasts rose-colored disks. I must stop here, also, to say that those, the homosexuals, were the only ones to retain some humor. They were courageous, kind, and often heroic. They set an example in how to bear injustice. There was dignity about them. The Jews had yellow marks; incurable loafers (*Arbeitsscheue*) were designated with blue tags, and habitual criminals, who were in supervisory positions and the most favored of the concentration-camp inmates, wore green. There was the most marvelous order. When I say that, I can't remember something because it was so terrible. I mean, for example, I can't remember how we managed to keep the floor in the entrance hall of the barracks, where we had to take our shoes off, as clean as it was. The floor was of a bright red, battleship linoleum composition. We came home from the moor pits and on rainy days our shoes were covered with mud, and the shoes had always to stand out in that entrance hall, orderly in line and always shined; even the strip of leather at the bottom of the shoe between the heel and the sole had to be shined, and somehow that was always done, they were were always clean and in a row, and the floor was shining. There was also a dental laboratory that cost one million marks to install and was the most modern in the whole world—but that was to show to people who came visiting, and to inspect the concentration camp, and when they saw how everywhere there were plots of grass and flowers, and they saw how neat the barracks were, and often they were shown through the dental laboratory, and saw painted on a wall WORK SHALL FREE YOU, they took pictures of it, and they said to themselves and to the people back home, "It is impossible to treat prisoners better than in Dachau. They have everything."

There were several forms of punishment, and the first time I ran into trouble was with the supervisor of the first barracks I was in. I was very well behaved and did everything exactly right and he watched me carefully.

One day as we lined up for mess this man took my mess kit out of my hand and said, "This mess kit is filthy." I had been extremely careful not to get in his way. I had been warned by the others, and I had painstakingly cleaned my mess kit. I said nothing.

"Don't you see how dirty that mess kit is?" said the capo, turning the metal dish this way and that in the sun.

The kit sparkled in the light and was spotless, and I said, "I beg your pardon Herr Unterscharführer, but I don't think that it is dirty."

He swung the mess kit by the handle. He hit hard and struck me across the face. "You see now, don't you, that this mess kit is awfully dirty?" he said mildly, like a father.

"*Ja,* Herr Unterscharführer," I said, "I see that this mess kit is awfully dirty."

He hit me with the edge of the mess kit across the mouth then and said, "You learn quickly. There's hope for you."

He reported me the next day for infraction of the rules and for lying, and my punishment was hard labor. That means that for three months I had to work every day until nightfall, and Saturday afternoons and Sundays I had to go out to the peat bogs as well. There were people among us who would have had the courage to jump at one of the S.S. men, or the capos, and bite them in the throat and kill them that way, and it was sometimes discussed, but it was impossible, because the consequences would have befallen the entire group. In that connection there was a man who was confined because he was a homosexual. He was in our group, and he had no time to finish his food, and so had put aside a small piece of bread at mess time. And because it was strictly forbidden to put any food into the pockets of the prison garb, he squeezed this piece of bread over his ear inside the rim of his cap. As we marched out to the peat bogs we met an S.S. man, and whenever that happened all the caps had to be pulled off quickly, and as this prisoner did this he lost his bread. It fell to the ground. The S.S. man saw it, and the entire company was sentenced to work for the next three months without caps. Our hair was cut short and the sun burned down on us, and it was a great punishment for us. Sentences of three months were a favorite stretch of time with them.

I also remember a scene that occasionally was enacted when a man who had succeeded in escaping was brought back. They were almost always caught soon after they left, and then at the end of the working day there was a parade. The band marched ahead through the camp, and in back of it the convict who had been returned. He was in his prison suit again, and around his neck was a string from which hung a sign. On this was written, *"Ich bin wieder da."* Normally that would be a nice warm sentence—"I am back again." With this he marched, and then he disappeared to the place where the screams came from and where they killed them slowly.

It was the devil himself who invented these things—or perhaps not even the devil: human bestiality only could think them up. There was also another disgraceful punishment. You had to report to the house where the administration offices were, and around this house, perpetually at attention, stood those who were ordered there, and any S.S. man who went in and out there and was in the mood came up to you and hit you in the face or on the body with just his flat hand, his fist, or anything he had in his hand. That was for a day, and if you fainted you were taken away, but you had to come back for another day until you served out the whole day.

When my sentence to hard labor was over I had another trouble. I had great pain in a tooth, in one of the molars on the right side of my jaw. The man who lay in the bunk beneath me whispered, "Why don't you go to the dentist?"

I said to him, "I would rather die," but he couldn't sleep below. He could feel how I twisted with pain in my bunk and how I turned from one position to the other all night.

"Go," he said, "go to the dentist."

The third day I reported on sick call. I was taken to the wonderful dental office, and the doctor stood there, an officer in a white dentist's coat, with a gun strapped around him outside his coat. I assumed the proper position and said, "Prisoner 783365 reports for treatment."

He put me into the chair and looked into my mouth. I only had the back teeth left, the others had been knocked out.

"How do you stand it?" he said, examining my jaw. He started to work on me, very carefully. After a while he drilled, and I twitched just once as he came on the nerve.

"Does it hurt?" he asked and stopped.

"*Nein,* Herr Doctor," I said.

"But you twitched," said the dentist.

"*Ja,* Herr Doctor," I said.

"But then it must have hurt," he said.

"No, Herr Doctor," I said, remembering the lesson with the mess kit. "It did not hurt at all."

"It isn't supposed to hurt," said the dentist. He continued to drill. A second later I twitched again. "But," he said, "you're not telling the truth. It does hurt, because you twitched again."

Oh, what new devil's invention is this, I thought, and I looked at him and said, "Yes, it hurts a little."

He said, "Why didn't you say so right away?" He stopped and got the needle to deaden the nerve, and I had to wipe my eyes because I cried. I thought I was dreaming, such a thing could not happen in Dachau. I sat up and looked at him carefully once more—at the white coat and the revolver strapped around him—and he stood there and he did nothing to me. He made me a very good inlay, which I still have today.

I would not give you a true picture if I did not tell you that some people were kind even in Dachau. I will never forget that dentist. Dentists until then were people to whom I did not pay particular attention. That happened in the fine dental hospital I told you about, with the most magnificent X-ray machinery and all the latest equipment.

"This isn't possible," I said one day later when I found myself in a room and there was a sign on the wall that said, "Work shall free you," and a picture of Adolf Hitler and some chairs on which twenty of us sat down. We never sat down, so it was an extraordinary occasion.

We jumped to attention as an S.S. man came in, and he sat down at a table, and looked at us, and then he folded his arms.

"You're going to be discharged by special kindness of the Führer—why, I can't understand. Before you leave, however, I want to brief you. We don't expect you to go back and tell them on the outside what a good time you had here. We don't want that at all because then they'll break the doors down trying to get into Dachau. Neither do we desire that you go back and tell them that you were mistreated, you understand."

"*Jawohl,* Herr Lieutenant," said the chorus with enthusiasm.

"We don't want you to say anything at all about Dachau, because, if you do, when we come for you you'll be able to say that you were really mistreated—you'll get twenty-five across the bare backside every day. And speaking of that, if it were up to me, before you got out of here, just before you left, as a reminder, I'd give you the twenty-five, but front-side, because the temptation to whine and talk will come when you're back with your women, in the night. Remember my words, and also remember that we have a long arm—it reaches all the way around the world. You can't run from us. There is no place on earth you can hide and no disguise that we won't tear from you. That's all I have to tell you. They'll give you a suit and a ticket home and some pocket money. Heil Hitler!"

I think one must be born German. Otherwise how is it possible that one can feel so thankful? I have never felt so grateful to anyone as to the capo who handed me a suit and money. There was a railroad station there, close to the crematorium, and it had also its ten-centimeter grass and its flowers, and we were separated from it by a fence. At this station was a fruit stand, and I said to the Gruppenführer, who was in charge of us, in the fashion in which permission for everything had to be asked: "I beg most obediently [*Ich bitte gehorsamst*], Herr Gruppenführer, may I buy myself an orange?"

And he said, "*Ja,* as soon as you have changed your clothes you may buy yourself anything you wish."

That is how close I was to freedom. In the room in which we were turning our clothes in, suddenly and terribly, my name was called, and somebody said, "Doesn't he go?"

"Yes, he goes," they said, "but not with this group."

I was then again hoping for the impossible error, saying to myself that a mistake had been made that I had been called for the wrong train, but they opened another door and I found myself with a contingent that went to another camp, and that was because I had stated, when I came to Dachau, that I was a precision mechanic, and there was a camp where such skills were needed.

I traveled with a group of people to Flossenburg and was assigned to a special unit.

I was put on a work table, and a tray of various delicate wheels was put before me, and I was to assemble them. It was perhaps something very simple, but I sat there and tried my best to put the puzzle together and couldn't. A prisoner came after a while and took away my tray—the one on which should have been the assembled mechanism—and brought me a new one, with new wheels and springs, and I sat again and stared at it, and then the Gruppenführer came, and stood by my side for a while and watched me. My face was hot. The water was running off my back, but with my untaught hands I was unable to assemble the mechanical puzzle. I was also forbidden to speak.

The Gruppenführer's face brightened as he watched me. He smiled and then he called an S.S. man who also stood awhile and watched me. Then they both left, and an hour later, after I had stared my eyes to a kind of blindness, looking at the tray, I was taken outside.

There stood a wooden horse, and in a triangle all the men of my barracks assembled about it. Next to the wooden horse was a big man who had a whip in his hand. My feet were tied to the wooden horse, and then I was told to remove my trousers. I was then strapped down over the horse and my coat pulled up, and I had to count loud, and if I had missed the count, then it would have started all over again. At the side of the horse stood a doctor with a white coat and a gun strapped around his waist, like the dentist. If a man fainted he listened to the heart, and he gave the signal when the punishment could be resumed. I received twenty-five lashes that day; the last was always a double smack, so one could really say that it was twenty-six lashes.

They left me alone for two days, and then I had light work for three more. There was a group that trimmed the lawn, which was to be kept as exemplarily as it was at Dachau, and there was another detail that kept the paths in order, but these paths were already so in order that nothing could be done to them, and the camp commander therefore had ordered that one of the prisoners was to fill his apron with little stones and rubbish and go ahead of the group, sowing the stones and the trash onto the path, and the others with small baskets followed and cleaned up again. We had to sing, and we had to walk in a bent position that was the invention of the particular commander of that camp. For a while my back burned, and when I lay still I thought of poor Papa and Mamma, and how they had begged me to learn to be a precision mechanic, and how all this would not have happened to me if I had listened to my parents. After my back had healed I was sent back to the workrooms, and they must have known that I wasn't a good mechanic, because I still couldn't assemble the pieces, and they assigned me to some simpler work.

There is a kind of collar button that is worn by officers of the German Navy, which is worn in back of the neck and has a double loop, one inside the other; the larger folds down over the cravat, once the collar is attached to the shirt, and the smaller folds upward. In the room in which I worked now, these collar buttons were assembled, and I was given a tray again on which were the parts of which the collar buttons are made. It's simple to put them together if you know how. But as I have said, my fingers are clumsy and I had no mechanical skill whatever, and while the others worked fast, the pieces on my tray turned very slowly into completed buttons. Although I missed my meals and thought of nothing but making these buttons quickly, I did not turn out the required number.

"I've watched him long enough," said the Gruppenführer to the S.S. man again as he stood in back of me. "He's obstinate, he hasn't learned his lesson."

And that afternoon there was again the triangle of comrades, and a small wooden footstool, and they wound a stocking around my wrists and then folded them in back of me, and tied them with a chain, and pulled my arms up—and then they kicked the stool from under my feet, and my arms were almost torn out of their sockets. They marched away and I was left hanging there. I hung thus for a long, long time, and my arms went to sleep.

"Ah, look who's here," said a voice I knew. I twisted my head in agony, because I had been given a shove, so that I swung back and forth like the pendulum on a clock. Franz Hinterwimmer was in the uniform of an S.S. Captain now.

"Congratulations, you've done a good job," he said. "The factory is gone, they came and bombed Regensburg, the Messerschmitt works too are gone." He looked at me for a while, then he said, "I'd like to stay longer, but I came here on business—I must leave you now," he said. "I have to pull out—I have to get back to work and repair the damage—we're back in the old house now at The Golden Opportunity, thanks to you."

As if he were my friend and shared his troubles with me, he added, "I had a terrible time getting on the four-o'clock train to Regensburg. I thought of driving here but then I figured it would take me away from home too long. I must tell you about your wife. She's gotten off her high horse. She doesn't make up any more. She's learned to conform—she's a clever girl and she understands the times. I think you should also know about your father—he died.

"I'm leaving now," he said, and gave me another shove. The pain in my shoulders was so great that I fainted. I don't remember when they took me down.

After, I was with the gang singing again and clearing the paths. We followed the man who threw the small stones from his apron and my arms ached as I picked them up. We were all bent, and once we came close to the fence that enclosed the camp. The Gruppenführer who supervised us told us to stop singing. He turned to me. "You're obstinate," he said, "and useless. You're no good to us here, but I'll make it easy for you." He tore the cap from my head and threw it into the wire enclosure. "Run, fetch it," he said, as one says to a dog. But I knew that the moment I would run and come near the fence, I would be electrocuted by the wire or shot by the guard in the tower. So I refused. "Oh," he said, "you want to live—you refuse to obey orders." And so I was punished, and that night I forgot where God lives.

They came for me and put me in a small dark room. It was filled with water to a height of two feet, and in the center of it was a stool. I sat down on this, and because they had taken my shoes away I pulled up my wet feet. They were cold, and I sat down on them, and then they became numb. I slept and prayed, and begged my parents' pardon, and I cried, and I forgot to think for long spaces of time, and I forgot time. I was sorry then I had not followed the Gruppenführer's order and made a run for the cap, and I remember that I thought of the agony of Christ, and I said, O God—after all, what was that compared to what happens here—Christ's suffering lasted only four hours. I thought of my wife and my child, and I cried for hours, and when they came and let me out, I collapsed from the light. And the comrades in my barracks told me that I had been away for six days. From then on I led a life so careful, so quiet, so without any sign of revolt or even the smallest violation. I did not even dare to show discontent on my face. I was left alone, and in steady, quiet fashion I became nimble, and actually learned to be an expert mechanic. I thought only of my work and of Sylvia. I had her engraved on my mind, on that dense screen of blackness that is before you when you close your eyes, and in the one thousand six hundred and eight nights that I was there she was always before me. No one knows love like a prisoner.

The war was going badly for us, then. There were many rumors—that the concentration camp would be evacuated, and that those who could make the journey would be marched to Dachau, and the others shot.

The Captain in charge of our unit, who was a friend of Hinterwimmer's, had me brought before him. He had arranged something very carefully. He had me brought to his office, and he spoke in almost conversational manner with me and did the unheard-of thing of asking me to sit down. And he asked if there was anything I wanted him to tell my wife. He looked at the door several times, and it opened, and a man brought in a package, and on it I could see my mother's writing, and a letter from my wife. He said to the soldier, "That one doesn't need anything any more—put it on my desk here." He took me by the arm and lifted me and said, "Stand over there. You can think about the message you want to give me while you wait, while we get a few more together." I said nothing. I floated in the air, as if I didn't care. I didn't feel any more. "Don't you have anything you want to say?" he said. I didn't answer him. I wanted to cry, but I kept my face dry. Not even my lips trembled, I wept inside. I think I cried with my stomach. They brought two others, and there was a guard for each, and so we marched out, along the barracks and plots of the nicely cut grass, and the clear path, and a man opened a gate and let us through, and there was a wall, and everybody had known all along by the sound of firing that regularly came from there what it was for. At that wall we halted.

Hinterwimmer suddenly was there, and his friend said, "Now I'll give you some good advice—lean forward, with your head touching the wall, then you'll fall right, and close your eyes. I promise you, you won't even hear anything. I'll do you a further favor, Herr Pappelmeier. I'll let you be the first."

I did as he said. I was without will. I waited, then I heard two shots that made me deaf, and I felt the blast and fell, and there was a great pause and then I heard him laugh. I was confused, not knowing whether I was dead or alive.

"He's still afraid to die," said Hinterwimmer, and then the guard yelled, "Get up, march, march, back to the barracks. We'll keep you for later." It was all a joke.

Two days after that the Americans came. Of that I remember only that one gave me an orange and that I went to a hospital.

"He weighed seventy-six pounds when he got home," said Pappelmeier Pepperl's mother. "But then everything was all right— all the people who came out of concentration camps were given a special identification mark, a crown of thorns, to wear, and they were immediately allowed to operate their business, and they received special food packages, and Pepperl was honored and the Americans gave him their wristwatches to fix, and everything was fine.

"It would have been all right, but then Franz Hinterwimmer was behind the wire now, in the S.S. compound at Dachau, waiting to be tried as a war criminal, and he needed some witnesses to say that he had never mistreated anybody and that he was there only for a short time and because he was ordered to be there and had to carry out orders. So his sister came, and cried, and said what a disgrace it would be if Hinterwimmer were to be hanged, and that if Pepperl would go to Dachau and testify before the Americans, as an ex-Ka-Zettler, then everything would be all right.

"But Pepperl refused, and so the Hinterwimmers got together and dug up the old story of Pepperl's having once belonged to the Nazi party, and denounced him to the authorities, and they proved that he was one of the first to have joined, and it was true. So his crown of thorns was taken away from him, and his privileges, and the food packages, and the time he had spent in Dachau was all for nothing. And he is behind the wire now. He will go on trial and get maybe a year or two in prison—but he can go to church, and he isn't beaten any more, and he gets enough to eat and has two blankets on his bed, and we can bring him a little something now and then. And this too will pass, and maybe the judges will take into account what he has suffered already. Oh, he is cured, and you know when he comes out he will get all of Papa's old customers—because now Pepperl is a wonderful precision mechanic. He can fix anything and put together the most complicated instruments—and also, he says, he doesn't want to travel any more, he just wants to stay in Regensburg, at The Golden Opportunity."

DOWN WHERE THE WÜRZBURGER FLOWS

I know about beer, because it flows in my veins; my great-grand-father was a brewer in the best hops country of southern Ger-many, and over the vast stone portal of the brewery was written:

> *Hopfen und Maltz*
> *Gott erhalt's.*

The peculiarly built, long, heavy wagons which cradle the oaken barrels were pulled by stout Lippizaners, weighing tons apiece, and the color of beer, with manes like foam. They moved with slow dignity—and when they came out of the brewery, pounding their heavy, shaggy hoofs on the creosote blocks of the pavement, sounded like thunder. This majestic tempo was kept up until the beer arrived in vast limestone caves, where it was rested or *gelagered* (hence the word "lager" beer) for six months. After that the barrels were carefully loaded again, and the beer was delivered to the various places which are called *Wirtschaften,* where it was poured and tasted with the ceremony and nervosity that is given in other regions of Europe to great wine.

As wine has a bouquet, so has beer. It is said of good, dark beer that it tastes like licking a dusty windowpane. That may not be everyone's idea of pleasure, but an experienced beer drinker knows what I mean; it is a dusty, a fine antique, dusty, musty—a taste that is perfection.

As does wine, so does beer reflect its native landscape. If you have been out in the vineyards of France, the wine will bring them back to you. You can see the flowered fields of Alsace with the aid of a glass of *Gewürtztraminer,* you can conjure up the faces of the *Bordelais* when you drink their wine; and the *Box-beutel* of Würzburg clearly reproduces for you the stony fields on which this superb wine grows.

Of beer, the same is true. The scene is more solid; it is a heavier canvas, determined in line and color. Not only does beer reflect; it is stronger, it also determines. It has created a certain kind of furniture, interiors, vehicles; influenced mores, dress, and the shape of people. It has even changed language, medicine, and the law.

In the south of Germany, whence the best brews come and where the cathedral of brewing, the Academy of Weihenstephan, is located, the number of breweries is easily determined in any given community simply by counting the church steeples. For every one there is a brewery.

Drinking here is a devotional rite, by people who have for generations given themselves to it. The South Germans are a kind of surviving Neanderthaler, with skulls of stone. In character, they are comparable to the Irish, of the same manic-depressive character. Their soul is a ponderous mechanism, and when set in motion by sentimental impulse or agitated anger it moves the man slowly at first but with mountain-moving might.

The heavy beer is blamed for that.

The beerpeople of the south of Germany should be of the greatest interest to the student of abnormal anthropology.

The children of beerpeople grow up normally, with here and there one that has an abnormally large head—which is called a

Wasserkopf, or waterhead. The local joke on this subject goes like this:

Two men stand on a street corner and one says, "Oh, look at the boy with the *Wasserkopf.*"

The other says, "That's my son."

"Looks good on him," answers the other.

As time passes, all but the *Wasserköpfe* look for girls to marry. The requirements are easily met, the conditions easy. They have to be sound in front and back, stand on solid legs, and have able hands. Beauty is not *ausschlaggebend* and the dowry is not as important as it is in France. The mating season is brief. The rites of love are an awkward kind of stumbling about, a dance of love as it is performed by the *Auerhahn,* a local bird that, with half-closed eyes, becomes ill with passion and almost topples off the trees. He is often shot during these exercises. The tail feathers of the *Auerhahn,* forming the outline of a *Lyra,* are a favorite decoration of the headgear of the man of the beerworld. He is married now, and produces children—statistics show an average of four—and, toward the last, he withdraws from woman as such. She goes to the *Kirch,* the *Kinder,* and the *Küche,* and he to the *Wirtschaft.*

The beer here has influenced the décor of the *Wirtschaft,* with heads of game on the wall and frescoes interwoven with poetry:

> *Leberwurscht für den Durscht*
> *Blunzeduft mit Kraut—*
> *Wenn der Bauer Hunger hat*
> *frisst ers z'amt der Haut.*

The author of this verse was my maternal grandfather, Ludwig Fischer. Translate it I cannot, but it wants to say:

> Liver sausage for the thirst
> the aroma of blood sausage and cabbage
> when the peasant is hungry
> he devours it ["fressen" is not translatable]
> "z'amt der Haut"—means with the skin.

The tables are solid and the influence of beer on the chairs is remarkable. They are heavy, made mostly of oak. The good ones have a face carved into the part against which you put your back. The seat is wooden also and so planed that it conforms to the anatomy of the local males; that is, you can place a large trunk on it and it will be safe and not wobble. Into the seat the four solid legs are placed, and here the Irish resemblance is again apparent. These legs are not glued or screwed into the seat, but merely inserted, so that with a good strong twist of the wrist you can remove them and work with them as with a shillelagh.

Now as to the man who sits on the chair—he is self-contained and quiet (unless enraged); he is honest, loves his country, goes to church. Beer has also influenced him. First of all, he is there on its account and on no other. He enters the *Wirtschaft,* goes to his chair, and a grunt and a nod serve him for the first half-hour. The waitress knows his wants and puts the first heavy stein in front of him.

During the first half-hour the true "Spezi," as he is called—and which perhaps means "specialist"—folds his hands and contemplates his beer. He might lift his head and look beyond his part of the *Stammtisch* to see if any hostile element is present. (Anyone from another city is a foreigner.) If he sees a friend there is another grunt. He does not call the waitress for another beer because when he wants one he merely leaves the cover on his mug open in upstanding position; that is the signal to the waitress to hit him again.

He usually eats at home. If he eats at the *Wirtschaft* he eats the same diet as his *Frau* prepares—radishes, pumpernickel, potato dumplings (which must be torn apart, not cut, or the cook's heart is broken), *Schweinebraten, Gänsbraten mit Rotkraut, Leberwurscht und Blutwurscht.*

All this gives him a liver like the geese of *pâté de fois gras* fame. He drinks himself to death at about the same age the American executive works himself to death.

He sits there like a frog that has swallowed a stone and is unable to move, his laughter is bitter, his words are few. The beer-world has formulated the language into a kind of ponderous audible shorthand. To illustrate this I will give here a quick sampler of this curious means of communication, of its meaning in High German and also in English.

How do you do?
High German: Wie geht es Ihnen?
Beer: Grüassdi

What are you doing?
High German: Wie geht hier vor?
Beer: Wastuastdenn

We're cleaning
High German: Wir machen rein
Beer: Ramma tamma

At home
High German: Zu Hause
Beer: Dahoam

My grandfather was an exceptionally well-preserved Neander-thaler. He was in the war of 1870, and was hit by a projectile at close range. It merely left a small dent in his skull. The brew-master was with him at the time and lost a leg. It worked a certain benefit for them, for they split their shoes, Grandfather wearing the right one and the brewmaster the left. O'Papa, as the grand-father is called in southern Germany, lost the use of his left leg— a martyr to his brewery.

He drank a minimum of thirty liters of beer a day, consuming this in one after the other of all the *Wirtschaften* in and around Regensburg, where our beer was sold. This is called *Kundschaft-trinken* and is related to the present-day practice of taking out the client. As a consequence he traveled in a wheel chair from tavern to inn to Rathskeller, one leg raised in a vast packing of cotton, the other down, with the foot stuck into an old-fashioned boot with elastic sides.

As he moved through the streets of the old city he waved his cane over the gouty leg to keep anyone from approaching it. He had a theory that every human being was filled with electricity and if too close to his leg started the pain. This pain was very curious, for he made sounds as if he heard jokes—he laughed from pain—hi-hi, ha-ha—and made faces.

The advanced age of O'Papa and the great volume of liquids he took posed a great problem, and it was again beer that con-ditioned the construction of the wheel chair. It had a tank at the bottom down to which a rubber tube led, a device that allowed O'Papa to ease himself without getting out of his chair.

The first time that my peculiar talents asserted themselves was in our beer garden in Regensburg. O'Papa was sleeping in his easy chair, the waters of the Danube lapped against the stone walls of the beer garden, the green candelabra of the chestnut trees were alight with white and pink blossoms. I crawled under the chair and I took the end of the rubber tube from the tank and stuck it into O'Papa's shoe. The only one who knew it was Fafner, an alcoholic dachshund—and also a Spezi on beer—he knew all the good ones.

All this, so long ago and far away, comes back to me with sharpest clarity when I sit with one of the good beers, with *Loewenbräu, Würzburger, Kulmbacher, Paulaner*—there isn't a bad one in that region, even in the places that have only one church steeple.

THE DOG OF THE WORLD

The fact that one can go into a shop and buy a dog has always depressed me. The windows of pet shops, especially on holidays, when the animals are altogether abandoned, are among the saddest sights I know.

After losing a fine dog I promised myself never to own another, for if you really love dogs they change your life. You have to cross oceans on ships, for you can't conveniently take dogs on airplanes, and you must use particular ships, which don't require them to stay in the kennels. I often travel on freighters so that my dog will not be left alone. If you live in the city you feel guilty; if you let your dog off the leash in a park you get a ticket. Then the dog gets sick, the dog dies, and all those troubles are forgotten; all you know is that you miss him.

I was still grieving for a departed dog when my friend Armand said, "The only way to get over it is to get another dog. I shall get one for you—the dog of the world—the greatest dog. I will get you the champion of all dogs, for I am president of the Club National du Bouvier des Flandres."

"What is a bouvier des Flandres?"

"*Alors,* the French have their poodles," said Armand, "the Germans the dachshund, the British the bulldog, the Swiss the St. Bernard, the Arabians the Afghan, and so on. But the Flemish —and you are half Flemish—have the bouvier des Flandres.

"Hundreds of years ago, the counts of Flanders wanted a dog of their own and they found that the only distinctively native dogs were working dogs—raw-boned, hard-working animals of no particular pedigree, accustomed to pulling carts and herding cattle in dirty weather. There was one great advantage to these dogs. They were simple, strong, intelligent, and healthy. There was nothing inbred or nervous about them. They usually lived in the huts of peasants as members of the family and were extremely pleasant companions as well as good protectors."

We saw a bouvier on the streets of Paris the next day. He was a fearful-looking creature with a rough coat and reddish eyes. He was black, gray, and sand-colored. There was nothing graceful about him. He looked like the hound of the Baskervilles.

"You have never owned a dog until you've had one of these," said Armand, and a few days later he telephoned that he had found the one for me and that we would drive out to see him.

Armand's car is usually being repaired, for he drives with slow deliberation and other cars frequently run into him. The last crash had taken off a rear fender, and on the day this was replaced we drove out of Paris in the direction of Reims. After thirty-odd miles without mishap we came to a village and stopped at a small stone house. A very old man opened the garden gate. There was deep barking, and then I was presented to madame, a son, a daughter, the grandchildren, and visiting relatives. The entire troupe followed us to the kennels, and there was my *"fils."* In France people refer to your dog as your "son." He was six weeks old and blue-black; he had the shapelessness of a half-filled hot-water bottle; he had an immense head, large opaque eyes, and a long pedigree. We had immediate rapport with each other. He gave me the first of many sad looks as I patted him and left to go into the house, where a glass of wine was offered, and where I became officially the owner of Bosy. I wanted to take him along, but Armand said, "He's only a baby. He must remain where he is."

I returned to America, and every ten days or so I received a letter in the thinnest pen line. It gave me long reports about my *fils*, how *sage* he was, what a lucky dog he was because he would eventually go to America. On one of these letters appeared his footprint by way of signature. He took on shape, and I looked forward to seeing him again and to having him with me.

Back in France, some months later, Armand drove me out to see Bosy. I had told the people at the good old hotel I stay at whenever I am in Paris that I was getting my dog, and I can highly recommend it as a dog-owner's hotel. Everybody there was happy, and a special dish with water was in a corner of the bathroom. The maid had changed the fancy rose-colored eiderdown for a less costly coverlet.

"For," she said, "he will want to sleep on your bed, monsieur. Also, don't be worried about the carpet—this one is old and will be replaced anyway." The tolerance for dogs at this hotel is due to the proprietress, who loves them dearly.

On the way Armand said, "You can't have him yet. You don't want an average dog, a dog that pulls on the leash, that gets into fights, jumps up on you, and misbehaves. I promised you the greatest dog in the world, and that is what you shall have. I know an old clown who had the most famous dog act at the Cirque Medrano. He trains dogs with patience and love. He is retired now, and has agreed to keep the dog for a year and train him. After that you shall have a companion who does all but speak. He will be gay or serious; he will console you in your lowest moods. He will be perfectly behaved and never leave your side. He will entertain your friends. He will rescue a child from a burning building or, if ever you are in danger of drowning, pull you from the water. He will watch your car, protect you against attack, carry your packages or umbrella, and refuse food from strangers. I have arranged for it all."

I enjoyed my "son" only briefly; we took him from his former owner, proceeded to Chartres, and I received the second sad look from Bosy, when he was handed over to the clown. When I returned to the hotel everybody was disappointed. I completed my European assignments and left for America.

The clown did not write, but the time passed and I came back again to France. At the hotel I was again given a room with an expendable carpet, and the eiderdown was changed for a blanket. Again Armand drove me out to Chartres, and the old clown asked us to hide so that Bosy would not be distracted. We watched from the window of a small garden house. The clown leaned a ladder against an open window a floor above the ground. Then he went indoors and reappeared with Bosy. The dog was now big, and reminded one of medieval missals illustrated with devils, gargoyles, and things that knock in the night. His eyes were red, his hair bristly. He wore a large collar and he was very mannerly, respecting flower beds, looking at the old clown, and sitting at attention when told to.

The clown addressed Bosy by the respectful *vous* instead of the familiar *tu,* giving him a series of commands which were carried out with precision and eagerness. Next the dog did some tricks, and finally the clown informed him that there was a fire in the house and a little girl was in a room upstairs.

"*Allez,*" he said to Bosy, "be nice and rescue the little girl."

Bosy went up the ladder, vanished into the room, and returned with a large doll in his mouth. He carried it carefully, coming backward down the ladder, and put it on the grass ever so gently. Then he looked at the clown, who patted his head but reproached him softly.

"Isn't there someone you have forgotten, Bosy?"

I could almost hear the dog say, "Oh, yes," as he turned and climbed once more into the "burning" building. This time he returned with a large tiger cat in his fearful fangs. He held it the way cats carry kittens, and again he descended. The cat was put down, and it turned, sat up, and licked Bosy's large black nose.

"We have seen enough," Armand shouted with enthusiasm and congratulated the clown.

There was wine again, this time in the little garden house, and then the clown brought out a statement on lined paper. He had written with a pencil the cost of training and of boarding Bosy. It came to sixty thousand francs. I gave the money to the clown, who counted it. As he came to the last five-thousand-franc note his mouth got wobbly and his eyes filled with tears. He sat down on an upturned wooden washbasin. "Bosy," he said, "come here for the last time."

The dog sat down in front of him and looked into his face.

"I've been good to you, haven't I?" The clown could hardly speak. "I've never had one like him before, so gentle, so courageous, so understanding."

Both the clown and the dog turned their heads in my direction.

"You are tearing the heart out of me," said the clown. "You are taking my brother from me," he cried, "the only friend I have in this world!"

Close by was the tiger cat, and I have never seen a cat so close to tears. It was all so terribly sad and desolate. A steady stream of tears ran down the clown's face now, and his face, even without make-up, was the saddest clown's face I had ever seen. I cannot look at people in tears, and certainly not clowns. I was all for letting him have the dog. I started to walk away, but Armand, who understands his compatriots better than I, said, "Just a moment."

He turned to the clown. "We shall leave him with you, but give us back the money for his board and tuition."

"Ah?" said the clown. He dried his tears and pocketed the money. He got up and, in slow, bent motions, walked toward the door of his house, without turning. He said, "Adieu, Bosy, go with your new master." Bosy gave me the third sad look and silently followed me to the car.

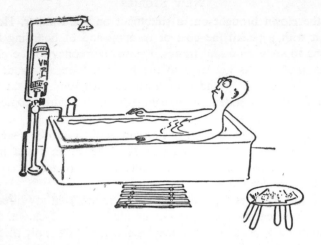

THE STREET WHERE THE HEART LIES

The most self-effacing and kindly gentleman of the neighborhood was Monsieur Camille St. Juste. He lived a steady and blameless life on the third floor of a six-story building in the Rue Git-le-Coeur, which, when translated, means the Street Where the Heart Lies.

He was the recipient, day in and out, of the concierge's smile, the only smile she had ever bestowed on a lodger. She said of him, *"C'est un monsieur tout à fait comme il faut,"* and if a Parisian janitress says of a man that he is altogether faultless, that is the highest possible character endorsement. Even the fox terrier of the concierge, who raised his right front leg as a preliminary to a furious fit of snapping at the approach of anybody, relaxed when he saw Monsieur St. Juste.

The children in the street who took pleasure in nicknaming everyone who lived there called him affectionately "Monsieur la Tortue," not only because he resembled one, but mostly on account of being as mute and self-contained as a turtle.

He was that anonymous type of neat and energetic French citizen who stalks along stiffly as a sandpiper, who may be anywhere between fifty and a hundred years old and be either an Academician, a duke, or the last violinist of the Concert Pas de Loup.

The appearance of this type in the street is uniform—always in black, never without dark gloves and a dark cane, a dark hat, a collar that is called "false," for it is not attached to the shirt, and a tie, dark and carefully knotted. The ensemble is completed with small marks of distinction, such as the red band of the Legion of Honor, the rosette of the Knights of Lorraine, or a ring of special significance.

Monsieur St. Juste was further distinguished by a pair of golden pince-nez and a carefully adjusted and always combed toupee, which he wore not so much out of vanity as for protection against the cold drafts of indoor and outdoor Paris.

He was extremely shy; he could not talk; he could not sing. But he could write, and for years he had supported himself by translations of French texts into English, and vice versa. During these labors he had often mildly wondered at the courage of authors. To the right and left of him lay volumes in which machine guns and revolvers spattered, in which women rose from the sidewalk to become atom spies, and in which the guillotine chopped forever through newly discovered characters in the French Revolution.

Eventually these tales had their effect on Monsieur St. Juste, and he developed a shaky trust, a wobbly hope, that perhaps, one day, he himself might walk out on the tightrope of authorship and write. "Write what?" he said to himself often, as he carefully knotted his tie. And he answered himself, "Nothing ever happens."

The urge of creation finally gripped him so strongly that he put on paper his own observations of the familiar things, the happenings in his neighborhood. He found a publisher, and the book, which was entitled *The Street Where the Heart Lies,* appeared and was a mild success. The publisher said it was remarkable that it sold as well as it did for, after all, nothing happened in the book that was very extraordinary. The royalties from this first effort were, however, sufficient for Monsieur St. Juste to buy something he had always wanted—a bath, complete with tub and a machine called Vulcan, which by means of a pipe coiled around a blue gas flame gave forth instant hot water.

On the morning of that long awaited day when the installation was finished and the Vulcan worked, Monsieur St. Juste reflected again upon the business of writing and he determined that in his next novel something tremendous and surprising would take place. He relaxed in his bath and was about to turn off the hot water when the concierge announced outside the door that there was a telegram for him. She pushed the telegram under the door, and a small corner of the envelope was visible.

Monsieur St. Juste stepped out of his bath and he tried to get the envelope, which he regarded with misgivings, for he belonged to that group of the population who receive telegrams only on the death of close relatives. He opened the door slightly and, seeing no one on the stairs, opened it wider to reach for the telegram. When the draft caused by the open door blew the paper out of his reach, Monsieur St. Juste took a step outside his premises to get hold of the wire. Just then he heard a sudden bang and found himself, without any clothes, in the stair hall.

The poor man was in panic, for he heard the clatter of a woman's heels coming down the stairs. He ran below and into the lady who lived on the second floor. Not recognizing Monsieur St. Juste without his clothes, his toupee and eyeglasses, she ran back into her apartment, slammed the door, and opened the window, screaming for the police.

The nude man, descending the stairs with the uncertainty of the myopic, felt his way along the entrance hall and, mostly by memory, gained the security of a drape that hid the entrance to the bedroom of the concierge, who, like janitors in France, occupied two rooms on the ground floor—one of which faces the street, and the second, mostly windowless, serves as a bedroom

There was shouting outside, and the tension grew with the crowd that assembled. The lady of the second floor had become the most important personage in the street. She explained, between the waves of tumult, that a maniac was loose in the house. The windows of every apartment in the street were filled with people, all except those of the apartment of Monsieur St. Juste.

Hard words had given way to ugly ones; the mood of the crowd was getting dangerous, and the police decided to ask for additional reinforcements before attempting to take the criminal. Soon the Paris police sirens, which go "Hoopaw, Hoopaw," sounded.

An inspector of the Brigade Mondaine arrived and took over. He detailed men to go up to the roofs of the adjoining buildings, commanded others to keep order in the street and to keep traffic, which had come to a standstill, moving, and he himself, with five men, entered the house, ready to pounce upon the criminal.

When they found him, he behaved typically. He cowered, wrapped in half of the ancient brown velour drape, which was attached with heavy wooden rings to a pole overhead. A scream came from the bedroom of the concierge when she saw where the fiend had hidden. She clutched her two children to herself and ran out the front door to inform the waiting mob that he had been caught.

Unable to remove the culprit as he was, or wrapped in the drapery, a policeman put his cape as protection around Monsieur St. Juste. It was fortunate that the police were there in large numbers and that Monsieur St. Juste was camouflaged with a blue cape and not instantly recognizable, for as he was brought out the fury of the mob was almost whipped into action.

The prisoner was quickly packed off into the dark blue wagon; two motorcycle police made way for it. The second wagon with police followed; and, after this, the car of the inspector of the Brigade Mondaine. "Hoopaw, Hoopaw," howled the cars, and the mob followed them across the bridge.

It was evident that this was a case for the criminal courts rather than for a magistrate, and, therefore, Camille St. Juste found himself facing the examining judge of the Parquet of the Seine. As he was seated there, shackled, and offered a cigarette, which he declined, as Monsieur St. Juste neither drank nor smoked, he merely shook with an inner excitement. Finally something had happened to him, and he had, he knew, a plot—the kind that fitted into the Rue Morgue rather than into the Street Where the Heart Lies. He wondered whether he should let life go on spinning the yarn for him or whether it was better to explain.

The Judge of Instruction, as the examining judge is called in France, disappointed Monsieur St. Juste, for he was a kind soul who seemed to be concerned about him. *"Voyons,"* he said, with reproach, to the inspector of the Brigade Mondaine. He said it so that it meant, "But you've made a mistake. This is evidently not a criminal." The inspector read off his notes. The judge became more sympathetic to the accused and ordered the handcuffs removed. "Tell me what happened."

Monsieur St. Juste made the gesture all Frenchmen use to denote that something fantastic has happened. He threw both arms into the air, thereby disrobing himself again. He quickly folded the cloak about his thin shoulders and, clutching it, retired into his shyness.

The thorough, patient judge finally drew out of him that it all had started with a bath. "You stated that you were about to take a bath, monsieur." He looked at the deposition. "You stated that you had turned on the hot water—"

"Bon Dieu," cried the accused, "it is still running—the hot water!"

"Well then, monsieur," said the judge, "the matter is very simple. You will be taken back to your house. If it is flooded, your story holds water, and you are restored to liberty and honor."

The judge stood up and shook the hand of Monsieur St. Juste. Again the "Hoopaw, Hoopaw" was heard and the police, in the same numbers as before, arrived in the quiet Street Where the Heart Lies.

The lady of the second floor was crying to the people, who reappeared at their windows, that water was coming through the ceiling. It was suspected that the criminal had killed Monsieur St. Juste. The children were running around the neighborhood, importantly whispering the dreadful news—that "Someone has drowned the turtle in his new bathtub."

The police were relieved to see hot water dripping down the stairs. The apartment was opened; the state of things written down in a full police report; Monsieur St. Juste, in his bathrobe, with his toupee and the golden pince-nez, identified and returned to his blameless status. All was respectable again, and the police left laughing.

Monsieur St. Juste waited until his apartment was in order and the floor dried—he smiled out of the window at the disappointed children who had stood waiting for his corpse to be removed— and then he decided that at last he would have his well-earned bath.

He let the water run and was about to step into the tub when he heard the voice of his concierge announcing the telegram which everyone had forgotten about. This time Monsieur St. Juste was extremely careful. He dressed in his bathrobe, put on his toupee and his glasses, and, furthermore, when he opened the door he braced it with a chair before reaching for the telegram.

Most things official in France are blue, like the telegrams. Also, it is true that when one opens a French telegram it is usually torn, for it is merely a sealed envelope on the inside of which the message is written. This telegram, having been thoroughly soaked, opened easily. Monsieur St. Juste read it carefully, once, twice. Then he prepared himself for his bath again. He added some warm water. As he stepped into the tub he was filled with mixed emotions, all of them those of success, of happiness, of hope— all of them so exciting that he could not lean back and relax.

The frugal man had calculated that with the cost of gas and water he would be able to afford a bath a week. Now suddenly he was able to bathe every day, twice if he wanted. He could afford several toupees and, by rotating them, give the illusion that he had had his hair cut and that it was slowly growing back again. All this on account of the telegram.

He picked it up and read it again. Yes, it was all true. It was from America, the place where the most exciting things continually happen in life as well as in books. Someone there—a colleague unknown—had translated the stories of *The Street Where the Heart Lies,* and the telegram was from a New York publisher, who was certain that the stories would be successful as a book, on the stage, the cinema, and on television. The prospects were tremendous. The publisher most anxiously wanted more stories of the same kind.

At last Monsieur St. Juste relaxed. He folded his hands in back of his head and he contemplated the vagaries of existence.

Now that at long last he had himself experienced an exciting, true story, formidable and filled with action, a story of an innocent suspect, of mistaken identity and the police present *en masse,* the publishers of that incredible country across the ocean asked him to write more stories of the Street Where the Heart Lies.

As Monsieur St. Juste started to soap himself, he sighed, as authors do, no matter what good fortune visits them. He realized, with overwhelming sadness, that his future lay in writing about the small, peaceful happenings; not, as he would like, about large, dramatic designs.

With a philosophic turn of mind he said to himself as he relaxed further into his bathtub, "I suppose that in America so much happens all the time that the little events of the quiet Rue Git-le-Coeur are wonderfully fresh and restful."

THE PARIS UNDERWORLD

There are many ways of getting to know the cities of the world. For me, the best way is through the eye. I look at a city much as I look at the face of a person. Some cities, as with some people, I take a liking to instantly; others, it takes more time to know.

The problem of the first look at Europe is a grave one, and people who have planned the trip often say, "I have been advised to go to such and such a place, to get to know it thoroughly, instead of flitting all over."

My advice would be to the contrary. For one's first look, I advise the traveler to take the guided tour within his means and flit all over. First impressions are strongest; you will discover what you like most and you will have a point of comparison. Later you can go back to those places that have impressed themselves upon you most.

My first visit to Paris depressed me. I hated it. I was then a bus boy in a New York hotel and my mortal enemies were waiters, waiter captains, and headwaiters. I worked my way over on the old S.S. *Rotterdam* and dutifully made my way to Paris. It seemed filled with battalions of my enemies. I left after two days and swore never to return. (I even circled around it to get back to New York.) I fled to my native Tirol, got into buckskin shorts and a green hat with the shaving brush. A photograph taken of me at that time is referred to by my daughter Barbara as the "Bing Crosby picture of Poppy." The buckskin pants have got too tight for me, the mood has changed. I have developed a tolerance for hotel personnel, and now my favorite city is Paris.

The hum of the engines changes, and afterward there is that always reassuring whine of lowering flaps and landing gear. A few rainclouds hang in the sky, violet on the underside, mother-of-pearl above. The plane banks, and now it sinks down over small houses and their kitchen gardens framed in neat walls against which fruit trees have been trained to grow. The runway is watered down by showers, the grass stands up like the hair on little boys' heads, and the morning sun shines on it all.

The door opens and you breathe the air of France. You are saluted by two of her officials, men with small mustaches and little blue capes barely reaching beneath the seats of their pants. And beyond them, as in a worn mirror, stands the Eiffel Tower, the capricious symbol of the beloved city. This way, please. Through a mildly fogged glass door you follow into a room filled with fellow passengers. *Thump, thump*—we are passed by the police. *Thump, thump*—we are passed by health. *Merci, monsieur . . . merci, mademoiselle.* To the customs now—no bottleneck here—merely the question, "You have nothing to declare?" and a chalk mark on each piece of baggage releases us to the bus.

The wind has done some brushwork on the sky and blown the clouds upward, and now we roll into the long avenue that leads to the Porte d'Italie, to the Esplanade des Invalides, where the Air Terminal is located. Sometimes one can wait an hour here before getting a taxi, so I always leave my baggage there and send for it later. For here Paris begins: the Pont Alexander III is in front of you. It shines in emerald and gold now, a bridge decorated with the makings of a bouillabaisse. Among its decorations are crabs, crayfish, conger eels, red mullet, hogfish, swordfish, sharks, pike, carp, and over a thousand scallops, together with seaweed and mermaids. One of its ornaments is a small crab that has become brightly polished because everyone tries to pick it off and take it home.

And in the next moment you see the Place de la Concorde, with its unbelievable vehicles and even more unbelievable congestion. Here also is the Obelisk whose hieroglyphs recount the glorious episodes in the life of Ramses II. It replaced the statue of Louis XV. Why do we take the time to stop to look at monuments? Because from their inscriptions Parisians learn their language and their history.

Turn around. There is the Eiffel Tower again, now close enough so that you can see the elevator climbing up to the first platform. It's a cockeyed kind of Toonerville trolley moving in a diagonal ascent. Has anyone written a song about the Eiffel Tower? Certainly—and there are songs about the heart of Paris, the wines of Paris, the streets and bus lines of Paris, the sidewalks of Paris, the bridges of Paris, the air of Paris, the rain of Paris, the girls of Paris, the skies of Paris, and the eyes of the women of Paris. It is the most sung of city in the world.

Every Parisian is an enthusiastic turntable for the long-playing records of praise and affection. This love of their home town is one of the ingredients of the glue that holds Parisians together. Penurious as they are, they are fully aware of the gift of beauty. The heavily jeweled finger of Louis XIV still points out what he has given them, and they enjoy it, whether they live in elegant quarters or under bridges. Another ingredient is their common love of pleasure.

Paris's love of pleasure is frigid at the top. The Parisienne of the *beau monde,* when seated at Maxim's close to a display of jewels better than her own, can lengthen her already long and fashionable nose into a dagger. The caviar in her mouth will turn to porridge and the salesmen at her favorite *bijouterie* will jump the next day with trays of stones.

At the bottom, it is warm. What matters government, what matter the thousand and one chagrins of life on earth? Forgotten is the standing in line—have patience—the strike will end. Anyway, one is prepared—there is a little pot simmering on the back of the stove and a bottle standing in a cool place.

Paris is a city in which women outnumber men—hence you see them pulling carts in the street, washing cars in the railroad yards, doing menial work everywhere. From his imperial tomb, his power radiating as from an atomic pile, Napoleon still influences the lives of the French, and especially the conditions of Frenchwomen. He decreed under the Code Napoleon that no woman may have a bank account or a passport without her husband's permission; that adultery is of consequence only when committed by her husband in her own home, and so on and on.

Under the French system of education, girls become well informed, but they are molded into a pattern of sweet women who sing off their lessons, believe them, and, although at times they are a little sad-eyed, in general they are happy.

Those in revolt fall into several classes. One is made up of the ambitious wives and mistresses of the *haut monde*. Another is a class peculiar to France—a monster in human form called the concierge. There is one to every apartment house. She lives on the ground floor near the entrance. She sits in what is called the *loge de la concierge,* which corresponds to the janitor's quarters in America, and she is installed there for life. "Beware of the concierge" would be a good sign to place on most apartment-house doors. She can answer for you the sometimes difficult question, "Where were you on the night of so-and-so?" She is ready to supply detailed answers to all other questions about you and the other tenants on her list. She has a dossier on the people of the neighborhood and adds to it by daily contact with the other concierges of the community. A cat and a snapping dog are always beside her. Her costume is never complete without a black knitted cape thrown over her shoulders. The loge smells the same, whether of food cooking or meals partaken.

If you are a Parisienne, young and beautiful, you will find a young man, also young and beautiful, and you will sit along the quais and dream of love—of marriage and children. That is the desire of most Parisiennes—and you see them in front of furniture stores, making their plans. The young man looks for a home, small and snug, which he and his bride will decorate, and in which they will install the comforts of life and where he will exercise a totalitarian regime of family and love. In Paris the young people do not share the American dream of ascending to a vice-presidential chair. Instead, they are happy in the domain of the small bourgeois. Great events to them are children, not many, and these are paraded on the streets in their Sunday best, like little dolls, with carefully tied shoelaces and clean white socks and gloves.

If you are a young and beautiful Parisienne and this domesticity does not appeal to you, then one day you can take off all your clothes and pass in review before a director of one of the hundred institutions devoted to the gaiety of Paris; and if you pass muster you may appear in your little skin on the stage, freezing in winter, and even in the best-paying shows you won't earn enough to take a vacation to get away from the summer heat.

If you are neither for marriage nor for the music hall, you can become one of the "little hands," as seamstresses are called, and work in an establishment of high fashion. What you are paid will help the family support you, but it is not enough to clothe, house, or feed you on your own. And you have to be very diligent, for there are so many.

And so, if you are young, and the old ones are eager to have you out of the crowded quarters, and you're not beautiful enough for the stage or the screen or the young man you love—then someday a man will speak to you, and you'll look at him and answer, and for once you'll get a full meal with champagne. Maybe the man is decent, and in this case he sees you again and he takes care of you. And things could be worse.

But maybe you're unlucky; maybe the stranger who speaks to you is kind only at first, and after a while you no longer go home, for somehow you find yourself providing him with clothes, silk shirts, perhaps a car—and although you may not feel gay about it, you also are adding to the gaiety of Paris.

Liberté, Egalité, Fraternité—the three words are written on almost all public buildings in France. *Liberté* Parisians do not want so much as the freedom to pursue a fanatically individual course. They have no desire to share either opinions or goods with anybody. The people of this ancient and restless city have a passionate interest in living, a constant renewal of ideas, and a vitality of optimism nonexistent elsewhere.

The mind of Paris is a split mind, constantly contradicting itself. You go into a shop and ask for something relatively simple and the shopkeeper will start to argue and convince you with elaborate logic that what you ask for is impossible, and even if it were possible, it would be of no benefit to you. You are content, you thank him and bid him good-by. Now he stops you, reverses himself, and with his index finger to his nose he pleads your case and convinces you and himself that what you asked for is the most important thing in this world. Similarly, the policeman who walks over to hand you a ticket ends up by helping you push your stalled car; he may even detect the defect and repair it.

The contrariness to a given issue, opinion, or condition of life is perhaps the most distinct and typical of Parisian traits.

The clearest example of this I found in the lowest quarters. I walked through the streets around the Place Blanche, in the company of a lawyer who had for a client a lady of the sidewalks who was over sixty. Her name was Gabrielle and she was of robust allure, starting out late at night when the clientele was dim-eyed and congenial. I wanted to interview her one Sunday morning, when she could usually be found drinking her coffee in a small place along the Rue St.-Dominique.

"She's not here," said the woman behind the bar. "She left this morning—and I wish you could have seen her. She had on a white organdy dress with leg-o'-mutton sleeves, a cartwheel hat, also white, with blue cornflowers on it. And naturally she had the little white sachet containing the white sugar almonds that one always brings, for she went to the First Communion of her niece. She went out to the suburbs, Marly-le-Roi. What a lovely day she has!"

A few of the girls came in.

"Ah, they love her so, she is like their *maman*," said the woman, indicating the girls.

All the faces in the bar seemed to shine with the light of the First Communion lace. In Paris girls like these don't bother much with introspection.

"This is the world as it is—and I live in it. Too bad it is as it is, but let's not waste time. *Je suis très jolie, monsieur.*"

Yes, très jolie.

I talked to Gabrielle later, and she gave me an account of her niece's First Communion in Marly-le-Roi that had all eyes moist. Then she stopped. "But the prices, my dears," she went on. "What I paid for the car, and the little dress for my niece—and the small *déjeuner* in the local inn. It is no longer possible for ordinary people to live decently in Paris."

I have long been interested in learning more about the *bas-fonds,* as the lowest depths of Paris are called, and I asked an old friend, Georges, if he would be my guide. Many years ago, when my child was three and a half, we used to sit outside the Café du Dome every morning, for breakfast. Barbara drank milk but always left half of it, and also half of her croissant. Georges, who was then a petty thief of great agility, sat nearby, and he invariably finished the milk and the croissant. Eventually we got to know each other, and I found out that he had been stealing for Barbara toys which I would not buy her. He had wit and his own code of honor; he never stole anything from me.

Georges is now the head of a syndicate that deals in foreign exchange. He is sedate and no longer sits on the edges of chairs. He has an office with his name plate on the door, he has important friends, and he talks of swindlers and small crooks with the same detachment he feels toward himself. He has not forgotten the friends of his beginnings, and he was glad to go with me on a tour of the lower depths.

The safest way to see apaches, gigolettes, and other underworld personnel is on a bus trip run by the American Express Company or other reliable tourist agencies. The cost of these trips, which take in four "naughty" and "libertine" cabarets and several carefully selected apache dives and St.-Germain cellars, is thirty-five hundred francs. The object of the various bus entrepreneurs is to help the sightseer to participate in the nocturnal Paris life, which has always been so famous or infamous throughout the world. In charge of an experienced guide, then, you will penetrate into an atmosphere extremely diverse—of moods varying from torpor to maniacal gaiety and extravagance. You will rub shoulders with inhabitants of the *bas-fonds* in their sordid quarters and breathe the same smoky air as the "smart set" that gathers there from all corners of the world. All this for ten bucks, which includes being returned to your hotel—perhaps the most important of the services rendered. The champagne (included in the trip fee) is only a little less bubbly than that served to non-conducted visitors at six thousand francs a bottle. Moreover, you are protected from assassination by headwaiters, doormen, coatroom attendants, and their greedy assistants. It is, perhaps, a grim form of merrymaking, but strongly recommended. If you are a student of the human form divine, take along a pair of powerful binoculars. It's worth the trouble.

To investigate the true *bas-fonds* by yourself is not advisable. For example, there is the matter of the passport. If you take it with you, it may easily be stolen, for bona fide U. S. passports have been sold for as much as ten thousand dollars. If you don't take it, and there is a police raid, you may have a few broken teeth, lose your watch and money, and spend the night in a detention pen. A word of advice should you be arrested: Never say to a French policeman that you are a friend of the prefect (chief of police). A man I know gave a party last summer in a respectable house in one of the best neighborhoods of Paris. It was very gay, the guests sang late and laughed too loudly, and the neighbors called the police.

Two *flics* (policemen) came, knocked on the door, and requested that the party quiet down. All could have been settled with a few polite words and some cigarettes, but one of the guests announced to the policemen that he was a great friend of the police commissioner and haughtily bade them leave. The policemen departed, but they soon came back with the salad basket (as the patrol wagon is called in Paris) and took the whole party to the commissariat.

There the haughty guest complained bitterly. The commissaire said, "Yes, yes, I believe you. It is, in fact, because you are a friend of the prefect that we are doing this so thoroughly. Your friend, the prefect, will want to know every detail about our interfering in your party." The night passed in the taking of depositions.

The police of Paris are no more or less corrupt than our own. The main difference is that the pickings are slimmer: the government skims off the cream. For instance, it recognizes the fact that man likes to gamble, and it is in the business of what is the equivalent of our numbers game—it runs the national lottery. Also, the government licenses, supervises, and taxes roulette, chemin de fer, trente et quarante, horse racing, and every other game of chance.

France is about to legalize prostitution again, having concluded that it is more injurious to the state when uncontrolled. The realism of this philosophy is so profound that Marthe Richard, the woman deputy who led the fight that brought about the closing of the bordellos, has now reversed herself. Hearing the golden trumpets of tolerance herself, she now says that the women engaged in this pursuit should be called "social workers" and thereby given the air of respectability with which the novelist and playwright Jean-Paul Sartre has dignified them. (Ever since the production of his play *The Respectful Prostitute,* they have been known as "the respectful ones" in Paris.)

Gambling and prostitution are the main corrupters of police everywhere. In America a third influence is liquor, but France is a wine-drinking country, and its drinking is traditional. Here and there a counterfeit label may be pasted on a bottle, but the deception is usually detected, and, at any rate, it is not big business.

Those of the police, then, who prey upon the outlaw, are reduced to petty thievery. The economic circumstances that govern the average Parisian are so hard that it is a game for pennies. Vegetables are wrapped in newspapers, each piece of string is carefully unknotted and saved, an empty bottle is redeemed, an old sack is mended, and cigar butts are commodities in a specialized commerce. It is perhaps the austerity of this life that stamps the criminal and the police alike with meanness.

The Paris policeman heartily hates the criminal, and the criminal returns the hate; in fact, it is said that he "sees flames" when he sees the police. It is possible to recognize a Paris policeman at a glance even in civilian clothes—his stance, his walk, his manner of speech, his way of looking. He knows his weight and uses it. He is unpopular with all classes of the population.

While the French enjoy political liberty, individual liberty is nonexistent, and the immunity of the police is absolute: they have always been the instrument of power rather than the friend and servant of the citizen. The friendly "cop" is not a usual part of the scene in Paris. The policeman in Paris loves nothing more than to bawl out someone. The Commissariat of Tourism alone has succeeded in making him lackey-polite to tourists from hard-money countries.

The above is a sweeping statement, as if one were to say, "All Italians have black hair and dark eyes." As there are Italians who are blond and have blue eyes, so there are in France policemen who are kind, who have humor, who do not consider themselves obliged to deal out punishment. But they are the rare exception.

The average policeman is a mediocre, small-minded individual; take such a one and pay him miserably, and you have a petty official, glorying in his small prerogatives; suspicious, endlessly on the defense, and happy when he can reach for his book and ask your name and address. He is happier if he can make an arrest, happier still if he can get a confession.

A young man arrested for the first time retracted his confession before the examining judge. The judge asked him why he had confessed in the first place.

"For three reasons," he said, and took three teeth out of his pocket.

Magistrates, prosecutors, and inquisitors are as poorly paid as the police, and, moreover, there are not enough of them to keep abreast of the ever-mounting legal tangle confronting them. Even their equipment is inadequate. The introduction of typewriters into the Palais de Justice is of recent date, and a number of district attorneys still are without them and have clerks to take down testimony in longhand. Not until 1929 was it considered necessary for each examining magistrate to have a telephone.

As the seasoning of French foods is distinctive, as the Parisian talent for women's fashion is unique and incomparably French, so are France's police and courtroom life intrinsically Gallic. If you speak the language only passably you will be more enthralled by a criminal trial in Paris than by the average drama in a theater.

When the examining magistrate asked the assassin of Henry IV the motive for his crime, Ravaillac replied simply, "I saw flames." The French are a race of "flame-seers"—especially Parisians.

The criminal trial is a lively show enacted by the flame-seer who committed the crime, the flame-seers who made the arrest, the flame-seer in the robes of judge. Add the flame-seeing lawyers and the flame-seers among the spectators, who are too excited to remain quiet, and you have a French courtroom scene where the judge leans so far out over the bench that he almost falls on the floor, and the accused has to be restrained by force from leaving his barrier. It is never objective, it is never dull, and frequently it leads to miscarriage of justice.

In practice the Frenchman is guilty until he proves himself innocent. If any tolerance is exercised, it is with regard to crimes of passion.

Machiavelli had said that a Frenchman is more covetous of his money than of his blood—an accurate observation. You will read of the slaying of a faithless mistress, a suspected husband, or even of poisonings in which revenge is taken on a whole family. Long-dead corpses are dug up and added to the list of arsenic murders. (Arsenic is the most often administered remover of objectionable relatives.)

In such crimes of passion the police and the judges are all understanding. The court listens with patience, even with sympathy. The punishment, in many cases, doesn't fit the crime.

Altogether different is a case in which a sum of money is involved. They sit up, they mete out terrible sentences, and they consider it a real, honest-to-goodness crime.

In the lower depths of the Paris underworld, streets are so narrow that dwellers can lean out their windows and shake hands with people in houses across the way. In daylight these streets are ill smelling, moldy-looking, and dung-colored, but night transforms the drab walls with an all-over cloak of charcoal and silver, the same lovely satin that is draped on Notre-Dame, on the Chamber of Deputies, and the buildings facing the Place de la Concorde. Close to you, the walls of houses are brushed with melancholy hues, and street lamps throw disks of soft light on sidewalks and gild the contours of the buildings.

Everything is filled with ache and misery. As the people of this district have their own language, a tough, simile-filled slang, so they have their own music. It is in the mood of the place, as melancholy as the color; the nasal whining of concertinas comes from small bars, called *bals,* meaning ballrooms. (The French have a compulsion to name things delicately: a brassière is called a throat supporter; a procurer is called a stand-by.)

Before going to the *bas-fonds* the visitor should be told that this form of sightseeing costs dearly in disillusionment; the misery is genuine, the women leaning against the wall or tapping their heels along the pavements, fiercely protecting their assigned stretch of sidewalk, are neither daughters of joy, temple dancers of fiction, nor the mascaraed houris of the Arab Paradise. With the rarest exceptions, they are gross, pitiful creatures, homogeneous to their surroundings.

"Allo, Georges," people said in all the *bals* as we entered.

"Allo," said Georges, my friend and guide. "I'm looking for René." People shook their heads, and Georges said, "He must have changed his *quartier.*"

We walked on. "You had left Paris," said Georges, "when I hit on a brilliant idea. It was at the beginning of the war. It goes like this: You read the newspapers and you see that this and that senator, minister, or industrialist has died. Naturally his picture is in the paper, so you get an artist to make a rough oil sketch of him. You go to the widow with the canvas and explain that, just before he died, the senator had commissioned you to make this picture. He had made a small down payment, but there is a matter of

ten thousand francs balance due, and for that the picture will be
finished and delivered as ordered.

"Occasionally you are thrown out. The widow screams that she
has enough souvenirs. But mostly it works, and no one can possibly prove that the senator did not actually request the painting.

"There isn't much swindling these days—just obvious stuff,
like changing dollars. But tourists are getting suspicious and they
all know that the hotel porter will change their money at black-
market rates. There is another trick that sometimes works. It's
done with the aid of elevators in small apartment houses. A
woman enters the elevator; between the second and third floor
it gets stuck, so she rings the bell. Nothing happens. Suddenly a
young man comes down the stairs. He opens the door on the third
floor and asks if he can help. Madame is panicky. 'Heavens yes,
get me out of here!' So he says, 'Of course. First of all, hand me
your bag and your parcels.' She hands them up to him, and he
runs. Naturally, he has stopped the elevator by forcing open the
door on a floor above."

Georges led me into another *bal,* but still there was no sign of
René. We kept walking toward the Boulevard de la Chapelle.

"It is curious how the oldest tricks," Georges said, "can be
worked again and again. A few days ago one was pulled on a
diamond broker in broad daylight. The broker was going to his
bank with a bag of diamonds worth several million francs. He was
just about to enter the bank when somebody called, 'Monsieur,
monsieur!' He stopped and turned. A respectable-looking man approached and informed him that somebody had spat on the back
of his coat. 'Thank you, thank you,' said the diamond broker.
And, being a thorough man, he put his bag on the ground and
took off his coat. He saw that the man had told the truth and decided to go into the bank lavatory, where water was available.
The stranger smiled and departed.

"The diamond broker picked up his valise and entered the
bank. At last he went to the safe-deposit vaults, and there, naturally, he found he had the wrong bag."

We were near the Place Blanche, in the Montmartre district,
and at long last the proprietor of a small bar knew where René
was. "You'll find him at the Angel or at My Little Chicken."

On the way to the Angel, Georges took me into a small bar at the foot of Montmartre. "This establishment," he said, "has changed hands three times in the last year. Three successive owners have been killed. The place is in disputed territory; both the Arabs and the Corsicans—two rival gangs—fight to 'protect' it. The Corsicans demand protection money; the owner refuses because he already pays the Arabs. His place is smashed—and he is killed by one side or the other."

"Do the police know who does this killing?"

"Yes, of course," said Georges. "I want you to meet that man across the room. He is a police inspector who killed a man outside this place three months ago."

"This war among criminals," said the inspector after an introduction, "is called *Le Gangsterisme*. It's like the American films. And our problems, too, are sometimes like those of American police. Often we know who is behind a certain crime but he is too big to take hastily. We pull in the little fellows and sometimes they talk. Then we pull in the big ones—but, usually, they are too clever—they have alibis. Once in a while we can change their minds about those alibis, but more often than not our hands are tied.

"Not long ago the owner of this *bal* was assassinated, and a new one took over. I came in with the brother of the victim. He pointed at a man standing at the bar and said, 'There he is.' The murderer had two bodyguards with him. I told him to come along, and we went out into the dark street. In my hurry to get him up to the boulevard where there is more light I made a mistake— I did not search him for weapons." The inspector led us to the street. "As we walked along there," he went on, "I noticed that we were followed by his two bodyguards, one on each side of the street, about fifty feet behind us. Suddenly the prisoner dropped to the ground, leaving me a target silhouetted against light. There was no time to do much choosing—I drew my gun and shot the prisoner through the head. It was the only thing to do. The others turned and ran down the street. The dead man was a Corsican."

Above Montmartre, snow white in the color of night and overlooking the squalid scene, stood the church called Sacré-Coeur.

"This is a lively neighborhood," said the inspector, pointing to an upper floor of a house. "Up there last week a man dismembered his mistress. He had the trunk all ready, addressed to Lyon. Paris trunk murderers have a preference for sending their victims to Lyon. Why, nobody knows. Perhaps Lyon is easy to write; maybe it's a pleasure to make a nice 'L' on a tag—I don't know. Good evening, messieurs."

At the Angel we found René, a fine, big man over fifty, with an honest face. He looked a little injured, as if someone had insulted him, making him feel sad rather than angry.

He wore a dark coat with sleeves that were too short, a blue shirt, and a bowler which sat close to one ear and high above the other. His eyes were blue, and he ordered his drink in a melodious voice. It had a poetic ring as he said, *"Une fine à l'eau, sans glace."*

"Ah, yes, I have been in the milieu all my life," he said when I met him. He waved his hand at the people in the room. "It is no longer what it was, it isn't Paris any more. It has become foreign —like everything else—and the Americans are the ones to blame.

"The crooks of today—bah—imitations of businessmen. They go for weekends in the country and get sunburned, they send flowers to women, they ride in cars and wear clean shirts and polished boots. They even go to the movies. In the old days it was different. The boss of the neighborhood, the chief of the gang, was known as the *caid* [many words in the language of the underworld are taken from the Arabic]. He didn't rob banks or hold up trains or stores—he never wanted vast sums of money. The idea of shooting a bank teller would have been revolting to him—he was a man."

René took a slow, thoughtful sip. "His life was simple," he went on. "He had a woman, and he engaged in small operations, enough to make himself comfortable. If he killed, it was somebody who tried to steal his woman or who double-crossed him. And usually he was content to mark him with a cross on the right cheek. Do you know how that's done? Very simple—not with a knife—with a piece of sugar."

"Show him," said Georges.

René took a lump of sugar from the bowl. "Observe," he said. "You break it diagonally, the long way, so—" He snapped the brittle lump and made a lightning motion with his hand. "It makes a better mark than a knife. It leaves a larger welt."

"No, it's not the same any more. You can have it." René sighed deeply, and we left.

As we went on toward the Arab quarter, on the Boulevard Rochechouart, there was a commotion. The salad basket was backed up against the sidewalk. Police were running after some people at whom they were swinging their capes. At first this seemed an amusing and typically French thing. It's like Keystone comedy, I thought—the cop runs after his quarry and hits him with his blue cape. Yet the quarry screams when hit, for the cape, on examination, is not funny. In its hem leaden weights are sewn, making the innocent-looking blue garment a potent assault weapon.

While some of the police were swinging their capes on the outer edge of the crowd, others were pulling various clients out of a large café. It was quick work.

Georges said, "Notice that the proprietor is absent; only Madame is standing by." The proprietress was sitting at her cashier's desk, and the head of the detachment of police was speaking to her.

Georges explained that in most bars the owner disappears the moment trouble starts. Many of these places are owned by men who have police records, so the property is in the name of the wife. The owner doesn't want to get "mixed up in anything."

When it was over, we went in for a drink. "Ah, *alors,*" said Madame, "this is the second time in a month that we have the cows here. The last time it was on account of opium."

Flics is the ordinary slang term for the police. *Vache,* which means cow, is a stronger term, used when the *flics* begin to annoy one. *Mort aux Vaches—Death to Cows—*is frequently found tattooed on the arms of *durs* (hard ones), as those who have served prison terms at hard labor are called.

The waiters righted the wicker chairs and upturned sidewalk tables. The proprietor reappeared, and I noticed that on his right arm was tattooed a sword around which a serpent wound.

Georges asked the proprietor about the opium incident.

A dealer in narcotics, so the story went, had succeeded in making an addict of a millionaire, for whom he had also procured women. After a year the Corsican announced that the only way the millionaire could be sure of getting the stuff would be for them to go into business together. The narcotics dealer then made him the following proposition:

For the sum of twenty-five thousand dollars, he said, he could lay his hands on sufficient opium in Naples to make a good-sized fortune in one move. This amount of opium, refined into heroin, would bring two hundred and fifty thousand dollars in Paris. (In America it would retail at two million dollars.)

The rich man decided to try it out and gave the Corsican five thousand dollars. It was arranged that they would meet in four days, when the first shipment would be delivered. Four days later the Corsican telephoned and set the hour and place of the meeting. Then he called the police, saying he wished to inform on a narcotics peddler. He gave a detailed description of the peddler (himself) and said that the peddler had a date to deliver a package of narcotics to a customer at a certain bar at six o'clock that night. The police dispatched plain-clothes men. The Corsican waited until his client arrived, and as he walked toward him he was arrested by the police. Naturally, he had come empty-handed. The client fled. At the police station the Corsican was freed, since there was no evidence on which to hold him. Not only did he gain five thousand dollars, he also retained the business of the millionaire.

The tables of Paris sidewalk restaurants become interesting once you get to know what passes. "Did you see the tattooing on the proprietor's arm?" asked Georges. "The snake around the sword? On the sword is written 'Vengeance.' The mouth of the reptile is open, which means that vengeance has been had. When the snake is pictured in repose, it means that vengeance is yet to be taken."

The most usual tattoos among the hard ones are found on the triangular patch of skin between the thumb and index finger of the right hand. This part of the hand can, with practice, be depressed. Into it tobacco or drugs can be placed to be sniffed, and it therefore is known as the anatomic tobacco pouch—*la tabatière anatomique.*

On this patch of skin one can find three tattooed dots, two toward the body and one forward, and these signify the three letters M. A. V., which stand for *Mort aux Vaches!*

This is the true sign of a member of the *durs.*

The next most frequent tattoo is the arrangement of five points, as found on dice. This means that the wearer has spent time in solitary confinement. "All alone between four walls" is the phrase. The third most frequent is a single dot on each of the three middle fingers. These dots are placed in a straight row on the backs of the fingers, halfway up the first joints, and indicate "My heart to my mother, my head to Deibler"—the executioner of Paris—"and the rest to the prostitutes." Nineteen per cent of the prison population wears the three points.

Marine cadets who were "hardheads" and placed in solitary confinement wear a fleur-de-lis tattooed on the wrist, and, for every day spent in solitary, a dot. Some have so many that they seem to be wearing blue bracelets.

Among the most frequent tattooed words and phrases are: "I suffer in silence"; "I want justice"; "Vendetta"; "Remember"; "To my Chicken"; "To you, Cri Cri"; and, spelled out large, the width of an upper arm; *"Mort aux Vaches."*

On that night of our visit to the boulevards of crime, I left Georges about two in the morning. He wanted to return at a respectable hour to his respectable flat and family.

"Before I go," he said, "I have to tell you something wonderful that happened the other day. There was a black-market money-changer, not one of the poor little crooks who stand on street corners and sell dirty postal cards on the side, but a clever man who did a good business with customers living in the fine hotels of Paris.

"The police finally caught him, but they promised to let him go if he would put them onto something big. After a week he telephoned the police and told them that a South American millionaire stopping at one of the best hotels on the Avenue Georges V wanted to buy seven million francs on the black market that afternoon. The police called the hotel, verified the fact that the millionaire was in suite number so-and-so, and a meeting was arranged for 3 p.m. The money-changer was given the money, and it was agreed that ten minutes after he went to the suite the police would break in. They did, but found nobody there. They are still looking for their informer and for the seven million francs.

"It does one good to hear a thing like that," Georges said in parting.

I went back to the Left Bank, where the unwashed youth of St.-Germain hangs out—the expatriate American boys with beards and the sloppy-looking girls who try to look like respectful ones. There are many little bistros, and Le Montana, where the beer is good, is as melancholy as the *bas-fonds*, but not really vicious.

A hanger-out in this place is Count Armand, who prefers the society of the unkempt. The place was so crowded that I found him sitting on a box out in the street.

"The other day you mentioned something about the local underworld," he said. "Would you like to see the real *bas-fonds*? If you are not easily scared I will take you to see the last apache in Paris, the last gigolette, and I guarantee that you will shiver at what takes place."

"Where?"

"Out near the Bastille."

That was the one place I had not yet visited.

"Well then, let's go." We drove to a moody street a few blocks past the Bastille, and off this was a dead-end alley called Passage Thiéré. We came to Le Petit Balcon, and got a small table and drinks, for which payment was demanded as we were served. The place was jammed. In the center of the floor an apache was dancing wildly with his gigolette. What he was doing to the girl was mayhem. He twisted her, choked her, banged her head on the floor. Finally a man sitting nearby jumped up in fury. He rushed, knife in hand, at the apache—and there was a fight and blood flowed; a pool of it appeared on the floor. People screamed and ran. Outside, a bus, with American Express written on it, waited for them.

"I own a share in this place," said Armand as the "blood" was being mopped up. "It's a gold mine. The next show starts in half an hour. The apache, the girl, and the assassin are not allowed to speak to anybody, because none of them speaks a word of French. They're two ex-GIs and a girl who used to be with a USO troupe. They all stayed behind because they love Paris."

The next morning, when I returned to my hotel room after breakfast, I found on my bed six shirts wrapped in pink paper. I glanced at the attached bill and discovered that what Gabrielle had said was true—it was no longer possible for the ordinary person to live decently in Paris. I went to the typewriter and put down: "The cost of laundering a shirt is seventy-five cents."

There was a knock at the door. It was Monsieur Sympatziarly of the ministry of Parisian enchantment. *"Bon jour, cher monsieur,"* I said. "Would you like a glass of champagne?"

"Ah, yes—champagne. Is it not the most precious jewel in the diadem of wines? The glorious plume of its foam, so light, so fragrant, so exquisitely suited to distinguished gatherings and gaiety. . . . Your health, monsieur. Coming down the corridor I heard the sound of the typewriter going—you were writing, perhaps, about *la belle France?* Perchance, about Paris?"

"Oui, about Paris."

"Ah, there is a surprise in store always for those who think there remains nothing to be said about Paris. They discover that nothing *as yet* has been said. Will you allow, *cher maître*—may I steal a glance?"

Monsieur Sympatziarly placed his stick, hat, and gloves on a chair, adjusted his pince-nez, and read aloud: " 'The cost of laundering a shirt is seventy-five cents.' Ah, it is about New York."

"No, it is about Paris. In New York, washing a shirt costs thirty-five cents."

The face of Monsieur Sympatziarly turned the red of the Legion rosette in his lapel. "Do you find, monsieur, that such an item is of interest to the man who crosses the ocean to visit Paris, the city of—"

"Yes, of great interest. For that man invariably wears a shirt, and he must send it to the laundry, and when he gets the bill he will be very unhappy about Paris, the city of the most expensive laundries and the most expensive—"

"Your argument, monsieur, provokes laughter."

"Why does it cost so much?"

"Ah, always enters the *point de vue économique*. Allow me, monsieur, have you ever had a shirt washed in France?"

"Yes, of course—just now some came back from the laundry."

"All the more sad. Here, let me explain. In a place of little light, so that the delicate colors will not be affected, there are the world's greatest and most experienced laundresses engaged in washing your shirt. They have spent their lives over tubs of water. Your shirt will not be mangled in the heartless drum of an automaton. It is tenderly rubbed, squeezed, and wrung out with solicitude. It is carefully hung, and at the proper temperature it slowly dries. And then it is sprinkled and reawakened. It is studied—and from a reservoir of ten thousand little buttons the one that matches exactly replaces the lost one. Like a little boat, the iron passes over the expanse of your garment. It is folded and with infinite care placed on a wicker tray, wrapped in rose paper as frail as breath. And then it is carried through the old streets of Paris by a girl who might have stepped out of a Renoir painting."

"Forgive me, Monsieur Sympatziarly," I cried. "I am a victim of the cruel phantoms of my imagination, and I have only recently arrived from America. I shall start my article on Paris all over again. For, as you say, nothing as yet has been said."